THE

SECOND

BLIND

SON

ALSO BY AMY HARMON

Young Adult and Paranormal Romance

Slow Dance in Purgatory
Prom Night in Purgatory

Inspirational Romance

A Different Blue
Running Barefoot
Making Faces
Infinity + One
The Law of Moses
The Song of David
The Smallest Part

Historical Fiction

From Sand and Ash
What the Wind Knows
Where the Lost Wander
The Songbook of Benny Lament

Romantic Fantasy

The Bird and the Sword
The Queen and the Cure
The First Girl Child

THE

SECOND

BLIND

SON

AMY HARMON

Published by 47North, Seattle

www.apub.com

Amazon, the Amazon logo, and 47North are trademarks of Amazon.com, Inc., or its affiliates.

ISBN-13: 9781542029728
ISBN-10: 1542029724

Cover design by Kirk DouPonce, Dog Eared Design

Printed in the United States of America

For when I am weak, then I am strong.

—*2 Corinthians 12:10*

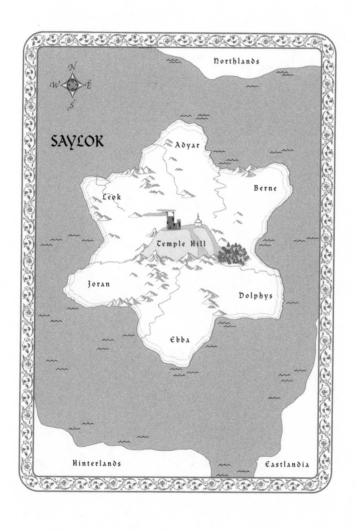

PRONUNCIATION GUIDE

Adyar: ad yahr
Alannah: a LAH nuh
Alba: ahl buh
Arwin: ahr win
Banruud: ban rood
Bashti: bash tee
Berne: burn
Baldr: bahl duhr
Bayr: bear
Dagmar: dag mahr
Dalys: da lis
Desdemona: dez de MO nuh
Dolphys: DAHL fis
Dred: drehd
Dystel: DIS tahl
Ebba: EH buh
Elayne: ee LAYN
Ghost: ghost
Hod: hoad
Ghisla: geese luh
Gudrun: goo drun
Ivo: EYE voh

Joran: YOR uhn
Juliah: YOO lee uh
Leok: lee awk
Liis: lees
Saylok: SAY lawk

PROLOGUE

In Saylok, the Tournament of the King happened every year when the harvest was over and the cold had not yet come. The clan chieftains and their warriors would gather on Temple Hill to compete in a slew of contests designed to measure strength and skill and determine the fiercest clan. The tournament winners became the fodder of legends, and for two weeks, the castle grounds and the temple mount became a carnival. Great swaths of color billowed in the breeze—green, gold, red, orange, blue, and brown for the six clans, and purple for the keepers of the temple.

The flags welcomed every citizen making the yearly pilgrimage to partake in the festivities, but the woman who struggled up the hill, her young son in her arms, had not come to watch the tournament or to sell her wares at the bazaar. She had come for a blessing from the Highest Keeper. She had come for a miracle.

During the tournament, the temple doors were opened and all were welcomed inside. The keepers were on hand to bless and advise, to pray and pardon. In Saylok, the king made the laws and the chieftains enforced them, but the keepers could mete out mercy. Those who received a hearing with the keepers were granted "new life" and absolution from their sins and sentences. Others were healed or comforted.

The absolution granted was usually spiritual and rarely criminal. Justice was swift and severe in the clans, and very few of the condemned actually lasted long enough to claim sanctuary or beg an audience with the keepers. Still, during the Tournament of the King, when the temple was opened, there was always at least one infamous fugitive who was granted pardon.

She was not a fugitive, and she would not seek forgiveness for her sins, though she knew they were many. She would not even ask to be healed, though she knew she was going to die. Her sickness had made her desperate. Brave. And she climbed with a single-minded purpose, heaving for breath.

The crowds were thick and the lines leading into the temple were long. She waited all afternoon for her turn, sipping from her water flask and trying to entertain the boy. He was good-natured and played at her feet, drawing pictures in the dust and eating bits of bread from her satchel. But the journey of days had taken its toll, and her vision swam and her spirits sank. She could not wait forever. She could not even wait for hours.

At dusk, the bells began to toll and the guards at the wide doors started to turn people away so they could close the temple.

"Return tomorrow," they insisted, shoving a persistent woman to the side. There were many desperate mothers in the crowd.

She hoisted her satchel and took her son's hand, searching for a bit of refuge, a place to shelter for the night. Stairs and columns ringed the front of the temple, and every step was filled with those as indigent as she. They would be first in line when the doors opened again in the morning. She staggered around the perimeter, hardly knowing where she stepped, clinging to the small hand tucked in hers. A door in the stone wall around the temple yard was unguarded, but when she pulled on the handle, she found it barred. Animals were housed beyond the wall; she could hear them. Smell them. She only needed a bit of straw, a little shelter, and a well where she could refill her waterskins. She rattled the door, hoping someone would hear, but no one came.

She sank down against the wall, trying to gather her strength. The sun had dropped behind the temple, and the stones were cool against her cheek. She pulled her son into her lap and closed her eyes. She would wait for someone to come through and beg them to let her bed down among the beasts. She'd done it before. Many times.

She must have slept, though it couldn't have been long.

A hand touched her head. She thought it only her son and reassured him wearily. "I am only tired, Baldr. Only resting. Stay beside me."

"Do you need help, woman?" The voice was gentle and deep, and she jerked, peering up at the man who stood over her. His hair was shorn close to his skull, and his robes were the deep purple that set the keepers apart from the clans. But it was the babe he carried across his chest that convinced her she was only dreaming.

The sling was dyed the same deep purple as the robe, so that it almost looked as if the child's tiny head floated at the keeper's heart.

She'd never seen such a thing. A man carrying a child thus was strange enough. Men did not care for infants. But a *keeper* with a child was beyond comprehension.

She closed her eyes and opened them again, but the keeper remained, his hand extended, the sleeping babe lolling in his purple pouch.

"I have come to see the Highest Keeper," she blurted, rubbing her eyes. "And I cannot wait until the morrow."

"I am not Master Ivo. I am only Keeper Dagmar, but I will do what I can."

He gripped her arm to help her stand. Baldr felt her efforts to rise, and stood as well, patting her leg, searching for her hand.

"Is this your son?" Keeper Dagmar asked.

3

The child was sturdy and handsome, with dark, curling hair and dimpled limbs, but his eyes were twin pools of empty green, clouded and cold, and people often stared at him in horror and hurried away.

"Yes. He cannot see," she explained. "Some say he is marked. His eyes frighten people. But he is not evil, Keeper. He is sweet, and he is smart. His mind is not slow."

"What do you call him?"

"Baldr."

"Baldr the Beloved. Son of Odin," Keeper Dagmar said.

"Baldr the Beloved. Baldr the Brave. Baldr the Good. Baldr the Wise. He is all those things," she said proudly.

The keeper gazed down at the boy without fear and patted him on the head. His kindness made her eyes smart; it also gave her hope.

"I am of Berne, Keeper. And I need a hearing with the Highest Keeper," she pled.

"You are sick?" he asked.

"Yes." She knew her eyes were bright and her cheeks were red with fever, and though she tried to suppress it, a deep cough rattled and escaped from her chest. "Yes. I have been sick for a while, and I am not getting better. I am in need of a blessing. But not for myself. For my son."

Master Ivo, the Highest Keeper of Saylok, was irritated.

The doors of the temple are open to all the citizens of Saylok during the Tournament of the King, but the doors had closed and the day was done, and he was an old man who needed his rest.

Yet this woman and her child had found their way into the sanctum, where no one but keepers and kings—and the chieftains on occasion—were allowed. Someone must have let her in.

"You must leave at once," Ivo hissed.

"I need only a moment, Master," she said, undeterred, and continued toward him. His perch was more throne than chair, with spikes that radiated out on the high back like rays of the sun or spokes of a wheel. It did not look comfortable, he knew, so it pleased him greatly that it was. It sat on the dais near the altar, and it was where he did all his best thinking . . . and sleeping.

The woman stopped a mere ten feet away, beside the altar, and folded her hands like a beggar.

"I would ask a blessing of you, Highest Keeper . . . and then I will go."

She had the courage of the desperate, and it radiated from her feverish gaze and pleading lips. Though the dust of long travel and the rags of destitution cloaked her thin frame, the child who walked beside her was healthy and relatively clean.

But there was something wrong with the boy's eyes.

The woman's mission was suddenly clear, and Ivo cursed whomever it was who had taken compassion on her. The Highest Keeper was not the only one who could bestow a token or pardon. Every keeper spent his days during the tournament healing and calling on the runes. Yet this woman had been brought to *him*, slipped into *his* sanctum without introduction, so that *he* would have to tell her that some ailments could not be righted with a rune. *Cowards.* He would punish the lot of them.

"Did he ever see?" Ivo asked, impatient, waving toward the boy.

"No, Master. His eyes were thus when he was born."

"He was not ill?"

"No."

"Then I cannot heal him. I cannot restore what never was."

The woman's shoulders sagged, and he thought for a moment she would collapse.

He cursed the Norns who delighted in tormenting him.

"I will give you both a blessing of strength. Then you will go," he relented.

5

He drew a half-hearted rune in the air, mumbling a blessing on the marrow and blood and sinews. He could not be expected to bestow more under the circumstances. The little boy let go of his mother's hand and cocked his dark head. Then he repeated the blessing, word for word, his voice high and sweet. Ivo's irritation disintegrated into the dust on the sanctum floor, but the woman was not comforted. Tears had begun to streak her cheeks.

"I fear strength will not be enough, Master," the woman whispered.

"Why not?" Ivo grumbled. She did not need to know his heart had changed.

"He is a fine boy, Master. But his blindness is a burden no one will shoulder. And I cannot take care of him anymore."

"Where is his father? What of your clan?"

"I am of Berne, my father is dead, and I have known many men, Master." Her voice was unapologetic, and he had little doubt she spoke truth, but she withheld something. Most women did when speaking of such matters. Especially to an ancient keeper who they assumed would not understand.

"Take him to Chief Banruud. It is the responsibility of the chieftain to provide for the children—all children—in his clan."

She was silent, resistant, and for a moment she hung her head, defeated.

He sighed, throwing his hands in the air.

"I cannot heal his eyes . . . but I can heal *you* so that you might take care of him," Ivo offered.

Relieved, the woman nodded, and he motioned her to approach him. Her hands shook with fatigue and her skin burned with fever. He would have to draw runes to ward off illness in every corner of the temple, but it was always thus during the tournament.

In his own blood, he drew three runes across her brow: a rune of breath, a rune of strength, and a rune to expel the sickness from her chest. The fates would decide whether or not to grant his request—life and death were not his to control—but already her eyes were clearing and the rattling in her exhalations was gone.

He waited, letting the runes sink beneath her skin before he wiped the residue away. He would not leave a mark for others to see.

"Go now. And take the boy."

She backed away, bowing gratefully as she did, but his rune had healed more than her body. It had restored her hope, and she made another request.

"There is word that there is a child, a babe, living among the keepers. Living in the temple. That is what I want for my son," she said in a rush.

"Word, eh?" He snorted.

Word all the way in Berne? He doubted that. But now he knew which keeper had allowed the woman entrance into the sanctum. Keeper Dagmar was a constant thorn in his side. A burr in his shoe. A canker in his mouth. And he had been from the moment Dagmar had come to the mount, a lanky, insistent boy, threatening to throw himself from the cliffs of Shinway if the Highest Keeper did not allow him to become a supplicant in the temple.

The worst part was, somehow Dagmar always got his way. Months ago, he'd brought a newborn babe, his dead sister's son, Bayr, into the enclave, and Ivo had relented again. Even though it had never been done. Even though it *should* never be done. Now this woman was here, demanding the same. Ivo had warned Dagmar of this very thing. The moment an exception was made, the rule ceased to exist.

"Can you not train him to be a keeper?" she pled. "He is so smart."

"A keeper," the little boy parroted. He stood beneath the altar, his arms extended as high as he could raise them, so the tips of his fingers could trace the carvings in the wood. The runes were all entangled, each figure indistinguishable from the others, except to the trained eye. It was the way they were protected, even in the sanctum. Even on the underside of the altar.

7

"Runes," the little boy said, marveling.

Ivo gasped. "He recognizes the runes."

"He knows naught of runes," the woman argued, shaking her head. "I know naught of runes. I swear it, Highest Keeper."

The runes were forbidden to all but the keepers. Her fear was justified, but Ivo did not scold her. He watched the child instead. The boy was entranced by the texture of the carvings beneath his hands. After a moment, the little fellow crouched, and in the dust of the floor, he drew a rune—two half circles, back to back, one that opened to the left and one that opened to the right. An arrow bisected the first crescent, and its shaft penetrated the second through the back. The rune was an exact replica of the one directly above the boy's head, if he remembered right.

Ivo frowned and then he gaped, dumbfounded. "He draws the rune of Hod."

The woman's brow furrowed in confusion.

"He draws the rune of Hod, the blind son of Odin," Ivo whispered.

"He knows naught, Master. It is what he does. He touches and he . . . draws. It is how he learns," his mother protested and rushed to erase the figure.

"Leave it!" Ivo hissed. The woman and the child froze.

The Highest Keeper did not believe in happenstance. A blind boy—a boy no more than four summers—had drawn the rune of a blind god.

"Bring him to me," Ivo said, curling his fingers toward the boy.

The woman hesitated, suddenly fearful, but she prodded the boy forward until they both stood in front of the Highest Keeper's enormous chair. The little boy reached out, tentative, and set his hands on Ivo's knees, almost as if he understood what was to come.

Ivo gaped again. No one touched him. Ever. The woman seemed to understand this.

"Baldr," she warned, drawing his hands back.

"His name is Baldr?" Ivo asked, stunned once more.

"Y-yes, Master," the woman stammered. "I am of Berne. It is a c-common name . . . in Berne."

"He is not Baldr . . . He is Hod," Ivo murmured. But the two names were inextricably tied, and it was just further proof to Ivo of a destined course.

"Turn his hands so I can see his palms," Ivo insisted. She did, gripping the boy's wrists and extending his small arms so he stood in a posture of supplication, palms up.

Ivo bent over the boy's hands.

"Runes hide on the palms of our hands, at each knuckle, in every line and whorl," Ivo muttered, providing explanation to the nervous mother.

The marks were already there, engraved on the boy's skin, though they were far more visible on him—particularly the rune of sound and of scent—than on most. The lines would continue to deepen as the boy relied upon them, but Ivo would make them deeper still. A gift to the child who would sorely need his other senses.

The Highest Keeper, with a flick of his sharp nail, took blood from the tip of his own finger and drew slumber on the boy's brow. The child immediately began to nod in his mother's arms. It would make the rest easier.

"He will sleep now. And I will bless him," Ivo explained. The child would need to be still, and he would not understand the sting of the runes on his skin.

He traced the tiny runes on the boy's right hand with the needled edge of his nail, and blood welled in the crevices.

His mother gasped, not comprehending the offering and uneasy at the sight of her son's blood.

"He will hear, smell, and sense far more than others do," Ivo said, completing the task. He curled the boy's bleeding fingers over his tiny palm. "Now take him away."

The mother lifted the sleeping child in her arms, her strength restored.

"Thank you, Highest Keeper. Thank you," she whispered. She stooped and swung her satchel over her shoulder and repositioned the child in her arms before turning toward the sanctum doors.

The fates screamed in Ivo's head, and he relented, throwing up his hands in surrender.

"Woman?"

She turned.

"You cannot stay here, on the temple mount . . . but I know a place where the child . . . can go," he said.

PART ONE

1

AND ONLY

Ghisla could no longer hear the shouts of the men on the ship or the screams of the women and children who'd been huddled below deck, trying to outlast the storm. She could only hear the howling of the skies and the crash of the waves, battling the tempest as they tossed her up and down. She had climbed up the ladder, opened the hatch, and thrown herself overboard into the water. No one had tried to stop her. The chaos had served as a perfect diversion.

Ghisla wanted to die. She wanted to end her suffering and her loneliness, to end the fear. She wanted that more than anything, but when a small barrel bobbed along beside her, she clung to it, hoisting herself over it, arms and legs wrapped around it like a babe on its mother.

Death would have to wait a bit; she had lost her courage.

The storm raged and Ghisla raged back, singing the songs her mother had taught her, trying to find that courage again. There were songs for planting and songs for harvesting. Songs for supping and songs for sleeping. There were even songs for death and songs to ward it off, but she knew no songs to welcome it. So she sang the song they'd sung at the end of each day before they'd closed their eyes to sleep. Hers had been a family of singers, in a village of singers, in a land of singers.

"Open up the heavens. Open up the earth. Open up the hearts of men, close the wounds and hurt. Hear my voice and hold my hand, help me rise and work again," she sang. "Mother, Father, Gilly," she wailed, throwing her voice into the gale. "Help me find you. I want to be with you."

"Your voice will open the heavens, Ghisla," her mother had always said. "Odin himself could not deny you, should you call him." But Odin did not seem to hear, though she begged him to come retrieve her.

"I will sing for you, Allfather, every day. If you will let me come and stay," she sang, her arms trembling around the cask. She could not let it go. She had no desire to live, yet . . . she could not let go. So she sang, harmonizing with the wind and the waves until exhaustion took her voice and her consciousness.

She awoke to light and warmth and a presence in the shadows.

"Am I dead?" she asked. She'd fallen to sleep cold and wet, bobbing on a forever sea, throat raw with salt and singing. She'd closed her eyes and succumbed to the darkness, beyond caring whether she lived, and here she was. But she didn't know *where* she was.

"No." The voice was young and newly deep. It reminded her of her brother, Gilly. His voice had sounded like that, cracking and quivering between man and boy. She tried to see the owner of the voice, but her lids were too heavy and sleep too sweet.

When she woke again, the warmth had changed, the light too, and the sun beat down on her cheeks, and something tickled her bare foot. She kicked at it, coming awake, frightened that a creature would scurry up her skirts or nibble at her toes. She peered down at the offending touch.

The creature was a boy, squatting on his haunches by her feet, silhouetted by the sun.

"Are you awake?"

She nodded, tucking her feet beneath her skirts, but he tipped his head to the side, listening, and asked her again.

"Are you awake?"

"Yes." Her tongue was heavy and her lips fat. She sat up, suddenly so parched she was desperate. He seemed to know, for he held a water flask in his hand and extended it toward her slightly, shaking it a little.

"Are you thirsty?"

Ghisla nodded again, but he simply waited, as though he expected her to take it from him. She did, grasping it before widening the distance between them. Then she uncorked the flask and drank until there was nothing left. She wiped at her mouth and wished for more, wished she had left a little to rinse the salt from her eyes. Her face stung.

"I'm sorry. I didn't mean to drink it all." She tried to hand the flask back to him, but he didn't take it. He waited until she nudged him with it before accepting it. Then he stood, still silhouetted by the sun at his back, and she shaded her eyes so she could stare up at him, though the glare made picking out the details difficult.

He was tall and thin, his shoulders broad but bony and draped in drab brown. His dark hair was cut close to his skull like a newly shorn sheep, and his eyes were averted, clinging to the distance, and she couldn't make out their color or intent.

"I can get you more . . . but we'll have to walk a little ways. Can you walk?" he asked. He had a long staff that pointed up at the sky, and he kept his hands wrapped around it as he waited for her to rise.

She took stock of her condition. She was sore and her dress was stiff with salt, but she was dry, and she was unharmed. She rose to her feet and shook out her thin skirts, brushing the sand from her sleeves and wiping the grit from her cheeks. The top of her head did not quite reach the boy's shoulders, and he reached out tentatively with one hand, his palm downward, and set his hand atop her head as though marking her size.

She jerked away from him, and his hand fell. He kept his eyes averted, looking at nothing. Now that she was standing, his body blocking the sun, she could see him better. His eyes were the color of the moss that clung to the stones, but they were coated in a white haze and they had no centers . . . or if they did, the milky white obscured them. She stepped back, wanting to run, but she had nowhere to go. The sea stretched out in front of her, cliffs and hills rose up behind her, and sand extended on each side. There was only this boy and this beach. And her.

"I heard you . . . singing in the darkness. Last night. I thought you were a nixie. But nixies are not so small," he said gently. "I was surprised by your height."

"A nixie?" she asked.

"A fish-tailed woman who sings and draws the sailors from their ships down into the depths of the sea."

"I don't have a fish tail."

"No. You don't." His teeth flashed, straight and white, but his eyes did not smile. "I tickled your feet, remember?"

"I am not a woman either."

"But you are . . . a girl?"

She frowned. "Yes. Can't you tell?"

"I've never met a . . . young . . . girl. There aren't many girls in Saylok . . . and there are no girls among the cave keepers."

"Who are the cave keepers? And what is Saylok?" she asked, but her throat was growing tight with panic. Where was she? And what was wrong with this boy's eyes? They reminded her of Gilly's eyes. And Gilly was dead.

"This is Saylok."

Saylok did not look so different from home. Trees, rocks, towering cliffs, and a white-sand beach rimmed in forest.

"This beach is Saylok?"

"This whole land. But we are in Leok, a part of it . . . though no one lives along this stretch because of the storms."

"No one but you?"

"No one but me . . . and Arwin."

"Who is Arwin?"

"He is my teacher."

"Where is he?"

"I don't know. He'll be back. Sometimes I feel him watching. But not now. Not for days. I think he's begun to believe I can manage without him. It is part of my training."

"You are training? For what?"

"To live on my own."

Why would he want to live on his own? Ghisla did not want to live on her own. Yet she did. She would forever be on her own. She swayed, already wearied, wanting to sink back down to the sand and fall back into the river of dreams that had brought her here.

"Come . . . I will take you to the stream," the boy said, turning away. She watched him for a moment, not certain if she should follow.

"I will not harm you," he called, but did not slow. "You have nothing to fear from me."

She hurried to catch up, toddling along behind him. He moved easily. Uprightly. But he led each step with the butt of his stick.

"Can you not see?" Ghisla asked, the realization seeping through her addled thoughts.

"I cannot."

She didn't know what to say. His voice was unconcerned, and he moved with surety and even grace, aware of his footsteps but not hesitant or fearful.

"How do you know where you're going?" she whispered.

"I have been here many times before. I live here." He smiled toward her, as though he thought her funny, and she stared up at his cloudy eyes once more, flabbergasted.

She was not watching where she placed her feet as she climbed past him and she tripped, falling heavily to her hands and knees. A spray of rocks tumbled down the slope.

He stopped immediately and extended a hand in her direction.

"Are you hurt?"

Her hands were raw, and her right knee was scraped. As she watched, blood beaded along the deepest welt, but no real harm was done.

"I am fine," she said.

"It might be easier for you if you follow behind. You will have time to stare at me after we've stopped."

She didn't try to defend herself but took his hand to rise and then fell in behind him, watching the path with more care.

He picked his way over rocks and up a small rise to a copse of trees where a small stream tumbled between the trunks.

"Here. The water is sweet and cold, but take care to stay on the banks—it deepens abruptly. You can wash your wounds as well."

"I am not wounded."

"You are not bleeding?" he asked mildly.

She frowned, caught in her lie and not certain how he could possibly know such a thing.

"Are you certain you cannot see?" She waved her arms to test his claim.

"The air moves when you do that," he said. "I can hear you . . . and feel it. And blood has a very particular scent."

She stopped flapping, embarrassed. "You smelled my blood?"

"Yes."

"Where am I bleeding?"

"I don't know that . . . but the flesh on the knees is much thinner than that on the palms. And judging from the sound of your fall, I'm guessing your knees are bleeding."

"Only one of them," she grumbled. "It doesn't even hurt."

"I think it does. Do you need my help?"

She ignored his question and moved past him to the creek. She paid heed to his instructions, though, and stayed on the bank, drinking her fill from the water that rushed over the smooth rocks. When she was sated, she rinsed the salt from her arms and legs and washed her bloodied knee, careful to do so without a wince or murmur. He waited nearby, his head tipped in such a way that she guessed he was listening the way most men watched, counting her swallows and marking each move she made.

"I will refill your flask," she offered when she had finished. "The one I emptied." But he approached, crouched beside her, and did it himself, his head still cocked, keeping track of her.

When he rose again, tucking the flask into his belt, she rose too, suddenly fearful she'd offended him, and that he would leave.

"I am Ghisla," she said.

"Ghisla," he repeated with a nod. "How old are you, Ghisla?"

"I have fourteen summers."

"Fourteen?" He sounded surprised.

"Yes."

"You are . . . small?" He asked the question as though he wasn't certain he was correct . . . or he wasn't certain she was being truthful.

"I am very small. My mother said all our people grow slowly."

"Your mother?"

"She is dead." Her voice was dull to her own ears, but the boy didn't say he was sorry or ask for further explanation. He was simply quiet, as though waiting for her to tell him more. She didn't.

"How old are you?" she asked.

"I am sixteen. We are not so different in age," he said slowly.

"You are tall," she said.

"Am I?" he asked, interested.

"Do your people grow big?"

"I don't know."

"You don't know because you can't see?" she pressed.

"I don't know because I . . . don't . . . know my people."

"Do you have a name?"

He seemed to think about that. "Yes."

She waited, but he didn't offer it.

"What shall I call you?" Her voice was sharp now. She was weary. Not scared. Not anymore. Just weary. Her bones ached and her belly growled in hunger, and the water she'd filled it with sloshed angrily against the hollows.

"You can call me Hod."

"Hod?" What an odd name. It rhymed with *toad*. She wondered if he would suddenly hop away. She hoped he wouldn't. She needed him. She had grown very tired all of a sudden.

"Yes. Hod. That is what Arwin calls me."

"Arwin . . . Your teacher?"

"Yes."

"Maybe Arwin can teach me too," she murmured.

Hod frowned, confused.

"But . . . you can see," he asked, halting. "Can't you?"

"Yes. But I don't know how to live on my own."

His face smoothed in understanding.

"I am very tired, Hod," she said. "I am very tired and very hungry. And yes . . . I need your help."

He brought her to a cave whose mouth yawned like that of a whale carved in the rock. He entered it without hesitation, the darkness almost immediately swallowing him whole.

"It is very dark in there," she cried, reluctant to follow. He answered immediately.

"I do not need the light . . . but I will make a fire, and you can rest there, near the opening."

She sank down obediently, peering into the depths, trying to find him, but the darkness was complete. She waited, anxious, weary, but comforted by the sounds that emerged.

Mere moments later, twin flames bloomed, one from a torch that protruded from the cave wall, another from the pit that lay deeper in the cave. Hod stood beneath the torch, his staff set aside, and he called her name.

"Ghisla, is the light sufficient?"

"Yes."

"Come inside, then. I will feed you."

The interior of the cave was as big as the home she'd lived in with her family. Bigger, if the tunnels that led off the sides opened into additional rooms. She would not be exploring them today. Skins lined the walls and the floor, and shelves filled with baskets and jars rose on every side. It was like no cave she'd ever seen before. A table with carved legs and four chairs was pushed to the side. Another table, long and narrow, was lined with candles and sundry things, and yet another was bare but for a row of knives.

"Sit at the table. It won't take me long," he instructed.

Hod unwrapped some meat from a waxy skin and cut a chunk of bread from a loaf in a cloth beside it. He had cheese and wine and honey too, and he set everything in front of her before he pulled out another chair and sat down.

"Please. Eat," he said, and she pounced on the offering.

She had eaten more than her share—half of the meat and more than half of the bread—when she stopped long enough to observe the boy across from her. He did not eat like her brothers. He ate carefully, neatly, chewing with his mouth closed and his elbows tucked to his sides.

She remembered belatedly that he was only blind . . . not deaf . . . and the happy noises she'd been making had most definitely been noted. She covered her mouth over an indelicate burp and set down her empty goblet. She waited for him to finish, keeping her eyes averted. He seemed to know when she was staring.

Now that her eyes had adjusted, she could see what appeared to be a bedroom through an arch to her right. A mattress on a wooden frame, fat and firm-looking, peeked out from beneath a giant pile of furs. Pillows encased in silk were stacked on top.

"Can I sleep there?" she whispered, trusting Hod would know of what she spoke.

"No. Arwin would not like that," Hod said. "But do not worry. I will make you a nest near the fire."

"A nest?" The words made her think of the rats that lived in the ship's hold. She did not want to sleep in a nest.

"It is what Arwin says I do when I prepare to sleep. I like everything just so. Anything else makes me feel like I'm floating away."

"Will you sleep by the fire too?" She wasn't sure how she felt about sleeping in his presence. She wasn't certain how she felt about sleeping alone either.

"I do not need to sleep now . . . but I have my own chamber. I will not be far."

He made a small circle of rocks and inside them placed a stack of furs as high as her knees. He covered it all with a wool blanket that smelled surprisingly clean—like cedar and salt air—and invited her to lie down.

She didn't question his rock circle or the marks he drew on their surfaces with a blackened stick from the fire. It was a simple circle with an arrow protruding out from above and below. It did not alarm her; it made her feel protected. She whispered her thanks, closed her eyes, and within seconds was asleep.

She floated for a very long time, back in the ocean but no longer cold, drifting back to her home, back to the time before, to people who existed only in her dreams.

She was thirsty. So thirsty. Her mouth was a crater filled with dust, and she coughed as she sought to fill her lungs. Her tongue lolled against the back of her throat—stiff and dry and useless. She rolled to the side and coughed again, gasping, and her tongue fell through her lips and lay against the pillow. But she could breathe. At least she could breathe, and she panted thankfully, her eyes still closed, gathering her strength to move again. She needed water. Gilly had brought water from the well just last night and filled the cup beside her bed. Or the night before. She could not remember now.

"That one is alive. What should we do?" The voice was afraid and the sound was muffled, like he held a hand over his mouth.

"Do not touch her. Do not touch anything. She will soon be dead."

Were they talking about her?

The voices retreated, and Ghisla fought to open her eyes.

"Mother?" she whispered, but the word was no more than a moan. Then she remembered.

Mother was sick. Father was sick. Peder and Morgana and Abner were sick too. She remembered that now. They were all so sick. But Gilly . . . Gilly was not sick. Gilly had brought her water.

She tried to say his name, but her tongue lay heavy against her teeth. She pushed herself up, swaying under the weight of her head and the resistance in her limbs. The water was there, and she drank gratefully, though it dribbled out the sides of her mouth and ran down the front of her shift. It was not cold and it tasted odd—like it had sat in the cup too long.

Someone had started a fire. She felt the heat at her back and the smoke in her lungs. The wood was too wet. She could smell the damp.

"Gilly?" She could see his boots just beyond the foot of her bed. He'd slept thus for nights on end. She braced herself and rose on teetering legs. He had tried to care for them all. Poor Gilly. She would bring him her cup.

He'd pulled a blanket over his shoulders and shoved a pillow under his head, but he was not asleep. He stared up at her with glassy disinterest, not answering, not responding, not moving at all. A fly landed on his eye and he didn't even blink.

The fire had escaped the grate. It was crawling up the wall between the rooms.

"Gilly . . . we have to go," she whispered. The fly on his face was joined by another, but the smoke billowed and the flies flew toward the open door.

She reached for Gilly's boots and began dragging him across the floor. His boots came loose with a wet swoosh, and she staggered back, still clutching them as she fell to the floor. She might have screamed, but the fire had begun to roll above her, popping and spitting, and she stared up at the ceiling, waiting to be consumed. Suddenly, a man was there, hoisting her up and dragging her from the room.

He set her beside the well, but he took Gilly's boots and threw them back toward the flames, an offering to the beast that had consumed her home. Other figures—more soldiers—flickered in the orange glow of the waning day. Red skies were mother's favorite.

But it was not the sun that made the heavens burn.

The soldiers were setting the village on fire.

Cottages and fields, barns, and wagons. Animals. People.

People were piled one atop the other, a teetering pyre of flesh and bone. They too were set ablaze.

Ghisla pushed herself up, coughing and groaning, and took two steps toward the house before her legs refused to carry her and she fell again. A long blade tickled her nose, but she could not find the strength to move or the will to open her eyes.

The voices came again, and she willed the soldiers not to spare her, but to take her swiftly. She did not want to burn, but she did not want to live. Mayhaps they could toss her into the well and let her sink into the cold darkness.

"Should we take her with us, Gudrun? She might live."

"Leave her there. If she lives, she lives. But I'll not be bringing her into my keep. You should not have touched her."

"I will burn my clothes."

24

"We will all burn our clothes. And then we will petition the gods that we aren't next."

"If she lives, she will be the only one," another voice grunted. "The only one in the whole village. All the Songrs are gone."

 ◦◦◦

"Ghisla."

Her name echoed from far away. She ignored it. She was ready to burn with all the others. She was not even afraid. But she would miss the nest Hod had made for her.

Hod. It was Hod who was speaking.

Memory settled as she rose from the deep well of sleep.

She was not home. She would never be home again. There was no home.

"Ghisla." He was closer . . . or maybe she was. She was rising through the layers of sleep, rising against her will to the surface of the sea and the boy who hovered over her.

"Ghisla, you must wake now." She felt a hand on her brow and fingertips at her lips, as though he tested to see whether she still breathed. She was not dead. Sadly, she was not dead.

"Ghisla. You must wake," he repeated. "Your lips are dry and your skin is too hot. You need water and food. Ghisla . . ."

She raised a weary hand and swatted her name away. She did not want to wake. She did not want water or food. Suddenly, she was floating again, and she jolted, panicked, but her arms were too heavy to flail and her lids were too weary to open. Something dug into her belly, and she realized groggily that he was carrying her over his shoulder. Hod. Hod the Toad, Hod the blind boy, was carrying her. She forced her eyes open, and the ground bounced below her.

"You are blind," she rasped.

"Yes. And you are sick. You are also very light. Which is fortunate for me. I have never carried someone before."

She was slung over his shoulder like a lamb, his right hand securing her legs, his left hand wrapped around his staff.

"It is not yet dark . . . Could you not have let me sleep a bit longer?" she groaned.

"You have been asleep for two days. I had to use a rune to make you wake."

"A rune?"

He did not answer but lowered her gently into the creek where he'd taken her to drink before. She gasped as the cold engulfed her, but he kept a hand beneath her head, keeping her face above water. It was not deep where she lay. She could feel the rocks against her shoulder blades and the small of her back. Her feet floated up, but she would not be swept away in the current.

"C-c-could you not just bring w-water to me?" she said, teeth chattering. "Why did you have to put me in the stream?"

"Your skin needs to cool. You need to drink . . . and you need a bath. This was the easiest way to accomplish all of those things."

"I do not need a bath." But she did need to relieve herself. The urge was terrible, but though the water would whisk it away, she could not do something so intimate with him looking on.

"Go away," she snapped. "I need some privacy."

"I cannot see you," he reminded her.

"But you can smell me," she grumbled.

His brows rose in surprise and his nose wrinkled. Belatedly she realized what she'd implied.

"I do not mean that!" she said. "I only need to empty my water."

He eased her upright as he rose and then released her hesitantly. She swayed and her head knocked against his knee. He waited a moment, like he didn't trust the creek or her strength, but she swatted at his leg.

"Go."

"You are already much better," he remarked, but he did as she asked, retreating downstream in search of their supper. He'd caught two shining, silvery fish before she'd summoned the strength to do anything but sit in the stream.

"My flask is on the rock near your head. A bit of soap too, if you like," he called out a few minutes later. She muttered to herself about him "listening and not leaving" but made thorough use of both.

"Are all young girls so ill-tempered?" he called when she didn't answer him.

"Are all blind boys so nosy?" she hollered back.

"I don't know any other blind boys. But I can't help it if I hear— and smell—better than others do."

"Ha. You don't smell any better to me." Actually, he did. He smelled quite lovely. He smelled of honey and peat and the bark of the needled trees near his cave. He smelled clean. It was an odd thing for someone to be so clean—almost as odd as his name. Her brothers had not smelled nice. Not ever. Mother had had to coax them to wash, and they never did a good job of it.

The thought made her ache.

"Your breathing has changed. Are you all right?" he called.

"You can hear me breathing?" she gasped.

"Yes . . . Are you still unwell?"

"I said I needed privacy, Hod," she whispered, but he heard that too. Suddenly he was back, kneeling beside her. He pressed his palms to her cheeks, checking for fever.

"I am fine," she said. "I feel fine."

"The heat is gone," he agreed. "Are you finished?"

"What . . . You can't tell?" she snapped.

"Only you know whether you are finished," he said softly. "I can't hear your thoughts. I wish I could."

"I have used all the soap, and your flask is empty," she supplied, trying to control her irritation. Beneath the prickling was a welling terror.

She wasn't tired anymore. She could not sleep away the hours ahead, and there would be nothing to distract her from her predicament. She was lost. She was alone. And she had nowhere to go.

"Can you walk?" he asked, like he'd done on the beach.

"Yes." But she made no move to stand. "Hod?"

"Yes?"

"I didn't want to wake up. I would like to sleep again."

"I know . . . but a bird must leave its nest."

"Why?" she sighed.

"To eat. To live. To learn."

"I don't want to live. You said you used a rune to wake me. Can you use a rune to make me sleep forever?"

He was silent for a moment. "I should not have done that," he admitted, misgiving ringing in his words.

"Done what?"

"I should not have told you about the rune. I am not accustomed to guarding my words. There is usually no one to hear them except Arwin . . . and he demands that I share them all. And master them."

"Master your words?"

"Yes. And the runes." He winced. "I've done it again."

"Where is Arwin?" Had she asked that before?

"He will be back. I would . . . appreciate it if you did not tell him about the runes."

"What can I tell him? I know nothing of such things. And you have not answered me. Can you make me sleep again?"

"I do not want you to sleep," he said. "I would like to talk to you. I would like to hear you sing some more."

"I do not want to sing."

"Come . . . You will feel better when you are dry and fed." He held out his hand. She took it, and he pulled her to her feet. She wrung out the skirts of her dress and he waited, his head tipped, listening to her. When he turned to go, she followed him.

2

SIDES

Hod worked like he'd gutted a fish a thousand times, and when she offered to help, he bade her sit, telling her it would be easier for him if she kept the space around him clear.

"I know what I am doing . . . but I can't see what *you* are doing. So you sit still and stay out of my way. You can talk to me. I am tired of my own thoughts."

"I don't like your name," she said, surprising them both.

"I am named for a god."

"Which god?"

"Hod." He laughed and she winced.

"I don't know this god. Are you teasing me? My brothers used to tease me. They were very good storytellers. They would persist until I believed them, and then they would laugh when I did."

"I am not teasing you. Arwin does not allow such things . . . though I have tried. He is almost as ill tempered as you are." His voice was kind, and a smile played around his mouth.

"You are teasing me now."

"No. Just trying to soften the truth. Where are your brothers? Where is your family? You said your mother was dead. Are your brothers dead too?"

"They are all dead. They grew ill, one after another."

"You didn't?"

"I did. But I got better. They did not."

"You are still very frail."

"Yes. I am easily tired. And I am even smaller than I was before."

"Why were you on the sea?"

She did not want to talk about the sea or what had come before. She shook her head and then remembered that he couldn't see her.

"Tell me the story of Hod," she insisted.

"Me . . . or the god?"

"Both. But first . . . the god. I still do not think he is real."

"I do not know if he exists . . . but he is real," Hod said.

She shook her head but found herself fighting a smile at his play on words.

"Do you know Odin?" he asked.

"I know Odin."

"And Thor?"

"Yes. His hammer makes the thunder."

"Then you know about Loki."

"I have heard his name. But I do not know Hod."

"Hod was a son of Odin. But . . . like me . . . he was blind." He was silent then, and she waited for more. She found she liked this story—and believed it.

"Did Hod have a weapon like Thor?" she asked.

"Arwin says his lack of sight was his weapon."

"How?"

"Everyone underestimated him. No one paid him any mind. They thought him weak . . . vulnerable, but Arwin believes our weaknesses and our strengths are the very same thing. Two sides of the same sword."

She didn't understand, but she didn't question him, and Hod continued with his story.

"Odin had many sons. Our land—Saylok—is named for one of his sons. I will tell you his story too, if you like."

"I have not heard of him either."

"Some are more well known than others, and some are not known at all. Some were hated, some beloved. Most beloved was Baldr, who was so loved by his mother that she convinced every living thing to agree not to harm him, though she forgot to negotiate with the lowly mistletoe. Even the fates looked kindly on Baldr and would warn him of all attempts to harm him before the attempts were made.

"Odin's son Loki hated that Baldr was loved and that he was simply tolerated. He too wanted to be loved, but instead of spending his energy making himself useful and worthy of Odin's affection and esteem, he spent his days trying to find the one thing that would destroy Baldr. Loki sent women to seduce Baldr with lips stained with the berries from the mistletoe. He sent warriors with weapons fashioned from the boughs. But all were unsuccessful because Baldr knew their intentions. Loki visited the Norns, the fates, at the base of Yggdrasil, the tree of life, and they laughed at his efforts. 'You cannot kill him, Loki,' they cackled."

Hod made his voice sound like a crone's, and Ghisla snickered. He was a good storyteller.

"Loki asked, 'If not me, who can?' But the Norns did not know. They said, 'We can only see what can be seen.' Loki thought that an odd response, and he left the fates with their riddle in his head. He puzzled over it for days until he came across Hod, who was hunting in the woods with his bow. He noticed how Hod listened for his prey, but never saw his arrows fly . . . or fall. Loki realized he had the answer to his riddle."

"A blind god . . . hunting?" Ghisla thought that unlikely.

31

"I hunt. I fish. I do many things," Hod said, slicing the fish he'd caught and placing it on the grate above the glowing coals.

"What did Loki do then?" she asked, sheepish.

"Only a god could kill Baldr . . . Only another god could get close."

"But why would Hod kill Baldr? Was he jealous too?" she interrupted again.

"No. But Loki thought he could trick Hod. Fate would not see him coming, because Hod would not know what he was about to do."

"The Norns could not see what Hod did not see?" she asked, trying to understand.

"Yes. If Hod did not intend to kill his brother . . . and if he did not even know he had . . . then the fates would not see it either. And they would not be able to warn Baldr."

"We can only see what can be seen," she parroted, and shivered a little. "I do not like the Norns."

"Loki and Hod went hunting. Loki told Hod to shoot. Hod believed he was killing a beast. He shot Loki's arrow, made of mistletoe, through his brother's heart. The beloved Baldr, killed by a blind man."

Ghisla gasped. She had not expected such an abrupt and tragic ending.

"Poor Hod," she whispered. "How evil of Loki."

"Yes . . . well. Loki was chained to a rock for eternity with a poisonous snake hanging over his face, dripping venom into his eyes. And that is where I got my name," Hod replied with finality, his story ended.

He threw the fish entrails onto the flame and washed his hands and his blade in a little pool that continuously renewed itself and emptied into crevices unknown. It was no bigger than a man's shield—not big enough for submersion of someone bigger than a babe—but it was a fascinating luxury in the stony enclosure.

"What happened to Hod after he killed Baldr?" she asked as he joined her once more beside the grate.

"His father banished him, and the heavens wept for the loss of two of Odin's sons: Baldr and Hod. Two gods . . . inextricably linked."

In the dirt he drew a character—two half moons, back to back, one that opened to the left and one that opened to the right. An arrow bisected the first crescent, and its shaft penetrated the second through the back.

"That is the story of the blind god, Hod, and this"—he tapped the ground—"is his rune. It is a good story, no?"

She frowned. "Why would Arwin name you Hod?" It seemed almost cruel.

"He says I must learn from his example."

"Huh. And why did Arwin name you . . . and not your parents?"

"I had a different name once, I suppose. But I do not know what it was. I was very small when I came to live with Arwin."

"You live here . . . in this cave, all the time?"

"Arwin is the cave keeper. There is one cave keeper in each clan."

"I did not know caves needed keeping," she said, doubtful, though it was a very fine cave.

"Only some caves."

"I think you are telling me stories again," she said.

"No," he said. "It is true."

"Well . . . I liked the story of Hod, the god . . . but I still do not like that name."

He shrugged. "It is only a name. It matters little. Who gave you your name?"

"Ghisla means *promise*. It means a sacred oath. But my mother and father never told me why they chose it. And they certainly didn't keep their promise to me."

"What promise was that?"

"They left me behind."

"But not by choice," he soothed.

"Then they should not have sworn to me that all would be well."
Her sudden anger felt good. It burned off the clinging sadness, sizzling
and snapping, and she considered it, feeding it with more thoughts of
injustice. Mayhaps if she hated her family she would not hurt so much.

"It is only a name," he repeated softly, almost defending them, and
her anger flared toward him. He sighed as though he felt the heat of it,
and for several moments they sat in silence, waiting for their dinner to
cook. It was not until they were finished eating, their plates washed and
dried and set neatly on the shelf, hot tea in their cups, that he spoke
again.

"Do you worship Odin where you come from?" he asked, steer-
ing her to new, cooler waters. She let them wash over her, dousing the
flame of her ire.

"The Northlands are very vast," she answered. "I cannot speak for
all who live there. I am from Tonlis. We sing songs to him . . . and to
Freya . . . and to the stars and the ground and the rocks and the plants.
We have music for all things."

"You're a Songr," he said, awe ringing in his words. "I have heard
tales of the Songrs."

"You have?"

"Arwin says the Songrs sing the runes."

"I do not know runes," she protested, frowning.

"No . . . not many do. But you know the songs."

"I know many songs."

"Will you sing one for me? Please?" he pressed.

"I do not want to sing right now. I don't know if I want to sing
anymore."

"But . . . why?" The note of pleading in his voice was sweet, and
she almost relented right then.

"It hurts too much," she rasped.

"It hurts your throat?"

"It hurts my heart."

34

He was silent, and she thought he'd accepted her refusal.

"Arwin says the pain will become strength if we embrace it," he said.

"I do not like Arwin."

Hod laughed, the hot brew he'd just sipped spewing from his mouth.

"I do not think he exists. I think he is like the blind god," she added, taunting him.

"You do not think *Arwin* is real?"

"You've never seen him, have you?" she countered.

He laughed again. "You are a very clever girl! And you are smiling. I can hear it."

She *was* smiling. How surprising.

"Why do you not have hair?" she asked, needing something new to talk about.

"I have hair." He rubbed his palm over the stubble that covered his skull. "I just prefer it this length. Hair holds scent. I don't want to smell myself. Hair also attracts crawling things."

Ghisla scratched her head and then winced when he grinned like she'd proven his point. The boy did not need eyes; he could hear her every move.

"There are no crawling things in my hair," she argued, but the mere suggestion had her shaking her locks and swatting at her head.

"Come here." He patted the ground beside him. "I will help you."

She frowned, considering, and then acquiesced, scooting closer to him.

He gathered her hair in his hands and parted it, tossing each weighty, tangled half over her shoulders, exposing her nape to him.

"What are you doing?" She tried to look over her shoulder, but he straightened her head so she was once again looking away, her hair curtaining her face on either side.

"Be still." He ran something sharp over her neck. It tickled and . . . stung. He soothed it with something wet and warm, smearing it with a swipe of his thumb.

"Are you drawing something on my neck? A rune?" she asked.

"There," he said.

Her skin crawled and she slapped at her forehead as a bug skittered across her brow. Another fell into her lap, its legs waggling in outrage, before it flipped over and fled.

"Ew!" Ghisla screeched. Two more, one a spider with spindly legs, crawled over her hands, and she squeaked and brushed them away.

"What did you do?" she demanded.

"It won't last, but for now, your hair is your own. I have nothing to help you untangle it . . . but I can comb through it with my hands and bind it. Like a rope." He added, "I am very good with my hands."

She could comb through it with her own hands. She could braid it too. But she was suddenly hungry for companionship. For touch. Her sister had often brushed her hair. It was something they had done for each other.

"All right," she agreed.

Hod was careful, starting at the ends of her hair and moving upward through the strands. His nails were short and his patience long, and her eyes began to droop as he worked.

"You are bending like a bowstring," he said.

"I am sleepy again." But it was not weariness that made her sway. It was comfort. She had missed the touch of gentle hands.

"It is not as neat or as tight as my weaving . . . but I don't want to hurt you. It will do for now," he said as he finished.

"Thank you." She scooted away but felt obliged to give him something in return. She had been taught to reciprocate kindness with kindness; a favor must always be answered with a favor.

"I suppose I could sing to you," she said. "One song."

"I would like that very much."

She opened her mouth and closed it again. She didn't know what to sing. All the songs in her heart and head were of her home and her family. Her thoughts raced, and the only song that came to mind was a song Gilly had sung about a toad. *I'll sing you a sad little ode about a sightless toad.* It had been stuck in her thoughts since Hod had told her his name. *Hod* rhymed with *toad*.

She sang the song without thinking, changing the words as she went.

> There once was a boy named Hod.
> He was a sightless toad.
> He croaked and hopped,
> To escape the pot,
> And ended up squished on the road.

Hod's brow furrowed, and his lips pursed, and Ghisla felt a wash of shame. Maybe her song was cruel. She had meant to make him smile, but he was not smiling.

"I look like a toad?" he asked.

"No! You look nothing like a toad."

"I did not think so. I have held one in my hands. They are slippery . . . and quite unpleasant."

"I've always liked toads," Ghisla said meekly, trying to fix her blunder.

"Did you compose it for me?" he asked. "Just now?" Hod's voice did not sound wounded. Only curious.

"No. It is a silly song my brother used to sing. Gilly was always crafting songs about funny things. Regular things."

"Surely he did not know a boy named Hod."

"No," she said. She sang the song the way Gilly had sung it, using the original words.

I'll sing you a sad little ode,
About a sightless toad,
He croaked and he hopped
To escape the pot,
And ended up squished on the road.

"That is a sad little ode," Hod said, smiling. "Sing me another. Sing me the one you sang in the sea."

"I sang many songs in the sea," she whispered. He had circled back to his original question.

"Why?"

"I wanted my family to hear me. I wanted Father Odin to hear me . . . and let me join them."

"You sang his name . . . Odin's name. I heard it. It is a song the keepers in the temple sing."

"Father Odin, are you watching?" she sang, knowing what song he spoke of. He nodded, eager, and she continued. "Father Odin, are you watching? Do you see me down below? Will you take me to the mountain, where the brave and glorious go?"

"That's the one. Sing it again," he whispered.

She did, adding in verses, supplicating Odin. She did not fear death, so she knew death would not come. Fear was like that. Fear called out to fate, and fate always answered.

When she was finished, her song still echoing through the cave, she looked at Hod. He had closed his strange eyes and his back was rigid.

"Hod?" she asked, startled. She reached out and grasped his hand. "It is a death song. I should not have sung it," she apologized. "Mayhaps you believe in such things. I did not mean to frighten you."

His hand curled around hers. "I was not afraid . . . but I could see the mountain. Your voice paints pictures in my mind. I thought your voice was a gift from Odin himself and listened all night in the storm.

I could hear you. But I did not see pictures. I did not see . . . colors. It's . . . wonderful."

"My voice paints pictures?" she gasped. She had never heard such a thing. But . . . she had never sung to a blind man before.

"Will you sing more?" he asked, still holding her hand.

She sang him the song of the harvest—the gold of the apples, the red of the wine, the blue of the sky, and the leaping orange of the flames they danced around. As she sang, Hod's hand grew tighter and the other joined it, until he was gripping her arm like he was afraid she'd escape . . . or leave him behind. His face was suffused with wonder, and the firelight glowed in his cloudy eyes.

"I did not know what they were called. The colors . . . I see them in my mind . . . but I did not know what they were called. Will you sing it again so I can see them?"

How could she refuse him? She sang it from the beginning.

"The gold of the apple," he marveled. "That is gold? What else is gold?"

She thought about that. "My hair is gold."

He touched it, rubbing a strand between his fingers, his brow furrowed in concentration, like he was memorizing it.

"And your eyes?" he asked.

"Blue. Like the sky in the song."

"Blue like the sky," he repeated. "Blue . . . is a glorious color."

"Yes. It is. Sometimes the sea is the same blue as the sky. But it changes its color. Sometimes it is green with white mist . . . like *your* eyes."

"My eyes are like the sea?"

"Yes. They are like no eyes I've ever seen before."

"Do you know a song about the sea?" he asked, hopeful. "I should like to see it."

She thought, and it came to her easily, the melody that rolled like the waves and reflected the grays of the sky and the purple of the mountains. Throughout, Hod sat, facing her, his legs crossed and his body still, turned to stone. Everything was frozen but his hands. She did not tell him to loosen his hold. His grip was a distraction from the agony of the songs. His wonder distracted her too.

"Please don't stop," he begged when she slowed, and she sang herself raw like she'd done on the sea. If she could not sleep, she might as well sing.

Hours later, she crawled onto the nest he'd built for her and left him sitting by the fire, his legs crossed and his appetite—at least for now—sated. She'd sung him every song she'd been able to conjure.

"Good night, Hod," she whispered, but he said nothing in return. It was almost as though he hadn't heard her at all.

When the sun rose, it lit the cave from the entrance to the first curve for several minutes before the angle changed and the light retreated once more. It was enough to rouse her for good. She groaned, unable to ignore her thirst and her discomfort any longer. She was sore, achy, as though instead of being tossed on the sea she'd swum to shore. She could see the prints of Hod's fingers on her skin. He must have bruised her while she sang to him. The marks were a deep purple like the circles beneath his eyes, and he was in the same position he'd been in when she'd retired the night before.

"Did you not sleep?" she said blearily, sitting up from her circle of stones. He shifted and shuddered, but he heard her this time.

"No. My head was filled with new things."

He didn't ask her to sing or reach for her arm again, but his hands trembled like he wanted to. He forgot his staff when they left the cave and stumbled like he was suddenly afraid. He'd been as sure footed as she the day before—*more* sure footed than she. He stopped and took a deep breath. Then he turned back to the cave, retrieved his stick, and walked beside her to the creek.

"You said your hair is gold and your eyes are blue. I know you are small and that you've been ill—your bones are frail and your skin is soft. You are bristly, like a rose, petals and prickles with a very distinct . . . scent."

"It is not kind to tell someone they smell." She was teasing him. He'd been nothing but kind.

"Is it kind to call someone a sightless toad?" he asked, tone mild. "I did not say you smelled bad . . . not anymore. I said you had a distinct scent."

"What does that mean?"

"Every living thing has its own fragrance, some more marked than others, but a scent is impossible to hide. I am not around people often enough to identify regions, though I suppose I could do that based on my knowledge of the flora and fauna from whence they came. I have been to all the lands of the clans—Berne, Leok, Adyar, Ebba, Joran, and even Dolphys—though I have been to Adyar and Leok most. They are closest. Each land and each people have a scent, and the scents merge from border to border, some notes fading, some strengthening."

"What do I smell like?"

"You smell of grain and grass and berry juice, though those smells are hidden beneath that moldering rag."

It *was* a rag . . . but she had nothing else to wear.

"You smell clean," she said.

"I cannot abide the smell of my skin or perspiration in my robes or mud or filth if it clings to my shoes," Hod said. "Those smells . . . blind me . . . to the scents around me. So I am always clean. It is for my own safety. We will have to find you something else to wear."

He sounded as if he meant for her to stay, and something eased in Ghisla's chest.

"Did your family till the earth and plant seeds?" he asked.

"Yes. Why?"

"You smell like the earth too."

"That is where I want to be."

"In the earth?"

"Yes. That is where my family is."

"You are not funny today," he sighed.

"I do not mean to be funny ever. There is nothing to laugh about."

"Are you sure you are a child? You sound like an old woman. You don't speak like a child . . . not any child I've ever heard. And you don't sing like one. Maybe you are really an old woman. An old witch, wearing the skin of a child to trick me." He frowned, but his voice was light with teasing. "Did Arwin send you? Is this one of his tests?"

"How am I testing you?"

"You have given me pictures . . . and now I want to do nothing else but see. My ears are dull, my nose too. It is like I am deep in the cave, all alone." He was not teasing anymore.

"I will not sing to you again," she promised.

"But I want you to," he whispered, the sound so mournful that tears pricked the backs of her eyes. She had thought her tears were all used up.

"Mayhaps it was too much at once. Too many songs," she said.

"Mayhaps."

"The songs have made you sad," she said. "They make me sad too."

"No. They do not make me sad. They make me . . . aware. They make me want to see."

"Did you not want to see before?"

"I did not miss what I never had. Now I *know* what I do not have."

"It is like having a family . . . and having them ripped away. I think it would be easier if I had never known them either."

"What were their names?"

"My mother was Astrid. My father was Wilhem. Morgana was my sister. She was the oldest. Abner and Gilbraig were my brothers."

"Were they older than you too?"

"I am—I was—the youngest. Abner was a man . . . Father always treated him like a man. Gilly was your age. But he was smaller than you are."

"Your people grow slowly," he said, remembering what she'd told him.

"Yes." And now her people did not grow at all.

"Gilly?" he pressed when she grew quiet. "Is Gilly . . . Gilbraig?"

"I could not call him Gilbraig. It did not fit. I called him Gilly, and he called me Ghissy."

"It is a sign of affection to alter the name like that?" he asked.

"Yes. I suppose it is."

"Then . . . will you call me Hody?"

"Hody?"

"Yes. To show . . . affection."

"It is still a terrible name."

"It is just a name," he said, repeating the sentiment of the day before. "It means little." But it clearly meant something to him.

"All right, Hody."

3

Runes

"I have a pair of hose that rise too high on my legs, and a tunic that pulls across my back. They are well worn, and I do not know if they will fit. But I've a length of rope to keep the trousers up if they don't, and they are clean."

She took the items from his outstretched hand. When she did, he stood by, waiting for her to try them on.

"Go," she insisted.

"I cannot see you," he reminded, impatient. "I wait only to hear if they will do."

"It feels like you can."

"I can't," he insisted, frowning. "Do you think I lie?"

She sighed heavily, relenting, and tugged off the long shift that wasn't much more than a tattered sack with a hole for her head. She tossed it toward him, intending for it to hit him in the face. He'd complained enough about the smell; she thought it would be humorous. Instead, he snatched it from the air and tossed it on the fire, easily, effortlessly.

She gaped and growled, rushing to cover herself with his old tunic.

"What?" he asked.

"How did you do that if you cannot see me?"

"I heard you."

She huffed, struggling to pull on the hose that were too long and the blouse that slid off her skinny shoulders. She folded the neckline in on itself and rolled the legs of the hose, cinching both at her waist with the bit of rope that Hod offered.

"Can you hear that they don't fit?" she marveled.

"I can hear you making adjustments."

"If you have a bit of thread and a needle, I can fix the hem and alter the neckline, though you've thrown my shift in the fire, so I have nothing else to wear while I do so."

"I cannot see you," he insisted again, a note of irritation in his voice. It made her smile to irk him.

"Yes . . . but what if Arwin returns and I am unclothed?"

He stilled, as though he'd forgotten all about Arwin. He cocked his head, turning his face toward the entrance.

"He has been gone longer than usual. Mayhaps there is something wrong."

Ghisla didn't know what to say, and so said nothing. For several seconds, Hod was frozen, listening, and then his shoulders relaxed.

"He is not near. The forest sounds different when he enters it."

"How does it sound?"

"The birds get quiet. The creatures in the trees and in the brush hear him . . . and I hear them. It is not sound as much as it is a cessation of certain sounds. The silence precedes him, and, if the breeze is right, I catch his scent when he is still a good distance away. He has never returned without me knowing he comes."

That evening when Ghisla sang for Hod, she flinched at his grip, revealing the soreness of her arms. Horrified that he'd hurt her, he tried to keep his hands in his lap as she sang, but the connection wasn't as immediate, and the images weren't as infused with color.

"My ears are overjoyed . . . My heart too, but it is like the night of the storm. I can hear you—your voice found me over miles of stormy sea—but I cannot see your songs. Not clearly. What fills my thoughts are more my own imaginings . . . a communion with your words and sounds, but not your . . . pictures."

She'd held both of his hands after that, and he made her promise to tell him if he was hurting her. When she sang she watched Hod's face, entranced by the emotions that danced there. He didn't keep his eyes closed—he had no need. His eyes didn't see; his mind did, as though she poured her own images into his thoughts with her songs.

He had his favorite songs, the songs of her people, the songs where the lyrics painted pictures, but he also enjoyed exploring.

"Sing me the one about the toad . . . the way your brother sang it. I was not holding your hand when you sang it the first time . . . and I was too distracted by the fact that you gave a toad my name." He smiled, letting her know she was forgiven.

She sang the silly tune, training her own thoughts to picture a croaking, odious little beast who hopped from one catastrophe to another, but her thoughts skittered away before he was flattened by a cart's wheel.

Hod laughed, throwing his head back. "I could see the toad. That was wonderful!"

"You are odd," she said, but she laughed too and sang him another one of Gilly's tunes, one about a talking trout with rainbow scales.

"A rainbow is many colors," Hod marveled.

"I will have to think of a better song—a more powerful song—to show you a rainbow, but I cannot think of one now."

"I don't think it is the songs that have power . . . It is you."

"Mayhaps it is you," she suggested. No one had ever "seen" her songs before. But Hod shook his head, adamant.

"Sing about your family," he urged when she grew quiet. "Show them to me."

"I don't want to. They are mine." She let go of his hands.

He sat in silence for a moment, his head cocked as though he contemplated her, and in a way he did, listening, listening, listening.

"Stop that," she grumbled.

"Stop what?"

"Prying."

"I want only to ease your sadness."

"I am only sad when I am forced to remember. Or sing," she said, her tone wry.

"You are sad all the time. It radiates from your skin and your voice. I hear it in the constant hitch of your breath."

"You have only known me three days."

"I have known you five."

"Two of those days I was sleeping."

"Yes . . . but the sadness was still there."

"My family is gone . . . and the sadness is all I have left."

"How did you end up in the sea, Ghisla? How did you end up here? Washed onto the shore?"

"I walked to a seaside village a day's journey from Tonlis, and I boarded a ship," she confessed.

"All alone?"

"Yes. I hid in the hold. I didn't know where the ship was going, but I didn't care."

"Why?"

"I thought drowning would be a pleasant death."

"It wasn't?"

"No. It was terrible. And I was afraid. And Odin did not hear my death song."

"I think he did. He brought you here. To this land."

Amy Harmon

"Is this land where people come to die?" she asked, wry, thinking he would laugh at her bitter humor.

"Saylok is dying . . . but mayhaps you will help us live."

"Why is Saylok dying?"

"There are no girl children."

"Why?"

"Master Ivo says the land was cursed."

"Who is Master Ivo?"

"He is the Highest Keeper. He is the guardian of the temple and the runes and is the conscience of Saylok."

"Is he the king?"

"No. The king is selected from the clans. There is a castle beside the temple. The king rules the clans . . . and the keepers rule the king, though King Banruud might disagree."

"There are no girls at all?" She could not imagine such a thing.

"In twelve years . . . only the princess. There have been no other daughters of Saylok born in that time. The men bring daughters from other lands . . . but it is not enough . . . and there seems to be no remedy or rune to cure the drought."

"There is a princess?"

"Princess Alba, daughter of King Banruud and Queen Alannah."

"You say the queen's name with sadness."

"Queen Alannah has recently died. The chieftains have been gathered to the temple mount. That is where Arwin has gone. I will hear all about it when he returns."

"Is Arwin a chieftain?"

"No." Hod smiled as though the thought humored him. "Arwin is a keeper—a cave keeper—but he was trained in the temple and often returns when councils are called."

"It seems a complicated system. Keepers and kings and cavemen and curses."

"Don't call Arwin a caveman," Hod laughed. "He will never forgive you. He fancies himself one of the anointed, a powerful keeper, and does not always like that he's been assigned to watch over a cave bedecked in runes."

"There are runes in this cave?" Ghisla asked, her interest piqued.

"Yes," Hod sighed. "I wouldn't mention that to Arwin either. He'll cut off my tongue for speaking so freely and cut off yours for knowing the secret."

"I will not speak of it. I have no interest in runes. I would rather talk about the princess." She would rather talk about anything other than Tonlis.

"Arwin says Alba's birth made Banruud king. There was great hope that the curse was broken. But it has been five years since Alba was born, and there have been no others."

"So Saylok . . . It is not a good place?" She was not certain there was any good place.

"People are afraid. Fear brings out the ugliness. It is easy to be kind and good when it costs us nothing. It is not so easy when it can cost you your life. So people are not kind, and often they are not good. And here . . . you are rarer than gold."

On the morning of their seventh day together—after two days of doing little but singing and letting Hod "see" to his heart's content—Hod proclaimed there were chores to do, and there would be no singing until after supper. Ghisla didn't mind the rest and trailed after him as he ticked off his tasks, helping him where she could. He had a system for everything, a system that fascinated her, and she watched him accomplish a dozen daily tasks with ease and quiet efficiency. He hung the furs that lined the walls and floor on a line that was strung between two trees and beat the dust from them with a broom. She did the same with the furs from her nest, but Hod was stronger than she, and the dirt plumed from his swings far more easily, so she retrieved a basket from the cave and picked berries instead, thinking it a task he couldn't do. But he wasn't a bad berry picker either; he ran his fingers lightly over the leaves, popping off the little balls that conformed to a certain size, and when they were finished, he'd gathered almost as many as she.

In the afternoon, he set his traps in the forest, chopped wood for the fire, and climbed an enormous tree to fetch some honey. He had no fear of heights or the massive beehive high in the branches and began climbing back down with dripping chunks of honeycomb in his basket and a cloud of bees circling his head. Ghisla knew a song about bees and began singing it—"thank you for your golden treasure, we'll not take more than we need"—hoping the bees would retreat. They did, almost immediately, but Hod fell from the tree, landing in a pile at her feet.

He lay on his back, stunned and gasping for air, his eyes fixed up at the branches above him, his basket of honeycomb still clutched in his hand.

"Hody!" Ghisla cried. "Are you hurt?"

"No . . . not . . . exactly," he gasped, searching for the breath that had been pummeled from his breast. "I've grown accustomed to their stings and their sound . . . but I am not accustomed to seeing them swarm."

"You saw them?"

"Only in your song . . . but . . . it distracted me. I wanted to . . . look. And I forgot I was still dangling in the tree."

"I made you fall," she said.

"It was worth it." He grinned. "They should not be able to fly . . . bees. They are fat and furry! And they have such little wings. They are black and . . . what is that color? Yellow? Yellow," he said, satisfied he had it right. "Yellow is like gold," he recited. "Like your hair . . . and grain . . . and the sun . . . and the flowers on the tomato vines and the apples in Tonlis."

He had his breath back, but he didn't rise. He was too caught up in his list making.

"I will try to remember not to sing while you are doing something dangerous," she said, looking down at him and chewing on her lip. "I was not even holding your hand. I didn't think you would . . . see . . . my song."

"But I did," he marveled. "I saw the bees . . . mayhaps not the bees around me . . . but I saw bees."

"Mayhaps . . . we are getting better at it."

"Like finding one's way on a well-trodden path," he said, agreeing. "Let's test it. Sing something else. Something simple . . . like the bee song, but not something you've sung before."

She knew a song about changing leaves and harvest dances that she hadn't shared with him. She remembered her sister laughing and twirling as she sang it, and Ghisla closed her eyes and sang along, swaying with the memory.

"Green and gold and orange and red, here and there and overhead, drifting down to touch the ground. In springtime they'll grow back again," she sang, moving like the falling leaves. The dance was one of turns and twists, and Morgana had loved it more than any other. Ghisla hopped and spun and dipped and bowed, and Hod lay at her feet, listening, rapt.

A roar, unlike that of any beast Ghisla had ever heard, broke their dreamy connection. A rustling and cracking accompanied the bellow, and a figure robed in black, his arms flailing and his staff swinging, rushed toward them.

Hod leaped to his feet in front of her, his stance wide, but the enraged figure was already upon them. The figure slapped at Hod's cheeks, knocking the boy back.

"What is the meaning of this?" the incensed stranger shrieked, the sound rattling her teeth. His cowl fell back, revealing his bald head and beaked nose. A braided white beard hung to his knees, and it bounced like a snake, writhing and wriggling as he struck Hod, who did nothing to defend himself.

"What have you done to my boy, witch?" the man yelled. "What have you done to my boy?"

Hod's nose was bleeding, and he swiped at it, leaving a streak of red across his hand.

"Arwin?" Hod asked, voice ringing with amazement.

"He does not know his own master!" the man wailed, gripping Hod by the shoulders and shaking him.

"No . . . Er-Arwin. I am f-f-fine. I am well," Hod stuttered, trying to pull free, and Arwin shoved him aside.

This was Arwin? Hod's teacher? He was not the wise and gentle figure Ghisla had imagined. When he turned on her, she felt a jolt of the same fear she'd felt when she realized she was not going to follow her family into death. He jabbed at her with his staff, the end punching against her belly, forcing her back against the tree Hod had climbed for his honey.

"Get back, witch."

She obliged, shrinking against the trunk.

"She is not a witch, Arwin," Hod protested. "She is a girl. A Songr. When she sings I can see. I can see, Arwin!"

This revelation seemed to horrify the man, and his black eyes widened in his wizened face.

With the sharp end of his stick he scratched a symbol into the dirt, mumbling words that sounded like a curse, and it was Hod's turn to gasp.

Arwin sliced at his hand, still mumbling, and held his dripping fist over the lines he'd drawn between them. Blood dripped onto the ground. Hod stepped toward her, his hands outstretched, one toward Arwin, one to her, as if to connect and calm them all. But the air sizzled and sparked like a heavy log tossed onto a flame, and Hod froze.

"Master . . . what are you doing?" he moaned.

"I have trapped the wench."

Ghisla tried to run, but the air crackled again and lightning shot upward from the ground when she took a single step. She fell back, clinging to the trunk of the tree.

"Let me go," Ghisla demanded.

"She has shown me her thoughts, Master. You have taught me to hear deception. She is afraid, and her heart races. But she has not sought to deceive. She is not a witch or a siren or a fairy. She is a Songr. A child. A girl child." Hod said *girl child* like she was a chest filled with treasure.

"She is Loki in disguise, here to trick you, just as he did with your namesake. She is here to destroy you."

"She is not Loki, Master. She has dwelled with me here for nigh on a week and has done nothing but sing to me."

Arwin gasped as if that were proof of her perfidy. "It is as Master Ivo said. The keepers will be destroyed. It has begun."

"Master Ivo? You saw the Highest Keeper?" Hod gasped.

Arwin shook his head, his beard writhing, but he did not answer Hod. Ghisla attempted to run again, darting in a new direction, and was knocked off her feet. Her head bounced off a rock, stunning her, and Hod cried out.

"She seeks to escape," Arwin howled. "Who sent you, witch?"

His voice wavered like he stood a long way off, and Ghisla's consciousness flickered. Unfortunately, her pain revived her. She whimpered, rubbing at the back of her head. Her hand came away bloody, and Hod cursed.

"She is bleeding, Master. You have hurt her."

"Your senses must be returning," Arwin said, his relief evident. "I have weakened her."

Hod scraped at the forest floor with the butt of his staff, and Arwin screamed in protest.

"Don't!"

A moment later, Hod was kneeling beside her, his fingers finding the lump forming on the back of her head.

"Are you all right, Ghisla?" he asked.

She was not all right. She was terrified. She swatted at his hands and staggered to her feet. Whatever barrier Arwin had erected around her was gone, and she lurched forward, temporarily freed, temporarily euphoric, her vision still spinning, and ran headlong into the trunk of another tree.

This time Ghisla succumbed to the deep well of unconsciousness.

When she surfaced again, she found herself on the bed Hod had made her in the cave, but her nest was no longer a sanctuary. Arwin had returned, and Ghisla was not welcome or wanted. Her head throbbed and her stomach rolled, but she didn't dare move. Hod and his master were in deep conversation, their backs to her. She observed them through the sweep of her lashes and closed her eyes again, not wanting to hear, not wanting to hope. Hod was pleading with his teacher, his voice low and urgent.

"I did not take her deep into the cave. She has stayed with me since I found her on the shore."

"You cannot *see* her! How would you know what she has *seen*, you fool!" Arwin scolded.

"I have not left her side, Master."

"You are slow. Dulled. She has to be destroyed."

"Destroyed?" Hod gasped.

"She has to leave," Arwin amended. "She cannot be near you. She cannot stay here."

"She is alone . . . like I was. She is from Tonlis. I told you; she is a Songr, Master. I heard her. Even through the storm. She was singing . . . and I heard her. I waited all night for the storm to end, and the waves washed her up onto the sand. I could sense her, even when she stopped singing. A vibration still rose from her skin. It is loud, Master. Louder than even you are, and I can hear you for miles."

"You did not hear me today!" Arwin reminded, silencing him. When Hod spoke again, his voice was pleading.

"Her life song is louder than any living thing I've ever heard. You could teach her. Like you teach me. She has nowhere to go. And she is a girl. She is precious. We cannot turn her away."

"She blinds you."

"No . . . she helps me see!"

"She blinds you, Hod," Arwin repeated. "All your other senses fade to nothing. You know it's true. I can see it in your face. I struck you, and you did not feel it coming. You did not hear *me* coming. I walked into the cave fearing the worst, and you were not here. I had to go looking for you. When I saw you . . . lying in that clearing, the witch dancing around you . . . I thought you were dead."

"It was innocent, Master. She is innocent."

"Innocent or not, for the first time in your life you were truly blind. She does not help you see."

"I need only to practice," Hod pled, but Ghisla heard the wavering in his belief.

"You will lose the sensitivity you have honed. If she is here, you will choose sight instead of insight. She will weaken you. She has weakened you already!"

"She is alone," Hod whispered. "She has no one. Nowhere to go. And she is a girl, Master. A girl! She needs protection."

Silence rose between them, and Ghisla didn't dare open her eyes to see what was unfolding. Her limbs were heavy, pain throbbed in her head, and she lay in dark misery, awaiting her fate. It was minutes before either of them spoke again.

"I have been to Temple Hill," Arwin said. "There is much talk. King Banruud has asked that a girl from each clan be brought to the temple mount. I will take the girl to Chief Lothgar in Leok. He will be relieved to have someone to send."

"But . . . ," Hod protested.

"It is a perfect solution. It is as if Odin himself delivered her."

"He did not deliver her to Leok . . . He delivered her to me," Hod argued, his voice so pained, Ghisla felt a twist in her own chest.

"You are already attached to her," Arwin lamented. "She has ruined you."

"I am not ruined. I am . . . I am . . ." Hod searched for the word and could not find it.

"She will hurt your training, boy," Arwin said, almost gentle.

"Then I will work harder. Please do not send her away."

"I do not have permission to teach her," Arwin yelled, all gentleness gone as quickly as it had come. "The runes are forbidden to her."

"But you would send her to the keepers?" Hod shot back. "To the temple?"

"Master Ivo is keeper of the temple and the runes. He will have to decide what to do with her . . . and the other daughters who are sent there. That is not my charge. She is not my charge. You are."

"Her heartbeat has quickened. She is waking," Hod said, his voice bleak.

A moment passed, and she felt them at her bedside, their combined presence blocking out the firelight that glowed beyond her lids.

"You put stones around her bed? And marked them with runes?" Arwin said, incredulous.

"I only used the runes to help her rest. And to help her wake. And . . . to rid her hair of bugs," Hod confessed, sheepish. "Three runes . . . was all."

"You mock their power with such things."

"What good are runes if they are not used when they are needed? She did not see the runes . . . or understand them."

"I did not raise you to be foolish," Arwin spat.

"You did not raise me to be fooled. I have passed all your tests, Master. I considered that she was disguised . . . that you had sent her. But there was no deceit in her. Not in her breath or her heartbeat. Not in her fear or her words. You must listen to her sing, Master. Then you will know."

"I don't want to listen to her sing. She will beguile me like she's beguiled you."

But there was doubt in his voice, hesitation, and when Ghisla opened her eyes he was there, hovering above her, Hod beside him. His beard tickled her nose.

"Where did you come from, girl?" Arwin demanded.

She groaned, and her head spun.

"She is hurt, Master," Hod said.

"Don't touch her!" Arwin yelled, slapping at his charge.

"Who are you, child?" Arwin asked.

"I am Ghisla," she whispered, and her head screamed.

"It would cost you nothing to take her pain away, Master," Hod said.

"Shh," Arwin growled. "Pain doesn't lie."

"Of course it does," Hod argued. "There is no liar as skilled as pain. Pain will say anything to save itself."

Arwin grumbled, but his fingers, probing and sharp, found their way into her hair. He traced the bump on her forehead with his thumbs and prodded the wound at the base of her skull with his fingers.

"She is a Songr. She has rune blood, Master," Hod said. "You need not use your own."

"Quiet," Arwin demanded, and Hod obeyed. A second later, the old man drew something on her brow, his fingers wet with the blood from her head. His mouth moved over words she couldn't hear, but Hod seemed to, for he exhaled in relief.

Her relief followed instantly.

She blinked up at Hod's teacher. She'd known she didn't like him. But the absence of the pain in her head made her feel slightly more charitable toward him, though he had caused it. She eased herself up so she was sitting with her back to the wall of the cave.

"Ghisla," Hod said, his voice kind. "This is my teacher, Arwin. You mustn't be afraid."

"He thinks I am a witch," she said. Of course she should be afraid. But she found her fear had fled with the pain in her head, as if Arwin's mark had freed her of both.

"Who sent you?" Arwin demanded, holding his staff like a spear, the sharp end only inches from her breast. He was afraid too, she realized suddenly. The thought was almost comical. He was bigger and stronger. He knew magical runes, and he was not bleeding, homeless, and huddling at the end of a sharp stick.

"Who sent you?" he asked again, prodding her ribs with his staff.

"No one sent me. There is no one left," she cried, swatting at the stick.

Hod's brow furrowed over his mossy eyes. She had not told him everything.

"No one?" Hod asked.

"My family is dead," she amended.

"How did you find him? How did you find Hod?" Arwin asked.

"I did not *find* him," Ghisla insisted. "He found me."

"This is true, Master," Hod interjected.

"Shh," Arwin spat. "She found you, Hod. She found us. She is here, isn't she?"

"I am here . . . but I know nothing about you . . . or this place," she said.

"Ask the runes, Master. Then you will know she speaks the truth," Hod urged.

"Silence, boy!" Arwin yowled. He reacted thus with every mention of the runes, as if he thought she had come to take them . . . or see them. Or learn them.

"How old are you, girl?"

"Fourteen summers."

"No," Arwin scoffed as if she'd lied, though she had no reason to do so.

"Yes," she answered.

"You are small. You haven't a woman's form. You look much younger," Arwin argued.

He was right. She had no breasts or hips. And though her hair was long, with Hod's old tunic and leggings, most would think her a boy.

"You don't have the face of a boy," he mused. It was like he read her thoughts. "Too pretty. Lips too pink, eyes too knowing." He nodded to himself, persuaded. "Aye. No doubt about it. You're a witch."

4

STEPS

It was not Ghisla's song that convinced Arwin she was not a witch. It was the fact that he was not nearly so affected by it as Hod, who sat in rapt stillness as she sang Arwin the ballad of the Songr, an anthem of her people and the place known for its music.

When she was finished, Arwin was frowning, confused, and even more suspicious. He'd been terrified to hear her sing, convinced she'd render him helpless and kill him in his stupor. He'd held a bow—strung, drawn, and aimed at her heart—throughout her ballad.

"I see images . . . but they are no more powerful than my own thoughts," he said. "The song paints a story. 'Tis all. It is beautiful, though. Sweet and clear. I should like to hear more." He frowned again, and his eyes narrowed in suspicion. "Mayhaps that is the trick, to hypnotize. To hypnotize . . . and destroy young Hod."

"There is no trick, Arwin," Ghisla said, but he did not believe her, and he guarded her all night, relegating Hod to other chambers, promising that on the morrow he would take her to the man named Lothgar.

She curled in her nest, willing herself to sleep, but could not do so with his eyes boring into her back.

"He is listening, you know. There is no place I can send him where he won't hear. Yet I walked through the forest and was upon him without him knowing I had returned."

She waited, uncertain. She didn't know what he wanted her to say.

"Lothgar will not harm you."

"I don't care if he does. As long as it is quick. And final."

He grunted. "You are an odd child. Lothgar may not accept you."

She was certain he wouldn't. She said nothing.

"He will want to know about your home. It would be better not to tell him."

Burnt fields and a razed village rose in her mind. Was home a country? The land beneath one's feet? Or was home people? She didn't ask him.

"I have no home," she whispered.

"Why are you here?" he asked, suspicious again. Fearful again. It was that note of fear that made her answer.

"I don't know. I did not choose this place. My family died, so I tried to die, but the sea would not have me. Odin would not have me. Even death would not have me. No one will have me. Not even you."

She heard the self-pity in her voice and loathed herself, but when Arwin spoke again, his voice had gentled.

"You cannot stay here, Songr."

"I do not want to stay here," she said. It was true . . . and it was a lie. She didn't want to be anywhere near Arwin, but she would very much like to remain with Hod.

"It is not good for Hod," Arwin added.

"Why?" she asked. But she knew what he was going to say.

"All his senses are dulled when you are near."

"*All* his senses?" That wasn't true.

"All his senses but his sight," he amended. "When he sees, he hears nothing. He feels nothing. He sits like a thirsty drunk, lapping up what he sees like it is elixir. You cannot sing to him forever. The moment you stop . . . he is in darkness again."

"Then I won't sing," she promised.

He scoffed.

"You keep speaking of runes. Is that what you are afraid of? I don't know how to write words. I can't read. I know naught of your silly runes," she said.

He glared, but she continued, desperate to convince him.

"Hod says you are a cave keeper. I don't want your cave. I don't want anything at all . . . except maybe somewhere to sleep and something to eat." She was hungry. Her appetite was returning. Mayhaps that meant she cared enough about her own life to feed it, which worried her. Caring—about herself and others—was not something she wanted to do. She had done that once before. Never again. But she did need somewhere to live.

"I know nothing of runes," she repeated. "I know only of songs."

It was the wrong thing to say. Or maybe he had already made up his mind because Arwin's face was hard and his voice firm.

"You will destroy him. You have to go. You cannot stay here."

Arwin sat in a chair near the fire throughout the night, guarding her, but he had been unable to keep sleep at bay and snored so loudly she lay awake much of the night, caught between indifference and indecision. Hod was powerless; she could not stay with him if Arwin would not allow it. But she could run away again. Hod might hear her go . . . but he would not bring her back. He had nothing to bring her back to.

"I can go anywhere," she said aloud, trying to buoy herself up. She was strong. She was brave. Arwin snorted in his sleep, and tears pricked her eyes.

"I can. And I will."

She rose from the pile of furs. Arwin did not wake.

She paused at the table where the knives were lined up in a neat row and took one, slipping it into the rope belt at her waist. Then she fled from the cave, out into the moonlit night, out into the trees that stood as a silent sentry. She would hide somewhere. Mayhaps she could find her own cave. Or mayhaps she would simply walk until she was too tired to think. She picked her way down the hill, back toward the beach where Hod had found her days ago. She would walk along the shoreline; it would be easier than going higher into the hills. She had made it to the shore when Hod spoke from behind her. She jumped but muffled her scream just in time.

"Don't go," he said.

She caught her breath, panting, but then continued on, out toward the place where the rocks became sand. Hod followed.

"It is not safe."

"He will not let me stay," she said. Her voice rang with accusation, and Hod did not defend himself, nor did he argue the truth of her statement.

"You must let him take you to Lothgar," he said quietly. "Lothgar is an honorable man, and a good chieftain. He has daughters of his own and a wife. He is loved by his people. You will be safe under his guardianship."

The tears were back, prickling and pushing against her eyes.

"I would rather stay with you." It was the darkness that wrenched the confession from her. She would not have said such a thing in the light.

"That is what I wish as well," he whispered. "But mayhaps . . . that is not what is best for either of us."

"I promise not to sing," she said, and the tears escaped, dripping down her cheeks and hiding in her borrowed tunic. She had promised the same to Arwin, and he had not believed her.

"I would not let you keep that promise. I would beg you to sing to me all day. And Arwin knows it. He is afraid, Ghisla. I am afraid too. Not of you . . . but of myself."

"Then I will go. Why have you followed me? Why did you not just let me go?" she cried, swiping at her cheeks.

"It is not safe for you out there. The only safety is in the clans or in the temple . . . and even then . . . there is no safety."

"I don't care what happens to me."

"If you don't care . . . then let Arwin take you to Lothgar. A life in the temple will be a better life," he insisted.

"A better life than a life in a cave?"

"I will not always dwell in this cave. Someday . . . I too will go to the temple. Arwin is teaching me about the runes. I am to be a keeper one day."

"And you will go to the temple?"

"Yes. I will come to Temple Hill and ask to join the keepers there. And we will see each other again."

"Do not promise me, Hody," she whispered. "I don't want to hate you."

"You don't?" Hope rang in his question.

"No," she sighed. She stopped walking. She could go no farther. The tide flirted with her feet.

"If there are no girls in Saylok, will I not be valued? Surely someone will want me. Why must I go to the temple?"

"Have you ever seen wolves fight over a rabbit?"

She was silent, shocked.

"Now imagine the wolves are starving and there are hundreds of them. Thousands of them."

"I found you, didn't I? You are not a wolf."

"No, I am a blind boy who has no way to protect or provide for you. Not yet." He sighed, the sound so heavy she staggered beneath its weight. "Mayhaps not ever."

"If I agree, if I let Arwin take me to this Lothgar, will you come with us? To Leok?"

"Arwin will not want me to come." He inhaled. "But he cannot stop me. I will come."

"How far is it to Leok?"

"We are in Leok now," Hod said. He crouched, and in the wet sand he made a shape like a star—fat and six-legged and rising at the center.

"We are here, where Leok begins to curve into Adyar. Adyar is the top of the star, Leok lies to its west, and Berne to the east."

"And where are the Northlands?" she asked.

He pointed out to sea. "You have already come a great distance, Ghisla. And Odin has kept you alive thus far. You have survived sickness and plague. You have survived the sea. You have even survived Arwin. The fates have plans for you, Ghisla. You will be a great lady."

When she didn't answer, he continued his lesson in the sand.

"The southernmost leg of the star is Ebba. The land between Ebba and Berne is Dolphys. The land between Ebba and Leok is Joran. Temple Hill is here . . . in the center of them all. That is where Lothgar will take you."

"And I will be safe there?" She sounded bitter.

"You will not be alone. There will be others, daughters like you, who will be brought to the mount. Arwin says the king has decreed it. He asked for a girl from every clan to be brought to the temple."

"Why?"

"As a symbol to the people . . . or for safekeeping . . . or for reasons only the Highest Keeper knows." He shrugged. "Arwin says the daughters will be taken to the temple and not the king's castle. That is good." He rose and crushed the star he'd made with the toe of his boot. "Lothgar has asked that every daughter in Leok be brought to the keep. So far, Arwin said no one has obeyed the summons."

"Why?" That was hardly a comfort.

"They do not want to part with their daughters."

No one would protest parting with her.

"I am not of Saylok . . . or of Leok. I cannot represent the clan," she argued.

"They need never know that." Hod's voice was firm and his marbled eyes reflected the moonlight. "You are a gift from the gods. And I believe you will do great things, Ghisla of Tonlis."

She did not want to do great things. She wanted a place to lay her head and a family to love her. She wanted a friend and a fire and a song that would make the ache go away. But that was not to be. Not now. Mayhaps not ever.

He reached out, touching her cheek with the tips of his fingers. She moved closer and reached for his wrist. He let her guide him. His fingers were sandy and cold from his map making, and his palms were broad. He had not yet grown into them, but, the gods willing, he would. He would grow into his hands and feet and his smooth cheeks would become whiskered and leathery like her father's had been.

The grief stole over her quickly and she bit down on her lip as he touched her carefully, the tips of his fingers learning her eyes, her nose, her cheeks, and the point of her chin.

"Now I've seen your face," he said, his hand falling away. "I won't forget it. I won't forget you."

She didn't believe him.

"We must go back. Arwin is stirring."

She hesitated.

"Ghisla?"

She knew what he was asking. She slipped her hand into his, and they began walking back to the cave.

"Will you remember me?" he asked softly.

"Yes, Hod. I will remember you."

"And do you promise me you will not give up?"

She sighed.

"I promise I will not give up today," she said.

They left for Lothgar's keep at dusk. Arwin had insisted that Hod stay behind, but Hod had refused, just as he'd promised.

"You will need me, Master. We must travel at night. Traveling with a girl will attract the worst sort. An old man and a blind boy are of no interest to anyone, but Ghisla will be," Hod said.

"Ghisla?" Arwin asked, spitting the word from his mouth. "You must cease calling her by that name. Ghisla is not a name of Saylok. She will need a new name, one with the sound of the clan of Leok."

Traveling in the dark didn't bother Hod at all. He didn't stumble or seem fearful, and he was the one who urged them to the side of the road to huddle behind the trees when another group approached. He heard people long before they were visible.

It took two days of traveling to reach the chieftain's village. Hod said it sat near the tip of the land of Leok, like all the biggest villages in Saylok.

"The clans sail from peninsula to peninsula, one leg of the star to another. It is faster by boat than by land."

Conversation between them had grown stilted and awkward with Arwin listening in. He was suspicious and wary and demanded silence and separation whenever they halted or slept. His mood grew more and more fretful, and by the time they reached the village around Lothgar's keep, he was bristling with impatience.

"We should wait for the morn to approach him," Hod suggested. "It will be safer for Ghisla when the keep is empty."

"We will go now," Arwin snapped. "I have not rested well in a week. I will take the girl to the edge of the wood and point her to the chieftain's lodge."

"Master . . . you must see if the way is clear. She will not make it ten steps in a crowded square. And what if Lothgar is not there?"

Arwin grumbled, folding his arms with indecision.

"Wait here." He looked from Hod to Ghisla, pointing a long, crooked finger at her nose. "I won't be gone long. No singing!"

As soon as he was gone, Hod reached out his hand. "Don't be afraid, Ghisla."

She ignored it and sank down to the dirt. Hod sat down beside her.

He handed her his flask and she drank deeply, hoping the water would wash away the despair bubbling up in her throat. She drank every last drop and handed it back to Hod.

"I . . . have been thinking," he said.

She said nothing, and he reached for her again, following her arm down to her wrist and tugging her hand into his lap. She pulled it away. A muscle twitched in his cheek.

"It is forbidden for anyone but the keepers to call on the runes," he began, hesitant. "But these are strange times, and Arwin says I am being trained for a wise purpose. Mayhaps . . . this is it."

"What are you talking about, Hody?" she whispered, and she thought for a moment he was going to weep.

"I want to put a rune on your palm."

"Why?" She made her voice hard. Her own emotions threatened to spill over, and it was easier to be cold.

"If you trace the rune with blood and sing, I think I will be able to . . . hear you. And mayhaps you will be able to hear me. Would you like that?"

"I will hear you . . . always?"

"I don't know. I think so. As long as the rune remains."

"How long will the rune remain?"

"If it is a scar . . . it will remain forever."

She gasped. Then she set her hand on his knee, palm up. He smiled, encouraged.

"It is called a soul rune. Soul runes require blood—as all the most powerful runes do. It will hurt. I will have to cut you. But if I put it on your palm, the lines will not be noticeable. Our palms already have runes imprinted on them. See?"

He traced the line from the base of her hand as well as the lines that intersected it.

"All right," she said. "Go ahead."

"Cup your hand so I can better follow the grooves," he said. She obeyed, curving her hand so the skin creased. With the sharp tip of his knife, he scored her palm, drawing a thin ridge of blood in the wake of the blade. It stung, but she did not protest. The promise of connection was too great. She would have severed her hand if he'd asked.

He made the same mark on his own hand and pressed it to hers, mixing their blood and curling his fingers through hers. "Now . . . sing to me."

She frowned. "You are sitting right here, holding my hand. You will be able to hear me without a rune."

"I mean . . . sing to me with your mind. Sing the song in your thoughts . . . and I will tell you what I hear."

It was hard to hear a melody in her head when his hand was pressed to hers. She was distracted by the warmth of his skin and the sadness in her chest and the wailing in her soul that had not quieted since she'd realized she was alone in the world.

"I can't do it."

"Of course you can," he said softly. "Do songs not stay in your head when you wish they would not?"

"Yes," she sighed. A song had already started to wriggle free. She screwed her eyes shut and focused her thoughts, hearing a melody without making a sound.

"That is lovely . . . but where are the words?" he asked after a moment. His voice was hollow, like it originated in her head and not from his mouth.

Her eyes popped open.

"I heard you," she marveled. She was holding his hand so tightly she couldn't feel her fingers.

"Yes . . . and I heard you. Try again," he pressed.

In Tonlis there is music. In the ground and in the air. In Tonlis there is singing even when no one is there.

Hod repeated the words of the song, though he did not sing them, and she heard each one inside her head, echoing in his voice.

She laughed but immediately sobered. "But . . . I will not be able to hold your hand when I am gone."

He released her and walked several steps. He extended his staff, rapping it against a tree to gauge its size and girth. Then he stepped behind it.

"Can you see me?" he called softly.

"No."

"Good. Now sing inside your head again."

My heart will be in Tonlis even when I leave her shores. My spirit will not sing again 'til I am home once more.

He repeated the words, and even in her head, his voice was sad.

"I hope your spirit will sing again, Ghisla."

She flinched. It was one thing to hear him, it was another to converse, to open her thoughts to respond.

"Must I keep singing? Or can I simply talk to you?" she said, speaking out loud. He stepped out from behind the tree and returned to her side.

"Arwin is coming," he said, his voice hushed, anxious.

Her heart galloped. She was not ready.

"Your hand will heal, but the mark will still be there," he whispered, rushing to get through the words before Arwin appeared.

"It will scar."

"Yes. Trace the rune with a drop of your blood and sing your song, wherever you are. Once you hear me, and I . . . hear . . . you, keep tracing the lines of the scar. It will keep us connected for a few moments, even when you cease to sing. And don't tell Arwin. Tell no one. I fear they will use your gift against you."

A moment later, Arwin's figure was visible through the trees, and Hod ceased speaking.

"He is there," Arwin said. "It is not yet time for the evening meal, and he has a man posted at the door. Let's go, girl." He wrapped his bony hand around her arm, pulling her up. Arwin arranged the blanket around her shoulders so her hair was once again covered as Hod rose too.

"Stay here, Hod," Arwin bade and urged her forward.

Ghisla didn't look back at him. She couldn't. She thought he said goodbye, but the thundering in her ears was too great. If he followed, she did not know, and Arwin gave no indication that his order had not been heeded.

Lothgar's keep was the biggest lodge on the square, and it was surrounded by stables and smaller dwellings on every side.

Arwin pointed at the man who stood beside the huge door, leaning on his sword, his long braid swinging as he turned his head from side to side.

He instructed Ghisla, "Go to that man. Ask for Chief Lothgar. Ask loudly. Insist. Tell him that you are answering Lothgar's summons."

"How will I know which one is the chief?"

"He sits on the biggest chair, and his hair and his beard make him look like a lion. He is loud, and large. He looks like a chief. The other men defer to him."

She hesitated, terrified.

"Tell him you are of Leok. Tell him you want to go to the temple. Insist. He has no one else to send. He will be relieved. And he will keep you safe until you are delivered there."

"And what about after I am delivered there?"

"You have nowhere else to go, child," he growled.

She had nowhere else to go.

"Let them believe you are young," Arwin reminded her. "It is better to be young. It will give you time."

The buds of her breasts were like rocks, hard and sore, so sore she could not sleep on her stomach as she preferred to do, and her legs ached with the pangs of growth. She would not be small—not this small—forever, and she would not pass for nine or ten much longer. Blood had begun to seep from between her legs. Not much. And not often. But she knew what it meant.

"Please let me stay with you." Her plea shamed her, and it did nothing to change his mind.

"I can't," he said, firm, and she knew he would not relent. "There will be questions if I accompany you. Questions I cannot answer. It will go better for you if you are alone. Do not speak of me or the boy. It will only bring us trouble."

She turned her head, searching the forest behind her, needing to see Hod one last time, but he was not there.

"They need not know about your songs either. It is enough to simply be a girl. That is gift enough. They need not know what you are capable of."

"What am I capable of?" she asked, stalling, desperate.

"You can make a blind man see," he snorted.

"Are there many blind men on Temple Hill?"

"No. But there are many ways that men are blind. Be careful, little one. Guard your songs."

It was the first time Arwin had called her anything but *witch* or *girl*, and she blanched in surprise. He sounded almost kind.

"Now go," Arwin insisted. "Walk straight to the door. Don't stop. Leave the blanket over your head. Go. Go." He pushed at her back, shoving her forward, and she took four stumbling steps. When she looked back, he too had disappeared into the trees. She pulled the sides of her makeshift cloak around her, keeping the hood over her hair.

There was nothing to do but go forward.

By the time she'd made it to the man at Lothgar's door, he was staring with a furrowed brow.

"I've come to see Lothgar," she insisted, avoiding his eyes.

"And who are you?" he asked.

"I want to go to the temple."

He pushed back the blanket over her hair.

"You're a girl," he gasped.

"Yes. And I want to see Lord Lothgar." She was suddenly, strangely calm. It had been harder to steal aboard a boat. At least she wouldn't have to hide with the rats.

"Come with me," he said, and abandoned his post at the keep's entrance.

Inside, the beams were high and the furnishings heavy and dark—everything made for big men. Horns and antlers and feathers and furs adorned the walls and covered a floor set with stone. The smell of bread and roasting meat came from deeper in the edifice, but the man did not take her to the kitchens. He took her to a hall where tables were arranged in a square, leaving the center empty. A few men milled about, but no one was eating. A fire crackled on a huge stone hearth and two dogs fought over a bone that had been fought over before.

A man with a full gold-and-gray beard that framed his broad face lounged in a huge chair on a raised platform, talking in earnest with a man who had a similar beard and a similar face, though he seemed to be listening more than he spoke.

"Chief Lothgar!" her escort interrupted. His voice was excited, triumphant even, and every head swiveled toward him.

The man in the chair looked up, irritation flickering across his features. The man beside him scowled as well, but when they saw her, trailing behind the big guard, their faces went slack.

"I've brought you a girl child, Lothgar," he crowed.

The only sound in the room was the popping of the fire in the grate.

5

YEARS

"Where did you find her, Ludlow?" Lothgar whispered.

"She walked right up to the door, Lord. She asked for you. She said she wants to go to the temple." The man laughed as though he couldn't believe it himself.

"How old are you, girl?" the chieftain asked. It was always the first question they asked. Hod's voice rose in her thoughts.

There have been no other daughters of Saylok born in twelve years. The men bring daughters from other lands . . . but it is not enough . . . and there seems to be no remedy or rune to cure the drought.

"I don't know how old I am," Ghisla lied. Her shoulders tightened and she stared down at her bare feet. They were black with filth.

"Where did you come from?" he pressed.

"I am of Leok."

"If you were born in Leok, we would have known," the man beside Lothgar said.

Lothgar held out his hand, as if to silence the man beside him. "Lykan . . . let me, brother."

"I am of Leok," she insisted, lifting her chin, doing what Arwin had counseled her to do.

"Why have you come?" Lothgar asked.

"I want to be sent to the temple."

A murmur rumbled throughout the room.

"Go. All of you. Leave," Lothgar ordered, and his command was immediately obeyed by all but his brother. Lykan stayed frozen beside him and Lothgar did not insist he go.

"Who cares for you, girl?" Lothgar asked when the room had cleared.

"I care for myself."

"Where is your family?"

"I don't know."

"What is your name?"

"I do not know."

"What do you know?"

"I am of Leok," she insisted, her voice rising. "And I am a girl."

Lothgar barked in laughter and his brother cursed in disbelief.

"The girl is small, but her tongue is sharp. She seems to have a firm grasp on the situation, young as she is," Lothgar said to him. "You look like a daughter of Leok," the chief conceded. "Your hair is fair and your eyes are blue."

"She looks like your daughters, Lord. Like our mother too," Lykan mused. Chief Lothgar studied her, his hand stroking the length of his beard.

"But she wasn't born in Leok," he said. "She is young, and we would have heard. Her parents would have brought her to me for the blessing."

"Mayhaps her parents were travelers between lands," Lykan suggested. "Mayhaps she belongs to the rovers."

"I belong to no one," Ghisla said. The two men gaped at her once more. It was as though they could hardly believe their eyes.

After a moment, Lothgar spoke again. "And . . . why . . . do you want to go to the temple?"

"Because I belong to no one," she repeated. "In the temple I'll eat."

Lothgar nodded slowly and his brother spoke again.

"We have no one else to send, Lothgar."

"No." Lothgar shook his head. "We don't. Not without raiding the homes of our people."

"You would have slain any man who tried to separate you from your daughters," his brother murmured.

Lothgar's eyes darkened, but he nodded his head. "That I would."

"Yet here is this child. A girl child. We don't know where she came from . . . but I find I don't much care," Lykan admitted.

Lothgar sat back in his chair with an air of relief. "Praise Odin," he whispered. "Nor do I." He tugged on his beard and studied her a moment more, but she held his gaze. It had gone just as Arwin said it would. They had no one else.

"You will have to have a name, daughter of Leok," Lothgar murmured. "What shall we call you?"

She had no idea what a daughter of Leok would be called, and she held her tongue.

Lykan spoke up again. "We should call her Liis. For our mother. Surely she sent her to us," he said.

"Liis of Leok," Lothgar grunted. "It is fitting."

"Come here, girl," Lykan demanded. She did as she was told, halting directly in front of the chieftain's chair.

Lothgar removed a blade from his boot and nicked the side of his thumb.

"The gods have spoken, and I will not refuse a gift so obvious." He smeared his blood across her forehead and rested his big palm over her head.

"Liis of Leok it is."

Chief Lothgar turned her over to his wife, a handsome woman about the age Ghisla's mother had been. The wife took one look at Ghisla and called for "Lagatha and Lisbet," two old women who came quickly, skirts swishing. They drew up short, tripping over one another in their surprise.

"Oh, Lady Lothgar! It is true, then? We were certain Ludlow was telling stories," they babbled, almost as one.

"We will draw a bath and find the child something to wear," Lothgar's wife instructed, and the women bobbed and nodded, accompanying Ghisla and the lady up a flight of stairs to a bedchamber with a small iron tub. A winch lowered a platform near the bath to the floor below. Buckets of hot water from the laundry were set on the platform and it was sent up again, and the old women had the tub filled in no time.

"Get in, child," Lady Lothgar instructed.

Ghisla tried to do so without removing her clothes, and the women clucked and scolded, descending on her like thieves, and Hod's tunic and hose were whisked away. She scampered to the tub and threw herself into the water, embarrassed by her nakedness. Her shoulders, ribs, and hips jutted out sharply, and her knees were the widest part of her spindly legs. She'd changed into Hod's tunic and hose in a rush. She had not looked at herself without clothes since . . . since . . . She could not remember when. It was before death had come to Tonlis.

"She's no meat on her bones!" Lagatha—or maybe she was Lisbet—exclaimed.

"Yes . . . and these clothes will not do," Lady Lothgar fretted. "Nothing I have will fit—there's not a gown in the village that will fit—but surely we can do better than these. We can't send her to the temple dressed as a boy."

The rune Hod had carved into her hand smarted as she sank into the water, but she didn't dare inspect it. Hod had said to keep it hidden, so she would. Just knowing it was there was a comfort.

"Surely not, Lady Lothgar. Surely not. She should be dressed in the colors of the clan," Lagatha said.

"But that will take time. When will the lord present her to the king?" Lisbet argued.

"Word is already spreading. Lothgar will take her to the temple in the morn. He says we will have no peace until she is gone, and I suspect he is right," Lady Lothgar worried, wringing her hands. "Where in the world did you come from, child?" she asked, her voice ringing in disbelief.

"I am from Leok," Ghisla said. Lady Lothgar waited, blue eyes searching, but when Ghisla refused to offer more, even after persistent questioning, the lady of the keep left her in the care of the old women and promised to return with suitable clothes.

"Do your best to untangle her hair. She must remain in here. Lothgar has put a guard outside to keep the curious away," she said, closing the door behind her.

The old women spoke excitedly as they soaped and scrubbed at her hair. They conversed as though she couldn't hear—the way grownups tended to do with children—about what it meant to have a girl child of Leok.

"She just appeared out of nowhere!" Lagatha marveled.

"She is a gift from the gods, surely," Lisbet added. "She looks like the daughters of Leok—she is not from one of the other clans."

"Yes, yes. Though she's a mite bit sickly looking."

"Nothing a bed and a few meals can't fix. And look at those eyes! She's a little beauty. Who *are* you, child?" Lisbet pressed.

"I am Liis of Leok," Ghisla said numbly, and the women grew quiet for all of ten seconds.

"Mayhaps she is touched in the head," Lagatha murmured.

"In these times, we are all touched in the head," Lisbet answered.

When she was sufficiently clean, Lagatha urged her from the tub and wrapped her in a blanket, directing her to a stool in front of a fire Lisbet had built. They rubbed oil into her hair and let it sit before picking their way up the length with combs and careful fingers. It lay shining against her back when they were finished.

They even cleaned between her fingers and her toes and buffed her nails with a small stone. She'd accidentally hissed when Lagatha grabbed her hand, but the women didn't seem to recognize the rune. They thought she'd defended herself against a whip. They clucked and murmured all over again, their sympathy stoked once more. They put a salve on it and bandaged it up when they finished with her hair.

Lady Lothgar returned with stew and bread and a nightshirt borrowed from someone's young son. It was clean and white, and it'd been worn into softness. They pulled it over her head and told her to eat.

By the time Ghisla was done she was so weary she could not keep her eyes open, and they tucked her into the bed in the corner of the room.

"Sleep, Liis of Leok," Lady Lothgar urged, and the awe was back in her voice. "No one will harm you here."

They left her for a time, and she was grateful for the solitude, though she knew they lingered outside the door.

She tried to sing a song for Hod, to reach out and test their connection, but she was asleep before humming a single note.

The women had found her a frock in what they called "Leok green" and dressed her like she was to be married to the king. Her hair was braided and coiled and her cheeks pinched for color, though they had days of riding ahead of them. The people of the village gathered to see them off and cheered and waved like she was a princess. Mayhaps they were simply grateful their own daughters had been spared.

Lothgar asked her if she could ride alone, and when she nodded, he placed her on an old horse so docile that the only thing that differentiated wakefulness from sleep were its plodding legs. Chief Lothgar rode in the lead. His long braid matched his horse's tail, one long rope running into another. It was even the same color.

All of Lothgar's men had long braids. Lykan explained that when the king of Saylok died, it was tradition for the men of the clans, in recognition of his passing, to cut their hair. The long, tight braid they wore down their backs was removed—a braid that had been allowed to grow for the entire reign of the king—to signify the end of one era and the beginning of another. In Saylok, one could ascertain the longevity of a king by the length of his warriors' hair.

"King Banruud has been the king for five years, but he is young; he will be king for decades more," Lykan said, and Lothgar grunted in displeasure.

"Easy brother," Lykan warned. Ghisla got the impression that Lothgar did not care for the king.

"The Keepers of Saylok never grow their hair at all," Lothgar said, throwing the words over his shoulder so she knew they were intended for her. "They keep their heads smooth. To grow a braid would be to show fealty to the king. Their duty is to remain separate. The daughters will be kept separate as well. In the temple."

They traveled three days, sleeping beneath stars, and each night the men formed a perimeter around her while she slept, not so different from Hody's stones.

"No one will hurt you while you are among my men. Not a hair on your head," Lothgar promised. It was a comfort, and she believed him. He was kind and boisterous, and his men seemed to like him. She liked him; he made sure she was fed and watched over, and he didn't insist that she speak.

Her appetite was returning, and she ate whatever she was given, but she'd stopped talking, ignoring the questions that everyone wanted answered. She was now Liis of Leok, and it had become her standard response when peppered with questions. She was certain that, just like the old women, Lothgar and his men thought her simple or suffering from something terrible. She supposed she was, but silence was her best response. If she did not speak, she need not lie, and she could not tell the truth. They all wanted a girl of Leok. They would not want a girl who had left plague in her wake.

Lykan seemed intent on instructing her, as though he knew she was not who they wanted her to be. He spoke of the chieftains at length—their clans, their colors, the beasts from which they all took their names. Leok the lion, Adyar the eagle, Berne the bear, Dolphys the wolf, Ebba the boar, and Joran the horse. Ghisla pictured the star Hod had sculpted in the sand as he spoke.

"Do you know the story of Hod?" she asked Lykan when he had finished. Lothgar looked back at her in surprise.

"She speaks," he grunted.

She immediately regretted it.

"Hod the blind god?" Lykan asked.

Ghisla nodded, just a jerk of her head, but it was enough to set Lykan off again. "Aye. I know of Hod. I know of all the gods."

"Some believe the Temple Boy is a god," one of Lothgar's men said, inserting himself into the discussion. "Some say he is the son of Thor. Many thought the keepers would make him king instead of Banruud."

"I've seen him battle several men at once," another man said.

"It is not battle if it happens in the yard," Lothgar grumbled.

"But, Chief Lothgar, he killed a man—several men—when he was still a child," another warrior argued.

"He is yet a child. Still a boy, though he is the size of a man," Lykan said. He looked at Ghisla, explaining as he was wont to do. "His name is Bayr. He has no clan. He's been raised by the keepers; everyone calls him the Temple Boy."

"His strength is not that of a regular man. His strength is beyond that of the natural world," Lothgar admitted.

"He can hardly speak, brother. He stutters like a mindless idiot," Lykan said.

"The gods are not perfect, Lykan. Odin's sons are as flawed as they are gifted."

"Hod was blind," she reminded softly, and for a moment the men were silent, thoughtful.

"Bayr is not a god. He is a boy," Lykan insisted after a while.

"Aye. A boy the king fears," Lothgar said, and he laughed as though it pleased him greatly.

∽

Temple Hill rose up out of the ground, so tall and green that the top was ringed in clouds, making it look as though the mount skewered the twilight sky. But Ghisla was the only one who gaped. The men of Leok had seen it before, though they seemed glad to see it again.

"That is the temple mount," Lothgar said. "On the left, you can see the spires and the dome above the wall. On the right, the king's keep, Castle Saylok. From the mount you can see in every direction, every clan. 'Tis not a bad place to live, Liis of Leok."

He said her new name like he was trying to make it real when they both knew it was not. *It is just a name,* she thought to herself. *It is only a name.* And it was not so different from *Ghisla.* It hissed off the tongue in a similar way, though she heard *Ghisla* in her mother's voice, and *Liis* was more like a curse, a whisper cut short. A life cut short. She did not *hate* the name. It was simply like wearing Hod's old clothes. It didn't quite fit. Mayhaps she would grow into it. Or grow out of herself.

"You will ride with me from here on out, Liis of Leok," Lothgar said. "I'll be better able to guard you, and I want King Banruud to see that you have my protection. Now . . . and when I am gone." Lykan dismounted and lifted her from her docile horse and placed her in front of his brother before climbing back onto his own horse. Lothgar's mount tossed his golden mane and chuffed his welcome. Lothgar wrapped his enormous arm around her waist, securing her against him, and they began the steep climb to the temple entrance and the edifices behind the walls.

As they climbed, the mountain grew. It was much bigger than it had looked from the King's Village below. The temple spires rising above the clouds had made the top appear elongated, but the mists had entirely disguised the top of the hill and the flat plateau behind the walls. It reminded her of a song where Odin took his sword and cut off a giant's head: *The giant fell to his hands and knees, his back as flat as it could be, and Odin made a table where all the world could come to eat.*

Temple Hill was a table where all of Saylok came to eat. Or where all of Saylok came to *meet*—at least all of Saylok's men. She had not yet seen any women. Everywhere she looked were men and horses, braided and bulging with leather and shields and weapons of war.

"Make way for Chief Lothgar of Leok," a voice bellowed from above, and bugles rang out as they rode beneath the portcullis.

The torches that lined the square shot light into the sky and shadows onto every face.

Tents were erected in the space beyond the castle—Adyar gold, Berne red, Dolphys blue, Ebba orange, Joran brown, and Leok green—but the light was being leached from the sky, robbing the flags and the tents and the outskirts of their color. There was only fire and stone, the temple and castle facing off across a cobbled square.

Half of Lothgar's men proceeded on toward the tents, talking of supper and swords and sore flanks. Lothgar and his brother, the only other face she had a name for, remained seated on their horses in the main square, and she remained with them.

"Are we the last to arrive?" Lykan asked, but his words were immediately interrupted by a trumpeter on the wall.

"Make way for Chief Aidan of Adyar and Queen Esa of Saylok," the watchman boomed.

A young man on a white horse draped in gold entered the courtyard, an aging woman riding at his side. The woman had a haughty lift to her chin and a yellow cloak that glimmered in the torchlight.

"Adyar has brought Alannah's mother, the old queen," Lothgar said, his voice rumbling above Ghisla's head. "The princess will need her, now that Alannah is gone."

A warrior helped the woman dismount, and she swept into the castle as though she belonged there. Her son watched her go before turning to his men and instructing most of them to set up camp. Like Chief Lothgar, he remained seated on his horse. His braid was as long and pale as Lothgar's, but that is where the similarity between the two chieftains ended. He was young enough to be Lothgar's son, and where Lothgar was square, Aidan of Adyar was sharp. His hair came to a deep V on his brow that echoed the tip of his nose and the point of his chin. He was handsome the way an eagle is handsome, and Saylok's animal sons took on new significance.

"He's brought the queen . . . but it does not appear he's brought a daughter," Lykan mused, searching the yellow-draped warriors that surrounded their chief.

"Banruud will not be pleased," Lothgar crowed.

"About the queen or the daughter?" Lykan asked.

"Both, brother. Both."

"Adyar is no threat to Banruud. He will never be king. He is a mouthy boy, intent on poking at the king simply because he thinks he can."

Ghisla was suspended between the desire to stare, unblinking, so that she wouldn't miss what was to come, and the need to close her eyes so she could hide from it.

"I do not care enough to be afraid," she whispered to herself, and kept her eyes opened.

Before long, Ghisla counted four other girls sitting on horseback in front of warriors, exactly like she was. Four girls with bowed heads and thin backs, and all looked to Ghisla to be younger than she.

Stone steps ringed the temple, and robed men with heads shorn like Hod's and their eyes rimmed in black stood in lines, their hands clasped and their gazes forward.

Those are the keepers, she thought.

"Aye," Lothgar answered, and she realized she'd spoken aloud. He patted her head. "Don't be afraid," he urged, but she heard guilt in his gruff words.

The faces in the square blended into one another. They were of a type—braided or bald, robed or riding—and when a trumpet sounded and the bells clanged, they seemed to turn as one toward the castle of the king, expectant and . . . resigned. The resignation, the sense of doom and quiet despair, rippled through the throng, and though Ghisla recognized it, she did not grasp the cause. It simply frightened her, and Lothgar's horse tossed his head, sensing her unease.

"I want to go now. I want to get down," she insisted.

"Soon, girl. Soon. The king is coming."

6

CLANS

"I did not bring a daughter of Adyar," Aidan of Adyar said, spurring his mount forward to greet the king. "You already have one, Majesty."

The king raised a brow and folded his arms. He was tall, with wide shoulders and powerful legs. He wore his dark hair swept back from his face and flowing around his shoulders, setting him apart from every other man on the mount, though Lothgar scoffed that it made him look like a woman.

He did not look like a woman. He'd been Chieftain of Berne, the Clan of the Bear, before he was king, Ghisla recalled, and he was as big as one. He wore a spiked crown on his head and unrelieved black.

"My sister, Queen Alannah of Adyar, gave birth to a daughter," the chieftain from Adyar continued. "That daughter lives here, on the temple mount. Princess Alba is of Adyar and can represent Adyar in the temple. She can represent our clan. Adyar has given enough, and we have no more daughters to spare."

"Yet you've come anyway, Adyar," Banruud said, scorn dripping from his words. "Why, brother?"

"I was curious. It seems the chieftains have obeyed their king."

"All but one," Banruud answered.

"I've brought you a woman," Aidan said, mocking yet mild. "Just not . . . a young woman. My mother, Queen Esa, has come to see to the upbringing of her granddaughter. Now that Alannah is gone, she feels you will need a woman to look after the princess. Unless . . . you intend to take another wife, Majesty? Mayhaps one of the clan daughters you've summoned?"

The king waved his hand, signifying his dismissal, as if Aidan of Adyar made no difference to him. The king moved on to the Chieftain of Ebba, who had already dismounted and stood next to a girl clad in a drab brown dress edged in orange ribbon.

"Erskin looks weary," Lykan remarked to Lothgar.

"The trouble in Ebba is worsening. He'll leave at first light. He has no time for this spectacle."

"This is Elayne of Ebba," the chieftain from Ebba said, introducing the girl and bowing slightly for the king. Elayne of Ebba curtsied deeply but didn't look at the king. Her hair was a deep red against her pale skin, and she looked as though she'd been crying. She was lean and long, though she'd begun to curve inward at the waist. She was much taller than Ghisla, though Ghisla guessed they were close in age.

"She was born before the drought," Lothgar murmured. Lykan grunted in agreement.

"She's the only one. Which means the others aren't from Saylok at all."

"We have no room to criticize, brother," Lothgar said.

Banruud moved on to the next chieftain, the chieftain from Berne. A girl dressed from head to toe in deep red watched the king approach.

"Her hair is coiled and her skin is brown," Lothgar said, chuckling softly. "She is no more Bernian than I."

"Who is this, Benjie?" Banruud asked. The girl did not seem intimidated by him at all. She stared up at him, expressionless.

"This is Bashti of Berne." The Chieftain of Berne put his hand on the girl's back and urged her forward. She planted her feet and pressed back.

"Bashti of . . . Berne?" Banruud questioned.

"Bashti of Berne . . . and daughter of Kembah, most likely," the chieftain replied.

"If she is a daughter of Kembah, she is not a daughter of Berne, Benjie. Plus, Kembah is a king," Banruud countered. "I doubt this girl is Kembah's. But if it suits you to pretend, cousin, I will not argue."

"Mayhaps when she is grown, we can make an alliance," Benjie offered.

"Mayhaps. If she has a womb she will grow into, it is enough." Banruud raised his voice. "Have you all brought me foreign wombs to beget other wombs?"

No one answered.

"You've brought me the cast off and the captured," he mocked. "All except Erskin, who has a better excuse than all of you. His warriors fight the Hounds even now, and yet he brought a daughter of Ebba as he was directed."

The chieftains regarded him silently, their resentment obvious.

"You said to find daughters. We found daughters, Majesty," Dirth of Dolphys grumbled.

"So you did," King Banruud said. He shrugged, granting them exasperated pardon.

The chieftain from Dolphys introduced the daughter he'd brought to the temple, Dalys. The little girl beside him was sloe-eyed and sooty-locked. She clung to the chieftain's hand and stared up at the king with tragic resignation. Outrage burned in Ghisla's throat and stiffened her spine. She did not like the king.

Banruud moved on to the Chieftain of Joran, his hands behind his back like he was inspecting horseflesh.

Chieftain Josef had brought a girl named Juliah, her long, dark hair braided tightly like that of the warriors around her, and the king asked if she'd been "raised by men."

"Yes, Majesty," the Chieftain of Joran said, eyes hard. "She was. Her grandfather is Jerom, the fisherman. He and his sons were casting their nets when the Hounds came ashore ten years ago. Jerom's wife and daughter were not spared. His wife was killed, and his daughter became . . . pregnant from the attack. She died in childbirth. Jerom and his two sons have raised the girl."

The king approached Lothgar last. Lothgar laid his arm around Ghisla's shoulders, but she shrugged him off. She did not belong to him. The king smirked at her rejection of the Chieftain of Leok, and she regretted her impulsive display. It was better not to let them—any of them—see her react at all. Her feelings were the only thing that were hers, and she vowed that she would not share them with strangers. And everyone present was a stranger.

She'd removed her braid before they'd made the climb to the mount, and her hair waved long and loose around her shoulders. She had wanted to look her best in the green dress Lady Lothgar had acquired for her. It was the nicest dress she'd ever worn, and preparing herself had calmed the nervous dread in the pit of her stomach. Now she wished that she'd worn Hody's tunic and his old hose. She wished she'd let her hair return to the tangled rat's nest it had been before the women in Leok had unraveled it. That girl would have still been Ghisla, even without her name. With her smooth hair and her borrowed dress, she was Liis of Leok, and nothing of Ghisla remained.

"King Banruud, may I present Liis of Leok," Lothgar said. The king studied her, his gaze flat, but when he spoke, there was begrudging admiration in his voice.

"How old is she, Lothgar? She looks like the clan—golden haired, blue eyed, ill tempered. Aren't all the women of Leok thus?"

"She has ten summers, Majesty," Lothgar claimed, though he knew nothing of the sort.

The king raised his brows, disbelieving.

"Where did you find her, Lothgar?"

"Odin gave her to me, Majesty." The men around him laughed, but the king grimaced, irritated by Lothgar's meaningless explanation.

"Where are you from, girl?" the king asked Ghisla.

"I am Liis of Leok," she said. She held his gaze—his eyes were black and unblinking. Looking at him felt like tumbling into a hole.

"Good. And now you are Liis of Saylok. Liis of Temple Hill. You will be a beauty one day. I look forward to watching you bloom."

"She is Liis of Leok even still, Majesty," Lothgar argued, but it was a meaningless distinction, and they all knew it. He would be leaving her on the mount.

"They will stay in the castle, under my watch," Banruud said, raising his voice to be heard throughout the assembly. Then he turned back toward his palace, as if he was through with them all.

"You said they would be raised by the keepers," Lothgar protested. "In the temple."

"They will be raised with my daughter, in my house," Banruud shot back. "Princesses of Saylok all."

A stunned hush fell over the clan representatives, and the king waved his guards forward.

"You will take the daughters to the castle," he directed them. "A feast awaits."

"They are supplicants to the temple," a voice boomed, and the guards hesitated.

An ancient man stood in the center of the courtyard, the light from the fat moon glancing off his face and hollowing out his black eyes and black lips like caves in pale sand. He and his brethren had descended from the steps while the king had made his inspection, and the crowd had been too distracted to notice.

"It is what was agreed upon. They will live in the temple and be guarded by the keepers," the man continued. His rasping voice raised the hair on Ghisla's neck, but she was not certain if it was from fear . . . or awe. Unlike the other keepers, he was dressed all in black, and he clutched a short, bejeweled staff in a clawlike hand. He had no hair, and his pale skin dripped from his face like he'd begun to melt in the moonlight. But his voice was strong and his influence stronger. The chieftains seemed to take courage from his presence.

"The Highest Keeper is right. It was what we all agreed upon, Banruud," Aidan repeated, still astride his horse. The king had dismissed him, but he'd remained in place.

The Highest Keeper. The ancient man was Master Ivo.

"You have no say in the matter, Adyar," the king shot back. "You have come to the temple mount with your hands empty."

"I have promised this girl's mother she will live in the temple and be raised in the safety—and holiness—of the sanctum," Erskin of Ebba sputtered.

"I have made the same promise to Juliah's grandfather," Josef said, his eyes touching on the girl with the warrior braid.

"These clan daughters will be raised like princesses," Banruud pronounced, pointing at the trembling children. "They will be raised beside my own daughter."

As if he'd choreographed his argument, a little girl in a tiny crown chose that moment to dash from the arched, raised entry of the palace. She came to a teetering halt in front of the assembled chieftains and their retinues and looked down on them like a performer on a stage.

A gasp rippled through the gathering; even Ghisla shuddered.

The little girl hardly looked real with her pale hair, dark eyes, and honeyed skin. Such coloring should not have existed in the natural world, but it did so in perfect harmony.

A young man with a long, black warrior's braid dashed out behind her, as if the girl had escaped his watch, but he drew up short when he saw her gaping audience. He was wide shouldered and lean hipped, with arms and legs that were thick with muscle, but his blue eyes were guileless and his skin was as smooth as the child's. He had the form of a man but the face of a boy.

He is the Temple Boy, Ghisla thought. And the little girl was Princess Alba.

The chieftains fell to their knees, Aidan of Adyar sliding from his charger without a word. Their foreheads touched the earth, and their braids, long again with the five years of his reign, coiled in the dirt beside their heads. The king walked up the steps and swept the princess up in his arms. Her small body stiffened in surprise.

Lothgar tugged on Ghisla's hand, urging her to her knees. The other girls slowly sank to their knees as well. They were in the presence of the princess, the hope of Saylok, and the king held Alba even higher, reminding his audience what he—not the keepers—had given them.

"The daughters will live in the castle with Princess Alba," he said again.

"No, Highness. They will be raised by keepers," Master Ivo insisted. The Highest Keeper had not fallen to his knees. None of the keepers had. They stood before the king, unbending, and the king glowered and raised his daughter even higher into the sky. She cried out and the Temple Boy grimaced, his eyes never wavering from her small form.

"Daughters of Freya, goddess of fertility, goddess of childbirth, wife of Odin the Allfather, we welcome you," Ivo cried, turning away from the king and toward the massive stone pyre that loomed cold and dark in the center of the square. The keepers moved behind him, as though they'd devised an entire ceremony beforehand.

"These daughters of the clans, these Daughters of Freya, will be guarded, their lives revered, their virtue defended. They will be a symbol to Saylok just like the runes," the Highest Keeper thundered. He cut his palm and painted upon the stone hearth with his blood. The rune became flame, whooshing up in a soaring column. The chieftains and their warriors gasped and Ghisla swallowed a scream.

"Saylok needs daughters," Master Ivo cried. "From this day forward, Chieftains of Saylok, these Daughters of Freya—your daughters—will keep the flame lit. As long as it burns, you will know that your daughters are tending it, that the Keepers of Saylok are tending them, and Saylok will live on.

"We will guard them well, just as we honor the princess," Master Ivo added, his tone placating but his gaze a challenge. The child in King Banruud's arms was lit by the glow, and the jeweled crown upon his head cast a glittering rainbow across the faces of the keepers. The kneeling chiefs began to nod, looking from King Banruud and his daughter to the Highest Keeper.

"Bayr of Saylok, a child raised here on the temple mount and blessed with exceeding strength, will be their protector as well, just as he has protected the princess," the Highest Keeper promised, extending his arms toward the boy as though he presented the chieftains with yet another miracle.

The Temple Boy simply dropped to one knee and bowed his head as though being knighted to the cause. But it was answer enough, and the chieftains rose to their feet, nodding and clutching their braids as though they grasped the hilts of swords slung across their backs. Bayr met the gaze of each one and stood, clasping his own braid in a posture of promise.

"The Temple Boy will guard them," Aidan shouted, releasing his braid and raising his fist. The chieftains of Ebba, Dolphys, Leok, and Joran did the same, though Benjie of Berne hesitated, his eyes shifting from the king's face to the men around him. Then he raised his arm slowly, almost fearfully, indicating his support.

"From this day forward, we will call them the Daughters of Freya, and they will be a light to the clans," Lothgar boomed beside Ghisla, repeating the words of the Highest Keeper like he'd composed them himself.

The princess was squirming to be released, and the king set her down with a look of disdain. She ran up the steps and into the arms of the Temple Boy, choosing him, completing the appearance of an anointing. Bayr rose and, holding the little girl's hand, bowed to the chieftains again. Then he bowed to the Highest Keeper and finally to the king himself. And still he did not utter a word.

"So be it, Master Ivo. I entrust the Daughters of Freya to your care and to the care of the Keepers of Saylok," King Banruud said, relenting, though his voice dripped with scorn. "Do not fail me. Do not fail them." He pointed at the five girls. "If something happens to one of the daughters, the chieftains and the people of Saylok will know who to blame."

Ghisla did not bid goodbye to Chief Lothgar or his men. She did not even spare them a second glance. She was too angry. Arwin said Lothgar had his own daughters, but Lothgar had not brought his daughters here to be raised by the hairless keepers in their purple robes and bottomless gazes. He had not brought his daughters to be used as pawns by a ruthless king.

Ghisla and the four other girls—Elayne, Juliah, Bashti, and Dalys—were herded up the stone steps and into the temple. The same resignation that had billowed through the clansmen and the keepers followed the girls into the stone edifice and settled on their small frames like little black birds with sharp claws and cawing beaks. Then the doors were closed behind them.

None of them cried, not even the littlest girl, Dalys of Dolphys. She seemed accustomed to being passed from one caregiver to another and was more at ease than any of them. None of them asked questions.

They all seemed resigned to their fate, whatever that was, though each girl handled her strain differently.

The keepers, so regal and silent in the square, scurried off like terrified mice when the temple doors were secured. None of them seemed to know what to do with five small females. The Highest Keeper barked orders at a man named Dagmar, who remained behind, and the girls were brought to a dining hall and served a simple supper in the cavernous and deserted room.

As before, everyone assumed Ghisla was far younger than she was. They thought she was younger that Elayne, mayhaps the same as Juliah, but older than Bashti and Dalys. Elayne said she was twelve. That made Ghisla the oldest girl there by two years.

Ghisla didn't bother correcting the assumptions. She had no intention of ever telling the truth again, at least not where it concerned her life and her past, and Elayne would be better in the role as oldest. She *looked* oldest. She also seemed genuinely kind and eager to make the best of things, though from her pale cheeks and red-rimmed eyes, it was easy to see that she'd succumbed at some point to fear and sadness too.

Juliah of Joran bristled with hostility when anyone looked at her, and Bashti of Berne was just the opposite. She wanted everyone to look at her.

She attempted to be the court jester, juggling the apples someone had placed on the table where the girls were instructed to sit for their supper. Bashti wasn't without skill, and Dalys clapped for her performance, but Juliah swiped one while it was in the air, throwing Bashti off her rhythm. Juliah took a huge bite out of it, the juice and bits of apple falling from her mouth as she chewed, insolent.

Bashti's temper flared at the rude interruption, and Elayne moved between the girls from Berne and Joran in an effort to diffuse the tension. They all ended up eating in weary silence, their eyes on their food, shivering in the candlelit hall while listening to Master Ivo and Dagmar discuss their predicament.

The two men had waited until the keepers on supper duty were gone, but like many men not accustomed to females, they assumed their conversation was being ignored or unheard. It wasn't. Though she bowed her head over her dinner, spooning in the broth of a weak soup and shoveling bread into her hungry belly, Ghisla was listening intently. She assumed the other girls were too.

"I had hoped the chieftains would not obey the king," Keeper Dagmar said. He was handsome, with pale-blue eyes and skin that did not have the pallor of so many of the other keepers. He seemed younger than most of the other keepers too, though the Highest Keeper looked so ancient, everyone was young in comparison.

"I knew they would. So did you, Dagmar," the Highest Keeper scoffed. "The chieftains are afraid. Saylok is afraid. A girl child from each clan—adopted by each clan—is their way of fighting back against a faceless foe, of preserving life, of bartering with the gods. Bringing a daughter to the temple is like storing gold in the ground, sewing jewels into a cloak, or hoarding food against a weak harvest."

"What do we do, Master?" Dagmar worried, his eyes on the huddled daughters eating in the flickering candlelight.

"They are supplicants, Dagmar. We will treat them as such," Ivo replied.

"They are not supplicants! They are children who have been ripped from their homes."

Ivo sighed. "We ask nothing of them, Dagmar. Nothing. We will simply keep them safe."

Dagmar shook his head and his tone was one of anguish. "I cannot protect Bayr. I cannot protect these girls. You saw the king this night. Bayr is at his mercy. These girls are at his mercy. He will use them to increase his power. It is a sham, Master."

"Only to the king, Dagmar. Not to me. Not to Saylok."

"They are just little girls," Dagmar said. "Can we do this, Master?"

"We can. We will. And when the king leaves for Ebba, you must retrieve the ghost woman from the fields and bring her here. She will help us."

∽

After supper, Keeper Dagmar laid five pallets by the fire in the kitchen. The keepers had not yet prepared a permanent space for them, and every other room felt dark and cold.

The littlest girls tossed and turned in their sleep. Elayne moaned as though she wrestled with bad dreams, and Juliah lashed out at invisible foes. But Ghisla lay perfectly still, contemplating nothing and everything.

The girl with hair like flames—Elayne of Ebba—slept next to her. Hody would be entranced by the color.

Why was she thinking of him? Why was she calling him Hody like he was one of her brothers and not just a boy she'd known for a handful of days?

She answered her own question: Hod was alive and her brothers were dead. Hod still existed, and her family was gone.

She traced the rune on her hand with the tip of her finger, wondering if she should try to reach him. But she dared not leave her bed, and she did not want to make herself bleed. Her heart bled; that should be enough. It wasn't enough, though, and she promised herself she would try in earnest soon.

Deep down, she was afraid it would not work, and Hod too would be gone forever. She could not bear that now. Not yet. So she held on to the hope of him and lay in the darkness, pulling the void into her chest and down into her belly until she felt nothing at all. Eventually, sleep followed.

7

BEAMS

The ghost woman Master Ivo had referred to at supper the first night arrived at the temple several days later covered in blood. Keeper Dagmar carried her up from the hillside, and she cowered against him, shielding her face with her hands as they entered the temple. Keeper Dagmar had looked almost as pale as the woman in his arms when he'd strode through the kitchen and into the apothecary.

"Do not be alarmed. She is fine. Just shaken. The blood is from one of the sheep, but she has a scratch on her arm. I'll patch it up. Please stay seated," he'd reassured them, leaving the daughters and the keepers with kitchen duties gaping. He'd shut the door firmly behind him, and when the girls saw the ghost woman again, the blood was gone but she was no less terrifying to behold.

She was young and unwrinkled, though her hair was white like that of an old woman. Her skin was equally pale, her eyes only a few shades darker; they reminded Ghisla of rain clouds. Ghisla was almost afraid to look at her, yet when she did, she struggled to look away. The woman was strange and . . . beautiful . . . the way Hod was beautiful. Master Ivo was fascinated by her too; the day she joined the keepers and the daughters for supper the first time, he'd drawn close to her and peered into her eyes like a thieving magpie. She'd met his gaze steadily, though her white hands twisted nervously in her robes.

"Your eyes are like glass," he pronounced. "A man will look at you and see himself. His beauty—or lack thereof—will stare him in the face."

Ghisla composed a tune in her head so she could show the ghost woman to Hod if she ever got the chance. The rune had already healed on her palm. The lines were fainter now, though they were also thicker and slightly raised. Each day she stored up images with corresponding melodies to sing to him . . . someday. If she ever dare try.

Ghost woman, white as snow, pale as ice from head to toe. From whence she comes I do not know, ghost woman, white as snow.

The ghost woman—Keeper Dagmar just called her *Ghost*—was perhaps a decade older than Ghisla, not old enough to be her mother, though that was the role she seemed expected to fill for all the girls. Dagmar said she was a shepherdess, and she'd come from the fields to help with the temple's "new flock."

The keepers emptied a room of relics and replaced the ancient artifacts with a row of beds. A small chest was set at the end of each bed, a place to store their possessions, though none of them had much. Ghisla had nothing but the rune on her hand and the green dress she'd worn the day she'd arrived. Though Ghost was not a child, they put her bed in the same room, at the end of the row, and provided her with an extra chest.

Then the keepers cut their hair. Every curl, every lock of red, gold, brown, and black was snipped away. The keeper in charge of the clipping took pity on them and, after consulting with the Highest Keeper, decided to leave them with close-cropped caps instead of stubble. Ghost submitted to the shearing alongside them, her heavy white hair covering the rest like a blanket of snow. Somehow, her loss just made theirs worse.

"At least we are not bald," Elayne said, though she'd cried as her hair fell around her feet.

"At least we do not look like keepers," Juliah agreed. She picked up her warrior's braid from the floor and refused to relinquish it. "I want it. It's mine. I will keep it in my chest," she demanded.

"We don't look like them . . . but we do not look like us either," Ghisla responded, grim. Ghost and the four other girls all looked at her, surprised she'd spoken up at all. She'd answered questions when they were directed to her, but never with more than a word or two.

They were measured for the purple robes as well as white dresses that gathered at their necks and at their wrists, to be worn beneath them any time they left the temple itself, even if it was just to walk in the square or on the temple grounds. The king's guard and the castle staff lived on the mount as well, and a distinction was clearly made: they were never to walk by themselves, even if they were all together.

"It is for your safety. All who see you must be able to immediately identify that you are a daughter of the temple," Keeper Dagmar explained. More often than not, he was in charge of their instruction. Apparently, he was the only keeper who had any experience with children; he had raised his nephew until King Banruud had assigned the Temple Boy to guard the princess.

Each girl was fitted for two sets of underthings, a shift for sleeping, and two smocks for daily wear fashioned from the drabbest gray Ghisla had ever seen. A woman from the village was brought in to sew for the daughters, though she wasn't allowed into the temple itself; she had to set up shop in the courtyard with her cart, pulled by a little burro as fat as he was tall.

The temple and the king's castle faced off across a large, cobbled square on the north end of the mount, but walls separated the king's grounds from those of the keepers. The king's grounds were vast, and they included stables and fields and barracks for his guard and a yard for training and sport. Beyond the king's grounds, the mount extended for a misshapen mile. During the Tournament of the King, which the keepers said happened after every harvest, that mile would be filled with tents of every color, and competition would abound for days.

On the east side of the mount, behind the temple, were corrals and gardens and outbuildings used exclusively by the keepers and walled off from the rest of the grounds. The keepers' grounds weren't nearly as vast as the king's, but the keepers made good use of what was theirs. They had a variety of skills and trades among them, and they did not spend all their time studying runes, reading scrolls, and pleading with the gods. Everyone had a duty—or several—and everyone contributed, though some more than others. It was a village of sorts, made up of bald men and strict rules, but Ghisla found she did not mind their severity. After long months of chaos and uncertainty, the order of the temple was a reprieve, even if it wasn't a relief.

The keepers weren't unkind, but they were awkward and aloof and often irritated by the new disruption. None of them had been fathers. None of them were comfortable with women—of any age—and they avoided the girls whenever possible, with bowed heads and skittering eyes. They avoided Ghost too. All except Dagmar and Master Ivo.

It was the Highest Keeper who insisted the girls be treated like little keepers—supplicants, he called them. They were instructed in reading and writing, and they were learning the songs and the incantations.

He reminded Ghisla of Arwin, Hod's teacher. Maybe it was their age or their stooped backs. Maybe it was the hook of the Highest Keeper's nose or the bright knowing in his eyes. Or maybe it was simply the way they both made her feel. Caught. Exposed. Unable to hide anything. Not her feelings, not her voice, not her loneliness or her aloneness.

"He is very ugly," Bashti said, mocking his bent carriage and his birdlike mannerisms.

"That is why I trust him," Ghost said. "I learned long ago the physical form is simply a shell for all manner of evil. Master Ivo looks evil. But he isn't."

"The king is very handsome," Elayne said, and her point was abundantly clear.

Master Ivo looked like a great, hunched vulture with talons and a beak of flesh. His black eyes and lips weren't as alarming as they might have been had Dagmar not explained their significance. He gathered them together about a week after their arrival, on their first full day as "supplicants," and answered as many questions as they had. Ghost sat with them too, though she knew far more than the daughters. It seemed that her questions had already been asked and answered.

"What is a supplicant?" Bashti asked. Elayne and Juliah seemed to know, but Ghisla was grateful for the direct question.

"Supplicants come from every clan," Dagmar began, "but they must have the support of their chieftain, and the Highest Keeper must grant them entry. Supplicants—most of them—eventually become keepers after their training."

"Will we be trained in all things?" Juliah asked, her eyes sharpening.

"You will be trained to read and write. You will learn history. You will learn philosophy. You will learn the language and the stories of the gods—not just the gods of Saylok but of many cultures and people, if only to better understand your own."

Ghisla wondered if they would be instructed in the ways of the Songrs, but she said nothing.

"Will we learn to joust and fence? Will we learn to fight?" Juliah asked.

Dagmar pursed his lips, contemplating that for a moment. "Yes. I suppose you will. Master Ivo said you should be treated like supplicants. All keepers are taught the basics of defense. So you will learn those things as well."

"Will we start today?" Juliah asked.

Dagmar smiled. "Soon. We will start soon. Mayhaps Bayr can teach you."

"You told me about the runes. You must tell them too, Dagmar," Ghost insisted, gently changing the subject.

"The runes are the language of the gods," Dagmar replied.

The mere mention of runes had five sets of eyes widening.

"But the runes are forbidden," Elayne whispered. She'd been raised in Saylok and seemed to have a grasp on things most of the other girls did not.

"You are supplicants now," Dagmar said. "But we will go slowly. Very slowly."

"But . . . don't you have to have rune blood to power the runes?" Elayne persisted, chewing on her lip. "What if we do not have rune blood? How will I—how will we—be keepers, then?"

"All who have rune blood do not become keepers. And all supplicants do not become keepers either. There are other paths . . . other worthy pursuits," Dagmar said.

"All the runes must be drawn in blood?" Ghisla said, her thoughts on the rune on her hand, the rune she had yet to use, though she thought of Hod every day.

"Yes. It is the blood that gives the rune its power."

"So if someone does not have . . . rune blood . . . the rune itself will have no power?" she asked. Hod had told Arwin she had rune blood.

Dagmar nodded.

"So why guard the runes if they are of no use to powerless people?" Ghost asked, pulling Dagmar's attention in yet another direction. There was too much to know, too much to learn.

"It is not the powerless people we must worry about. Just because a man or woman has rune blood does not mean they have a pure heart. Power tends to corrupt."

"Does it corrupt . . . keepers?" Elayne asked. That was the question, after all. If keepers were no better than the clansmen, none of them were safe.

"Of course. Keepers are just men. But that is why we live here, without riches or reward, without the temptations that would make us susceptible to such corruption. It is a delicate balance. We don't use the runes for power or dominion. We do not use them for gain or glory. We seek wisdom, understanding, and patience."

"Bayr has rune blood. That is why . . . he is so strong," Ghost said, and her eyes met Dagmar's as if they shared a secret. The people in the temple were full of secrets. Ghisla didn't trust any of them, but she listened to the conversation intently. Talk of the runes reminded her of Hod and crazy Arwin.

"Will Bayr become a keeper—or a supplicant—someday?" Bashti asked.

"He is a warrior!" Juliah scoffed, as though the idea of the Temple Boy wasting his strength was laughable. "Warriors do not become keepers. They fight. That is what I want to do."

"Do girls have rune blood?" Elayne asked, still worrying her lip between her teeth.

"Of course. My sister . . . Bayr's mother, had rune blood. There are many women who do."

"So why aren't there any keepers who are girls?" Juliah asked.

"Women are keepers of a different sort."

"What do you mean?" Juliah frowned.

"Women are keepers of children. Keepers of the clans." Ghost spoke again, like she was repeating something she'd heard.

Dagmar nodded. "Through the ages, women have been needed elsewhere. We men were more expendable. We are *still* more expendable."

"What is expendable?" Dalys asked. At six, much of the conversation flowed over her head, but they were all beginners. None of them knew how to read. None of them knew how to write. So they would all be taught together, regardless of the difference in their ages.

"Expendable means not as . . . precious."

"What is precious?" Dalys asked.

Dagmar smiled but Juliah groaned, impatient to ask her own questions.

"Precious means there are very few. Precious means special. You are all . . . precious."

"Why did we have to cut our hair?" Elayne asked softly. Of everyone, she had not recovered from that loss.

"We shave our heads to show we are separate from the world, but we wear robes of the same hue to show we are one with each other," Dagmar answered her, his eyes compassionate.

"Why do you put black around your eyes?" Juliah asked.

"It is symbolic."

"Of what?"

"Of our own . . . lack of vision and understanding."

"Master Ivo blackens his lips as well," Juliah reminded. "But *you* don't. None of the regular keepers do."

"As the Highest Keeper he has great power, more power than any other man, but next to the gods and the Norns he is nothing. He is flesh. He is subject to fate and death and evil. So he blackens his lips to show his words are not the words of a god. He blackens his eyes to signify his sight is not omniscient."

"What is aw-awm-ni-shunt?" Dalys asked, struggling over the word, and Dagmar stood, clasping his hands, signaling an end to the inquisition.

"It means all-knowing. None of us are all-knowing. Not the Highest Keeper. Certainly not me. There will be time for more questions tomorrow, and the day after that. For now, let us just try to get through the next few hours."

⁓

Master Ivo slowly began including them in keeper life, molding the pattern of their days into a likeness of the brotherhood. They had their own quarters, and they played more and prayed less than the keepers. They did not go into the sanctum but were schooled in their own hall, often by a rotating gaggle of grumpy keepers who took turns instructing them in various dry subjects in unvaried, dry tones. Keeper Dagmar was their favorite, and he seemed to enjoy teaching them too, though Ghisla caught him watching Ghost sometimes, a peculiar expression on his face. It looked like fear and fondness, an odd combination. Mayhaps it was fear *of* fondness, which Ghisla understood. It was better to not get too attached; she'd learned that lesson well.

Ghost was their constant companion and caretaker. She slept in their room and ate at their table and sat through all their lessons. Ghisla was surprised to learn that she did not know how to read either. Nor did she know how to make or use runes, and no one—save mayhaps Dagmar and Master Ivo—knew her story or how she'd ended up on Temple Hill living among the keepers. She was as quiet about her past as they all were and offered only the barest of histories.

"I was left in the woods as a babe," she said. "An old woman found me. She was almost blind and didn't realize I looked as I do. She was lonely, and her children were all grown. I stayed with her until I was five. When she died, her son made me a servant in his house. I've been in many houses since then . . . but I've never lived in a temple."

They'd all been afraid of her at first, especially when she darkened the area around her eyes like the keepers did. Ghisla suspected she was trying to be one of them, to blend in, but it just made her all the more terrifying to behold.

But little by little, the daughters relaxed around her, and she around them. The little girls clung to her, especially at bedtime. They moved their beds closer to hers and followed her like little ducklings.

Ghisla kept her bed where it was. She slept on the end nearest the door. Each night she planned to use it, to creep out into the temple to a hiding place, where she could muster her courage and summon Hod. But each night she lay silently, listening to the others sleep, too afraid to try.

No one spoke of their lives before, and Ghisla was not the only one who seemed unaccustomed to answering to her name. Poor Dalys answered to everything. Elayne was of Ebba—a true daughter of Saylok. Juliah was too, though her father was a marauding Hound. Bashti was not a Bernian name, though it began with the sound of the clan. Sometimes in her sleep, she chanted in a language Ghisla didn't understand. Mayhaps they were the songs of her people, the songs of the people who'd loved her once, a lifetime ago. Like Ghisla and the Songrs. But they did not speak of their lives before.

Two months after Ghisla and the other clan daughters were brought to the temple, the Temple Boy and Princess Alba came for a visit. Evening meditation had commenced, the bells had tolled, and everyone had retired to their private quarters for quiet contemplation. It was one of the hardest hours of the day for all of the girls, but especially for Juliah. She could not hold still unless she was readying to pounce and sat on her bed rattling like a pot prepared to boil over. Bashti wasn't much better, though she considered it her mission to make the others laugh with her grimacing and get them in trouble. Dalys usually fell asleep, Elayne sat in obedient silence, and Ghisla used the time to compose songs in her head that no one would likely ever hear.

When the door to their room opened with a slow screech, the girls looked up from their assigned spaces to see the Temple Boy, with the princess perched on his shoulders, standing on the threshold. The door was tall, but Bayr still raised his hand to protect Alba's head as they ducked through the frame.

"It is Alb-ba's b-b-birthday," he said, as if that was enough to explain their sudden presence. He closed the door behind them. "We w-wanted t-t-to m-m-meet you."

The girls looked at him with varying expressions of fear and fascination. They'd not been officially introduced, but they'd all seen him pledge his protection in the courtyard the night they arrived, and they knew his story.

Elayne stood and took a step toward him and Alba, assuming the role of hostess. She curtsied deeply and Ghisla and the other girls followed her lead, rising and bobbing their own welcomes.

"Happy birthday, Princess Alba," she murmured. "I am Elayne . . . of Ebba." She pointed to Juliah, the next oldest. "This is Juliah from Joran and Liis from Leok." Ghisla forgot who she was for a moment and failed to do anything but stare rudely, unaware that she had been introduced. Elayne rushed on, as if trying to cover her silence.

"Bashti is from Berne. Little Dalys is about your age, Princess. She's from Dolphys . . . like you are, Temple Boy. Keeper Dagmar too."

"He is Bayr," Alba corrected kindly, patting his cheek from where she was perched. "Not Temple Boy. His name is Bayr."

"Why have you brought her here?" Juliah asked, peevish. Ghisla suspected her bad humor was jealousy; Bayr had not yet been available for weapons training, though Dagmar kept promising.

"It i-i-is Alb-ba's b-birth d-day," Bayr stammered again.

"You said that," Juliah snapped. Elayne flinched and Bayr stiffened. Slowly he brought Alba down from his shoulders. He touched Alba's pale hair, as if trying to shield her from Juliah's unwelcoming behavior.

Alba walked to Juliah and, without hesitation, took the girl's hands and tipped her head back with a smile. Ghisla had thought her breathtaking by moonlight, but she was even more so in the light of day. Her hair was as pale as corn silk, but her eyes were so brown they appeared black. Sooty lashes brushed her honeyed skin, and her lips were the color of the berries that grew on the bushes near the eastern wall.

"YOU LEE UH!" Alba sang Juliah's name. "I am here to see *you*." And just like that, Juliah wilted.

They stayed an hour, Alba singing and hopping from bed to bed, making the girls smile in spite of themselves. Bayr hung back, watching, listening for prayers to end and the sun to set, and when the bells tolled again to signal meditation was over, he scooped Alba up and bowed to the girls.

"Th-thank y-you," he stammered.

"Will you bring her back, Bayr?" Dalys asked.

He nodded swiftly, and little Dalys wasn't the only one who smiled in response.

"I don't want to go, Bayr. Not yet. I want to stay here, in the temple," Alba begged.

Bayr patted Alba's leg, dangling over his shoulder, but he still turned to go. With Alba's protestations trailing behind them, he whisked her away.

⟲

Hod had to put Ghisla's pictures away. That is how he thought of them; they were Ghisla's, not his. Ghisla's eyes, and Ghisla's memories, all colored with Ghisla's songs. If he didn't put them away, tuck them behind a door in his mind, they became his world, and he wanted only to visit them.

They were not his world.

His world was one of sound and silence, one of sense and scents, one of hearing and heeding. And when he looked at Ghisla's pictures—especially in the beginning—those things fell away. He had begged Arwin to let her stay—who gave a miracle, a gift from the gods, away? But in the part of him that was not heartbroken at the loss, he understood his teacher.

When Ghisla sang, he was useless. Useless to himself. Useless to her.

So he locked her pictures away until he was alone and Arwin thought he was sleeping. Only then did he study the color and the cast. But before long, they began to fade.

The rune on his hand was silent; it only seemed to work one way. He did not have her gift, and the thread between them was not one he could pull. He was afraid for her, the little songbird with the frail bones and bitter words. But beneath his fear for her was despair for himself. For one perfect week, he'd had a friend. A friend, and music and pictures. But she was gone, and she took her songs with her.

For months he waited and listened, hoping. He and Arwin traveled to Leok for supplies, and talk of Liis of Leok had still rippled through the streets. That's what they called her now. *Liis.* It was not so different from *Ghisla*, and he was glad. There was talk of all the Daughters of Freya, the way there had been talk of Princess Alba years ago. In another five years, the Highest Keeper or the king would have to find something—or someone—new to keep the people from losing hope. For now, the daughters were the new gods—Liis of Leok, Juliah of Joran, Elayne of Ebba, Dalys of Dolphys, and Bashti of Berne—and the people raved and prayed as if the girls would save them. Mayhaps they could. Ghisla had saved him for a time.

At least he knew she was alive. That much gave him hope. Arwin did not speak of her, not to Hod, though Hod knew he sought out news in the villages when he thought Hod was out of earshot. If Hod concentrated, he could hear great distances, especially if the speaker had a voice he was accustomed to and the conversation took place out of doors. He could hear a flock of birds a mile away. He'd tested the distance. Crickets and all crawling creatures were quieter, but the more distinct their sound, the farther off he could hear them.

People were the easiest to hear. They did not move with the same stealth or suspicion. They were predators instead of prey, and they stomped and sang and spoke loudly, even when they were alone. He'd grown accustomed to the distortions of the wind and the water, to the way both tossed sound about and muted or amplified it. He could hear a leaf fall—that pleased Arwin immensely—though what good it did him, he wasn't sure.

But he couldn't hear Ghisla. And for months he waited, doing his best to forgive his teacher for sending her away, and to forgive himself for not fighting harder for her to stay.

8

TONES

Time passed and the days ran together in leaps and lurches. Life was not terrible. Ghisla had lived through terrible. But it was not sweet. She'd lived through sweet too and recognized the absence. The keepers lived in constant companionship, and they expected the same of the daughters. They moved as one through their days—chores, chanting, study, and sleep. Even in meditation or contemplation they were expected to dwell together, though they were instructed not to speak at all. Ghisla had grown up in the fields and in the forest. Even as a child she'd had far more freedom than the cloistered temple life allowed, and it grated on her patience and poked at her frayed nerves. Only in her thoughts was she able to slip away into dark corners and quiet nooks where she could breathe for a moment all by herself.

At least they were in the gardens; the harvest had begun, and all hands were needed. Ghisla had blisters from all the picking and pulling. Bayr and Alba were with them—the old queen had given permission for the princess to be educated alongside the daughters—and Bayr had cut their work in half, but Alba was demanding to be entertained. Dalys had painted her a picture, Juliah had walked on her hands, though her knotted skirts rose up around her knees and embarrassed Bayr. Elayne had wreathed flowers in her hair, and Ghost had convinced a bird to eat out of her palm, but they were all things Alba had seen—and done—before. She wanted something new.

"Liis should sing us a song," Elayne suggested. "She has a lovely voice. She tries to hide it, but it is obvious. Even when she hums it is beautiful."

"Yes, Liis!" The princess clapped. "Sing us a song."

"I do not want to sing," Ghisla said, shaking her head.

"Are you bashful?" Alba asked. "I am never bashful, am I Bayr?"

"N-no," Bayr stammered, shaking his head. "N-n-never."

"Mayhaps it is because I am so smart. I am good at many things. I am good at everything I try. That is what Bayr says."

"He is right," Ghost said, smiling at the little girl. "You are very smart."

"You just need to try harder, Liis," Alba insisted. "You need to sing more, so it will become easier and you won't be so bashful."

"I am not bashful," Ghisla insisted, stiff with discomfort. "I just do not want to sing."

"She is not bashful. She is secretive," Juliah grumbled. "And cross and selfish. She does not want to entertain us, though we entertain her."

"I will entertain you," Bashti offered. "I am not the least bit shy."

"I want to hear Liis," Alba insisted. "I want to hear her beautiful voice. My mother used to sing to me."

Any mention of the deceased queen made them all rush to attend to Alba's every request, especially Bayr, who had endless patience and affection for the child. She'd watched him run for hours with her on his shoulders, her arms outspread like she was flying. But he could not give her music.

Bayr turned pleading eyes to Ghisla, and she wavered under his gaze.

"I . . . do not know what to sing," she muttered. Since she'd arrived, she'd not dared to sing the songs of Tonlis. Hod and Arwin had known about the Songrs, and she had little doubt the other keepers would know about them too. They would know she was an imposter and not of Leok—or Saylok—at all.

What if her songs made images dance in their heads? What if the keepers cast her out? Where would she go then?

"Sing the song of parting. You know that one," Elayne suggested. "I heard you sing it with the keepers just last night, though you hardly did more than whisper."

It was a mournful dirge, a chant with little variation that the keepers sang at dusk. Eight tones, repeated in ascension and descension, to put the sun to bed. It was not of Tonlis, and there were no words. Mayhaps she *could* sing that one.

She didn't look at her rapt audience and sang softly, not allowing the sound to fill her throat or resonate in her chest, yet they all fell silent anyway, listening to the rise and fall of the notes.

"Do it again, Liis. Please?" Elayne begged sweetly when she was done. Her lips were trembling. "Your voice is so beautiful, I could cry."

"I don't want to cry," Alba said. Her eyes were wet as well. "Don't you know a happy song? Please sing a happy song."

"I know a song about a toad," Ghisla said. That song too would be safe. She trilled out Gilly's song about the unfortunate toad, and Bayr and the others laughed, but Princess Alba wrinkled her nose in confusion.

"I don't think that is a happy song," she argued. "The poor, squished toad is not happy."

The bells began to toll, signaling meditation had ended, and saving Ghisla from performing something else.

Bayr scooped Alba up unceremoniously and dropped her on his shoulders. One day she would be too big to ride thus, but that day was still a long ways off. She was never happy to go, but she'd learned not to argue when Bayr signaled the end of the day. It did no good to argue with him. He never said anything. His tongue was hopelessly tangled, and he only spoke when there was no way to avoid it.

Alba waved goodbye as Ghost ushered the girls from the gardens to join in evening worship. The keepers had moved from the sanctum and out onto the temple steps in a long purple line to sing their songs of supplication after the bells tolled.

Ghost and the daughters did not stand among them, but behind them in the shadow of the temple columns. The keepers sang the song of supplication, the one most commonly raised in evening worship. The daughters raised their voices in obedience as well, as they had been instructed to do, but half-heartedly.

Mayhaps singing in the garden had broken through a layer of fear and ice, but for the first time, Ghisla let herself sing with them—truly sing—her voice piercing the air the way her silence usually deflated the room.

Mother of the earth be mine, father of the skies, divine.
All that was and all that is, all I am and all I wish.
Open my eyes to see, make me at one with thee,
Gods of my father and god of my soul.
Give me a home in hope, give me a place to go,
Give me a faith that will never grow cold.

Her voice was crystalline and cutting, sitting above the tenor tones of the complacent keepers. It grew and climbed, and she did not rein it back. It felt good to sing. It felt right, like rebirth, and she sang the prayer, beseeching the gods to protect her secret even as she revealed herself. The voices of the keepers, raised in habit, became voices hushed in awe, and still Ghisla sang, hating the words for making her ache yet reveling in the musical resurrection within her breast.

No one stopped her or cried out, and many continued to sing with her, though their voices softened as hers rose. Those around her listened and even marveled, but they did not seem shocked or afraid or even entranced, and the reticence that had been her constant companion for months abated. She let her eyes drift closed, surrendering to the music. One song rolled into another, the song of supplication followed by the plea to Odin, a song they'd sung in Tonlis too. She'd sung it for Hod, but she'd not dared to sing it since, even though the keepers knew it and regularly sang it. She sang it now as though she were alone.

Father Odin, are you watching? Do you see me down below?
Will you take me to the mountain, where the brave and glorious go?
I'm not strong and I'm not worthy, but I trust you'll make me so.
Father Odin, are you watching? I am lost and I'm alone.
Will you take me to the mountain, where my heart now yearns to go.
Will you take me to the mountain, where my heart now yearns to go.

When she finished, dulcet tones still piercing the air, she breathed deeply, momentarily freed, and then she opened her eyes.

The keepers' faces were slick with tears, and Ghost and the daughters were weeping with bowed heads.

None of them would look at Ghisla.

Guilt and fear rocked her, and for a moment her knees weakened beneath the weight.

"I'm s-sorry," she stammered, gazing in horror at the trembling lips and streaming eyes. They hid their faces and mopped at their cheeks, as if they were embarrassed by their emotion.

What had she done?

"There is no reason to apologize," Dagmar said, climbing the steps and stopping beside her. Master Ivo followed him, his black gaze boring into her, and Ghisla's knees buckled again. Dagmar's pale eyes were wet, but he smiled and steadied her. "Weeping is good, Liis. It eases the pain."

"Then why will no one look at me?" she said, searching for reassurance and finding none. Ghost had disappeared into the temple without a word, and Juliah sat with her head on her knees. Elayne, tears dripping from her chin, was wiping the eyes of the younger girls, who cried like their hearts had been torn from their chests.

"There has not been enough weeping among us. None of us are accustomed to the relief of tears. But you have given us a beautiful gift. You have lightened our hearts."

"It is true. So you must sing to us again, songbird," Master Ivo rasped, the claw of his hand curling around his scepter. If there were tears on his cheeks, they had lost themselves in the creases of his skin, for he appeared unmoved. Of course, movement of any kind was not his habit. He tended to observe and opine.

"Don't fear your voice, Liis of Leok," Ivo insisted, emphasizing the hard ending of Leok. "There will come a time when you will need it, and if you do not use it, if you bury it inside you, it will grow weak and small. There is power in your songs."

"Yes, Master," she said. He rapped his scepter on the stone steps, indicating the matter was settled and entered the temple without looking back. It was suppertime, and the keepers moved from the steps to the temple and continued on toward the hall. Ghisla held back, needing a moment to collect herself. She'd sung . . . and she'd survived. Mayhaps she would be able to sing more often.

She released her breath and relaxed her tightly clenched fists. A large blister on her right hand had burst, and blood and fluid had collected in the well of her palm. She hadn't even felt the sting. *She'd been singing.* For the first time in months, she'd been singing. She climbed the stairs and stepped through the temple doors.

"Ghisla."

She stopped and turned, thinking someone had called her name.

All the girls had gone ahead, and the temple doors were now closed behind her.

"Ghisla?"

She started and looked around her again.

No one here knew her name. Not her real name. They called her Liis. Half the time she didn't even realize they were talking to her. More than once one of the girls had tugged on her sleeve or waved their hand in front of her face to alert her.

"Ghisla? Are you there?"

It was Hod.

"Hod?" For a moment she felt dizzy. Disoriented by the disembodied voice that resonated between her ears.

"Ghisla, I heard you singing."

Hod.

Hod was inside her head. She needed to be alone. She couldn't do this standing in the corridor.

The dining hall was filling, so the sanctum would be empty, and she rushed to the door. The candles were always burning in the sanctum, midnight to morn and morning to midnight, and she sank down on a bench in the darkest corner.

"Hody?" she whispered. The blood on her hand was dry and the voice in her head was gone. She screwed her eyes shut and sang the lines she'd sung when he'd first drawn the rune: "In Tonlis there is music. In the ground and in the air. In Tonlis there is singing even when no one is there."

She said his name again, louder. "Hody?"

"Ghisla?"

His voice was faint, like a voice from another room, but it was there. Dagmar made them use saliva to make the sun rune. She spat on her palm and mixed it with the blood, tracing her scar frantically.

There! She could hear him better now. He was speaking quickly, like he was afraid the connection would be lost, and she held her breath, straining to hear.

"I heard you singing. So much singing! It was so beautiful, Ghisla. I saw the sky and the keepers—they wore purple. I saw purple! It is like the grapes you showed me. I saw things I don't understand. Shapes and images and people. I think they were people. Girls with shorn hair. Have they made you all supplicants, Ghisla? Where have you been? Why have you not called out to me?"

His voice broke, and she thought he was gone.

"Ghisla?" he moaned, and she realized he thought the same.

"Hody, I can hear you," she cried. She was almost shouting. She could not speak to him in her head the way they'd done in the clearing. It was too hard to focus, and her heart was hammering too loudly in her ears. "I can hear you."

"You can hear me." Joy rang in his voice. *"Where are you?"*

"I am here. In the temple. I have so much to tell you." She tried to moderate her voice, but she could not quiet her heart.

"Ghisla, why have you not used the rune? I feared the worst."

"I w-was afraid it would not work. I did not . . . I did not dare try," she confessed.

"You promised me you would not give up," he said, but she heard a smile in his censure.

"I was afraid to hope. But it is . . . it is . . . so good to hear your voice." She was suddenly flooded with grief and . . . joy. Joy like she'd never felt before. It was like Princess Alba's hair and eyes: things that should not go together, but somehow did. The two emotions trod hand in hand across her heart, and tears began to stream down her cheeks.

She brushed her hand across her face, wiping at them, and Hod's voice became even clearer still. Tears worked in the rune! Tears and spittle and blood, the stuff of life.

"Arwin is coming. I must go," he said, regretful.

"Oh no. Not yet," she begged.

"Promise me you will not give up." His voice was fading.

"I will not give up today," she said, the joy and grief still warring.

"And promise me you will sing to me again."

"I will sing to you again. I won't be afraid to try."

"Liis?"

She jerked, pressing her hand to her heart.

"Hody?" she squeaked, disoriented all over again.

"Liis of Leok, who are you talking to, child?"

Master Ivo stood near the doorway to the sanctum, his hands wrapped around his scepter. She hadn't heard him enter. She'd been too lost in her miraculous conversation.

She rose in respect, her hands clasped before her, her mind scrambling. What had he heard? What had she said?

"I see none of the other daughters. They are at supper where you should be. So . . . who . . . were you talking to?" He enunciated the word *who* like a whip.

"Only to myself, Highest Keeper," she said. "To myself . . . and . . . to Hod."

He gaped. "To Hod? The blind god?"

"Yes, Master."

She'd stunned him. She'd stunned herself. She'd told the truth, but it wasn't the truth at all, and she feared the old wizard would hear her lie.

"Of all the gods, why do you speak to him?" he asked.

"Because he . . . he is the best . . . the best listener, Master."

The Highest Keeper stared and then he laughed, a cackle that made him sway with its power. He laughed, bent over his scepter, and she waited, trembling, and held her tongue.

"He is the best listener," the Highest Keeper crowed, still snorting with laughter. "This is true. Imagine. Such a thing had never occurred to me. Hod hears better than Odin himself." He laughed again. He shook a clawed finger in her direction. "You are a clever girl."

"Thank you, Highest Keeper."

"Now go. You should not be in the sanctum. You can pray to Hod elsewhere." He laughed again, and she curtsied and fled, his chortle following behind her.

⌒୨

It was only after midnight on the following day, when the temple and all its occupants had retired to their quarters and the watchman on the mount wall cried out that all was well, that Ghisla dared to creep down to the stores beneath the kitchen and summon her friend. It was the only place in the temple where she trusted no one would hear.

The mice and spiders would hear, and some might come out to inspect. The thought made her shudder, but she wasn't deterred. She lit a candle in the kitchen before pulling the door closed behind her and descending the stone steps to the nethermost chamber where meat was hung, dried, and salted before being stored. She'd thought about sitting in the room where the jarred fruit was shelved and casks of wine were kept but thought that room was more likely to attract late-night visitations. The hooks that extended from the ceiling were adorned with unrecognizable carcasses, and the room smelled of flesh and blood, but the keepers were nothing if not fastidious, and every surface had been scrubbed and every corner swept. It would do.

She was deep enough beneath everything else that no one would hear her, and she didn't want a repeat of the episode with Master Ivo in the sanctum. She had no excuse—conversations with a blind god would not work again—for being out of her bed. With two doors and earthen walls between her and the floor above, she perched on the workbench and used a needle to prick her finger. She didn't let herself think or doubt. She simply smeared the blood into the lines of her palm and called out.

"Hody?" she sang softly. She suspected one word was not enough, and she began to chant his name using the eight tones of the song of parting, hoping it would suffice.

Ho dy, Ho dy, hear me, Ho dy.
Ho dy, Ho dy, hear me, Ho dy.

It was no longer a name but a pealing summons. She closed her eyes and waited for the darkness behind them to merge with his. Her heart was banging so loudly she was afraid she wouldn't hear him. Afraid he wouldn't hear her. Afraid he would not answer. She kept singing, out loud, and traced the rune again.

"I am here, Ghisla."

His voice was as clear and discernable as her own, as though he sat with her in the macabre chamber, with only candlelight between them. She laughed in wonder.

"I have been waiting. Hoping."

"I am never alone. I called out as soon as I could."

"You must tell me everything."

She could not keep the words in her head, the way they'd done in the clearing. Her thoughts were filled with his voice, and it was easier to speak naturally than to waste time and concentration on forming silent sentences.

"They call me Liis. Liis of Leok."

"To me you will always be Ghisla of Tonlis. I know who you are."

"Yes." Emotion rose suddenly in her throat. "And you are the only one."

"Are you well?"

She hesitated. What was well? She had not been well for a very long time. She doubted she ever would be again.

"I am fed. I am clothed. I am taught. I am learning to read. Do you know how to read, Hody?" She did not want to talk about herself.

"I cannot see the words on the scrolls . . . but I can make them, the way I make runes. I see the shapes in my mind and in the sand."

"I am learning the runes, though the runes we have learned are simple and meaningless."

"You have rune blood. Surely they know that by now. One only has to hear you sing."

Talk of blood reminded her to prick her finger again.

"Ghisla?"

"Arwin told me to guard my gift. So I have. No one knows I am a Songr. I'm afraid they would cast me out or . . . worse. I must be Liis of Leok now."

"You are happy there?" he pressed.

"I am happy now." And she was. In that moment, she was perfectly, serenely happy.

"I am happy now too, Ghisla." His voice was warm and pleased, flooding her mind and dripping down into her chest. For an hour they talked of the temple, of the people in it, and she sang him the songs she'd composed. She had a verse for each of the clan daughters, as well as Ghost and Alba.

"I can see them, Ghisla," Hod exclaimed. *"I can see them all."*

"Princess Alba is a beautiful little girl. Her hair is like moonlight."

"You have shown me moonlight."

"I have shown you moonlight *and* sunlight."

"Your hair is like sunlight."

"Yes."

"Like grain," he added.

"Alba's hair is pale . . . but her skin is not. It is warm . . . like bread."

"Like bread?"

"We knead and roll and twist and pull and let it sit upon the stone," she sang slowly, reminding him of a song she'd sung in their days together in the cave.

"Ah yes. I remember now. Bread is . . . brown." He said the word with the confidence of a child mastering a new skill, and her heart grew in her chest.

"She is glorious. And loved . . . and best of all, she loves."

"That is good."

"Yes. She is nothing like her father."

"The king. The mighty Banruud. You will have to tell me more about the king. Is his hair like moonlight too?"

"No. His hair is like midnight. And his skin is pale. She looks nothing like him. He is a beast. He loves no one but himself."

"I cannot see midnight."

"Midnight is darkness. King Banruud is darkness."

"Ah . . . I am well acquainted with darkness."

He was silent for a moment, and so was she. Their time had come to an end, and her fingers ached from pricking them, though she'd smeared the rune with spittle too, to make the blood last longer.

"Next time, I will sing a song about the chieftains. And about the king," she promised. "I have many more verses. I've been saving them for you."

"Next time," he agreed, wistful, though he did not ask her when that would be. *"And . . . next time . . . you must sing me a song about Ghisla of Tonlis, so I can see your face."*

9

Days

Ghost was always watching, always wakeful, and nine days went by without Ghisla reaching out to Hod again. When she did finally seek him, late at night, he answered immediately, though he warned her not to despair when he didn't.

"Arwin cannot know. If I do not answer, it is because I cannot, not because I want not."

But he had not failed to answer her yet.

They grew more accomplished at the connection each time. Hod said he could only see the things she sang about, and even then he did not see them with his eyes but with his thoughts. She became adept at crafting songs to describe her world.

She always called out to him with a song—any song, though the anthems of the Songrs seemed to work best, and he saw those images most clearly. Mayhaps it was the ancient words or the melodies that had been sung so many times they became part of the wind that moved over Saylok, songs soaked up by the clouds and released again in rain, the cycle continuously renewing. Mayhaps it was just Ghisla herself, and the heritage in her blood and bones, the heritage of a people that had sung the songs for centuries and passed them on through life and death.

She and Hod never spoke as long as they wanted to. They were both terrified of discovery. The daughters were, by design, shut off from the men of Saylok. Fraternizing with a boy—even one who lived far away—would not be tolerated. She also knew that the rune on her hand and the gift that made the connection possible would bring devastation down upon both of them.

The keepers had their work and their runes and the companionship of the brotherhood. The daughters were expected to limit their companionship the same way and were kept isolated from everyone but the keepers, the king, and, of course, each other. The chieftains demanded to see them whenever a council was called, and the daughters would be paraded in front of them like cattle so the chieftains could report back to their clans on their welfare.

After one such visit, Ghisla complained to Hod, "Chief Lothgar says I am fattening up nicely. He seemed so proud, like it was his doing."

"You were the size of a tiny bird. I cannot imagine it. You must show me."

Ghisla imagined sheep, thick with winter wool, shuffling into the temple enclosures and used a gruff voice, mocking the big Chieftain of Leok. She wasn't as good at mimicry as Bashti, but she tried.

Liis of Leok,
How you've grown,
Since you left your long-lost home.
Let me pinch your puffy cheeks
And watch you waddle like a sheep.

Hod laughed as she expected him to, but he wanted to hear about the council in detail.

"I cannot tell you much more. We are brought in, looked upon—sometimes I sing—and then we are escorted out. We are not privy to the conversations of the men, though Keeper Dagmar tries to answer our questions when we ask. He is the only one who does."

She sang the lines she'd crafted for Dagmar, his pale eyes, thin face, and patient ways.

"Keeper Dagmar reminds me of you. He is wise and kind. Mayhaps it is his mannerisms more than his appearance."

"I remember. Keeper Dagmar is of Dolphys. He is the uncle to Bayr, the Temple Boy, who watches the princess," Hod recited. Hod was fascinated with the Temple Boy, and they talked of him often—his strength, his size, and his stuttering tongue. It seemed to comfort Hod that a boy so gifted had such a weakness.

"Two sides of the same sword. Just like Arwin always says."

"He is so powerful, yet he can hardly speak. His tongue is cursed. I have thought perhaps . . . if he would learn to sing it would help loosen his words."

"You must teach him," Hod pressed. But Ghisla doubted such an opportunity would present itself.

"Tell me more."

"Dagmar is his uncle, yet no one talks of his mother or father. Juliah says he is the son of Thor, and someday he will kill the king and break the curse upon the land."

"Juliah of Joran. The daughter with the warring spirit."

"Yes. She does not want to be a keeper. She does not like being a woman either, I don't think, though Bayr has taught her how to throw a spear and shoot a bow and wield a sword. He has tried to teach us all, but Dalys is so small she can barely lift one off the ground."

"Smaller than you?"

"Much smaller. I am growing, remember? And I am mean. Both seem to have helped me in swordplay."

"You are mean? This is not true. You are simply irritable. Like Arwin. He is quite skilled at swordplay as well, though I have begun to defeat him regularly. He says he will bring me a new teacher to teach me what he cannot."

"You are skilled with a sword?" Ghisla gasped.

"I am skilled with a sword and a spear and a bow, though I will never be a warrior."

"You will be a keeper. And someday you will come here, to the mount. Just like we planned."

He was silent in her head, and she thought for a moment she had lost him.

"Arwin says there will be no more keepers from the clans as long as the daughters are in the temple."

"What?"

"The king has decreed it. There will be no young male supplicants until the drought is over. I will not . . . be going to the temple any time soon, though I am seventeen now, and I am of age."

She was too shocked to respond immediately. She did not know all the ways of the keepers or of Saylok. It had not occurred to her that there were no young keepers entering the brotherhood.

"It used to be that one supplicant was selected each year from the clanless and one from each clan. All were not young, but all were willing. Some years, no supplicants were sent because there were no men who wished to be keepers. But since the drought began, more men have become warriors, and the clans have lost their belief in the keepers and the runes. Now the king has forbidden it altogether."

"But . . . what does Master Ivo think? Can he not override the king on matters of the keepers?" she cried. Hod *had* to come to the temple.

"You would know better than I."

"The Highest Keeper does not tell me what he thinks, Hody."

"Yes . . . but he is your teacher, is he not? Does he think Bayr is a god? The son of Thor? Does he think Bayr will break the curse upon the land?"

"He loves Bayr . . . All the keepers do. He was brought to Temple Hill when he was a babe and he has been raised among them ever since. He is their child, the only child, the only son any of them will ever have. He is beloved. Ghost says that is why he is loathed by the king. The king hates anyone who could challenge his authority or his throne. He wants to dispense with the keepers and continues to blame them for the lack of daughters. He claims they have not lifted the curse or healed the scourge. The people . . . the clans and the chieftains . . . have started to listen to him. Master Ivo fears at some point they will turn on the keepers and the temple will be destroyed."

"If there are no more keepers, the chieftains and the king will have sole power over Saylok. There will be no balance or ballast. No checks on the authority of the king. And there will be no one to use or protect the runes."

It was more than Ghisla could comprehend. She was only a girl from Tonlis, after all. The machinations of the king and the keepers made her head spin. But one thing was perfectly clear in that moment, and it filled her with hopelessness.

"If you cannot come to the temple . . . I will never see you again."

∽෧

It was not uncommon for the keepers to clasp hands during one particular song at the end of the day, though they did so only with each other and invited the daughters to do the same behind them. Ghisla always resisted the ritual and kept her own hands together so no one would reach for her. She and her family had often clasped hands as they sang; it was common among all Songrs, and she did not want to sing with anyone else. Deep down, she was also afraid Ghost or one of the daughters would feel the scar on her palm. It was a silly fear. The scar was well hidden among the lines of her hand, just as Hod said it would be, but it was a fear nonetheless.

Since the day she'd reduced everyone to tears at worship, the other girls had started jostling each other in order to stand beside her when she sang, even though she'd reverted back to barely singing at all.

"We want to hear you," Elayne had explained when Ghisla protested the new attention. "If you would sing out, we wouldn't have to stand so close."

Ghisla just kept moving away from them until Ghost put an end to the constant repositioning and assigned spots to stand during worship, putting herself at the end of the row. That evening, Ghisla was distracted when the song changed, and when Ghost reached out and took her right hand, Ghisla did not pull away.

The clasping song was not much more than a drone, a collective amen sung with conjoined hands, but it had a way of centering the mind and calming the spirit. The keepers would break off into harmonies above and below the melody line, but the word sung never changed.

"Amen. Ah ah ah men. Ah ah ah men," Ghisla sang, keeping her voice muted, and her eyes forward. If Ghost sang, Ghisla did not hear her, but she did not release Ghisla's hand.

"I love him. I love him. And I wish that I didn't," Ghost said.

Ghisla looked up at her, confused, but Ghost was mouthing *amen*, as her eyes drifted over the keepers. Keeper Dagmar stood a full head taller than the old men around him, and her gaze stopped on his face.

It was forbidden to converse during worship, and Ghost was not one to break the rules . . . at least with the girls. Ghisla began singing once more, but she watched Ghost from the corner of her eye.

"Ah ah ah men. Ah ah ah men," Ghisla sang.

"It hurts to love him." Ghost's voice bounced between Ghisla's ears, but her mouth did not move. *"Just as it hurts to love Alba. I loved her from the moment I felt her in my womb, and I will love her until I die. I fear it will be the same with Dagmar. That the pain will continue to grow, and he will never be mine. Just as Alba will never be mine. Some days, I cannot bear it."*

Ghisla jerked again, and Ghost frowned down at her, unaware that she'd just poured her private thoughts into Ghisla's head.

"Ah, Liis. What a strange, sad girl. She reminds me of myself," Ghost thought, and Ghisla gasped, dropping Ghost's hand like it had burned her.

"Liis?" Ghost questioned. Her voice no longer had the hollow effect, and it was muffled by the droning all around them.

"I don't want to sing anymore," Liis murmured. Her legs wobbled and she sank down to the steps.

"Are you ill?" Ghost asked. The keepers had started to turn, their faces wreathed in frowns and disapproval.

"Are you unwell?" Ghost pressed, stooping down beside her. Her silvery eyes were concerned, and Ghisla saw herself reflected in the twin mirrors. Her short blond hair stuck up in tufts around her head, and her blue eyes were rimmed in dark circles. She hadn't slept well for so long. She looked almost mad.

"Yes . . . I am unwell," she whispered, afraid that she truly was.

៚

She'd heard Ghost's thoughts, and as alarming as that was, the content of her thoughts was just as disconcerting.

Ghost loved Dagmar, and Ghisla was not greatly surprised. They were careful around each other, but they were always aware, as though they danced without touching and watched without looking.

But the revelation about Alba was shocking.

It occurred to her that perhaps Ghost was using the word the way it was applied to all the girls—Daughters of Freya, daughters of the temple—and they were nothing more than a cast-off assortment of females. But Alba was rarely included in their number. She was the princess, not a daughter, and there was always a distinction.

Alba's eyes were so different from Ghost's. Her skin too. But when Ghisla studied Alba through new eyes, the resemblance between them was there to see if one only knew where to look. Moonlight hair and bow-shaped mouths and smiles that dimpled their cheeks. Ghost so rarely smiled . . . but she smiled when Alba was near.

Ghisla did not want to know Ghost's secrets. She was horrified by the knowledge, and for several days she wouldn't touch anyone, bristling when someone sat beside her or settled a hand on her sleeve. She refused to hold hands at worship and sang so softly no one could hear. They all thought she was being selfish and silly and whispered about her among themselves. She didn't need Hod's superior hearing to know she was being discussed. The whispers made her angry. She was trying to protect them, and they complained about her. That evening at worship she sang a little louder and extended her hand to whomever would take it. If she heard their secrets while she sang, why should she care?

But Elayne's voice was one of only concern.

"Liis is troubled. We all are troubled. I wish she would sing. I think if she would sing . . . it would soothe us all. We are all so afraid. I miss my mother. I wish I could go home."

Ghisla was overcome with guilt, and she stopped singing, squeezing her eyes shut and willing the door to close.

Just like Ghost's, Elayne's thoughts tumbled in a disjointed stream, one slipping into another, but all were spoken in her voice, and as long as Ghisla kept singing and holding her hand, the stream continued. It was the same with all the girls. And one by one, she heard them too.

During evening meditation, when Ghost left them in their room, she approached Juliah and held out her hands as though she sought her forgiveness. Mayhaps she did, for what she was about to do.

"I will sing to you," she said stiffly. "Choose a song."

"Do you know the fishing songs of Joran?"

She knew the fishing songs of the Songr, and she sang her one of those instead. And she cast her net, collecting Juliah's inner musings.

Juliah wished for escape and dreamed of having Bayr all to herself. *"We will go to Joran. We will fish with my grandfather. Bayr will teach me to fight, and we will leave this temple and this hill and live wherever we want. Everyone will be afraid of us."* But almost immediately she despaired because she knew Bayr would never leave Alba behind.

"I will go to Joran myself. Soon. Soon I will go. When I am bigger and stronger, and I can wield a sword."

Bashti wanted a dancing song, though she frowned at Liis throughout. Bashti was competitive, and she did not like the attention Liis received.

"I can sing, and I can dance, and I make everyone laugh. Liis only makes people cry." But almost immediately, those words were replaced by awe, and she began to sway to Liis's song, her little brown feet shuffling and her hands clasped in Liis's.

"Don't stop, Liis. Don't stop yet, please. I want you to sing all day."

Dalys was the only one whose thoughts were not communicated in words. She saw color, spilling and moving, and shapes emerging from the paint, as if she were creating as she listened. She let go of Ghisla's hands and went in search of parchment so she could draw, begging Ghisla not to stop.

That night, in the darkness of the cellar, she called out to Hody to confess what she had done.

"I can hear them, Hody. I can hear them all."

"What do you mean?"

"I was holding Ghost's hand during worship as the day ended. I was singing . . . and for a moment, singing at her side, our hands together, I heard her thoughts . . . as if she were speaking to me. But she wasn't."

"You heard her?" Even in her head, his voice rang with shock.

"I immediately stopped singing and released her hand, and I could not hear her anymore."

"Does she too have the power of song?"

"No. Though I think she has rune blood. She has an affinity for the animals. Wild things do her bidding. I've seen birds eat from her hands and deer walk alongside her."

"Did she hear you too . . . the way I do?"

"No. I think I would have . . . heard her . . . hear me." It was confusing, but Hod seemed to follow her reasoning.

"And Ghost is not the only one. The same thing happened with Elayne, Juliah, Bashti, and Dalys," she confessed in a rush. "I had to know if it was only Ghost. It isn't. When I sang and clasped their hands . . . I could hear them all."

"Ghisla . . ."

"Is it the rune?" she asked. She had linked hands with her family in song many times, and never heard anything but music ringing from their lips.

"Perhaps. But I think it is more likely . . . you. One who does not have your talent would not be able to use the rune in such a way. Do you have to trace the rune to hear their thoughts?"

"No. I just have to be touching them while I sing."

"The runes unlock different things in all of us. It is why we study them. Why they must never be misused or abused. Why they must be protected. In the wrong hands . . . they can be very destructive."

"What if *my* hands are the wrong hands?" she moaned. "What if I am destructive? I do not want to know the things I heard."

"What did you hear?"

"Ghost loves Dagmar."

"That is not so bad. Is it?"

"No. No. That is not so bad." Her stomach roiled. "But that is not all."

"Ghisla?"

"The late queen was not Alba's mother. And I am not at all convinced that King Banruud is her father."

～

Ghisla had never sought Dagmar out for conversation before. She did her best to observe and listen and let the questions others asked answer her own. But she was troubled. More troubled than she'd ever been, and she had questions that needed answering.

"Dagmar?" she asked, approaching him as he bent over his scrolls. He raised his head, surprised by her voice.

"Can I speak to you for a moment?" she asked.

"Of course. What is it you need, Liis?" He extended his hand to her, but she did not take it. She was afraid to touch anyone right now.

"You say we—the daughters—are the salvation of Saylok," she blurted out.

"Yes," he said, eyes searching, hand still extended.

"How . . . exactly . . . are we the salvation of Saylok?"

"Without women, Saylok will eventually . . . die," Dagmar said softly.

"But . . . if we are kept in the temple, none of us will ever become mothers."

Dagmar's eyes cleared and his mouth twitched as though someone so young should not be contemplating such things. He folded his hands together and sat back in his chair.

"Is that why you are worried? There is time enough for that, Liis, in the years to come. You are a child yet."

"I am fifteen!" she snapped. "Soon I will be sixteen."

He frowned in disbelief. She'd never told anyone how old she really was, but the words spilled out, angry and hot. She was *not* a child anymore. She had not been a child for a very long time.

"Will Chief Lothgar or King Banruud decide what happens to me? Or will the Highest Keeper?" she demanded.

Dagmar seemed shocked by her questions, and his surprise made her even angrier. Did the keepers understand nothing?

She stared at him coldly, waiting for an answer.

"I don't know," he whispered. "I don't know who will decide."

It was as she thought, but at least he did not lie.

"And what will happen to our children?"

"What do you mean?"

"Will they be taken from us, the way we were taken?" *The way Alba was taken from Ghost?* She did not say the words. They were not her words to say. But she thought them.

"Daughter . . . ," he said, stunned. "Where is this coming from?"

She turned to leave, but he called out to her as she neared the door.

"Liis." His voice was sharp.

She stopped.

"My sister, Desdemona, Bayr's mother, felt as you do. As if she had no choice. I did not protect her as I should have. But I will do everything in my power to protect you."

She believed him. But there was no real safety within the walls of the temple, and no safety without. There was only waiting. Waiting for time to pass and for the powerful to determine what happened next. Gods, kings, and keepers would decide their fate. And there was little she could do about it.

Hod had given up hope of ever hearing Ghisla sing again.

And then one day, she was simply there, her voice ringing in his head.

"Give me a home in hope, give me a place to go, give me a faith that will never grow old."

The rune on his right hand, the rune he'd drawn to mirror hers, began to burn, and he'd walked from the cave and out into the waning day, feeling the light on his skin, and lifted his face to better hear.

Arwin had followed him, but when Hod had waved him away— "'Tis just a new bird, Master"—he'd grown bored and returned to his supper.

For several minutes, it was just her voice. No images. No colors. Just her voice, like she sang with her eyes closed. But it was enough, and he stood, enraptured, listening. Rejoicing. Then the song ended and he heard her speak. He heard her ask a question, but she was not talking to him.

"Why will no one look at me?" she asked.

"Ghisla?" he whispered, afraid Arwin would hear. He scrambled down the path to the beach, needing distance and space and the roar of the water to muffle his voice.

He was almost running, moving too quickly on a path that would never be clear enough for a blind man to run down; he could not hear rocks, after all. He broke out onto the beach without mishap but stumbled in the sand.

"Ghisla?" he said, louder, terrified she was gone again.

"Hod?" the word was so faint, it was hardly there, but he shouted in response.

"Ghisla! I heard you singing. I heard you singing, and it was so beautiful."

"Hod?" His hand was still burning, and he cried out again, babbling in joy and disbelief.

And then her voice was there, as clear as if she stood beside him, and he fell back on the sand, his face to the sky.

That day, he'd made her promise to use the rune again, to call out to him when she was able, and she had, many times since.

She didn't tire of his questions, and she never refused him a song.

She gave him so many songs.

With her songs, he saw Elayne of Ebba with her fiery hair and her gentle ways, but he didn't just *see* her, he *knew* her. He knew them all.

He knew Bashti; he saw the brown warmth of her skin and the bright flash of her mind. She was a marvel at mimicry, both mannerisms and voices, and she made Ghisla laugh. That was a wonder too—Ghisla's laugh. Rare and rippling, it never failed to rob him of breath; he *loved* Bashti for that, for giving Ghisla laughter.

He knew dark-eyed, little Dalys and experienced all her colors. Ghisla composed songs as Dalys painted, just so he could see them too.

Through Ghisla's music, Juliah danced in his thoughts with her sword and shield, pouncing and punching, and he delighted in her antics, though she and Ghisla were often at odds.

"She does not understand me," Ghisla said. "And I don't know how to make myself understood. We are very different."

"I think it is more likely that you . . . are the same," he suggested gently. "You are both warriors. Both fighters. You just fight in different ways."

"I'm not always certain who I am fighting. Who the enemy is. All I know is that you are my dearest friend, Hody."

"And you are mine."

"I could not bear it if I could not talk to you."

Hod often wondered how he'd borne a single day before she'd washed up on his shore. When Ghisla sang he saw the world. Her sisters and the keepers, the castle and the king. He saw the gardens and the gates and the wall that separated them all from the rest of Saylok. He saw the sea and the sky and the mountains and the trees. He even saw himself.

It was a beautiful world to look at, though he knew, for Ghisla and her sisters, it was not always a beautiful world to live in. Sometimes Ghisla's songs were washed with grays or infused with shadows. Sometimes her loneliness and despair made the images she drew for him waver like the sands after high tide.

And yet she kept on singing, and he kept on listening, doing his best to shoulder her sorrow and speak relief to her soul.

He did not tell her how he missed her or how he suffered when she could not visit him. He did not tell her how the darkness wore on him, and how he worried there would never be a better day, a better Saylok. He did not tell her that he fought his own hopelessness and could not see his own path. He did not reveal that he feared the reason for his existence and begged each day that the gods would make it clear.

He greeted her with only joy whenever he heard her voice and made her promise to not give up.

PART TWO

10

LULLABIES

"You have grown so much, Liis. You hardly look like the same girl I met two years ago. There is some flesh on your bones, and your cassocks are so short, your ankles are showing," Ghost remarked one morning as they worked side by side in the garden.

"I will let the stitches out of my hems," Ghisla said.

Her sleeves were too short too, and she'd begun to bind her breasts in a length of cloth to keep them from swaying beneath her shapeless frocks, but she didn't mention that. She thought Ghost had probably noticed. She was sixteen summers now, and she'd begun to look her age, though no one commented on it. She was still not as tall as Elayne—she never would be—and she was still too thin, but the swell of her breasts and the curve of her hips was much more pronounced; she would not pass for a child any longer.

"I will ask Dagmar to fetch the seamstress again. All of you girls are growing," Ghost said as they shook out their aprons and washed their hands. Ghost never ventured out of the temple or down into the village. She rarely even walked the mount. She was afraid of the king. They all were, but even when the king was gone and Temple Hill breathed easy, Ghost did not change her habits.

Ghisla was not the only one who had noticed Ghost's tendencies. Bashti had a theory and shared it with her sisters—as they'd begun to call each other—while they prepared for bed.

"She doesn't want to be seen because she thinks she is ugly. People stare . . . and it makes her sad."

"People stare at all of us, Bashti," Elayne said. "But at least our hair has begun to grow." Elayne had surprised them all when she'd refused to cut her hair again. She'd promised to keep it covered until it was long enough to weave into a tight circle around her head, and the Highest Keeper had relented. The chieftains had complained to the Highest Keeper and the king that they were ugly; Ghisla had heard it in a keeper's thoughts. She'd clasped his hand at mealtime with a song of worship still ringing in her head, and his voice was loud and clear.

They are girls. And the people want them to look like Daughters of Freya, not keepers. They are hideous this way.

Their hair had all grown long enough now to braid it around their crowns. It did not flow down their backs like that of most women in the clans, but it set them apart from the shorn keepers, and it was a vast improvement from the early days. Even Ghost wore her hair thus, though she continued to blacken her eyes like the keepers. Ghisla thought her magnificent, regardless of what Bashti claimed.

Bashti rolled her eyes. "They do not stare at us for the same reasons, Elayne. They stare at you because you are beautiful."

Elayne smiled, pleased, but Bashti was just getting started.

"And you will soon be old enough to wed. They stare at Liis because she is beautiful too, and everyone is hoping she will sing. But people stare at Ghost and me because we are outsiders. We can't pass for clan daughters. She is too pale, and I am too dark. Yet here we are." Bashti folded her arms with a harrumph and stuck out her lips, daring the others to disagree.

Elayne stood and coaxed Bashti to take her hands. "You are Bashti. You are not an outsider. You are one of us. A Daughter of Freya."

"I am Bashti, but I am not of Saylok. I do not even remember where I'm from."

"It is better not to remember," Liis said tremulously, drawing the eyes of her sisters. She turned away, folding her dress inside the chest at the foot of her bed.

"I do not look like a Daughter of Freya," Bashti cried, and Liis relaxed. She hadn't meant to interrupt.

"The keepers all attempt to look alike," Elayne said. "But I think . . . it makes them . . . disappear."

"Disappear?" Juliah scoffed. "I sometimes wish Keeper Amos would disappear. He drones on and on and never ceases."

"The keepers want to disappear as individuals," Elayne explained. "They want to blend into each other. To present oneness. But I like that I am different. That we are different. None of us are the same. Not me, or you, or Juliah, or Dalys, or Liis. I do not want to disappear. Do you?"

Bashti shook her head. "No. I want everyone to look at me." They all laughed because it was true. Bashti wanted to be the very center of attention, all the time. The only one who got more attention was Alba, though she was happy to share.

"I do not know why Ghost hides," Elayne said. "But you should never hide. If people stare, it is because you are special. You are Bashti, the performer. Bashti, the dancer, and Bashti the jester. You are a daughter of the temple, and there is only one of you. You are rare and wonderful."

"Rare and wonderful?" Bashti said, her pout giving way to a grin.

"Yes. And beautiful, though rare is far better than beautiful. Rare is *never* ugly," Elayne said, smiling too. "Now, please . . . can we go to sleep?"

Elayne doused the light and they all crawled into bed, and for once the dark silence was not a relief. It felt more like . . . disappearing.

"Will you sing to us, Liis?" Dalys asked sweetly. "When you sing, I see the colors."

When Liis did not answer immediately, Juliah grumbled.

"Liis does not want to be rare and wonderful. She wants to be invisible. She wants us to be invisible too."

I don't want you to be invisible. I just don't want to see more than you want me to see, she thought, but as usual, she said nothing. She'd found most thoughts were not usually kind. Not because people were unkind, necessarily, but because feelings were unguarded and . . . true. At least, they were true in the moment they were felt. She didn't want to dislike her sisters. And she didn't want to hear their dislike for her.

"You are being unfair, Juliah," Elayne murmured, always the peacemaker.

"I am being honest," Juliah retorted.

Bashti grunted her agreement and Dalys sighed in gusty disappointment.

"All right . . . I will sing you a lullaby," Ghisla relented. She was safe from their thoughts underneath her covers, the soul rune tucked beneath her chin.

"I want ten lullabies," Dalys pled, but her voice had already grown sleepy.

"I will sing until you are asleep," Ghisla bargained, and five rare and wonderful girls drifted off to places unknown as the room reverberated with Songr lullabies.

⁓

"Liis . . . Liis, wake up."

For a moment she was still lost in the lullaby, in soft breezes and long grass, and her mother was there. But Ghost was not her mother, and the soft sounds of the girls sleeping around her were not Gilly and Abner.

"Bayr is here. The king sent him to get you. Pull on your keeper's robe and your shoes."

"Why?" Ghisla said, suddenly wide awake, but Ghost laid a finger across her lips.

"Shh, do not wake the others."

Liis slid from beneath her covers and pulled her purple keeper's robe around her shoulders and shoved her feet into her leather slippers.

"Bayr will go with you. Don't be afraid. Nothing will happen to you with Bayr near."

"What does the king want?" she asked, following Ghost from the room. No one else even stirred.

For a moment Ghost didn't answer, and her silence only increased Ghisla's fear. As if she felt her terror, Ghost reached out and took her hand.

"He wants you to sing to him," Ghost said as they descended the east staircase to the huge entrance below. Bayr was waiting for them.

Ghisla had sung for the king and the chieftains at the council many times before. Usually just worship songs and a simple song of Saylok that Dagmar had taught the daughters.

Take my eyes and give me wisdom.
Take my heart and give him strength.
I will fight beside my brothers.
I will battle with my men.
We will fight to see the day
When the daughters live again.

The song was meaningless to her. Silly. She'd meant not a word. But the chieftains and their warriors always banged their feet against the floor and lifted their swords in appreciation and patriotic fervor, and Ghisla and the daughters were then escorted back across the square, appearances made, their duty done.

But this was different. It was late and the other daughters would not be with her. And there were no chieftains on the hill.

"The k-k-king i-ins-sists," Bayr stuttered in explanation, his eyes weary. His braid was rumpled and his face creased, like he too had been pulled from sleep to do the king's bidding, but he had not awakened any of the keepers. Only Ghost. Or mayhaps she had not yet been to bed.

"If we tell Dagmar or the Highest Keeper, they, of course, will refuse to send you," Ghost explained, her eyes pleading forgiveness. "And there will be . . . bloodshed. Bayr says the king has not slept in days, and he is . . . desperate."

"The k-king is ill. B-bet-ter to s-sing than . . . f-f-fight. But I w-will s-stay with y-you," Bayr promised.

"But what can *I* do?" She still did not understand.

"He does not trust the keepers to administer the runes, though Ivo could ease his suffering," Ghost explained. "Bayr says your voice soothes him."

"I w-will n-not leave y-you," Bayr promised again. He extended his hand, waiting for her consent. She took it, but instead of leading her through the temple doors, he entered the sanctum and pushed against the wall behind the altar. The wall rattled slightly, the scrape of stone brushing stone, and an opening appeared. Bayr entered without hesitation, though the darkness was absolute.

"There are t-tunnels all over the m-mount," he stammered. And he left it at that.

The distance felt interminable, though in truth it probably took mere minutes. When Bayr stopped and thumped the stone, the rock rumbled and an opening emerged before them, depositing them in the throne room of the king.

He was pacing and groaning, his advisors and a few of his men standing by, nervous and perspiring. The one named Bilge eyed Ghisla's bare ankles and her messy hair and smirked as though he liked what he saw.

Bayr tried to announce her presence, but King Banruud cut him off, impatient.

"Go," he roared, waving at the room. His advisors were eager to be gone, and Bilge swiped a bottle from the table and slinked for the door, shooting another look at Ghisla and her silent escort. Bayr did not leave.

"I w-will s-stay," Bayr said, firm, though his stuttering tongue made him sound unsure.

"You will go."

Bayr did not even flinch.

Banruud strode toward him—toward them—and swung at the boy. The air whooshed over Ghisla's head and Bayr grunted, absorbing the backhand to his cheek, but he did not move. The king tensed to strike him again.

"What would you like me to sing, Majesty?" Ghisla cried, stepping in front of Bayr, and the king frowned down at her, his eyes ringed with exhaustion and shot with blood.

"You would cower behind a woman, Temple Boy?" he spat.

"Bayr says you want me to sing," she rushed. "I will sing anything you wish."

He glowered at her, his brow shining with perspiration, and turned away from them. Bayr's face had already begun to swell.

The king threw himself onto his throne, rubbing at his temples and pulling at his hair, and Ghisla almost pitied him in his misery. She pitied Bayr more.

"Come here, Leok," the king ordered, addressing her by the clan she represented. "Stand here. Next to me. Sing until I tell you to shut up."

She looked up at Bayr and he nodded at her, trying to smile, but it looked more like a grimace. He did not trail behind her when she did as the king ordered, but he did not depart either.

She began with the song of parting, the mournful dirge that seemed most soothing, but the king swore and threw a wine-filled goblet against the floor, the deep-purple liquid dousing her feet and the strip of bare leg extending from her nightgown.

"Not keeper song," he yelled.

"If not keeper song . . . what?"

"I do not want words. Only sound. I need bloody sound," he ground out.

She formed her mouth in the shape of an O and pealed out the melody of several songs before the king's head started to droop and a sigh of relief escaped his mouth. When she faltered, he lunged for her, dragging her closer.

"Do not stop," he insisted.

She started over, her voice a wordless harp, and his hand remained a manacle around her wrist, keeping her going. The base of his big palm pressed to hers, and his mind opened like the stone wall of the tunnel.

She could hear him.

He'd had too much to drink. The wine smeared his thoughts and scattered his internal dialogue. And beneath the mess was the tinny bleating that was driving him mad.

It would drive *her* mad. She fixed her eyes on her wine-spattered feet and pushed onward, her voice moving over the melodies, no words, only sound, as the king had requested.

Ghost's face and Alba's name bounced through his dream. And another woman. Desdemona. Desdemona . . . Dagmar's sister. Bayr's mother. Her hair was a black tumble and her eyes were blue and filled with scorn. Desdemona's face became Bayr's, and Ghisla faltered again, shaken.

Banruud's hand tightened around her wrist. She sang louder, trying not to see what was in his tormented head.

There were other names. Other faces. Flickering like flames, licking at the king's dreams, and then . . . the ringing in the king's head faded, bit by bit, like it too had fallen asleep. His fingers became lax and his hand fell away, dangling over the arm of his throne.

Ghisla finished her song, her final stanza so light it barely caressed her lips. She stood, staring at the slumbering king for several minutes, afraid to move and too weary to continue singing. When he did not wake, she eased away from his throne.

Bayr had fallen asleep sitting against the wall, his arms propped on his knees, his head against the frame of the door. His cheek had blackened while she sang. She walked toward him with a careful tread, but he opened his eyes when she drew near. Without a word, he rose, his gaze flickering beyond her to the sleeping king, and together they entered the tunnel in the wall and walked in the darkness back to the temple.

Someone had lit fresh candles in the sanctum, though it was well past midnight; it was closer to dawn. Ghisla guessed it was Ghost and hoped the woman had gone to bed.

"P-please do not t-tell," Bayr whispered, pointing at his face.

"Why?"

"It w-will only c-cause them p-pain. They c-can do n-nothing." He was fourteen years old, two years younger even than she, yet he was the protector of everyone on the mount.

"Is there *anyone* who can do something?" Her anger and helplessness welled again.

"Y-you d-did," he whispered. "Y-you sang. You f-fixed him."

"For now, but I wish I hadn't."

He cocked his head, his brow furrowed in question.

"He will need me again."

He nodded sadly, admitting the truth. "Y-you are of u-use."

"I have drawn attention to myself. That is never a good thing."

"I w-will n-not t-tell if y-you d-don't." The swelling on his left cheek made his smile crooked.

"You are wise, Temple Boy. I am not fooled by your stutter."

"And I am n-not f-fooled by your s-size, L-Liis of L-Leok. Y-you are p-powerful."

"If you sing . . . mayhaps your words will not stick to your tongue," she suggested.

Bayr laughed and shook his head. He touched his throat while he raised one brow and made a yodeling sound that cracked and creaked.

"I didn't say it had to be beautiful," she laughed.

He shook his head again and turned to go.

"My mother sang away my bruises," Ghisla said. "It might . . . help."

He looked back at her, hesitant, but then he nodded.

"All r-right. S-sing."

She closed the distance between them and laid her right hand on his cheek.

> Cry, cry, dear one, cry,
> Let the pain out through your eyes.
> Tears will wash it all away,
> Cry until the bruises fade.

"Her song is like a rune," he thought, and his inner voice did not stumble at all. She tried not to be distracted by it as she continued with her tune.

> I'll sing until you're whole again,
> No more ache and no more pain.

Bayr's eyes immediately began to stream, just as hers had always done when her mother sang this song. He pulled away, embarrassed by his weeping, and she scowled up at him.

"It will not work so quickly," she snapped. "Come here."

"It f-feels b-better," he admitted. It already looked better. "You h-have r-rune blood," he said.

"It is not me," she protested. "It is you. It is your tears. It is you who has rune blood." She didn't know if what she said was true, but he allowed her to put her hand back to his cheek and sing the song again.

Bayr's thoughts were as kind as Elayne's.

He was grateful that he would not have to hide his face from Alba and Dagmar, that they would not see the king's mark. He also wanted to ask about Liis's mother, but his reluctance to talk kept him blissfully silent. She decided his stutter was one of the loveliest things about him. It made him especially good with secrets.

Ghisla sang the tune a third time, softly, swiftly, and his tears tumbled over his cheeks and dripped off his chin, taking the swelling and the angry color from his face.

"There," she said, dropping her hand. "It will not work for illness or serious wounds . . . but it is a tonic for the little aches. Next time . . . you can sing it yourself." She hoped there would not be a next time but feared the king's treatment of him was all too common.

"Th-thank y-you."

"You will not tell?" she pressed, though she knew he wouldn't.

He shook his head.

"Good. Master Ivo might try to make me a keeper . . . and I would like to keep my hair."

He laughed.

"He fears you. The king . . . he fears you," she told him. She didn't tell him how she knew, but Bayr nodded once, like it was something he already understood, and ducked into the tunnel. The wall scraped closed behind him.

"He did not hurt you?"

She heard the fear in Hod's question when she told him about her night singing for the king.

"No. He did not hurt me. He hurt Bayr. But Bayr did not leave me."

She had not returned to her bed when Bayr left her in the sanctum. The dawn would be coming soon. The cock had already crowed. Instead she had walked out into the garden and through the rear gate, invigo-rated by her sudden freedom in the lavender-colored dawn.

Hod would be awake, she was almost certain. She'd drawn her finger over a thorn and watched as a drop of blood fattened on the tip. Tracing the rune, she'd begun to call out to him, singing the same lul-laby that had accompanied her through the night.

"Why does Bayr not fight back? He has killed men with his bare hands. Surely he could defend himself."

Hod sounded as if he wanted to kill Banruud himself, but he knew the answer to his question.

"He is the king," Ghisla said. "And Bayr is not interested in defend-ing himself."

"He wants to protect everyone else."

"Yes." She felt close to tears and blinked them back. Her tears would not make her whole again, and tears could not fix what was wrong in Saylok.

"Is there not something more than this, Hod?"

"More than what, Ghisla?"

"More than suffering? Even the king, who causes so much pain . . . is wracked with it."

"What did you see when you sang to him?"

"I saw Desdemona."

"Desdemona?"

"Bayr's mother."

"Can you show me?"

For a moment she just hummed the lullaby, not singing the words, just like she'd done for the king, and she concentrated on the flickering image she'd seen in his head—the black-haired beauty, a sword in her hand, and a child swelling her womb. Then she released the image and let the old Songr melody score the changing sky in her here and now. She was too weary for the king's demons.

"I am looking at the most beautiful sky," Hod whispered.

"You can see my sky?"

"Yes," he breathed. *"What color is that?"*

"It is many colors."

"Rainbow?"

"No. Blue and black and purple—violet—and there at the bottom, lining the hills, it's—"

"Gold."

"Yes. The sun is rising."

For a moment she hummed the melody, letting him see through her eyes.

"Your power is growing, Ghisla."

Her laugh was dry. Hard. "It is odd, isn't it?"

"What is odd?"

"I can hear a king's thoughts and sing him to sleep. Yet I am still his prisoner."

"Yes. I suppose . . . in a way . . . we all are. Ghisla?"

"Yes?"

"Promise me you will not give up."

"I will not give up today."

෧

Hod's conversation with Ghisla had left him shaken, and when he climbed up from the beach to return to the cave, he was in no mood for Arwin's announcement. He had not yet slept. He rarely slept when Arwin slept.

"We will leave for Adyar soon."

"I do not want to go to Adyar."

"But I have found you a new teacher. He will teach you to better use your stick as a weapon."

153

Arwin had secured yet another warrior to try to kill Hod for a month while he did his best to not be killed. He would be bruised and battered when he returned, and no closer to ever putting his training to any real use.

"Someday the Highest Keeper will call on you, Hod. You must be ready," Arwin warned. He had said the same thing a thousand times.

"Why will he call on me, Master?" he sighed.

Arwin huffed at Hod's pessimism. "I have told you. Repeatedly, I have told you."

"Tell me again."

"Your mother brought you to the temple. She was ill. She was desperate. And she asked Master Ivo to heal you. But the Highest Keeper recognized you."

"He recognized me?" Hod almost laughed. Each time Arwin told the tale, it became bigger and more dramatic.

"Yes! He knew you were sent by the gods. By Odin himself."

"So he sent me here to you to await the day when Saylok needs me," Hod parroted. He was tired. Saylok needed girl children, not blind men who could wield a stick and draw runes.

Arwin was angry now. "Do not mock me, Hod."

"I do not mock you, Arwin. I only mock myself."

"You will see," Arwin snapped. "Someday you will understand. And you will thank me for my faith and your mother's sacrifice."

"My mother's sacrifice," Hod whispered. He had not thought of Bronwyn of Berne for a long time. He had no face to match the name. He remembered very little at all of his mother, but Arwin said she was pretty and young and alone in the world. She'd died not long after delivering her small blind son to the cave keeper, and Arwin had buried her in a clearing near the cave. A boulder marked the spot where she lay.

Hod tried to summon her memory, but instead an image rose. Not his mother, but the woman—Desdemona—Ghisla had shown him from the king's thoughts. Desdemona. A shield maiden. Bayr's mother.

She too was dead. She too had sacrificed for her son, Hod was sure. Mayhaps he and the Temple Boy had that in common.

"We will go to Adyar," he sighed, relenting. At least it would distract him for a time.

"That is best," Arwin said, immediately mollified. "Trust me, Hod. Trust me, and when the time comes, you will be ready."

11

TUNNELS

The Tournament of the King had turned the hillside into a wash of color. A rainbow. Ghisla showed it to Hod in her mind's eye, the tents and the teeming horde, the citizens of every clan lining up to see the daughters and seek a blessing from the keepers.

"Those who make the pilgrimage are mostly men now. Lines and lines of men," Ghisla told Hod. "They want to touch our hands, and some throw flowers at our feet. One man threw himself at Elayne and knocked her to the ground. He was dragged off by the temple guard and put in the stocks in the square."

"Is Elayne all right?"

"Yes. But yesterday, three men approached on their knees, as though to worship us. They were clanless—no warriors' braids and no sashes—but all at once they stood, daggers in their hands, and one grabbed Dalys and ran. An archer on the wall shot him as he fled. The other two were hung on the north gate as an example to all those who would seek to take a daughter of the temple."

"I am horrified . . . and I am glad," Hod confessed.

"Poor Dalys screamed in her sleep last night. I sang to her, but I dared not touch her. I did not want to see her dreams."

"You should not be on display. It is not safe."

"Master Ivo barred the temple doors and refused to bestow favors and blessings, but people have waited so long. The keepers are supported by the public, and he opened them again this morning. The king and the chieftains insist the people see us. And Dagmar agrees. He said the people's adoration is both a bane and a blessing. It endangers us even as it keeps us . . . safe. We are symbols of Saylok, and Master Ivo claims we will not be touched or traded or given away in marriage to the clans or the chieftains, though there is always talk."

"You are all young yet, and supplicants do not marry," Hod said, but she heard the same concern in his voice that shivered in her belly when such things were discussed. She saw the way Elayne was looked upon. The pressure on the keepers and the king would only get worse as they came of age.

"Dirth of Dolphys has died. The clan will pick a new chieftain." She did not want to talk of marriage anymore.

"Arwin told me. He heard the news in Leok last week. Word is that Dred of Dolphys will take his place."

"Dred is Keeper Dagmar's father. The relationship is strained, though I don't know why."

"They have not spilled all their secrets to you?"

"I have kept my hands and my songs to myself. I do not wish to know anyone's secrets."

"But I do. So you must tell me when you know."

Hod was teasing her, trying to keep their conversation from straying into the heaviness that always lurked in the shadows. The weight of people's secrets wore on her. Her knowledge was not power; it was pain. What she knew she could not tell, and what she knew she could not forget. So she carried others' secrets around, like rocks she couldn't put down. Telling Hody was her only relief. So she told him everything and said not a peep to anyone else.

But she worried about the day when she would hear something she could not ignore.

⁓

The melee was the final event of the tournament, and it was a contest open only to clansmen. Each chieftain chose ten warriors to compete, and all six clans were represented. Sixty warriors took the field in their clan colors, and only one clan could claim victory. The object was to be the last clan standing, even if it was only one warrior. There were no weapons and no rules but one: take every man down. Once a man's body hit the ground, he was required to leave the melee until only one man—or one clan—remained.

"We've only nine, Majesty," Dred of Dolphys called out, striding forward. "We're a man short."

The crowd groaned. They'd been hopeful the melee was about to begin. Ghisla groaned with them. She was weary, her skin was sticky and hot beneath her purple robe, and she did not care for sport in general. The melee was one of the few events the daughters were allowed to attend—everyone attended the melee—but she had no interest in it. Juliah had been talking about the melee for weeks; she was rooting for Joran, obviously.

The king raised his arms to quiet the commotion.

"Then choose another, Dred. Surely you have another warrior from the Clan of the Wolf willing to enter the melee."

"I claim him. I claim the Temple Boy." Dred raised his arm and pointed at Bayr, who knelt behind Alba not far from the king, guarding her, ever present, ever faithful.

Ghisla was not the only one who gasped and gaped.

The king shook his head in immediate refusal.

"He is not of Dolphys. He has no clan. He cannot fight with you. Choose another," the king replied.

"I claim him," Dred insisted, planting his feet. "We have not yet chosen a chieftain. But I speak for my clan, as the oldest warrior on the field, and I want him."

The crowd grew quiet, confusion rippling in silent waves. Dred of Dolphys was a seasoned contender, and he knew the rules of the melee. It was a contest among the clans. The clanless were not allowed.

"What are you babbling about, old man?" Banruud growled. He was sitting up straight in his seat, bristling with annoyance. "He is not qualified."

"He is of Dolphys," Dred replied.

"He is not," someone yelled.

"He is the son of my daughter, Desdemona, shield maiden in the Clan of the Wolf."

The king grew eerily still and the crowd followed suit, the hush of a thousand held breaths. No one knew why the king had turned to stone, but none of them dared break the spell.

"He is fourteen years old, Dred of Dolphys. Why have you not claimed him before? This is highly suspect," Aidan of Adyar murmured.

"I did not know he lived," Dred shot back. "His mother—my daughter—is dead. She has been dead since his birth fourteen years ago, Aidan."

"He is naught but the Temple Boy," the king ground out.

"That may be true, Highness, but he is also of Dolphys. And I claim him. We claim him. It is my right as acting chieftain unless . . . he has already been claimed by a clan or . . . a king?" Dred's voice was mild and the onlookers nodded.

"Is this true, boy?" the king sneered. "Are you of Dolphys? If you accept this claim, you must live among your clan."

The crowd shifted in protest and Juliah muttered under her breath. No one was required to live among his clan, but no one would argue with the king.

"Highness, it is a ploy," Aidan of Adyar interrupted. "Dred knows he cannot win the melee with his pack of aging wolves. He thinks the Temple Boy is Odin's hound. He'll abandon him when the battle is over. Leave the boy be." The warriors stomped and thundered their agreement. They wanted to begin the contest.

"What'll it be, boy? Do you want to live in Dolphys?" the king pressed as if it mattered little to him. But Ghisla knew different. Banruud cared. His loathing was almost love.

"I a-am a s-servant of the t-t-temple," Bayr stammered, and the king sneered at his stuttering. Ghisla wanted to slap Banruud, to spit in his face, to scratch at his eyes in defense of her friend. But such fantasies were folly, and she gritted her teeth and willed the confrontation to end for Bayr's sake.

"Do you withdraw your claim, Dred of Dolphys?" the king asked.

"I cannot withdraw my blood from his veins, or his from mine, Highness. But I'll not take the boy from his home . . . or his duties. We will play with nine. And we will win."

The warriors behind Dred—clansmen and opponents alike—reacted, cries of denial and protest rising to chase away the awkward encounter, and Dred of Dolphys turned away, abandoning his claim.

The melee ensued but Ghisla did not watch. She watched Bayr. His eyes were fixed upon his feet, and when Alba began to droop on her little stool, Bayr stepped forward and, with his typical care, lifted her into his arms. Queen Esa rose as well, trailing him to the castle, calling to the handmaid who waited. Ghisla doubted the queen cared which tribe prevailed. Ghisla did not care either. She sensed that Bayr had lost, and that was all she knew.

$\sim$

The melee signified the end of the tournament, but the celebration afterward stretched well into the following day, when drunk and stumbling clansmen and citizens found their way off the mount for another year, often leaving the keepers with a mess to clean up.

Ghisla and the other daughters had gone to bed with music and laughter echoing up from the square and woke to a temple in mourning.

Dred of Dolphys had made another claim, and Bayr, his face bruised and battered, spent the day being prepared to leave for Dolphys.

"What has happened to Bayr?" Juliah asked.

Ghisla thought it likely that the king had taken out his rage on the boy, and Bayr had been unable to keep it from his uncle, and Dagmar and Dred of Dolphys had joined forces to remove Bayr from his clutches.

Bayr did not want to leave.

"Who w-will w-watch over the d-daughters?" he protested again, looking over his shoulders at Ghisla and her sisters as he was urged forward, out of the temple, to his waiting grandfather. His eyes met Ghisla's, panicked, and she knew what he was asking. Who would watch over *her*? Who would protect her when the king summoned?

"We will. I will," Dagmar said again. "I will watch over them all." His voice was firm but Bayr shook his head, doubtful, despairing. Bayr didn't believe his uncle *could* protect her. Ghisla didn't think so either. But the matter was clearly out of Bayr's hands.

Master Ivo and the purple-robed keepers descended the stone steps of the temple, surrounding Bayr and Dagmar. Ghisla and the other girls trailed behind them, trying to hold back their tears.

Dred and the warriors of Dolphys were mounted and waiting, their postures as grim and apprehensive as those of the keepers.

"Word has spread. We must go now, Bayr. We must go now," Dred urged, waving him forward.

But it was too late.

The chieftains, led by Erskin and the king, were striding into the temple square, three dozen warriors following behind them.

"You cannot claim him, Dred," Erskin shouted as they drew near. He sounded fearful and almost desperate, as if he too could not imagine the mount without its protector.

"I can and I have," Dred returned. "He is my daughter's son. He is my kin. I have no other. I would not deny you, Erskin. Why do you seek to deny me?"

"He is the Temple Boy. He swore to guard the daughters of the clans," Lothgar of Leok brayed. "We stood on these steps, gathered around this flame, and Bayr of Saylok promised to protect them the way he has protected the princess. He cannot break that vow. He must remain on the temple mount."

For a moment, Dred was silent, as if stunned at the development. Ghisla realized suddenly that Dred had not been present the day the daughters were brought to the temple. Dred had not seen the Highest Keeper light the Hearth of Kings and promise that it would continue burning in their honor. He had not seen Bayr swear to serve the daughters of the clans.

Bayr stepped out from among the robed keepers, his warrior's braid so long it touched the new blue sash tied around his waist.

"Why does he wear that sash?" Ghisla whispered. She still understood so little about the customs and traditions of the clans.

"Because he has been claimed. Now he wears the colors of a clan," Juliah said, almost wistful. "I wish I could wear the colors of Joran."

"You cannot deny a clan their chieftain," Dred said.

The Dolphynian warriors beside him grew still. Bayr drew to a halt halfway down the steps, and Dagmar froze beside him. The king and the chieftains balked as well, and the metallic whisper of swords being drawn shivered through the square.

"Return inside, Daughters!" Keeper Amos insisted, as if afraid that a skirmish was about to ensue. But none of them moved.

"What chieftain?" King Banruud hissed.

"Dolphys has yet to choose a chieftain," Dred said. "The boy must present himself to the clan to make a claim."

"You will be chieftain, Dred of Dolphys," the king retorted. "We all sat at council when it was decided."

"One old man for another?" Dred asked. "That is not in the best interest of my clan." His clansmen shifted again, uncertain, but still they did not protest.

"You have the blessing of the keepers, the support of the chieftains, the nod of a king. Why do you insist on claiming the boy?" Aidan of Adyar asked, his voice thoughtful, his gaze narrowed.

"I am not the best choice. If given the opportunity, I have no doubt my clan will choose him." Dred pointed at Bayr, and all eyes followed his finger.

"He is not yet grown," Erskin argued. "How can he lead a clan?"

"Have you killed a man, Bayr of Saylok?" Aidan asked.

Bayr nodded once. "Yes."

"Have you bedded a woman?" Lothgar boomed.

Bashti snickered and Elayne gasped.

"Th-there w-was no b-bed," Bayr stammered.

Lothgar grinned, and the men at Dred's back relaxed infinitesimally.

"Sounds like a man to me," Aidan said. "Looks like one too."

"He has protected the temple and the princess since the king was crowned. He has not failed or faltered. But he has a clan, and his clan has claimed him, and you cannot deny us our chieftain," Dred pressed.

Ghisla watched Dagmar wrap his hand around Bayr's arm, as though willing him to yield, to trust.

"The clan has not made their selection. Your people have not spoken. You cannot speak for them, Dred of Dolphys," the king argued.

"I can't. But the boy must come to Dolphys and be heard," Dred insisted.

"This is a farce," the king argued, his tone glacial.

"It is not," the Highest Keeper intoned from the shadow of his hood. "Dred of Dolphys is a man of vision."

Erskin scoffed and Lothgar folded his powerful arms in disbelief.

"Dred of Dolphys forsakes his own claim to the chiefdom for another, better man," the Highest Keeper argued. "Would you do the same? I can think of many warriors in Ebba and Leok who would lead their clans with great distinction."

"The clan will choose him," Dagmar's voice rose, strong and sure. "I am a keeper of Dolphys. In the temple, it is I who represent the clan. Bayr of Dolphys has my blessing."

"He cannot forsake Saylok for a single clan," King Banruud protested.

"He is not a slave, not a supplicant, not the son of the king," the Highest Keeper said. "He has fulfilled a duty and will now fulfill another. When you were chosen as king, Sire, you did not break an oath to Berne. Someone took your place. Someone will take his place." The Highest Keeper's voice was so mild—and cutting—none could disagree.

"And if he is not chosen?" Lothgar interrupted.

"If I am n-not chosen . . . I w-will return," Bayr promised, and Dred of Dolphys looked at him like he wanted to clap his hands over Bayr's mouth.

But Bayr's vow eased the tension in the chieftains, and Aidan of Adyar grasped his braid with one hand and his sword with the other. "He's been claimed. Let him go. If the Norns will it, he will return."

Lothgar of Leok echoed the motion, but Erskin of Ebba and Benjie of Berne did not. The king's face was a mask of indecision, his big legs planted, his arms folded, his shoulders set. Still, no one stepped forward to impede the boy's progress as Dagmar escorted Bayr the final steps to Dred's side.

"To Dolphys," Dred shouted.

"To Dolphys," the warriors behind him hollered, and as one they turned for their horses.

"To Dolphys," Dagmar ordered Bayr, his voice firm.

Bayr swung up onto his mount, his eyes clinging to his uncle's. Then he looked at the keepers and the daughters, a fleeting glance filled with pain and apology.

"No," Juliah moaned beside her, and Elayne clutched her hand.

"What will we do without him?" Elayne wept.

"I don't know," Ghisla whispered. "Odin help us." Odin help *her*.

∽

The moon was full and the hour late when Ghisla picked her way down to her favorite overlook on the east face of Temple Hill and sat in the grass, tucking herself back into the shadows so she could call out to Hod. Below her was the long, grassy slope spotted with rocks and trees that eventually flattened in the Temple Wood below, but she could see in every direction. If she saw anyone or felt any danger, she could scurry back to the tunnel in the hillside and be back inside the temple in minutes.

Eleven tunnels crisscrossed the mount. Tunnels from the temple to the castle, from the sanctum to the throne room, from garden to garden, and from the cellar to the hillside. Bayr had shown her all of them.

But now Bayr was gone. The occupants of the temple were reeling. Dagmar had shut himself in the sanctum, and Ghost had disappeared after supper, though Ghisla thought she was probably with Alba, who had been inconsolable since saying goodbye to the boy who had guarded her since birth.

Poor Alba.

What would they *all* do without him? Elayne's question had echoed continually. Ghisla would have to face the king alone. She would have to sing for him without Bayr nearby. The thought made her innards twist in terror. She'd sung for the king a handful of times, and had managed, after the first time, to keep her distance and not touch him at all.

And yet . . . Ghisla rejoiced that Bayr had been saved. That he'd been protected at last. He would be in Dolphys, away from the king. He would be safe—as safe as a warrior of Saylok *could* be—and he would be free. Free. Dolphys would make him their chieftain—she had no doubt—and all of Saylok would be better off for it. The chieftains were the only ones who could truly challenge Banruud, and someone would have to challenge him eventually.

Ghisla pricked her finger and had just begun her song to summon Hod when two figures appeared below her, emerging from the side of the hill as if they too had made use of the network of tunnels from the temple.

Ghisla ceased her song, slinking down into the grass, her palm bleeding, her heart galloping. With the tournament ended, Temple Hill had emptied of her visitors, but Ghisla knew better than to believe she was safe. She peered out over the ledge in front of her, trying to gauge the danger of discovery.

It was Dagmar and Ghost, hand in hand.

Hand in hand.

When they stopped, directly below her, and collapsed onto the grass, she moaned in apprehension and discomfort. She did not want to witness a tryst or eavesdrop on a highly personal conversation, but she was well and truly stuck.

It was them, no doubt. Ghost's pale skin glowed like the moon, and Dagmar was speaking, his voice strangled as though he fought tears.

"Twenty years ago, when I was the same age as Bayr is now, I left Dolphys for the temple," Dagmar choked out. "I was so confident. So sure. I knew where I belonged. Now I know nothing. I am powerless. Unsure. And my heart is, at this moment, traveling back to Dolphys."

He paused, and Ghisla realized she was not witnessing an illicit tryst but a confessional.

"Bayr is the king's son, Ghost. He is Banruud's son," he said, and his tears began to fall.

Ghost swayed, as if in shock, and Dagmar pulled her down to the grass, enfolding her in his arms as though he was desperate not to lose her too.

He would not lose Ghost. Ghisla knew that much. Ghost loved him, she worshipped the ground he walked on, and Ghost had her own secrets. She would not leave him.

"Oh, Dagmar," Ghost gasped, holding him, stroking his shorn head.

"Bayr does not know," Dagmar wept, the sound so raw and wounded that Ghisla wept with him, pressing her hands to her lips so she would not reveal herself.

"And the king?" Ghost asked. "Does he know?"

"My father claimed him as Desdemona's son. The king is not a fool. I think he has suspected all along," Dagmar moaned.

"You must tell me everything from the beginning," Ghost begged, and after a brief hesitation, he relented.

Ghisla thought about covering her ears. She should shield herself from his burden. But she didn't. She listened as his words spilled out, giving her more secrets to carry, more sorrow to shoulder.

"When my sister died . . . she drew two blood runes," Dagmar explained. "Runes she should not have known. One of them required her life in exchange. But she was already dying. And she was angry, bitter. She cursed all the men of Saylok. She said there would be no girl children, no women for such men to love. She cursed Banruud by name."

"How?" Ghost gasped. Ghisla bit back a moan, and the rune on her hand burned. Hod was waiting. She could feel him as though he stood on the other side of a wall, but she could not call out to him.

"She said Bayr would be his only child," Dagmar continued. "In the second rune, she said Bayr would be powerful, so powerful that he would save Saylok, yet his father would reject him."

"His only child?" Ghost repeated numbly, and Ghisla knew what she didn't say: Alba was not the king's child, and Ghost knew it.

"The runes are not all-powerful. Clearly," Dagmar answered. "Banruud has another child. A daughter. He has Alba. Yet . . . the curse continues. The power of my sister's blood rune persists. I don't know how to break it, or if it *can* be broken."

"Have you told Ivo . . . of the runes?" Ghost asked, her shock evident.

"No," Dagmar breathed. "I can't."

"You must. He will know what to do."

"I can't," Dagmar insisted again, and Ghost said nothing, her hand still stroking his head.

Dagmar straightened, releasing her so he could look down into her face, and his agony was on full display to Ghisla. To move would expose her to view, so she lay, helplessly listening, painfully witnessing all.

"If Ivo knows, he will be forced to act," Dagmar said, his voice harsh with the truth. "As Highest Keeper he will do—he *must* do—whatever is necessary to destroy the power of Desdemona's rune." Dagmar paused briefly and then choked out, "I cannot take that risk."

"But . . . is that not . . . what you want?" Ghost asked.

"What if Bayr is the only one who can break the curse?" Dagmar cried.

"I don't understand," Ghost said. "What are you telling me?"

Dagmar began to weep again, his sobs the scrape of metal on metal. It was the worst sound Ghisla had ever heard, and she buried her face in her arms, but she had to know. *What curse?*

"What do you mean, Dagmar?" Ghost asked.

"Bayr's birth marked the beginning of the drought." Dagmar spoke as though he impaled himself on each word. "What if his death marks the end?"

Ghisla did not rise and go back to the temple through the long, dark tunnel when Dagmar and Ghost left. She was too depleted. Too frightened. And too numb.

She needed Hod. She had to tell someone. The blood on her hand was dry and her throat even drier. She jabbed at her finger and watched the droplet form and trickle down her finger and pool at its base. She smeared the blood through the lines of the rune, trying to sing. It was no more than a whisper, but Hod was there, waiting, as she finished the simple verse. And she told him everything. She told him about Dred taking Bayr to Dolphys. She told him about Ghost's silence, Dagmar's secrets, and Ivo's ignorance. And she told him Dagmar's dilemma.

"Dagmar has not told Ivo about the runes. He is afraid if Ivo knows, he will be forced to act. He is afraid the end of the scourge will only come with Bayr's death."

"He's afraid the Highest Keeper will try to kill Bayr if he knows about the runes?" Hod asked.

"Would you? Would Arwin? If you thought it would end the drought?"

He was silent for a moment, considering. He did not answer directly.

"You must tell Master Ivo."

"I can't."

"You must. Tell him what you heard. Tell him about Desdemona's curse, about her rune. Exactly what Dagmar said. He will know what to do."

"But what about Bayr? What if Dagmar is right?" she moaned.

"Bayr is in Dolphys. Bayr is safe . . . for now. But Saylok is not. The temple is not, and you are not."

"But . . . would you do it, Hod? If it would break the curse, would you kill Bayr?" She needed to know.

Hod sighed, the sound vibrating in her thoughts like wind in the eaves.

"I don't know."

"If it would break the curse . . . would you kill me?" she asked.

"What are you talking about, Ghisla?"

Mayhaps it was her fatigue. Mayhaps it was her fear, but after this day, honesty was all she had left, and so she gave it to him. "I love you, Hod. You are my dearest friend. My only friend. And I would do anything to keep you. Do you know that? I would trade all of Saylok for you."

He was silent for a moment, as though she'd shocked him, but when he finally spoke, he sounded almost reverent.

"I would trade all of Saylok for you too, my little Songr."

"That is how Dagmar feels about Bayr."

"Yes . . . I imagine it is."

"I want to go home, Hod."

"You sound so tired."

"I want to go home," she said again, urgent, and he understood, the way he always seemed to.

"You want to go to Tonlis."

"Yes. But there is no Tonlis."

"Of course there is."

"It was burned to the ground. Every cottage, every field. Every man, woman, and child. Everyone but me."

Hod gasped. *"Everyone?"*

"I saw no one else. I saw only death. Families dead in their homes. In their fields. The bodies were piled, and everything was set on fire. The dead, the animals, the homes, the fields."

"Oh, Ghisla."

"They were trying to stop the disease. I don't know why they let me live. Mayhaps because they thought I would die. But I didn't die. I didn't die. I just wanted to. Now I am here. And it is happening again. Must I sit by and watch everyone die in Saylok too?"

"It is not the same."

"No. This scourge is slower." She was close to tears, but even tears felt like too much work.

"You must rest now. Nothing must be done tonight."

She was so weary, she didn't trust her legs to take her back through the tunnel and up the stairs to her bed, but she rose and made her way to the hatch hidden behind the rock.

"Promise me—"

"I will not give up," she sighed, finishing his sentence. It was how they always parted.

"And Ghisla?"

"Yes?"

"I love you too."

12

Hours

Days later, just after the night watchman wailed, Ghisla crept down to the cellar to call out to Hod. She had just pricked her finger and begun her song, her back to the door, when strong arms wrapped around her, and a hand covered her mouth.

For a moment she was too stunned to do anything but blink into the darkness. She could not see who assailed her. She could not see anything, and she flailed, throwing her head back, but he was tall, much taller than she, and her head thudded off his chest. She tried to bite at the fingers covering her face but bit her lip instead, and blood pooled in her mouth.

With his hand over her mouth, he could not control both of her hands, though his weight against her back made her flailing useless. She started to choke on the blood that dripped down her throat. She couldn't breathe, and she clawed at his hands.

When her legs buckled, her assailant stepped back, creating space to push her down to the floor. His hand moved from her mouth to her clothes, and she coughed and choked, spitting up blood and gasping for air.

"No one can hear you, Daughter," he whispered.

She screamed in response, sending her voice pinging off every surface.

"No one can hear you," he insisted, but she screamed louder, finding a note so high and sharp it stabbed at the backs of her eyes and tore at her throat. She pressed her hands over her ears and screamed louder, the song of terror and outrage one she'd never sung before. And the man who clawed at her legs and pinned her to the floor was suddenly singing with her.

Screaming with her.

Then he was gone. His weight was gone. His hands and his heavy limbs were gone. A draft brushed against her bare legs, signaling the cellar door had been opened, but she did not stop. She simply curled her knees into her chest and screamed harder.

Light bloomed moments later.

"Liis. Liis. Daughter, stop. Stop!" It was Dagmar. Dagmar and Ghost. And she was saved.

"Who was it, Liis?" Dagmar asked. His pale eyes were bleak, and he kept a distance, letting Ghost tend to her. Her lip was battered and her throat was raw, but she was otherwise unharmed.

"I don't know," she rasped. "I was singing . . . and I didn't hear him come down the stairs. I hung the torch on the sconce in the corridor. He shut the door behind him, and it was so dark." She traced the scar on her hand with her thumb. She'd been singing to Hod. That was why she hadn't heard the man.

"Was he a keeper?"

"I—I don't think so. He was big in the way a warrior is big, not a keeper. And I think he had . . . hair. It was pulled back, but I fought and kicked, and a few strands came loose and brushed my face."

"Thank the gods," Dagmar exhaled. Ghisla wasn't certain if he thanked the gods for her safety or for the reassurance it had not been one of their own who'd attacked her.

"Why did he run? Did he hear you coming?" Ghisla asked.

"He was gone before we came," Ghost answered. "Otherwise we would have passed him on the stairs. Your scream was not just a scream, Liis. It was a blast. I thought my ears were going to burst. Dagmar's did."

A thin trickle of blood stained the shoulder of Dagmar's purple robe.

"I'm sorry," Ghisla said, but she wasn't. Her screaming had saved her life.

They alerted Master Ivo and the other keepers, as well as the king and his guard, but nothing was ever done to find her attacker. It was an attack of opportunity, more than anything, but he had been in the temple—or mayhaps he had been in the cellar all along—and Ghisla and the others felt even more vulnerable than they'd been before. Ivo did not think it a coincidence that the attack had come after Bayr had gone.

"Word has spread that the Temple Boy has left the mount. We will have to be more vigilant than ever before, and I will petition Banruud for better protection."

Ghisla felt as though she teetered on a ledge, unable to breathe deeply, to step left or right. To simply balance over the abyss was her only goal. To exist without falling. She sensed the same in the faces around her. Strain. Tension. Unease. It permeated the air and the keeper song. It billowed in the wind. She wondered if Hod could hear it in his cave, hissing with the insects and humming beneath the soil. Mayhaps they had cursed the land with their fear, created a truth from their belief.

For weeks she considered what she'd learned the night Bayr left and the advice Hod had given her. She vowed to tell Master Ivo about Desdemona's blood rune only to second-guess the wisdom of her decision moments later.

Dagmar walked the halls of the temple in a grief-stricken daze. One evening, she offered to sing to him, to sing to all of them, eager to comfort but also desperate for the direction she might get from seeing their thoughts. She ended up holding Dagmar's hands, singing senselessly while he showed her his memories. She saw a tiny babe, bloodied and newly born, clutched to Dagmar's chest, the babe's dead mother lying on the forest floor. The babe became a toddler who scaled walls and hoisted rocks bigger than he was. The toddler became a boy not much older than Alba who tackled a bear in the wood and stuttered a tearful promise that he would "always p-protect you, Uncle." Then the boy became Bayr, surrounded by warriors from Dolphys, who had not looked back as he was sent away.

Ghisla had ripped her hands away and fled the room when her song was done, leaving Dagmar to his terrible pain and her sisters and Ghost to wonder if she was as unfeeling as she seemed. Dagmar's images brought her back to where she'd started from, convinced someone had to protect Bayr, even if it meant the drought in Saylok continued. Bayr had protected everyone else . . . and she must protect him.

The king left the mount not long after Bayr was taken to Dolphys. The borders of Ebba and Joran were overrun by Hounds from the Hinterlands, and warriors from every clan joined in the battle to beat them back. When Banruud returned months later, snow was on the ground and ice hung from the temple eaves. Ivo had blocked the tunnel from the sanctum to the throne room. He did not want the king's guard, which had grown continuously less circumspect in their dealings with the temple and the keepers, to be able to enter the sanctum at will. That didn't stop the king or his men from entering the temple.

The night Banruud returned, he sent a guard named Bilge to retrieve Ghisla. She awoke with fetid breath in her face and a hand over her mouth, and she was thrown headlong into the nightmare she'd experienced in the cellar.

"The king is asking for you," he whispered. He pulled her from her bed and told her to walk. The fact that he knew exactly where to find her was almost as alarming as being found.

The other girls were motionless shapes around her, but Ghisla saw Ghost peering out from beneath her covers, as if she feared Bilge would see her. Ghisla felt a flash of outrage that she would not intervene but tamped it down as she left the room. Ghost was hiding from the king, that much was clear, and Bilge was the king's man.

Ghisla just hoped she would fetch Dagmar or Master Ivo when she was gone.

"The temple mutt is gone, isn't he? No matter. I'll watch out for you, girl," Bilge said, patting her bottom like she was a mare. She lashed out at him instantly.

"Don't touch me. Keep your distance."

"Spirited, aren't you? Not demure and sweet at all. I didn't think so. Too much fire in those eyes." He tried again, brazenly palming her breasts, and she let out a shriek that made her own hair rise.

He slapped her.

"Stop that. Shut up!" he sneered. "Now your nose is bleeding. The king won't like that."

"Don't touch me."

"Bilge!" the king grunted from where he lay, sprawled across his bed, and Bilge ran his sleeve over Ghisla's face, trying to clean up his mess.

Ghisla pushed past him, hoping the king would see and Bilge would be punished, but the king did not lift his head.

"Sing to me, daughter of Leok," he groaned. "Sing until I'm asleep."

She did so, grateful that his request was the same, even now that Bayr was gone. He never wanted words and he never wanted worship. He simply wanted music to combat his raging headaches and the incessant ringing that often accompanied them.

It didn't take her long before Banruud was snoring softly. When she stopped, he did not wake.

But Bilge was still waiting outside the king's door.

She did not hesitate, but dashed past him, reaching the stairs before he had time to react. But he was quicker than he looked. Ghisla was down the castle steps and halfway across the square when he caught her, lifting her up off her feet and burying his face in her neck.

"Let me go, Bilge. The last man who tried to take a temple daughter rotted on the north gate," she reminded.

"One of the clanless, I'm sure. But I don't want to kidnap you. I just want a kiss. Just one from that pretty, pink mouth. And I promise to look after you as well as the Temple Boy did. I'll bet you gave him kisses. I'll bet you let him touch your breasts and pet the curls between your legs. That's all I want. And I'll take care of you just like he did."

She could tell by his wheedling that he expected her to cry and fight him a little, and then let him have his way. What he didn't expect was the bloodcurdling scream-song that she released, throwing her head back and alerting the entire mount—castle, temple, and all the grounds—that something terrible was occurring.

"Stop that!" he hollered, releasing her in his surprise. He should have run then, but she'd made him angry and he slapped her. She wobbled but didn't lose her volume. She got louder, the sound so earsplitting that the bell in the tower began to hum with the vibration.

Bilge hit her harder, slugging instead of slapping, and she fell, smacking her head against the cobblestones. It was then that he chose to make his escape, dashing across the courtyard to the palace steps and disappearing back the way they'd come.

Suddenly Dagmar was there, and Master Ivo too, helping her up from the cobbles. Ghost must have alerted them after all. She hovered by the temple door, her cowl pulled over her white hair, watching.

"Who was it, Daughter? Who has hurt you?" Dagmar asked.

"His name is Bilge. He is a member of the king's guard."

"It is not yet dawn . . . What is the meaning of this?" Ivo stammered.

"I sing for the king . . . when his head aches. Bayr used to go with me. But . . ."

"But Bayr is gone," Dagmar finished, his voice hollow.

"Yes."

"Why was I not told of the king's request?" Master Ivo was angry.

Ghisla looked at Dagmar who looked back at Ivo.

"I did not know, Master. Bayr did not tell me."

"And Ghost did not tell you?" The Highest Keeper was having trouble making sense of it all.

"Ghost was afraid if we said no . . . there would be trouble," Ghisla explained, not wanting Ghost to incur the Highest Keeper's wrath. "It was an . . . innocent request. I was not hurt . . . until today." She did not tell them Bayr took the abuse for her.

"How often have you sung for the king?" Ivo asked.

"In these last years, mayhaps a dozen times," she answered.

"And I was never told!"

"No, Master."

Master Ivo glared from Ghisla to Dagmar with quivering outrage.

"I need to speak to the king. You will both come with me." He pointed a clawed hand at Dagmar and Ghisla.

"He is asleep," Ghisla said. It would not be wise to rouse him.

"Then we will wake him up," Ivo raged.

But when they walked into the throne room, Bilge was already making his case to the irate Banruud. Banruud's hair was matted and his eyes so bloodshot they appeared red in his sleep-swollen face. He was a handsome man, but pain and sleeplessness had made him ugly, and his mood was foul.

"Your shrieking has disturbed the king," Bilge spat.

"Your men seem to think the temple daughters are here for their pleasure," Master Ivo roared without preamble.

The king glowered at the Highest Keeper and rubbed his temples.

"Months ago, Liis of Leok was attacked by an unknown warrior. She did not see his face. It was dark, but he wore a warrior's braid. She screamed and startled him, and he ran. We never discovered who it was. Now we know the likely offender. The temple daughter cannot sing for you, King Banruud, if she is not safe in your service."

"She screamed so loud, my ears bled," Bilge whined. "I thought she was having a fit. I only hit her to make her stop."

The king studied her bleeding face.

"Did Bilge strike you?" he asked.

"Yes."

"Why?"

"Because I screamed."

"Why did you scream?"

"He put his hands where he should not."

Bilge protested again, but the king leveled him with a look that made even Master Ivo step back.

"Ring the bells. I want everyone here, in the hall. Everyone. Even the keepers. Now," the king ordered. A sentry rushed to obey, but Bilge was directed to stay put.

Minutes later, the king's guard stumbled into the hall, sleepy eyed and rumpled, but they were dressed. She supposed they could be forgiven for their confusion and fatigue considering many of them had returned only the night before. The keepers looked no different than they always did, save the bags beneath their eyes and the discomfort of being summoned at dawn. The daughters, their braided wreaths not as tidy as usual, were huddled together beside them. Ghost was not present.

Master Ivo had not moved from his position in front of the king's throne. Dagmar and Liis stood on either side, and she could feel his tension though his face remained serene and his hands were folded around the ball of his scepter. The king stayed slumped in his chair, his hands on the hilt of a sword he kept sheathed next to the throne. When all were assembled he began to speak.

"I have not slept in days. I have traveled from Ebba where we battled the dogs of the Hinterlands for two months. Yet even when I am home, in my own bed, I have no peace."

He eyed the gathering with bloodshot contempt. Then he raised a hand.

"Daughters of the temple, step forward so my men can all see you."

Elayne, Bashti, Dalys, and Juliah moved to stand behind Master Ivo, who had not lowered his eyes from the king.

"These daughters have lived under my protection, on this mount, for almost three years. They represent the clans. They belong to the temple. You will not look at them. You will not talk to them. You will not touch them."

Master Ivo grunted in surprised approval.

"Liis of Leok, come here," Banruud directed.

She stepped forward onto the dais, and the king pointed out to the assembly. "Turn so my men can see your face."

She did as she was asked, her eyes running past the tired guard and the frightened keepers, before snagging on Bilge who remained nearby. He had lost his smirk.

"Who bloodied your face, Liis of Leok?" the king asked, projecting his voice so the crowd could hear his every word.

Liis raised her hand and pointed at Bilge. "He did."

The king curled his fingers toward Bilge.

Bilge hesitated, but then walked forward until he stood next to her. Ghisla did not shrink, but she stepped away.

"You thought you could touch a daughter of the temple, Bilge of Berne?" the king said, his voice silky and mild.

Bilge did not deny it. Ghisla's face condemned him.

"Did you touch her breasts?"

An uncomfortable murmur spread through the men.

180

"You will cease this spectacle, Banruud," Master Ivo ground out.

Heat and mortification rose in Ghisla's chest, but she refused to give the king or Bilge the satisfaction of her humiliation.

"Yes. He did," she said, calm. Cold.

"It was . . . it was . . . it was in jest, Sire," Bilge stammered. "I did not hurt her."

The king unsheathed his sword and shoved it into Bilge's chest just left of center.

A collective gasp ricocheted around the room and Elayne screamed. Bilge gurgled and groaned, clutching his breast as the king yanked his sword free.

"And there? Did he touch you there?" the king asked, pointing the tip of the sword between the man's legs. Bilge moaned and tried to ward off another, more terrible blow.

"No," Ghisla said, shaking her head, emphatic. Her vision pulsed and bile swam in her stomach.

Blood was dripping from Bilge's mouth.

"You don't touch them anywhere," Banruud boomed. "You do not touch the temple daughters. Is that clear?"

Bilge staggered and fell from the dais onto the floor. Blood began to pool around him.

"Get him out of here," Banruud ordered, pointing to the dead man at his feet. "Leave. All of you, go."

The exodus from the throne room was an almost silent stampede. No one spoke, no one protested. Ghisla stood on hollow legs until Dagmar stepped forward to escort her from the room behind the keepers.

"She stays," Banruud grunted, pointing at Ghisla. "Her screams woke me up . . . she can damn well sing me back to sleep."

Two hours later—the king had been slow to settle—Ghisla staggered back to the temple, escorted by a guard who said nothing and kept his eyes locked straight ahead. Banruud's message had been received.

Bilge's heavy body had been strung up on the north gate for all to see, but Ghisla kept her eyes averted. She was not *sorry* he was dead, but she was horrified by it.

She entered the temple through the main doors, stepping into the huge foyer with the rising stone staircases on either side, and paused, dropping her chin to her chest and allowing herself a moment to breathe.

She was famished, and she marveled at the normalcy of the sensation. Life continued. The keepers would have already gathered in the dining hall, and breakfast would be over. They were nothing if not structured, nothing if not punctual. A man had been slain in front of them, but naught could be done about it now. And the fact that he was not a good man made it easier to overlook.

She ignored her hunger. She could not eat with the stench of blood and death in her nose, and her face ached with every beat of her heart. She needed to wash and she needed her bed more than she needed food. Her nightdress stank of sweat and terror, and her purple robe was splattered with the blood from her nose. She did not want to consider that it was Bilge's blood.

"Liis of Leok," Master Ivo said from the shadows.

She raised her head and found him, standing near the entrance to the sanctum.

"I need to speak to you, Daughter."

She did not have the strength to commune with the Highest Keeper, and she hesitated.

"Come," he ordered, entering the sanctum. She followed, but when he sat in his throne, she collapsed onto a stone bench not far from him and lowered her eyes.

"I mean no disrespect, Master. I am weary."

"There is a great deal I don't know about you, Liis of Leok."

"There is a great deal I don't know about you, Master." She sounded impudent, and his response was cold.

"I am not your enemy, child."

"I am not a child, Master."

"No. You are not. And you have caught the king's eye. That is not good."

"I have not caught his eye. I have caught . . . his ears."

"Yes. This is true."

She closed her eyes and willed him to be finished with her.

"Why were you in the cellars, Liis? So late, and all alone."

She had not expected the question, and her eyes snapped open.

"I was not in the cellars, Master. Bilge of Berne summoned me from my bed."

"No. Months ago . . . when you were attacked. You were in the cellars in the wee hours of morning. Why?"

"Sometimes I want to sing, just to sing. It comforts me. I don't want to wake anyone, and often I don't want company." It was a poor excuse, and it fell from her lips with a disingenuous ring.

"It is hard to know who to trust, isn't it?" the Highest Keeper mused.

She did not answer him.

"It is even harder to know what is right," he added.

"I am not sure there is . . . right. Only . . . good." Bayr was good. Hod was good. Elayne, Alba, and her sisters were mostly . . . good. But everything else—everyone else—was a roiling pot of secrets and self-preservation. Including Ghisla herself.

"But there is truth. The truth is right. The truth is good. And that is what I seek."

He held out his hand, his gnarled fingers trembling. She had never touched the Highest Keeper before. She was afraid to do so now. She didn't want to hear his thoughts. She didn't want him to hear hers . . .

and she knew, somehow, he would. But she took his hand, unable to resist the pull of his will. He stilled, and his eyes fluttered closed.

"Will you tell me the truth, Liis?"

"Will you use it to harm?"

He seemed taken aback by the question.

"For every truth you give me, I will give one back."

"I don't want your truths, Master." She had pockets full of cold, hard truths. They were heavy. She did not want more.

He laughed. "And yet . . . you have just given me one."

She had, and she felt lighter for it.

"You are not from Leok . . . are you, child?"

She wanted to release his hand, but his fingers were a vise, and her walls began to crumble. Whatever he asked, she would tell him. She would tell him about Desdemona and her blood rune. She would tell him about Ghost and Alba. She would tell him about Hod.

"Do not be afraid," he soothed. "My father was from Ebba. That is where I was born—a lifetime ago. But my mother was a Songr. Have you ever heard of the Songrs, Liis of Leok?"

"Yes," she breathed, almost weeping the word.

"My mother could sing . . . not like you . . . but well. Her song comforted. But her scream was deafening. She leveled grown men with her scream. Just like you."

Was that all he wished to know?

"Are you a Songr, Daughter?" He asked so kindly . . . so easily . . . and she gave him the answer he already seemed to know.

"Yes. Will you send me away?"

"Of course not. We are all from somewhere else. From other clans. No one is born on the temple mount. No one, that is, but Bayr. He is a true son of Saylok."

"And he has been sent away." She should tell Master Ivo. She should tell him about the blood rune now, but Bayr's face swam in her thoughts.

"He will return one day." He released her hand, and Ghisla released her breath on a sob. The only secrets she'd revealed were her own, and she suspected they were things the Highest Keeper already knew.

"Mayhaps, if the blind god wills it, you will return home too," he said, a hint of a smile around his lips.

"I am confused, Master." She was more than confused. Her throat was tight and her eyes burned, and the strain of the last twelve hours was suddenly more than she could bear.

"I know, Daughter. The blind god listens . . . but he cannot see. Odin sees but he does not speak. I do not have the answers, though I have sought them all my life."

"I am weary," she whispered. She rubbed at her arms, chilled, and Ivo dipped his fingers into a goblet of water beside him as if to wash her truths away. He seemed weary too.

"Things are not always as they seem, Liis. They seldom are. Do not trust the king. Today he appeared a hero, a protector, but he only protects himself."

13

Maidens

Ghisla did not tell the Highest Keeper about Desdemona's runes. Not the next day, or the next, and not in the weeks after that. Her indecision eased, though not entirely. In the eighteen months that followed, her knowledge plagued her. She dreamed about it, her mind conjuring the odd symbols and characters from Dagmar's tortured thoughts. But she did not tell Master Ivo, and though she told Hod about everything else, they did not speak of Desdemona's runes again.

It was too troubling, and they avoided discussing their worries and their woes, though they had many. It was not that they kept them from each other; they simply chose to speak of better things: musings and meanderings that were not pressing but felt essential, because in them lived beauty and hope. What they spoke of seemed to grow, and so they spoke of their dreams and not their doubts, their joys and not their pain. They were even careful not to let the discussion of others intrude upon the time they had, though sharing their lives sometimes meant sharing the people in them.

Hod knew Ghisla sang for the king. He knew she dreaded the encounters but had managed to survive them unscathed since Bilge was skewered and hung from the north gate. He also knew she'd grown closer to Elayne and her sisters but was still leery of everyone else—even Master Ivo, Dagmar, and Ghost—because she knew too much, and everyone was sheltering enormous secrets.

"I don't trust anyone. And they don't trust me. I can't blame them. They don't understand me . . . and I can't explain myself. To do so would only make things worse. They would trust me even less. It is better that they dislike me than they reject me altogether."

She didn't have to explain herself to Hod. She told him everything, and in return, he bared himself to her, giving her everything he could in the snippets of time and space they spent together.

Ghisla knew all of Arwin's foibles and faults. She knew of his tests and his tricks and the way he tutored and trained Hod, convinced that someday the blind god would complete his penance and rise again.

"I fear his disappointment will be great if I simply end up being a man with sharp ears, a good nose, and a steady hand," Hod said one evening.

"What does he want you to be?"

"He wants me to be a hero."

"What kind of hero?"

"He is convinced someday I will be the Highest Keeper."

"Is that what you wish?"

"I thought it was, once. I had no ambitions of my own. I was happy to let Arwin dream for both of us."

"And now?"

"Now . . . I have my own aspirations."

"Tell me."

"I dream of breaking the curse. And I dream of being near you."

"Will that ever happen? Will I ever see you again? I know nothing about runes. But I speak to you through a rune on my hand. Sometimes I think I am crazy. Am I crazy, Hod? I hear voices. I hear *your* voice. But are you even real? Or are you just a figment of my imagination?"

He laughed, though she was half-serious. *"It will happen soon."*

"How soon?" she asked, too cautious to give in to the excitement she sensed bubbling beneath his words.

"I am coming to the Tournament of the King. I am coming to Temple Hill."

༄

Ghisla watched for him all day. He'd said he would be here, in the square, when the temple doors were opened to the people of Saylok on the third day of the tournament, but when Ghisla, Elayne, Bashti, Dalys, and Juliah were escorted onto the dais in front of the temple, she could see nothing but the same endless crush of people trying to position themselves to obtain an audience with the keepers and see the daughters.

A platform had been erected between the columns to the left of the heavy temple doors. Their hair was twisted with ribbons and wrapped around their heads, and each daughter wore a new robe in the color of her clan. Princess Alba had even joined them for a while, wearing a yellow gown to represent Adyar.

Elayne of Ebba wore orange; she looked like a tall, thin flame with her red hair and fiery robes. Juliah complained about the brown of Joran, though it was the same chocolate as her eyes and echoed the richness of her hair. The color contrasted with the cream of her skin and complemented the ruby of her lips.

"Brown is like soil—deep and warm and rich. You look like the goddess of the harvest," Elayne soothed, always knowing what to say. But she was right. Juliah was now fifteen, and she'd become a beauty overnight, though she seemed confused and even resentful of it.

They were *all* a little resentful and more than a little apprehensive. They were looked on differently, and there was new tension in the temple. Ghisla was eighteen, Elayne sixteen, and Bashti thirteen; Dalys and Alba were the only daughters who still looked like children, though

Alba at almost ten was already tall and towered over tiny Dalys, who was a year older.

Master Ivo had grown exceedingly pensive as the tournament had approached. The chieftains would be assembling, the people gathering, and the changes in the daughters would be well noted.

The new robes were his idea.

"We cannot hope to hide you in purple any longer, not at the tournament. You are not keepers of the runes . . . You are kept by the runes. You are becoming women, but we must remind the people that you are their ambassadors. That you are symbolic, like the goddess Freya herself, separate and unattainable. You are women . . . but you will not be wives. That must be made abundantly clear."

Bashti wore the red of Berne and had stained her lips to match, much to Ghost's horror. She looked too fierce and too . . . female, but the Highest Keeper said to let her be.

"She looks like she's sipped the blood of her enemies . . . and enjoyed every drop," Ghost argued.

"I know. That is good. Better that people fear her, in my opinion. They will keep their distance."

Dalys wore the blue of Dolphys and looked as delicate as Bashti looked immortal. Ghost put tiny white flowers in her hair and demanded she stand nearest the guard, afraid that someone would swoop her up like in years past and try to escape with her. As always, Ghost remained inside the temple throughout the tournament, watching from shuttered windows, hiding her pale face from public view.

The green of Ghisla's robe was not the silvery green of pines or the yellow-green of the autumn grass. It was the green of fields after days of rain, the green beneath the mists of Hody's eyes, and she loved it. She couldn't wait to tell Hod all about it—to show him—while he sat beside her. Soon they would be together, and she could hardly contain the horrible joy and dread that swelled in her breast.

It was hot beneath her new green robe; the platform was shaded by the temple, but the heat from the continually burning Hearth of Kings made the square too warm in the waning summer sun. They stood in the square for hours. Master Ivo and the king were agreed on that.

"You give the people hope that there will be daughters again . . . that daughters can still thrive in Saylok," Dagmar said, though standing in the heat being observed for hours on end did not feel like thriving.

During the tournament, people came from every clan and swarmed the mount for days. Beggars, peddlers, musicians, and thieves were all welcomed. The crippled and the sick were brought to the temple as well, hoping to be healed. Criminals seemed more prevalent than ever; to be pardoned by a keeper meant a clean slate in the new year, and the keepers collected coins and confessions from the condemned in body and spirit. The crowd was filled with both the piteous and the dangerous, and Ghisla feared for Hod, moving among them.

And then she saw him.

Her gaze should have bounced over him, but it caught and stayed. He too wore a robe, but the hood was pushed back from his face, and it hung open over his tunic and hose. He held a staff like he'd done years before, but he did not prop his weight against it or let it fall loosely at his side. It was as straight and upright as he was, his touch upon it light, like he was prepared at any moment to jab it or swing it round.

He lifted his head like he was tasting the air, and her heart leaped and her thoughts sang in a jubilant chorus.

Hody, Hody, Hody, Hody.

His hair was still shorn. He looked like the keepers—no braid swung between his shoulders like the warriors from the clans. He didn't wear their colors either. All around him was a sea of bouncing colors, and he should have been drab, standing among them, but the absence of color, the gray of his clothes, the rough brown stubble of his hair, and the stillness of his form served as a beacon for her eyes.

He was tall, but not terribly so, and he was still thin, though his shoulders had widened and his neck was corded with strength.

Hody, Hody, Hody, Hody.

She dare not sing his name out loud; her sisters would hear. And she could not prick her finger to trace the rune on her hand. Her palms were wet with perspiration, which might be enough, and she pressed her right hand to her heart, willing him to hear her summons, as close as they were.

Hesitantly his right hand rose, though he did not turn toward her, and he copied the motion, pressing his palm to his chest. Almost immediately, she heard a muted drumbeat in her head, steady and strong, like his heart said her name: *ghis LUH, ghis LUH, ghis LUH.*

There was no way he could approach her. No way they could speak. Not now. The keepers encircled the daughters, and temple guards were posted to keep the clansmen and villagers from being too familiar. He would not be able to get any nearer.

And she could not approach him.

A surge of despair welled with the heat. She could see him. He was so close. And yet . . . there was nothing to be done but wait. Wait. Until when? Her despondency grew.

"I am ill," she insisted, drawing the startled gaze of her sisters. "I feel faint."

"It is very hot," Elayne agreed.

"Dagmar," Ghisla raised her voice, adamant. "I am ill. I must go inside."

"We will all go inside," Dagmar said, his voice revealing a note of relief. "You have been on display long enough."

❧

The day was interminable and made even longer by the reluctance of her sisters to retire when the evening deepened. Alba had spent the afternoon in their company, not yet old enough to preside over the festivities or observe the events, and not nearly as well protected as she had once been. The king put a cadre on her every time she moved about the grounds, but his guard was spread thin across the hill. Many of them were competing in the events as well, which meant the daughters and the princess stayed behind locked doors when they were not on display.

"I am not tired. I wish we could wander the mount," Alba mourned. "There is so much to see, and we are stuck inside. If Bayr were here, he could accompany us. No one would dare approach if he were watching."

"But he is not here . . . and I am weary," Ghisla said, her tone cross, though her stomach knotted with guilt at her lie. She had no intention of sleeping.

"The queen says I can stay here with all of you tonight," Alba said, cheering up slightly. She only referred to Queen Esa as *Grandmother* when she addressed her directly, which was not very often. The woman held herself apart and rarely left her quarters in the king's castle.

Ghisla almost groaned. Alba's presence would make it that much harder to slip away.

"You can sleep with me, Princess," Ghisla offered. "Then Ghost will not feel compelled to let you have her bed." And when she retired, all the beds would be full, giving Ghisla a little more cover.

"I don't want to sleep yet," Alba complained.

"I will sing to you."

She would sing until they were all drunk with sleep. Her stomach twisted again. She did not like to manipulate her sisters, even with slumber, but she was growing desperate. The rune on her palm pulsed with Hod's nearness, and she feared he would give up on her and retreat to his tent or whatever lodging Arwin had secured.

"Sing the one about the little bat," Dalys begged. "That one always makes me smile."

"I have not heard that one!" Alba squealed, wriggling down beside Ghisla. Elayne, Juliah, and Bashti were slower to convince, but there was nothing else to do and the day had been wearying.

They stretched out over their beds and let Ghisla sing them into dreamland, climbing and soaring above the mount with the little bat whose only mission was to be himself, a bat, free to fly and flit about, without a care in the world.

He cannot see, but he's not scared.
He swoops and glides up in the air.
The sky is dark but he is light,
And though his eyes aren't blessed with sight,
His joy is full, his wings are strong.
He dances to a distant song.
He flies, and he is free to play,
And at the end of every day,
He folds his wings and draws in close,
To all the bats who love him most.

Before long, the room was a symphony of deep breaths and soft snores. Her own eyes were heavy, but the rune on her hand was hot, and she knew if she rose from her bed and tiptoed out of the temple to the hillside, she would find Hod, waiting.

She'd been serious when she asked him if he was real. In her four years on the mount, she had almost convinced herself that Hod was like the blind god—like *all* the gods: invisible and nonexistent but for folklore and legend. Invisible and nonexistent but in her own mind. And it hadn't mattered at all. Sanity—reality—was too painful not to have someone to talk to, even if that someone was a voice in her head. But he wasn't an illusion. He was here. She'd seen him. And she was going to find him.

She rose from her bed, splashed her face with water, and traded her nightdress for a frock. With a prick of her finger and a quick tracing of her rune, she glided from the room, down the stairs, and out of the temple through the tunnel in the sanctum, singing his name in her mind, calling him to her.

It didn't take long. She watched him pick his way across the hill, using his staff to inform his steps, and when he was a mere ten feet away he stopped and cocked his head, reminding her of the boy she'd first met on the beach. He was not a boy anymore. His eyes reflected the moon like water, making them more gold than green, and she rose from her crouch, wanting to greet him, but unsure of what to say. How did one greet their own soul?

"You've stopped breathing . . . and your heart is shouting," he murmured. "It is even louder than your song. Are you afraid?"

"I am . . . overjoyed," she confessed.

His smile bloomed, parting his lips and creasing his lean cheeks, and her happiness spilled out of her eyes. He sheathed his staff the way other men sheathed their swords, securing it across his back. Then he opened his arms.

She ran to him, and he swept her up, laughing as she wrapped her legs around him. It was not dignified or ladylike, but she didn't care. He was solid in her arms. Hard and whole, his heart singing with hers, his legs planted to keep them from rolling down the hill. She rained kisses over his cheeks, his brow, and the lids of his eyes. She even kissed his laughing mouth, panting like a pup too long from its master, and he bracketed her face in his hands, his thumbs tracing her features like he was seeing her too.

"Stop wriggling," he laughed. "You're going to knock me over." He unsheathed his staff again and laid it down as he sank to the grass, keeping her in his arms and making a nest for her with his legs.

When she remarked on his tendency to shelter her with nests and runes, he laughed but did not release her, and for a moment they sat, their arms wrapped around each other, trying to catch their breath, but she could not stop looking at him.

"Where is Arwin?" she whispered suddenly, fearful that he would have to leave soon.

"He is snoring like your sisters. He honks like a goose when he sleeps. It makes my head ache. I do not ever sleep at his side. I can't if I want to sleep at all. Mostly, I do not sleep at night. I will sleep tomorrow when he is awake. It is customary for us."

She gaped, though he couldn't see her surprise. "You can hear my sisters snoring?"

"Not now. But I heard you. Singing to them. I have been outside the temple all day. All evening. Waiting for you to come out again."

"You heard me?"

"Yes. And I didn't even need our rune. I liked the song about the bat."

"I wrote it for you . . . Have I never sung it to you before?" She couldn't believe it.

"Sing it again, but hold my hand, like old times."

His strong cheeks and deep-set eyes were shrouded by dark brows and bristly black lashes that made shadows like tiger stripes on the whites of his sightless eyes. She tipped his face toward her so she could look at him while she sang and then slid her hand into his.

"The sky is dark but he is light, and though his eyes aren't blessed with sight, his joy is full, his wings are strong. He dances to a distant song," she sang, but she could not focus with his face so near. When her voice trailed off, he cocked his head, waiting.

"I hardly recognize you," she whispered.

"I am the same. Only bigger."

"No. The shape of your face has changed," she murmured.

"Tell me."

"There is no softness round your cheeks."

"I no longer resemble a toad?"

"No . . . you still resemble a toad . . . just an older toad."

He grinned, the shape of his face changing again, sharp bones and unseeing eyes softened by the smile.

"You are quite handsome, truthfully," she offered, surprising herself.

His smile slipped, like she'd surprised him too.

"Has the shrew left with the little waif?" he asked, touching the point of her chin.

"No. They are both here. I am still a shrew . . . and still a bit of a waif."

He tested her weight in his arms, bouncing her like a child.

"You have grown."

"Yes. I am eighteen now, and I look my age, though I will never be tall."

"Your mother was right. Your people grow slowly."

She'd forgotten, but as soon as he said the words, she remembered the moment her mother had said them to her, mending the hole in a dress she'd worn out long before she ever grew out of it.

"You remember everything."

"Yes . . . but I remember you the way you were. Not the way you are. I suspect your face has also changed." His fingertips ran over her face again before skimming the coil of her hair, feeling each woven section that made a circle around her head.

"It is a crown," he marveled.

"Yes. It is how all the daughters of the temple wear their hair."

"Will you take it down?"

With shaking hands, she unwound her braid and ran her fingers through the strands. His fingers followed.

"It is soft . . . and it waves like the wind on the water." The palm of his hand followed the length down her back, and something warm curled in her belly. His hand immediately fell away, as if he'd heard the hitch in her breath, but his attention was elsewhere.

"They are looking for you, Ghisla. The king has sent a guard for you, and no one knows where you are. A woman is calling your name."

Ghisla scrambled up, but Hod was frozen, listening. "She has sent Dagmar to look in the cellar."

She turned toward the hatch, terrified that a member of the king's guard would suddenly emerge from the door in the hillside, calling her name.

"You cannot be seen with me," she warned, suddenly far more afraid for Hod than she was for herself. She'd been so foolish. "The king will kill you."

"Don't worry, Ghisla. I am just a blind man. Everyone looks past me."

"I didn't."

"No . . . I felt the moment you saw me."

"You put your hand on your heart," she whispered.

He nodded, and a new emotion flitted over his features.

"Will I see you tomorrow?" she whispered, aching. Scared.

"Tomorrow and the day after that and the day after that. We will stay all week. I have entered the archery contest, and I plan to win."

"How will you see the target?"

"I won't. I will hear it."

"How will you *hear* the target?"

He grinned. "Arwin will stand beside it, and I will shoot to the left."

∽

He could hear Ghisla singing—not in his head but with his ears. And yet . . . it brought him no joy. He was afraid for her. She'd gone back through the tunnel and into the temple, and before he'd gotten back around the wall and through the entrance gates, which were kept open for tournament traffic, she had already been escorted to the castle. She'd lied easily, saying she'd fallen asleep on a bench in the sanctum where the air was cool and quiet. The woman—Ghost—was too relieved to question her.

It was so late, and she was kept too long, her voice soaring through melodies that had no words—or if they did, she did not sing them. Hod knew she sang for an audience of one and the rest of the occupants of the mount could not hear her like he could. He would have been able to hear her from the hillside—her skittering heart and her soaring voice—but he hugged the walls of the castle until he was as close as he could get and listened until she stopped. She did not move after she ceased singing but waited as though she needed to make sure the king was truly asleep. Her heart settled and the whisper of her small feet on wood floors moved through the room, out into a corridor, and down a flight of stairs, the sound changing as she descended into an entrance hall that echoed like a cavern.

Two guards escorted her across the empty cobbles, the clap of their longer strides bracketing hers. The temple doors creaked opened and swished closed behind her, and the two guards retraced their steps, *clop, clop, clop, clop*, talking quietly to each other.

"During the full moon, the king cannot sleep without her," one muttered. "It is a pattern I have noticed."

"He cannot sleep without her . . . and he cannot sleep with her," the other quipped. "Lothgar and the other chieftains would not stand for it."

"He is the king. He will do what he wants."

"Aye. It's just a matter of time, though he'd better tread carefully. The whole country is about to blow."

"He cannot take one of the daughters to wife. The moment he does—"

"The moment he does, the whole kingdom will fall."

"The dam will burst. They are either off limits to all—even the king—or none."

"The other daughters won't be safe for a single day. Not just the daughters of the temple . . . but the women in the clans. It is a fine line he's walking."

"'Tis a fine line we're all walking."

"There are thirteen maidens in the village, all of marrying age—"

"An uglier lot I've never before beheld."

"And you've beheld so many!"

The critical guard had the grace to laugh.

"Ugly or not, they have their pick of men."

"And they aren't picking us, though we are members of the king's guard."

"No . . . they want to marry into the clans. My two sisters chose warriors from the clans, though they had no feeling for them."

"Protection?"

"Aye. One went to Joran, and one to Dolphys. My father was glad to see them go. It was an endless duty keeping the wolves at bay. He received a fine bride-price for both."

The two guards did not seem to notice Hod as they walked back to their posts inside the palace; he could usually hear a hitch in the breath or a surge in the blood that signaled awareness, but the guards thought the square abandoned in the wee hours of the morning.

A handful of inebriated warriors approached. He suspected they were from Adyar from the tilt of their tongues over their words, but their voices were slurred and their footfalls stuttered, and they did not react to him either.

He listened for Ghisla, hoping she would call out to him again, but she must have been too afraid . . . or too weary . . . and she was silent. He circled the mount several times, walking the perimeter and winding in and out of the camps of the visiting clans and tournament goers while the world was quiet. He measured distances and determined the dangers, learning the lay of the land and making note of the sounds and scents that marked each footstep. It was what he did in every new place. People presented different challenges than animals. Mountains were harder than valleys. Wind distorted smells, and rain could quickly change the terrain. He was adept—more than adept—at taking it all in stride while listening and learning and altering his course based on experience and instinct, but he always familiarized himself with his surroundings, and he never took his abilities for granted.

He did not allow himself to doubt them either. To doubt was to falter, to falter was to fail, and in almost every situation, he knew what to do. But he did not know what to do about Ghisla.

He whispered her name, just to release it from his thoughts, and a portion of his earlier happiness swelled in his breast. She'd been so thrilled to see him. *Overjoyed.*

He'd held her in his arms while she'd talked to him—not in his head, but mere *inches* away from her. He could hardly believe it had happened. That it was real. They'd had so little time, but every second had exceeded his expectations.

He had not worried that they would have nothing to say; they had never struggled with that in the four years they'd conversed. His love for her was not the fondness of a new friend or the novelty of a forbidden relationship. It was deep and abiding. For four years, he had beseeched the fates for her welfare and begged the gods to watch over her, but he had wondered if his love for her would manifest itself differently now that they were older. Now that they knew each other so much better.

If anything, his feelings had grown. She had grown.

The little bird she'd been was gone; he'd been almost afraid to touch her when he'd found her on the beach that first day. She was still slender, still dainty, but her hips were rounded, her breasts well formed, and her legs long. A man noticed such things when a woman wrapped herself around him.

He berated himself and halted, needing to put her out of his thoughts. She was too distracting, and he could not afford to have his attention elsewhere while he crept among the camps. He breathed deeply, attempting to clear his mind, but her words rose up, unbidden.

The sky is dark but he is light,
And though his eyes aren't blessed with sight,
His joy is full, his wings are strong.
He dances to a distant song.

For four years, she had been his distant song. Now he was here, and he didn't know how he would part with her again.

14

Stars

"I see nothing . . . and you see so much. I can hear a nest full of little birds, calling for their mother from the wood below, but I cannot hear a man's thoughts," Hod said as they sat together the next night, tucked into a natural alcove on the hillside. He was subdued and troubled, and he kept asking questions about the king.

"It is more confusing than clarifying most of the time. I only see pieces . . . parts . . . and those pieces don't tell the whole story. I hear Master Ivo's dilemma. I hear Dagmar's determination to protect Bayr, and Ghost's loyalty to Alba. I hear my sisters' worries and the keepers' fear."

"And their troubles become yours."

"Yes. Each piece of knowledge is like an invisible sliver in my hand or a stone in my shoe—something I feel but can do nothing about."

"I know," Hod said, taking her hand. "I am sorry."

"No one knows how to end the scourge . . . or if it can even be ended. Everyone is plotting and maneuvering and keeping secrets. But not out of hate, out of love." She sighed. "Everyone but Banruud. There is no love in him."

"What do you see when you hold the king's hand?" he murmured, tracing the rune on her palm.

"His thoughts are twisted and blurred, like listening to someone through water. Sometimes a thought will be perfectly clear—his irritation, his desire, his rage—but when he's riddled with headaches and bad dreams, his thoughts are muddled and tangled, and I try my best to ignore them. Most of the time, I don't touch him at all. My songs are usually sufficient." King Banruud only touched her when his pain was intolerable, and he was afraid she would depart too soon. Then he kept his hand wrapped around hers, keeping her at his side until sleep swept him away.

"I do not wish to speak of the king," she murmured. "You must tell me how you fared in the competition."

"I won the day of competition," he said. "Keeper Dagmar was among the spectators. He spoke to me afterward. He was very kind."

"You won the day?" she gasped. "You must tell me everything."

"The chieftain from Berne and a warrior from Dolphys—Daniel—accused me of cheating . . . though neither could explain how so. Daniel said he didn't think I was truly blind." He laughed. "I reminded him that everyone else could see. It would hardly be cheating if I could see too."

"Why didn't they believe you? One has only to look at your eyes to know."

"I think it is because I do see . . . in my own way. I use my ears the way everyone else uses their eyes."

"How?"

"It is actually quite simple. Every heart sounds different. And every heartbeat is distinct."

"But . . . how do you remember which heart belongs to whom?"

"I suppose it's like recognizing a face. We all have two eyes, two ears, a mouth, a nose, yet none of us look exactly alike. Or so I'm told."

He grinned. "It is the same with our hearts. It is not strange to remember a face, is it?"

"No. I guess not," she marveled.

"Dred of Dolphys wanted to know how I accomplished it as well. When I explained I could hear his heartbeat, he spent the hour after the competition ended demanding I shoot at him."

"And did you?"

"Yes. I hit his shield every time. He was quite fearless. I imagine Bayr is much like him. I had hoped the Temple Boy would be here. Though I can understand why he is not."

In the soil beside him, Hod drew the blind god's rune: the half circles, back to back, and the arrow that pierced them through. Melancholy had settled on him once again, and she rushed to distract him.

"But a target does not have a heartbeat."

"No. But if Arwin stands beside the target—two feet to the right— I can use his heartbeat to gauge my shot. I would not be able to do it otherwise."

"Is he not afraid he will be skewered?"

"When I was young I would warn him before I released the arrow, and he would lift his shield. Now he only worries about the other archers on the course."

"The king was also in attendance," he said softly. "His heart is easy to pick out. I thought about killing him. Saylok would be better off. You would be better off."

He heard the horror in her silence.

"I have upset you," he said.

"You would be slain. Immediately."

"Yes."

"I can endure the king. I cannot endure a world without you in it."

He sighed heavily, and she searched his face, anxious.

"Hod . . . Tell me you are not serious," she whispered. "Surely you jest?"

"I have thought of little else since last night. I am scared for you, Ghisla. Mayhaps it is my calling to kill Banruud . . . Arwin is convinced I have one."

She gripped his hand and forced it back to the rune he'd just made in the dirt. "If this is Hod . . . then this is Ghisla," she insisted, tracing the two halves of the rune and the arrow that connected them. "You cannot harm yourself without harming me."

He pulled her into his arms, burying his face in the plait of her hair.

"I am sorry. We have so little time, and I am scaring you. Forgive me."

"We are bound, Hod." She pressed her hand to his, feeling the scrape of his scar against her own. "I am yours. You are mine."

"With this rune, I thee wed," he said, but his smile was bleak.

"With this rune, I thee wed," she repeated, urgent, but she could not quiet her racing heart, and he cursed softly, pressing his palm to her chest.

"Shh, Ghisla. I am here."

She laid her hands on top of his, keeping his hand clutched to her heart. She stared up at the stars, her eyes skipping from one to the next, counting the brightest ones as she caught her breath. Fourteen stars were brighter than the others, and a tendril of a melody surfaced in her thoughts.

"There was a song my people used to sing . . . when they wed," she murmured.

"Sing it for me."

"I do not remember it. There was a line about stars." But as soon as she said the words, the lyrics curled up from the place in her heart she rarely let herself visit.

"Two of us, two of us, two lives, two," she said, hesitantly. She hummed the bit of the tune, fitting the phrase like a key to a lock.

Hod listened, his hand still caught beneath hers, and she tried again.

"Two of us, two of us, two lives, two. Now we're one, just begun, new lives, new."

Figures danced in her memory, and she let them come.

"Take my hand, tie the bands, one step, two," she sang, piecing the words into a line. That is how they'd danced when the ceremony was done, all in a line.

"Make a wish, on the stars, say I do." In her mind, the long row became just the bride and groom. She could see Morgana, the way she'd looked that day, her hair loose and her skirts swinging, but the image was blurred.

"Is that . . . your sister?" Hod asked.

Ghisla fought the grief that warred with the joy but pressed on. She *wanted* Hod to see. "Yes. That is Morgana . . . on her wedding day. Morgana and Peder."

"Morgana and Peder," Hod breathed.

"Now we're one, just begun, me and you," she sang. The Peder in her mind stooped to kiss Morgana, and someone cheered. *Gilly.* Gilly had cheered. But she could not see their faces.

"I cannot call their features forth," Ghisla murmured.

"You are trying too hard." Hod's fingertips were gentle on her face. He urged her eyes closed, and she sang the song from the beginning. By the time she was done, the memory had become sharp and shining, playing out as if she were once again in Tonlis, dancing with her family.

"Peder could not stop kissing her. He did not want to eat or dance. He wanted to kiss . . . and Morgana did not mind. No one minded terribly, though my father grumbled and my mother fretted that they would disappoint the guests who wanted to drink and dance with the couple. Singing, drinking, and dancing are all Songrs want to do."

"It is beautiful."

"Spin and skip and take a sip, then sing whilst you walk back again," she sang, one tune melding into another. "That was a song the men sang. Every gathering they sang it—that silly song. It gave them a chance to drink and dance at the same time. Usually the groom would sing with the men, but Peder sang it once and walked back—just like the song says—to Morgana. And the kissing continued."

Ghisla laughed, the recollection crystal clear.

"He is devouring her," Hod said, incredulous. "Like a hungry beast."

Ghisla laughed harder. "I thought it disgusting . . . and . . . wonderful too. I was twelve. Not yet ready for romance . . . yet not immune to it either."

Hod was as entranced as she, and for once she had no trouble letting the memory run its course. Peder had knocked over the table in his desire to reach his bride—wine had something to do with his dramatics as well, she was sure, but it had made their guests laugh and had brought the women to the rescue. The women had a song of their own.

Men who need kisses
Make babes who need kisses.
Babes who grow up
Become men who need kisses.
Men who need kisses
Chase women for kisses.
And . . .
Begetting begins again.

The music never ended that night, and Ghisla trilled and tripped lightly over every song, a smile on her lips, her eyes closed to take herself back, and her hand pressed to Hod's.

"There are your parents," Hod said, his voice awed.

"Yes, whenever we parted, we sang the same song. But that night as we sang it, they did not stand hand in hand like we usually do. They danced like they too were young and in love."

Think of me when we part,
I'll send you with my heart.
Keep it tucked next to yours,
'Til you return once more.

"He does love her. He holds her gently," Hod said, as though the vision was now.

"Sometimes he held her gently. But he held her tightly too. She would complain that he kissed her too hard, but she was always smiling and swaying when he finished."

They watched together a moment more, Ghisla humming the song that had played while her parents danced.

"I have kissed a woman," Hod said softly.

"You have?" she gasped.

Her shock and dejection chased the happy memory away, and the connection was lost—the connection to her past and the connection to Hod.

It seemed to stun him, the return to darkness when his mind had been flooded with color and story.

"Come back, Ghisla," he said. He turned her in his arms, his fingers searching and settling on her cheeks, his palms cupping her jaw.

She stilled, and his fingers flexed, as though he didn't trust her not to jerk away.

When she did not, he inched toward her until his face was too near for her to make out his expression, until his forehead lay against hers. He did not try to turn her face or tilt his chin to align their lips. He simply hovered there, so close, their heads touching but their minds their own.

"Yes. I have kissed a woman. Several. In Berne. It was quite distasteful. Arwin thought it educational. They were not gentle . . . and they were not shy. I suspect the women were old and weary of men. Some did not have teeth. Some had far too many. Arwin made certain the whole experience was as unpleasant as possible."

His breath tickled her mouth, and her stomach flipped. Imagining him with another woman—even one without teeth—was oddly, inexplicably, painful to hear. He was *her* Hody. He was hers. And she had expected him to be as inexperienced as she. She had thought they might learn together.

"Why are you telling me this?" she moaned.

"Because . . . I did not expect to want to do it again," he confessed. "But I very much want to kiss you."

"You do?" she asked.

His forehead lifted so their mouths could meet, and his lips brushed hers.

It was not unpleasant . . . not at all . . . and she forgot her pain.

For several moments, their lips fluttered and flitted as they learned how to best fit their mouths together, but fit they did, and the fluttering became a settling and a seeking. It was a new dance, one they choreographed as they moved their mouths together and apart, over and against. It was a dance Ghisla never thought she would tire of. She raised her hands to Hod's face to hold him to her.

"I want to see you," he whispered against her mouth.

"And I want to kiss you," she murmured back. "I cannot sing and kiss you at the same time."

"Then we will have to do it my way," he said. He did not withdraw his lips, but his fingers glided over her face and down her throat. He continued across the bony ridge where her shoulders dropped onto her chest, and her body began to hum.

His kiss deepened.

"Open your mouth, Ghisla. I want to taste you."

She pulled away slightly, uncertain. His sightless eyes were closed, and his voice was sweet. Pleading. And he pulled her mouth back to his.

If it had been anyone but Hod she would have grimaced. What an odd thing to say. What an odd thing to *do*. But it was Hod, and she obeyed, parting her lips against his.

His tongue was tentative, the way his hands had been, as though sensation was dependent upon it, and she opened her mouth wider, welcoming him in.

The humming within her became a quake, and his exploration became her own. Then the music changed, the movement changed, and their kiss took on a new tempo.

They were not so careful and not so sweet. Tasting became suckling. Suckling became plundering, and kissing was no longer enough. She wanted to be closer. She wanted to crawl inside him. She wanted to sink beneath his skin.

"I want to be inside you," she said, panting against his mouth. "And I want you to be inside me."

Hod's hands and mouth stilled. A shudder moved through him, and he moved his lips to her brow.

"That is not wise, Ghisla," he whispered.

She repeated the words in her head and realization dawned. She knew what women and men did to make children. Morgana had explained in great detail.

That is what sisters are for, Ghisla. Mother will not tell you. Father will not tell you. And Gilly and Abner do not know. At least they don't know it from a woman's perspective. But there is pleasure in it for you too, if you aren't too bashful to take it, and if your husband wants to give it. If you love him, and he loves you, he'll want to give it.

Ghisla had had no interest in imagining Peder and Morgana giving each other anything, and she'd been horrified—and a little sickened—by her sister's descriptions. But she thought of them now, and the images drew her up short.

"I did not mean . . . I did not mean that," she stammered, morti-fied. She'd only wanted to be closer. To get as close to him as she pos-sibly could.

"I do not want that," she insisted, twisting his jerkin in her hands.

For a moment they simply listened to each other breathe, his lips on her forehead, her hands over his heart.

Maybe she *did* want that. Maybe that was exactly what she wanted.

There was nothing and no one to stop them. The world was sleep-ing, and at present, they were the only two people in it. They had only each other, and their time would soon end. The thought made Ghisla ache, and she reached for him, desperate. For a moment, his kiss matched her own. His hands and mouth clung, frantic and frenetic, but then he lifted her from his lap, pushed himself away, and stood.

"Hod?" she whispered.

He extended his hand to help her stand, and she took it, wanting only to touch him again, but he released her as soon as he felt her rise.

"You have been the light in my world from the moment I heard you singing," he said, and his voice was bleak again, back to where they started. "And I want nothing more than to be with you. In whatever way I can. But you are a daughter of the temple. What do you think would happen if we were discovered?"

"I don't know." But she did. He would be flogged or put in the stocks . . . or worse. An image of Bilge and the other men swinging from the gates rose in her mind.

"We will not be discovered," she said, refusing to entertain the idea. "That will not happen."

"No. That will not happen," he whispered, and she heard the words he did not say. He stepped back, and she stared up into his unseeing eyes. The moonlight made them glimmer like glass, like the fourteen stars that shined brighter than the rest. And like the stars, she could not reach him.

"Will I see you again?" she asked, knowing their time had, once again, come to an end. He turned his palm and she pressed hers into it. The work-rough ridges of his hand scraped against hers, and emotion tickled her nose.

"Yes. Tomorrow. But I am always right here." He ran his thumb over the rune on her hand and then tugged her close. He embraced her quickly, fiercely, and melded back into the shadows. She closed her eyes, unable to watch him go, but he left silently, and she heard nothing but her own longing.

∽

She traveled back through the tunnel, but when she neared the opening in the sanctum, there were voices on the other side, and she froze, fearing that they were looking for her again. She listened, trying to determine who occupied the sanctum at such an hour. A metal grate in the stone door allowed her a narrow view of the room beyond.

Master Ivo and Keeper Dagmar were deep in conversation, and neither of them mentioned her name. They were not looking for her—or anyone—and she wilted against the wall, prepared to wait them out, but when she heard the Highest Keeper's query, she straightened once again.

"Do you remember the woman with the blind child, Dagmar?" Ivo asked.

Ivo sat in his throne, his back to the opening in the wall, but Dagmar faced him, and she could see the frown that furrowed his brow.

"I do not."

"You let her into the sanctum. You *should* remember," Ivo grumbled.

Dagmar shook his head.

"It was during the Tournament of the King, only months after Bayr was born. You were distracted." Ivo waved his hand like it was yesterday.

"The child's eyes were cloudy. No irises. He was just a little boy. Three or four years old. Old enough to talk."

Dagmar's face cleared in remembrance. "I do remember. I found the woman sleeping against the garden wall. She was sick and asked for a blessing."

"A blessing for her son," Ivo corrected, his voice dry.

"Yes . . . well."

"I could not fix his eyes. But you knew that. That boy . . . is now a man. He is the blind archer they call Hod."

"No!" Dagmar marveled. "I met him just today. He was extraordinary. The talk of the mount. He reminded me a little of Bayr. Mayhaps it was just his humility about his own prowess, but he was a pleasure to watch."

"Hmm," Ivo grunted. "He has an aptitude for many things. I thought he might be a keeper someday. He showed a great affinity for the runes at our first meeting."

Ghisla tried to moderate her breaths, the dust from the tunnel tickling her nose.

"He came to see me today—he and his teacher—and pled for me to make him a supplicant."

She covered her mouth, moaning into her hands. *Oh, Hod. Why did you not tell me?*

"He is not the first since the scourge," Dagmar said. "He will not be the last."

"No. And I turned him away as I have turned away all the others."

She could not breathe. She would go back to the hillside. She would find Hod. But the conversation continued beyond her hiding spot, and she was frozen in place.

"Our mission has changed, Master," Dagmar said. "We have to think of the daughters."

"Yes . . . but I would have turned him away, regardless."

"Why? You say he had an affinity for the runes."

213

"He has been trained by Arwin, the cave keeper. In truth, he has been a supplicant all his life. His knowledge is already vast, his skills great. And that frightens me too."

"Why?"

"I have not decided if he is good or evil."

Dagmar's gasp cloaked Ghisla's. "Why would he be *evil*, Master?" Dagmar asked.

Ivo sighed. "Mayhaps evil is not the right word. He drew the rune of the blind god there, beneath the altar, in the dust. A child. A little, blind boy. Now he is grown, but his eyes are still as empty."

"The blind god was not evil."

"No . . . but evil used him. Evil uses the ignorant."

"And you think evil might use the blind archer?"

"That is what I have not decided. I know it is foolish to ignore the signs. And there are many."

"But the woman—I remember her now—she said you blessed him. She said you blessed her. When she left the temple, she was greatly restored."

"No thanks to you," Ivo grumbled.

"No thanks to me," Dagmar repeated, a smile in his voice. They both grew quiet, thoughtful, and Dagmar stood, as though the matter was done.

Ghisla wanted to sink a blade into both of them. Her hands trembled with her rage. She would scream until their ears wept with blood, until she begged her for the mercy they had not shown Hod. *How dare they? How dare they reject him? How dare they judge him?*

"I will rest better when he is gone," Master Ivo grumbled.

"He has unsettled you that much?" Dagmar asked, his interest piqued again. "I am surprised, Master. I sensed no darkness in him."

Master Ivo harrumphed. "That may be . . . but I cannot ignore the signs."

"So you have sent him away."

"I have sent him away. There is no place for him here."

Ghisla turned back to the tunnel and fled, not caring whether she was too loud, not caring whether she was discovered, not caring whether she ran headlong into a stone wall and ceased living altogether. By the time she reached the hillside and tumbled out through the hatch, her lungs burned, and her eyes were as blind as Hod's, but she did not stop.

The Temple Wood stretched out at the base of the hill, and she staggered toward it, not even pausing to take the trail to ease her descent. The mount rose and ran in grassy shelves, and she tumbled over one side and down another before she thought better of her decision and picked her way across a clearing to the well-beaten path that led to the bottom of the hill. She didn't know where she was going, but when she reached the woods she continued on, losing herself in the trees.

I cannot see, my tongue is a traitor.
My flesh is a foe, my heart a betrayer,
My eyes will I blacken, my lips will I close.
And let the runes lead me down paths I must go.
No man can follow. No man can lead. No man can save me,
no man can free.

It was the Prayer of the Supplicant, the prayer of all keepers, and a verse that Hod had always felt was written just for him. He had learned it at an early age, preparing for this day.

He had gone before the Highest Keeper and pled for entrance into the brotherhood. He'd sung the song, said the words, and he had been rejected.

Arwin was as devastated as he. His teacher had been so convinced it was time and that Ivo would make an exception. He'd petitioned the Highest Keeper in Hod's behalf, but his pleas had fallen on deaf ears.

"You cannot refuse him, Master Ivo," Arwin had argued. "I cannot teach him anything more. I have not been able to teach him for ages. He knows far more than I. You sent him to me more than fifteen years ago. How long will he be made to wait? He should be here, learning from you, a keeper in truth."

"The temple has become a sanctuary. It is no longer what it was. We have new challenges, Arwin. And I have no place for him here. Not now."

"But . . . Master. It is what he has been trained to do. All these years. I have done what you asked. You said he was special. Chosen."

"I cannot see the future, Arwin. I did not see this future. In sixteen years, not a single girl child, save the princess, has been born in Saylok."

"Yes, Master, I know."

"Do you know why, Arwin?"

"No, Highest Keeper," he whispered, dejected.

"Nor do I. I have petitioned Odin. I have looked into the well. I have carved runes into the dust and runes into my skin. I have sheltered daughters in the temple where there were no daughters before. But still . . . there are no daughters in Saylok. And I have no answers."

The Highest Keeper was adamant and unbending. And Hod had accepted the verdict with hollow resignation. It permeated him still, and he knew Ghisla had felt his despondency.

He had not told her why they'd come. He'd been afraid to raise her hopes, to raise his own. He'd used the tournament as cover, but the contest would end on the morrow, and he would have no excuse to stay.

He should have remained with her longer. He should have soaked up every second and kissed her until the cock crowed. But he had not trusted himself in her presence. He did not even trust himself on the mount.

Arwin had drowned his disappointment in a bottle and lay dreaming about a path that would never be.

"When the scourge has ended, we'll come back," he'd mumbled, patting Hod's shoulder. "Tomorrow we'll go home. We'll go back to the cave. It is better there. Your purpose will be made clear. The time has not yet come."

He walked aimlessly, erratically, listening for Ghisla even as he tried to steel himself for the farewell to come.

And then he heard her crying. The wail was no more than a droplet in the sea of sound that was the mount, but it was Ghisla, and he halted, finding her in his mind.

The crying was not centralized; it bobbled and weaved, like she was walking—falling?—and getting farther away. Dread pooled in his belly and apprehension rippled down his spine.

She had left the mount.

15

PROMISES

Ghisla did not hear Hod until he was almost upon her, and she was too despondent to cry out when she saw his shadowy form. She sat in a clearing with her back to a tree, her legs sprawled out in front of her, her head down. She'd not gone far; the stars she'd counted the night before still littered the sky above her, framed by the circle of trees that ringed her resting place. She'd grown tired an hour ago, and once she stopped, she could not find the will to keep going. Her sobbing had ceased, but somehow her anger had not ebbed. It burned, hot and sour, in the pit of her stomach.

Hod knelt beside her and gathered her up in his arms, pulling her into his lap as he stole her position against the tree. He made her drink from his water flask until her stomach sloshed and her skin cooled. Then he washed the salty streaks from her cheeks and smoothed her tumbled hair. Finally, he asked where she was going.

"I am going home," she said.

He did not argue that the Songrs were gone, that Tonlis had been reduced to ash.

"Where is home?" he asked gently.

"Home is wherever you are," she whispered. "And Master Ivo has denied you. He cannot decide whether you are good or evil."

He sighed, his breath stirring the tendrils of hair that clung to her forehead. He didn't ask how she knew, and he didn't deny it.

"You must go back to the temple," he said, but his voice broke on the words.

"I want to go with you."

"The women are protected by their clans . . . And I have no clan to protect you."

"You have no clan, and I am the property of the temple. The property of the king," she said, her voice as shattered as his.

"We all live under the oppression of these circumstances," he whispered. "All of us."

"I am not comforted by our collective suffering," she shot back.

"The population is frantic, and the chieftains are frenzied. It is not just a famine or a drought. People fear it is permanent, the end of Saylok." She could not tell if he was trying to convince her or himself.

"I do not care about Saylok."

"If the scourge does not end, there is no hope for us, Ghisla," he said, and for the first time in her memory, his voice was sharp. Bitterly so.

"There is no hope for us anyway," she mourned.

He pressed his forehead to hers, gripping her face like he could make her believe through the force of his will.

"Promise me you will not give up," he ground out. "Promise me."

"Oh, Hody." It was what he always said, and he always said it with such conviction, like it was enough to just say the words.

"Promise me you will not give up, Ghisla."

"Give up on what, Hod?"

"Give up on life. Give up on . . . me. Give up on us."

"Will there ever be an us?"

"There is an us now. There has been an us for four years."

His voice echoed the anguish in her breast. "But you are leaving," she groaned. "And I cannot bear it."

"I will come back."

"When?"

"I don't know. But I will return. I promise."

She did not believe him, and the agony in her chest screamed louder.

He kissed her forehead, her eyes, her cheeks, and the tip of her chin before he settled his mouth on hers, trying to extract the meaningless pledge from her lips. She kissed him back, hungry. Frantic. Hopeless.

She broke away, panting, and twisted her hands in his tunic. He could give her fifteen promises and countless kisses, and it would change nothing.

"You have destroyed me," she whispered, the realization so sharp and sudden she gnashed her teeth to keep from crying out.

Hod flinched.

"You have destroyed me. You have made me long for a life I cannot have. You have made me love you. What a fool I've been. What a fool!" she said, shuddering. "Tomorrow you will leave, and I will be here, wanting you. Wanting what you cannot give me and what I cannot give myself."

He did not even defend himself, and his willingness to shoulder her condemnation, to bear her irrational wrath broke her all over again. She clawed at him, crazed, and sank her teeth into his shoulder. He moaned and buried his face in her hair, and she bit him again, so angry she did not even know herself.

"You are right. I have nothing to give you but my heart, Ghisla," he ground out. "But it is yours. Every beat. Every bloody inch. You have ripped it from my chest. If I have destroyed you, you . . . have . . . obliterated . . . me."

He rolled so she was pinned beneath him, trapping her flailing fists and bruising hands. Then his mouth captured hers, and he held her face in his hands as she raged and railed against him. She snapped at the softness of his lips, but he did not retreat. Instead, he bathed her mouth in gentleness, in worship, and slowly . . . softly . . . her terrible rage became crippling remorse.

He must have tasted her contrition, for when she pulled away to beg his forgiveness, he simply drew her back, taking her penitence and turning it into redemption.

They did not speak for a long while, their mouths communing, their bodies shuddering with need and desperate devotion. Beneath his hands, her pain became unbearable pleasure, and agony gave way to awe.

Suddenly, there was no tomorrow. No parting. No pending farewell.

She dare not speak for fear he would stop; she dare not open her eyes, afraid it would end. But when Hod hesitated, his mouth hovering over hers, his body cradled in the well of her hips, she looked up at him, at his shuttered eyes and his beloved face, and she begged him for the only thing he could give her.

"There is no joy but this, Hody," she whispered. "I have no joy but you."

His mouth returned, and he sank into her, giving her what she asked of him, and she did not close her eyes again.

A humming grew beneath her skin, and the stars above her winked and grew as Hod moved. Their brilliance pulsed and pressed in concert with the swell inside her, and with each breath, she pulled their shining tails into her chest and down into her belly.

"I can see you. I can see you, Ghisla," Hod moaned into her mouth, and his moan became part of her symphony.

"Those are stars, my love. Those are stars," she thought, but she was past speech. She was shooting across the sky, part of the firmament, leaving a trail of light behind her.

Finished.

Spent.

⌒๑

"Master Ivo, Liis is gone."

Elayne of Ebba stood on the threshold of the sanctum, her red hair streaming around her shoulders, her feet bare. The higher keepers assembled for early blessing and confession gaped at her, bleary-eyed. The Tournament of the King wreaked havoc on the enclave, and the day ahead would be as long as the day before. The lines had already formed outside.

Master Ivo rose from his chair and motioned Elayne forward.

"Come, Daughter."

"I saw her leave not long after we retired and thought the king must have summoned her. I went back to sleep. But when the cock crowed, I woke, and saw that her bed had not been slept in at all."

"I will go to the castle," Dagmar offered, his lips hard and his countenance dark. "I have feared this."

"I will go with you," Ivo whispered. "The rest of you, search the temple. Liis of Leok has been known to seek out her solitude."

"We have looked, Master. All of us. We did not want to tell you until we were sure," Elayne said, pointing toward the door of the sanctum. Bashti, Juliah, and Dalys stood watching, their toes as bare, their eyes as wide. Juliah had not stopped for her shoes, but she'd strapped on a sword.

"Your weapon will not be necessary, daughter of Joran," Ivo said, but it was evident from her frown that she did not believe him.

"I will keep it until Liis is found," Juliah said.

Five of the higher keepers, including Dagmar, accompanied Ivo to the castle to find the king. The crowd in the square cried out and clamored, thinking the keepers had come to attend them, but the temple guard closed in around the purple-robed men, keeping the congregants at bay, and they moved as one, up the steps and into the palace without mishap.

"Say nothing to anyone until we know. It will do no good to alarm the mount if she is . . . here," Ivo instructed the keepers around him. No one stopped them as the procession climbed the stairs to the king's chambers. A guard stood beside the door.

"I need to see the king, sentry," Ivo demanded. "Is he inside?"

"What has happened?" the guard asked, fearful. The death of Bilge of Berne was a result of the Highest Keeper's last early morning visit to the king, and none of Banruud's men had forgotten it.

"Did you escort Liis of Leok to the throne room last night?" Ivo asked.

"No, Highest Keeper. She was not here last night. The chieftains were assembled . . . some are still assembled . . . in the hall, though most are not . . . awake. The king retired to his bed not an hour ago . . . and he is not . . . alone." The guard was doing his utmost to be discreet.

"A daughter of the temple is missing. I need only to know if she is here."

"I see," the guard said. He turned and rapped on the door, calling out as he did. "Liis of Leok is g-gone, Majesty. The Highest Keeper has come to see you."

A moment later, the king wrenched the door open. His tunic gaped and his pants hung low on his hips like he'd hiked them up to attend to the interruption.

"Where is she?" he asked, as though the Highest Keeper was just there to torture him.

"We do not know, Highness," Ivo replied, his voice level, his hands folded beneath the long sleeves of his robes. "You did not summon her?"

"I did not," Banruud grunted. His jaw hardened, and his eyes swung to the sentry, who stepped back in fear. He began to snap orders, sending his men running.

"Tell Balfor. Alert the watch. Rouse the chieftains. Ring the bells. Get my bloody horse. Find her."

When they returned to the temple, Master Ivo expelled everyone but Dagmar from the sanctum and drew a seeker rune in his blood on the fleshy part of each of his palms.

"We should not use the runes to gain information we can achieve by using our own two feet, Dagmar. But now that we know she is not on the mount, we must do what we can to find her quickly and find her . . . first."

"Yes, Master. I agree."

Chanting Liis of Leok's name, Ivo pressed the runes to his closed eyes, but after several slow breaths, he lowered his hands, frustrated.

"That is not her name," he whispered. "She is not Liis of Leok. Not in her bones or in her blood. The fates will not honor my request." Crimson streaked his hooded lids.

He washed his hands and face in the basin of water beside the altar. In fresh blood, he drew the runes again and pressed them to his eyes once more.

"Show me . . . the Songr of Temple Hill," he muttered. "Show me the little Songr."

Dagmar waited, barely breathing.

"Ahhh." Ivo leered. "The Norns like specificity." But within seconds, his grin became a grimace and then a hiss. "She is in the Temple Wood. In a clearing . . . and she is . . . lying beneath . . . Desdemona's tree. The very same tree where your sister gave birth to Bayr."

Dagmar inhaled sharply, but Ivo was frozen, observing what the rune chose to reveal. He was silent for too long.

"Is she hurt, Master?" Dagmar cried, impatient.

"No. She is with . . . a man," Ivo whispered, his obvious horror raising the hair on Dagmar's neck. "She is with a man. He is lying . . . beside her. He is holding her. And she is . . . holding him."

The Highest Keeper lowered his hands and looked up at Dagmar, blinking like the blood burned his eyes, and his lips trembled with his next words.

"She is with . . . Hod . . . the blind supplicant."

From the chatter of the birds in the treetops, Hod presumed the dawn had broken; the light never changed for him, but the air did. The sound did, and he knew they were out of time. They'd fallen asleep wrapped around each other, sated and exhausted, and even still, Ghisla slept deeply, her head tucked against his shoulder, her body boneless and warm at his side. She'd pulled her robe over them at some point, and his was rolled beneath his head.

He should wake her. They would need to make a plan. But he did not move. He did not even adjust his aching arm. The ache was too sweet. A moment more would make no difference, and he could not part with her yet.

He had endangered her. If a child grew from their union—the thought made his heart swell and his loins tighten. *Their union.*

If his child grew in her womb . . . he would . . . he would . . . he would . . .

His mind had ceased to function at all. He was caught up in the remembrance of flesh and feeling and euphoria, and he could think of nothing else. Not while Ghisla still lay beside him, smelling of woman and seed and warmth and hope. And the idea of a child made him more ebullient.

There is no joy but this, Hody. I have no joy but you.

He could not find it within himself to regret his actions. Not yet. She was a woman, protected by the temple and by the king. If a child swelled her stomach, the keepers would call it miraculous and praise the gods. It would be Saylok's child. Mayhaps it would even be . . . a girl child. It would be Saylok's child. Not his child. He and Ghisla could not be together.

With that thought, reality tried to intrude. He was a fool, and there would be a consequence for the joy they had taken. Every action begat a reaction.

Men who need kisses
Make babes who need kisses.
Babes who grow up
Become men who need kisses.
Men who need kisses
Chase women for kisses.
And . . .
Begetting begins again.

He grinned up at the boughs above him. He was not thinking straight.

He was flat on his back, Ghisla on his right, his staff on his left, and he stretched his hand, patting the ground beside him, trying to find it without disturbing Ghisla.

The pads of his fingers brushed a whorl in the dirt, a singed circle, like the fairies had gathered beneath the tree and danced around a tiny fire. The grass that bristled around the edge of the circle was sharp, and he cursed as a blade nicked his middle finger. It was the curse of the blind to be constantly bleeding. His hands were as scarred and calloused as the bark of the tree above him, but still he bled. He perused the area more carefully, using the palm of his hand instead of his fingers. There were two singed circles . . . but where was his damned staff?

His finger stung with all the ferocity of a tiny cut. He'd found dogs and wounds were alike; the little ones barked the loudest. He curled his finger toward his palm and searched the tip with his thumb, looking for a sliver or a thorn.

An image flashed behind his eyes—trees, earth, sky—and he froze.

He realized with a start that he was bleeding into his rune. But Ghisla was asleep beside him—she was not singing—and he'd never been able to see anything without her. Was it his rune? Or was it his rune . . . and his blood . . . dripping onto the strange circle burnt into the earth?

He turned his hand and patted the ground once more, careful. Careful.

The whorl of burnt earth sizzled against his bloodied rune. The image flashed again, and this time, it held.

He was in the clearing. *This clearing?* It felt the same. It sounded the same. The tree at his back murmured the same low tone.

But the woman who lay beside him was not Ghisla. Her hair was dark, her skin was pale, and her dress was . . . blue. Blue like Ghisla's

eyes. Blue like the sky. Like the mountains near Tonlis. Like the robes
of Dolphys.

She held a babe to her chest.

The babe was covered with gore, like he'd just been born. His little
arms flailed, and his cry was lusty, and the woman said his name.

*"You must take him, Dagmar. And you must call him Bayr. Bayr for
his father's clan. Bayr . . . because he will be as powerful as the beast he is
named for."*

Hod withdrew his bleeding hand with a gasp, and the image was
instantly doused. He wiped his bloody hand on his breeches. He did not
want to see more. He knew who the woman was. He knew her story.
He knew her child.

The circles in the earth were Desdemona's runes.

Ghisla stirred, and he heard her indrawn breath and the quickening
of her heart as she woke. His movements had roused her.

She said his name, the word full of love, like she was remembering
what had transpired between them. He instantly abandoned the woman
in his thoughts for the woman in his arms. He turned to her, rolling
onto his side, and gathered her close.

Ghisla's hand curled against his chest and he pressed his lips against
her brow, greeting her. She moaned and burrowed her face into his
neck, wrapping her arms around him. She opened her mouth against
his throat, as if she wanted to sink her teeth into his veins and draw
him—blood, body, and soul—into her lungs.

His love for her was an inferno, scalding his throat and burning
his chest, and he ran his hand over her rumpled hair and down her
back, memorizing the way she felt against him, the swell of her hips,
the length of her legs entwined with his. He would relive their union
on an endless loop, the stars exploding behind her eyes, the silk of her
skin, the depth of his devotion, and the moment nothing else in the
world had mattered.

Awareness skittered down his back like a spider inside his clothes.

He stiffened, the inferno becoming a glacier.

Ghisla felt his frisson of alarm, and her lips stilled on his throat.

The chatter of the birds continued. The buzz of bees, the flow of water over stones from the river nearby. But something—someone—was watching. It was a sensation he easily recognized—especially in a setting like this.

He knew better than to react with fear or flight. It was what separated man from beast. A deer would bolt. A wolf too. But running away from the unknown was always a mistake. Better to face it—to name it—than to run headlong in circles that could only bring one back into its clutches.

The sensation continued; the spider had grown. It skittered up his back and over his face leaving ice in its wake. Yet the birds gossiped and the trees hummed, and the earth beneath him was still. Not a single footfall or even the shifting of a man's weight rippled over the ground.

Then the sensation was gone. The ice of the unknown gaze disintegrated against his warm skin and the spider legs up his spine became nothing more than the press of Ghisla's hand. For a moment they didn't speak, even though they knew their time was up. To speak would be to come back to earth, to step into the future that lurked just beyond the silence.

"I have to go," she whispered. "Don't I?"

He nodded, his emotion making speech almost impossible.

"Then I will go back. And I will wait for you. However long it takes."

She had become the brave one, the believer, and he found her lips, kissing her with all the gratitude and grief he could not express. It was a kiss of solemn swearing, an oath of teeth and tongues.

With a final press of his hands and his lips, he ripped himself away from Ghisla and rolled to his feet. Ghisla rose silently beside him.

The chatter in the trees suddenly ceased and the leaves shivered. Then the bells began to ring, the clanging easily discernible even with the distance of the temple walls.

Ghisla moaned in dread. "They know I am gone."

From beyond the treetops Hod heard the pommeling of hooves and the blaring of horns. It was too far away to know how many or how fast they were moving, but not all the seekers would be on horseback. Even now he could feel the creep of company, the hush of the forest, and the expectant silence of the trees.

"You must go, Hod," Ghisla begged, pushing at him. "Go deep into the wood. Go now. If you are found with me . . ." Her heart thundered with her fear for him, and for a moment he could hear nothing else.

"If they find me, they will not keep searching," she said. "And you will be safe."

"I love you, Ghisla," he whispered.

She was in his arms for a moment, and then she was gone, running toward the mount, her skirts whooshing and causing her to stumble. She cursed and gathered them, impatient, and she was gone again, her small feet dancing over the soft ground, the crack of branches marking her flight.

She was singing softly as she fled.

"Hody, Hody, Hody, Hody."

He did not leave the clearing to plow deeper into the forest as she had demanded, but stood, listening, sensing, her taste on his tongue, her musk rising from his skin.

It was better this way, an easier goodbye. To prolong it would have been unbearable, but he could not go until he knew she was found. Until he knew she was safe.

She was one hundred yards away. Two hundred, weaving and winding through the trees at an angle to the mount. She would not come out at the bottom of the east face of the hill, but farther north, nearer the entrance to the mount. A search party on horseback would descend that way, and she was purposely running right for them. It was not more than half a mile to the edge of the wood from the clearing. He'd marked it as he'd entered the night before.

He heard a muted bellow of triumph. She'd been spotted.

16

Warriors

Hod was so intent on Ghisla's flight, the sound of her song, and the vibrations coming from every quarter—the mount, the horses, the bells, and the men who spilled down the mount to search for the stolen daughter—that he did not hear the keeper until it was almost too late.

Hod could have eluded him. He could have turned then and slipped back into the trees and hid until it was safe to come out. Arwin would worry about his absence, and he would miss the final day of competition, but there was no help for that. He could not return to the mount now, not yet; he would have to wait until the fervor had died and Ghisla was safely ensconced inside the temple.

Hod recognized the keeper—the sound of him, both the rhythm of his heart and the echo it made in his chest—and he wasn't afraid. So he waited, turning in the direction of the man's approach, and kept his staff and his feet planted. He didn't close his eyes to make his visitor more comfortable. He knew his strangeness disconcerted most people, and he didn't yet know if Dagmar was an enemy. He hoped not.

Dagmar paused when he was still some distance away. He whispered Odin's name like he was preparing himself or pleading for intercession.

He couldn't have known that Hod could hear him far better than the Allfather.

"You don't need to fear me, Keeper. Do I need to fear you?" Hod called out to him.

He heard Dagmar put his hand to the blade at his waist, fingering the handle.

"You are considering your dagger. Mayhaps I do," Hod said.

"You can hear a man's heartbeat . . . I suppose I should have known you would hear me approach and . . . reach for my knife," Dagmar said.

"Aye. You should have known. If I were as evil as Ivo fears, you would be dead, Keeper."

"I've come for Liis."

Liis. The name did not sit right in Hod's chest. He didn't like it, and he was suddenly angry that Ghisla had been made to answer to it.

"Liis of Leok has returned to the mount," he said, his voice bitter. He did not bother to explain himself or make up a story. He simply told the simplest truth and left it at that.

"But she was here. With you." It was not a question.

"She came here alone. She left alone."

"Was she the reason you entreated the Highest Keeper for supplication?" Dagmar asked.

"I have trained my whole life to be a keeper."

"That is not what I asked, Hod."

When Hod did not answer, Dagmar continued as if it was obvious.

"And if Ivo had allowed you entrance . . . what then? Keepers are not allowed to love. We are not allowed wives or families. Your feelings would have been immediately discovered."

"Have yours been?" Hod asked. Turbulence trembled in his chest, but his voice was mild.

Dagmar hissed in surprise, and Hod continued, unable to bear the hypocrisy.

"You love the ghost woman. She loves you. And yet you live, year after year, pretending otherwise. I could have pretended too."

"Who *are* you?" Dagmar whispered. Hod had revealed too much, and he tried to gather his thoughts and calm the anxious bubbling in his veins.

"I am just a blind man with an exceptional pair of ears."

Dagmar was silent, as though he considered this. "Must we talk thus? Or do you trust me to come closer?" he asked.

Hod cast his senses to the mount, to the song that was Ghisla. She was on horseback now, a warrior at her back. They were climbing the hill and the bells were clanging again, though the cadence had changed from frantic clamor to sedate signaling.

"All is well," Dagmar said, exhaling. He could hear the difference too.

"All is far from well," Hod whispered.

Dagmar closed the distance between them, his breathing cautious, his gaze tangible, and Hod lowered the tip of his staff toward him, warning the keeper not to come too close. His nerves were raw, his emotions frayed, and the numbing effects of his euphoria were fading the higher Ghisla climbed. Soon she would be behind the walls.

Again.

And they would be apart.

Again.

"She left her robe," Dagmar said softly.

Ghisla had left her robe? Oh, gods. She'd left her robe.

He heard Dagmar stoop to retrieve it from the ground.

"How is it that you came here?" Hod asked. "Of everywhere you could look, you came here. To this spot."

"The runes can be useful," Dagmar said.

"Ahh. So that was you. I thought I felt someone . . . watching."

"We were afraid for her."

"Afraid . . . of me?" Hod asked. The irony was laughable. He was powerless against the enclave. He had nothing. He *was* nothing.

Dagmar ignored the question. "Master Ivo says our Liis is not of Leok at all. She is a Songr. Did you know that, archer?"

Hod should not have been surprised; Ghisla had told him the Highest Keeper knew, but Dagmar's query startled him, and he did not like the way he called her "our Liis."

"Yes. I know . . . she is a Songr."

"Did you know her before . . . before she ever came to Temple Hill?" Dagmar pressed.

"Yes."

"Ahh. I see," Dagmar breathed.

"Do you?" Hod whispered. He wished he did. The gates had closed. Ghisla was within the walls, and he could no longer hear her heart. She was too far away.

"Master Ivo says you have an affinity for the runes. You have been trained to use them . . . though their use . . . is forbidden to all but the keepers."

"The Highest Keeper sent me to be trained. My knowledge was sanctioned . . . and yet . . . he has rejected me." Hod could not keep his attention on the conversation at hand. He was in agony.

"He does not trust you, Hod," Dagmar said, his tone like a whip. It stung, and Hod snapped back to attention.

"Does he trust *you*, Keeper Dagmar?" he shot back, defensive.

Dagmar's heart stuttered, his conscience clearly tweaked, and Hod continued. "I've done nothing to warrant the Highest Keeper's distrust or suspicion. I was born blind and clanless, the son of a harlot. And I am strange. Those are my crimes."

"Those are your crimes?" Dagmar scoffed, incredulous. "You . . . slept . . . with a daughter of the temple. You took her from the mount during the tournament. The countryside is crawling with the clanless and the depraved. Have you any idea how much danger she was in? How much danger she is still in?"

"You must tell Master Ivo," Hod murmured, his tone sardonic. "Tell him I am in love with a temple daughter, and I have used a forbidden rune. Tell him so that I will be banned from the temple, banished from the mount, and my eyes burned out of my head."

"Have you no remorse? You are lucky you are not swinging from the north gate," Dagmar said.

Hod straightened his staff, signaling his readiness to leave. "Be that as it may . . . It is a long way back to Leok. I would appreciate it if you would tell my teacher that I will wait for him along the route. Unless . . . unless you would like me to accompany you back to the mount to stand trial?"

"I did not think you a villain or a fool, blind archer. But now . . . I'm not so certain. I thought you like my nephew. But I realize now . . . you are more like . . . the king." Dagmar sounded genuinely flummoxed, and his heartbeat underscored his distrust and dismay.

"I want the robe," Hod insisted. He wanted it, and they were past pretense.

Dagmar turned to go, dropping Ghisla's robe at Hod's feet as he did.

"This robe condemns you. If you love her . . . as you say you do . . . you will not return to the mount. Ever. And you will pray to Odin she does not suffer for your selfishness."

His disapproval was more than Hod could bear.

"There are two runes beneath this tree. The rune of strength and another, one that I don't recognize. When I touched it, it rattled like a snake. Do you know anything about them, Keeper Dagmar?"

He regretted his words immediately.

His anger had caused him to lash out. His knowledge—Ghisla's knowledge—should not have been used thus. He was not in control of himself, and every word from his mouth oozed menace. He was acting like a threat, and Dagmar treated him as such.

"If you come back to the mount, I will see that you get the punishment you deserve. Do you understand, Hod?" he whispered.

"I am not who you think I am," Hod said, repentant, but even his contrition sounded ominous.

"No . . . I fear you are far worse." Dagmar spoke the words with such conviction, Hod almost believed them true.

With that, Dagmar left the clearing, giving Hod his back.

Ghisla didn't climb the hillside to the east gate but ran along the edge of the wood, searching for the horses and men Hod had heard. She needed to be seen, and she didn't stop to consider or fear what was to come.

A cry went up. A watchman on the wall had seen her. A trumpet blared, then another and another, and before long, sixteen mounted warriors, including three chieftains and the king, thundered toward her, shields raised as though they expected a volley of arrows from the trees.

She halted and squared her shoulders. She would not run toward them as though she fled a conquering army, and she would not behave as though she'd escaped a murderous horde, though she probably looked it.

Her cheek felt bruised and there was a long scratch across her brow that she'd acquired in one of her tumbles down the hillside. She tried to smooth her hair and found it adorned with sticks and bits of grass, too many to remove in the seconds she had. The tie that gathered her neckline was gone, making the round neck hang too low on her breasts. She gathered the extra cloth in her hand and noticed a tear at the seam where her shoulder met her left sleeve. Her skirts were speckled with drops of blood and a dirty handprint at her thigh.

She'd left her robe behind.

Her new green robe was still in the woods. She'd used it to cover Hod while he slept; she desperately wished she had it to cover herself now.

The king called a halt and the party pulled up, shading their eyes and staring down at her with scowls and wary disbelief.

Lothgar of Leok was the first to spur his mount forward.

"Are you all right, Daughter?" he asked, his dread evident.

"Yes. I am quite . . . well," she said.

She had not thought what she would say. Mayhaps she should say nothing at all. It had worked for her more times than not.

"There is blood on your skirts, Liis of Leok, and blood on your face," Lothgar said gently.

She stared numbly down at her ruined gown and tightened her hand at her bodice.

"Even so . . . I am fine. 'Tis but a scratch from a tree branch."

"Fine?" the king snapped, reining his horse to a stop beside her.

"Yes."

"Where . . . have . . . you . . . been?" he asked, enunciating each word like he pounded a spike into the ground.

"I took a walk in the Temple Wood. It was quiet. Peaceful. And I was weary, Majesty. I do not sleep well . . . and I have no one to sing to me."

Banruud glowered and Lothgar laughed, his perennial good nature lightening the mood. The chieftains had all heard of the king's reliance on her songs. A few of the other warriors snorted but swallowed their mirth when Banruud raised his hand, demanding silence.

"You fell asleep in the forest," he stated, unconvinced.

"Yes, King Banruud. But I heard the bells and the trumpets, and I knew you were . . . looking for me."

"The whole bloody mount is looking for you, Daughter," Lothgar interjected. "A thousand citizens—contestants, chieftains, and clansmen—were awakened by alarm bells and the news that a daughter was missing."

"I regret that," she said quietly.

"You regret that?" Benjie of Berne jeered. His braid was unkempt and bits of food were caught in his beard. He looked as though he'd been dragged from his bed or his table. They all did.

"You are not to leave the mount, Daughter," Lothgar interrupted. "You are fortunate to have only tangled with a branch."

"She should be lashed," Benjie of Berne grumbled. "She should be tied to the whipping post and lashed. Publicly. She'll not run away again."

"You'll not lash a daughter of Leok, Benjie of Berne," Lothgar shouted.

"Someone should," Benjie snapped.

No one disagreed.

"You will ride with me, Liis of Leok," Banruud demanded. "Punishments—whatever they may be—will be meted out later."

"I will walk," she argued. "If I ride, the people will think me injured or weak. I am neither. So I will walk, Majesty."

She could not go around him. There was nowhere to go. The chieftains made a wall in front of her. The king bent and swooped her up, tossing her across his saddle, her belly to the horse, her head and shoulders hanging off one side, her legs off the other. She flailed and her bodice slipped, and she was certain more than one warrior caught a glimpse of her naked breasts. She clutched at her dress and pushed herself up with one hand, trying to sit, and almost toppled over the other side. Banruud put a hand on her back, pressing her back down.

"Banruud," Lothgar warned, but the king ignored the chieftain from Leok.

"A good shaming is what she needs, Lothgar," Benjie said. She loathed him almost as much as she loathed Banruud. For a moment she thought about screaming, the way she'd done in the cellar and the square, when Bilge had raised his hand to her. But the horses would likely bolt, and she was in no position to withstand that.

"If she can sleep in the woods, she can ride like this," Banruud replied, and Lothgar held his peace.

She was made to ride thus to the top of the hill, her head and feet bouncing with every step. The motion and the press of the saddle against her stomach made her ill, but she kept her eyes shut and her teeth clenched. She would not be sick. She would not be "shamed" in that way.

Trumpets heralded her triumphant return, and Lothgar demanded she be let up before they passed through the gates.

"She is a daughter of the temple," he boomed. "That is enough!"

Banruud wrapped his hand in the cloth at the back of her dress and yanked her upright in front of him. She kept her eyes forward even as her stomach rolled and her bodice gaped, but she managed to keep her seat and to keep her breasts covered.

"You smell like you slept with a man, daughter of the temple," Banruud growled into her ear.

She flinched and recoiled but said nothing. He smelled like he slept with the dogs.

"You are a liar, little girl."

She kept her eyes aimed above the people in the square. She cared little what any of them thought and even less what any of them said, but the keepers stood in their purple robes against the backdrop of the temple, Master Ivo a black crow perched among them. Her sisters were there too, their pretty new robes little spots of color in the purple sea. She would have to get a new robe . . . or mayhaps Hod would find a way to return it to her.

She felt her control crack, just the tiniest bit, at the thought of him, and her eyes jumped to the place where she'd seen him standing the first day of the tournament, three days—and a lifetime—ago.

A gray robe, a tall staff, and a shorn pate made her look twice.

It was not Hod, but Arwin. For a moment, their eyes locked and his back stiffened. Then he began to run toward the king's party, twirling his staff round his head like he was scattering sheep . . . or running off the wolves.

"She's a witch, Majesty. A witch!" Arwin screeched.

Ghisla shrank back against the king and immediately bristled and arched away.

"What have you done to my boy, witch?" Arwin cried, his eyes wild. "What have you done with Hod?"

Arwin was talking to *her.*

"What have you done to him, girl?" Arwin ran in front of the king's horse, his palms up, entreating him to stop.

"Get out of the way, Keeper," Banruud shouted. His horse pranced and the old man ducked, his braided beard dancing, but he did not retreat.

"I am not a keeper. There are no keepers anymore." Arwin spat on the cobblestones like the term offended him.

"Go away, old man," Benjie demanded, halting his horse. He slid from the saddle and dug at the seat of his pants, shaking one leg like his breeches had climbed too high. The other warriors began to dismount as well, but Arwin continued, outraged.

"There are no temple keepers. There are only temple daughters." Arwin said *temple daughters* with dripping disdain and spat again, and Benjie stopped, sensing a compatriot in the old man.

"They are more trouble than they are worth," Benjie said. "I will not argue that, Keeper. And this one should be pilloried." Benjie pointed at Ghisla.

"There *are* no keepers!" Arwin repeated. "There are no supplicants, no study of the runes. We have a bloody plague, and instead of dedicating our most powerful keepers to solving this problem—to beseeching the gods—we house daughters in the temple and turn away supplicants."

Arwin was drawing a crowd, his passion and volume turning heads, even from the temple steps. Master Ivo had started to descend, a purple line behind him.

"For years we've turned them away," Arwin mourned. "My Hod—my boy—what have you done to him, witch?" He pointed at Ghisla with his staff, and all eyes swung to her. "You've hypnotized him. You've entranced him with your songs . . . just like you do for the mad king."

The gathering crowd gasped at Arwin's words. To call the king mad to his face was a death sentence. The king's guard was pushing through the crowd, but Banruud's ire had been raised.

He slid from his horse, leaving Ghisla cowering in the saddle. He grabbed Arwin's staff and swung it at him, knocking the man to his knees. The crowd gasped and the horse beneath Ghisla shimmied.

"The mad king?" Banruud said, and swung again, delivering a blow across Arwin's back.

"Stop!" Ghisla shrieked, but Arwin had not stopped pleading his case. He gazed up at the king, warding off the next strike.

"It is her fault you are mad. She'll make you lose all your senses like she did my Hod. She'll sing you to sleep, and then she'll cut your throat."

The gathering crowd gasped at Arwin's babbling accusations, but Banruud tossed the staff aside and lifted the man from the cobbles by the neck of his tunic.

"I am mad, Keeper?"

Chief Lothgar was suddenly beside her, pulling her down from the king's horse. "Come, Daughter," he urged, pulling her from the irate king and her desperate accuser.

"He is your son, Majesty. Can't you do something for him?" Arwin pled, wrapping his hands around the king's wrist. "He should be Highest Keeper. He's never asked for favor or even for acknowledgment."

"I have no sons," Banruud said, twisting the cloth at Arwin's throat so the man was hanging from his clothes. Yet Arwin persisted, speaking in choking, nonsensical pieces.

"Son . . . he is . . . Hod . . . blind god."

"Hod, the blind god?"

"Yes . . . Yes . . . Hod."

The king released Arwin abruptly, and he fell in a heap.

"The blind god is my son?" Banruud asked. He had begun to laugh. He threw up his hands to the crowd.

"Do you hear that, people? I am not a mad king. I am Odin himself! I am Odin, father to Hod, the blind god."

The crowd began to laugh too—warriors and clansmen throwing back their heads. Lothgar laughed with the rest of them, his big hand on her shoulder. But Ghisla was quaking, and her legs were slowly turning to liquid.

"I am the father of daughters and gods!" Banruud brayed, his arms still raised in triumph, and the crowd cheered.

"Yes. Yes, Majesty. Hod is your son!" Arwin beamed and tried to rise. "Yet he is turned away from the temple."

The guards had reached the king, and with a wave of dismissal, he turned from Arwin.

"Put him in the stocks. I will not kill him today. At least he has made me laugh."

The guards dragged a sputtering Arwin away, and the crowd groaned like they'd wanted the fun to continue.

"And what about the daughter of Leok?" Benjie of Berne shouted. "What will her punishment be, Majesty? She has endangered herself and dishonored the temple. She too should be punished."

A ripple of both interest and discomfort surged through the crowd. Lothgar stiffened beside her and pulled the gathered blue sash from around his waist, draping it over her shoulders like a shawl. It only served to draw the eye to her dishabille.

"She is a daughter of Leok," he yelled, his hand raising to the hilt of his sword, which was slung across his back.

"She is sullied," someone said, and the word was like a whip, snapping and breaking over the crowd, and the surge of condemnation swelled.

"She should be whipped," Benjie cried, and others spoke up around him.

"Pilloried!"

"She should be made to carry a hot iron."

"She should be made to wear the irons. She will not leave the mount if she is in irons."

"The daughter will be returned to my care," Master Ivo boomed, parting the crowd. He was alone but for two of the temple guard. Ghisla could not see the steps of the temple any longer. The crowd was too thick.

"She fled your care, Highest Keeper," King Banruud sneered. "And I had to bring her back." The king never missed an opportunity to turn the hearts of the people against the keepers.

The crowd rumbled and pushed, trying to get a better view of the confrontation.

"She is a Daughter of Freya," Master Ivo insisted. "Everyone, stand aside." He extended his hand toward Ghisla. "Allow the daughter to pass and return to the temple."

But the crowd at the back could not hear and began to press forward, trying to get closer, and the circle around them became smaller. Lothgar cursed and lifted Ghisla up onto the low stone wall that circled the Hearth of Kings to get her out of the way. The hearth rose behind her, as wide as it was tall and crowned in continuous flame, and she steadied herself against it as she searched for a path through the excited crush.

"Stand back," Ivo yelled, throwing his arms to the side. His palms were red with blood and he drew frantic shapes in the air. The flame above her whooshed and spit, sending sparks raining down in a wide arc into the crowd.

It was an impressive but meaningless bit of theater, and the crowd cheered the show, but did not move back.

Ivo tried again, calling a blast of wind that funneled down into the square and whipped the flags on the perimeter wall, but he could not maintain the gust with runes in the air, and the crowd wanted more.

The king bounded up onto the platform beside Ghisla, vying for the attention he had lost.

"This is the last day of the Tournament of the King. Today we will battle in the melee, and tonight we will feast," he yelled. "Go. And prepare."

The people shifted and some turned to go, but Benjie of Berne would not relent.

"The daughter has not been punished," he yelled, insistent. "Bilge of Berne—my clansman—was skewered and hung from these gates for daring to touch her. Yet she does not suffer a single mark for her sins."

Master Ivo shoved his way forward and took her hands in his, streaking them with his blood.

"She has been marked for the temple . . . with my blood. Now be done with this madness, Benjie of Berne."

"It is her blood that should be spilt, Highest Keeper. Not yours," Benjie shot back, and the dissent began again.

"She is a daughter of Saylok," the king answered, raising his voice for dramatic effect. "And she will bear *that* mark . . . to remind her who she is . . . and who she represents."

The king pulled the chain with the star of Saylok from around his neck and dangled it high, letting the flames of the Hearth of Kings lick at it. Slowly he lowered it, so the flame and the golden spires of the star seemed one. The sun had just risen above the temple, and the gold of the amulet caught its rays and reflected them back. The murmuring in the crowd turned to awe and marveling. The heavy gold amulet had been passed down from one king of Saylok to the next, and Ghisla had never seen Banruud without it. He kept the amulet dangling in the fire until the chain in his hand grew too hot to hold. He set the amulet on the ledge of stone and reached for Ghisla's hand. She jerked it away.

The people fell silent.

"Hold out your hand, daughter," Banruud insisted.

"I will not."

"Hold out your hand, or I will press this amulet into your brow," he said, his voice low but his eyes burning. "They will have their justice one way or another."

Ghisla held out her hands. The king grasped her right wrist and turned her palm up. The lines of her rune were puckered white stripes amid her pink flesh, but if he saw her scars, it did not deter him. Using the chain, he lowered his amulet onto her palm and pressed her fingers closed around it.

She tried to scream, but images flashed behind her eyes, shifting and shivering at the speed of light, as if she held the hand of the god Saylok himself. Five hundred years of kings, embedded in the gold, spoke to the rune on her palm. And then pain raised its white-hot head, obscuring every color, every line, and she saw nothing but fire.

The king released her fingers and yanked the chain away, his amulet bounding from her burnt flesh. He raised her wrist aloft, showing the star seared on her palm to his bloodthirsty citizens. Her vision swam and her knees buckled, and for a moment she dangled from his grasp, just like Arwin. Just like the amulet.

"There it is. There's your mark. Now let the games . . . begin," Banruud said, and he released her into Lothgar's arms.

17

BLOWS

Master Ivo drew runes to ease Ghisla's pain and promote healing, but it was not the burn on her hand that made her frantic. Her palm was a deep, weeping wound, but there were other wounds he could do nothing about.

He did not seek explanation for her absence; it was as if he already knew everything. When Ghisla asked if he would look after the keeper Arwin's welfare, he had simply nodded and promised he would. But his hands trembled when he drew the runes, and though the lines to see the keepers grew outside the temple, he barred anyone from entry and set guards at every door.

"There will be no more blessings or favors today. The keepers and the daughters will remain in the temple until the tournament has ended and the mount has emptied."

It was Ghost and the temple daughters who pled for explanations. Elayne had discovered her gone and alerted the entire temple. They held their questions as her wound was attended to, Ghost washing her feet and face and Bashti brushing her hair. But when she climbed the stairs, donned a clean nightdress, and climbed into her bed, they all followed.

"Who took you, Liis?" Dalys asked, running a small hand over her brow.

"Did you run away?" Juliah asked.

"I have run away before—but I always come back," Bashti confessed.

"It is not running away if you never leave the mount, Bashti," Juliah snapped.

"Was it the blind archer, Liis? I saw him in the square. You looked as though you would faint when you saw him the first day of the tournament," Elayne said softly.

Elayne was far too perceptive, and her observation made Ghisla's stomach churn and her pulse race. If she had noticed, others might have noticed too. Her fear for Hod grew, and it was all she could do to simply breathe.

"A blind archer?" Juliah gasped. "Is he any good? Why have I not heard of him?"

"He sought supplication in the temple. With his teacher," Ghost said, studying Ghisla with her rain-soaked gaze. "He was sent away."

"He is an archer . . . and he is blind?" Juliah stammered. "And he was sent away? Why? Could we not have at least seen him shoot?"

"Juliah," Elayne sighed. "This is not about archery."

"He was sent away because there are no male supplicants being taken into the temple. This must remain a sanctuary for daughters. Ivo says more will be coming," Ghost murmured.

"Where did you go, Liis?" Elayne asked.

"I wanted to be alone," Ghisla whispered. She rolled over in her bed and closed her eyes.

Her sisters grew quiet, but they did not leave, and when she woke in the night, her hand throbbing in agony, it was Ghost who drew the runes to soothe, and Bashti who sang them all Songr lullabies.

The king sent for her three nights later, but Master Ivo turned his sentry away. She could hear the uproar echoing through the corridors.

"She is unwell," Ivo said.

The sentry came back, frantic, telling the Highest Keeper the king was threatening to send a hundred men to retrieve the girl if she was not immediately dispatched.

"He is in terrible pain, Highest Keeper. Since the tournament. His head is what ails him."

"She is in terrible pain. Tell the king her hand is what ails her."

Ghisla rose from her bed and dressed. It would serve no purpose to refuse him. He would only cause misery to those who could not help him.

"Do not go, Liis," Juliah said from the darkness.

"He is a bad man," Dalys whispered.

Ghisla said nothing. She simply pulled on her purple robe and left the room.

"Why does she do it?" she heard Bashti wail as she started down the corridor.

"Because she loves us," Juliah answered.

Ghisla drew up short for a moment, surprised. Juliah always acted as though she didn't understand Ghisla at all. She turned back to the room, back to her four sisters who deserved more than her silence.

They stared up at her, surprised by her return. Their eyes were bruised with worry and their hair—each hue and texture so different— hung around their shoulders like the new robes they'd been so excited to wear. They had so little to look forward to, and because of her, they'd missed out on the melee and the tournament feast, the one day of events they actually got to attend.

"I do . . . love you," she said. Then she turned and descended the stairs to attend to a king she did not love at all.

◦◦◦

Hod waited at the fork, where the roads to Leok and Adyar diverged, all day and late into the evening, listening to the rattle of carts and the clopping of hooves as the mount emptied and clansmen and villagers headed for home.

Some chattered and some stumbled, too drunk to do anything but put one foot in front of the other. He listened to their tired conversations and kept his ears attuned for Arwin. He feared he would have to return to the mount and find him, despite Dagmar's threat.

The warriors from Adyar had won the melee—the young chieftain's first victory—and the citizens of Adyar were the last to leave and the most inebriated. A group of seven—six men and a woman—talked loudly all the way down the hill and past the spot where he waited, tucked from view.

"It's about time he won. He's been chieftain since he was seventeen."

"Seventeen cheers for Aidan of Adyar!"

"I had seventeen drinks for Adyar," a farmer belched, and the stench caught the wind, making Hod wince in his spot beneath a tree. He guessed the man had also partaken in pickled pig and lamb chops at the feast.

"Feels like seventeen blows to my head," another grumbled. "You should have tied me down and lashed me for drinking those last five pints."

"I thought we'd see a lashing," the woman mourned. "It's not a tournament without a good lashing."

"Or a public hanging. Last year we saw a dozen."

"The king and the Highest Keeper almost came to blows."

"And the daughter of the temple was burned at the hearth."

"Yes. That's true. I suppose it was a fine year after all."

He'd listened for Ghisla too, but he'd lost her heartbeat in the clearing, and he'd not drawn close enough to find it again. Too much distance and too many stone walls separated them now. But the villagers' talk of the daughter of the temple had him rising to his feet.

He'd heard comments all day that he had no context for, but not like this.

He walked toward the group, careful not to approach too quickly or startle them as he stepped out from the trees.

"Pardon me," he said, keeping his distance. "I could not help but overhear. What happened to the daughter of the temple?"

Their hearts skipped and settled, and one man swayed and stumbled to the left.

"Hey . . . it's Blind Hod!" the belching man chortled, and the others paused, processed, and then burst into raucous laughter.

"Son of Odin," the middle fellow mocked, wheezing.

"Son of the king!" the woman added, and their guffaws grew.

He didn't understand their mirth, but he doubted they knew his name. They were talking about Hod, the blind god, and they found themselves hilarious.

"What happened to the daughter of the temple," he insisted, his voice louder, his hands tightening on his staff.

"The king did not like her running away," the belching man said.

"Go on now, Blind Hod. Your father is calling."

More laughter.

One of the men tossed a coin at his feet like he was a beggar, and the group began to move away, dismissing him.

"What did he do?" he shouted, and they halted, huffing in offense at his perceived belligerence.

"Shut up! For Odin's sake. Yer makin' my noggin pound," moaned the man who'd complained about seventeen blows to his head.

The belching man took a swing at him that he heard and smelled a mile away. The man who'd tossed the coin tried to pick it up again, while another made a grab for the purse that hung from Hod's belt. Hod jabbed his staff into the thief's belly, swung it around to the side of his neck, and leveled the five other men in similar fashion. They helped, by tripping over themselves and each other in their attempts to run away.

It was not a fair fight . . . not at all. They were drunk and he was not. But he'd not started it. The woman was the meanest of them all, and he hadn't wanted to strike her. He swung his stick beneath her feet and buckled her elbow with the end of his staff every time she tried to rise. On the third attempt, she bounced her forehead off the ground, and he left them all in a groaning pile and headed for the mount.

He heard Ghisla's heartbeat halfway to the top, and as he neared the gates, he found Arwin too.

Arwin's gait was altered, and his breathing labored, and he wept when Hod called his name. Hod slung the old man across his back and carried him to the bottom.

"I thought you dead. I thought you dead," Arwin wailed, but when Hod tried to get answers as to what had occurred, Arwin stopped talking altogether.

They slept at the spot where he'd waited at the fork, but by the next morning, Arwin was weak with fever, and Hod bought a cart and a horse from a farmer in order to get his master home.

∾

"It is healing quickly," Ghost marveled a week later when she changed the bandages on Ghisla's hand. "Does it hurt very much?"

"It does not hurt at all," Ghisla replied, regretful. The pain of her hand had shrouded other hurts, and as it healed, her despair grew.

Her rune was gone.

The star-shaped scar and the fibrous web of healing skin obscured it completely. Ghisla couldn't trace the lines in blood; there *were* no lines. She'd bathed her hand in tears and blood and sang until she was hoarse, but Hod did not answer.

Yet she had not lost her ability—if an ability was what it was—to hear the thoughts of others while she sang. She'd tested it while Elayne sat at her bedside, clasping her left hand. Ghisla had warbled but a single verse, and Elayne's thoughts had poured into her head like water over the falls. Whatever the rune had once unlocked—if the rune was indeed the source—still remained, embedded beneath her new scar.

She thought that when her hand had more time to heal she might be able to re-create the lines of the soul rune; she'd traced it often enough. But it was much harder to carve with her left hand than she anticipated, and the pain to her healing palm was intense.

The cuts she made became infected, and she suffered for a week before Ivo asked to see it. The oozing mess had him cursing the Norns and the king, but he drew his runes and mumbled his words, and her hand began to heal once more.

She practiced the soul rune when she was alone, drawing the character in the dust, but though she remembered the angle and shape of the mark, she didn't know which line to draw first; a rune could not be crafted any which way, and the soul rune was forbidden. She could not ask for instruction.

She worried Hod would think her affection had waned, then she worried that something had befallen him, and that fear was worst of all. She missed her menses two months in a row, but on the third month, her bleeding was so heavy it soaked her bed coverings and woke her. She cried then, though she did not cry in relief or even despair.

She simply cried for yet another love that would not be, for yet another life that had been denied her. The king, as fate would have it, sent for her that night, and when her songs were done and he lay sleeping, she left a puddle of blood in the middle of his bedroom floor where she'd stood for an hour, humming to soothe his splitting head.

Not long after that, Master Ivo summoned her to the sanctum, and when she stood before him, her hands folded demurely, he made a surprising confession.

"I realized some time ago that I am a fool," he said.

She raised her brows in question but did not argue with his assessment.

"All this time—all those years—you were communing with a blind boy . . . not a blind god."

She blinked at him, neither confirming nor denying it.

"I admit. I have laughed about your cleverness these last months . . . when my heart did not ache for you."

"Why would your heart ache, Master?" she whispered.

"Do you think me so unfeeling?"

He had sent Hod from the temple with nary a second thought. *I will rest better when he is gone.*

"The cave keeper . . . Arwin . . . told me many things when I sought his release from the stocks. He was quite adamant that you are a witch."

"I never said I wasn't."

Ivo chortled.

"He said you have addled all our brains, though he is hardly one to talk. He is quite mad himself. He did not thank me for the mercy I showed him, though I blame him, in part, for your hand."

"He was not terribly injured?"

"I watched him walk through the gates myself. I am confident he left the mount and rejoined his apprentice."

She had worried about Arwin finding Hod and was grateful for that meager bit of news.

"Arwin said you washed up from the sea and beguiled young Hod. He said it was he who took you to Lothgar," Ivo added, his tone careful.

She nodded once, and Ivo grew pensive with her admission.

"Is it your song? Is that how you talk to him?" he asked, grave. She didn't ask to whom he referred. She knew.

"I don't know. He does not . . . talk to me anymore."

"You do not know . . . or you do not want to tell me?"

"I do not know," she insisted.

"I want to believe you, but you have fooled me before."

She considered her secret for a moment; it seemed pointless to protect it now.

"Before I left Leok, he carved a rune on my hand. A soul rune. It matched the rune on his. When I sang he could hear me," she said quietly.

She had shocked the Highest Keeper, and his mouth fell open, giving him the look of a baby bird awaiting a worm. "He used a soul rune?"

"Yes."

"That is forbidden. It is . . . forbidden. How . . . how did he . . . That is forbidden!" Ivo stammered. He pounded his staff, but his pronouncement mattered little now.

"Show me," he hissed.

She stepped toward his throne and uncurled her scarred fingers, letting him study her palm. The star-shaped imprint of the king's amulet made him wince, but it didn't hurt anymore. It just made her angry.

"I can't show you. It is gone. I have only this ugly star, and my dearest friend is gone."

"You cannot trust him." He banged his staff against the stones once more.

"But I do," she said. "And I miss him terribly."

To admit it loosened something in her chest, and the pang of release was sharp . . . but sweet.

Ivo steepled his hands and closed his eyes, and for a moment she thought she was being dismissed.

"Do you know the story of Hod?"

"Yes."

"Tell me."

"He was a son of Odin. A brother of Baldr the Beloved. And he was blind."

"Yes. What else?"

"Loki tricked him into slaying Baldr."

"It is believed that he was tricked into killing his brother. But I'm not certain that is so. Hod knew what he was doing."

Ghisla waited for him to expound. Master Ivo always spoke slowly, as if giving his pupils a chance to formulate their own theories in the space he provided. But she was too rattled to do anything but wait.

With a flick of his nail, Ivo drew a bead of blood on the pad of his finger. "Give me your hand, Daughter."

She extended it, palm down, and Ivo began to paint on her skin.

"It is not enough to know the shape of a rune, Daughter. You must know how it is drawn, and you must not deviate from that order. The power comes not just from the hand that wields it, but from following the rules of each rune with exactness. The rune of the blind god is formed from top to bottom, left to right."

Ivo drew two half circles, back to back, on the back of her hand. One circle opened to the left and one opened to the right. An arrow bisected the first crescent, and its shaft penetrated the second through the back, the tip extending like it had skewered them both.

"That is the rune of Hod."

She raised her eyes to the Highest Keeper. She wanted to clutch his hand and sing so she could see his thoughts. He spoke in riddles and innuendo, and she didn't dare respond, even to admit she knew it well.

"Tell me what you see when you look at it," Ivo insisted, directing her eyes back to the figure he'd drawn in blood.

She stared, trying to gather her thoughts and tamp down her trepidation. She could not help but remember the conversation she'd had with Hod about this very rune.

"The partial circles look like two bodies," she ventured. "Two bodies, bowed in pain . . . back to back . . . pierced through by the same arrow."

"Yes," he breathed. He drew another rune. Again two crescents, back to back, but this time one sat atop the other. One crescent was a mount, the other a valley, and the arrow that connected them was vertical, the rounded tip creating a head, the shaft, a body.

"What do you see now?" Ivo pressed.

"It looks like a spider with only four legs . . . or mayhaps a man, his arms raised, his stance wide."

"Yes. That is Baldr's rune. The god of war."

"Baldr is the god of war?" she asked, frowning in disbelief.

"Yes."

"But . . . he was beloved."

"He was both."

That made little sense to her.

"Tell me what you see now, Daughter."

The Highest Keeper pushed her hand back toward her chest, bending her arm at the elbow, changing the angle with which she gazed down at the two runes he'd drawn on her skin. And she saw what he intended her to see.

"The runes are the same," she said. "One is just turned on its side."

"Yes. The same rune for both gods. For both brothers. One is upright, one is toppled. They appear different, and they tell different stories. But it is the very same rune."

"Why are you telling me this, Master Ivo?"

"So you will understand my . . . fear. For you and for the temple. For Saylok. I cannot ignore the signs. Especially when there are many. Especially when the cave keeper is convinced Hod is the son of Banruud."

It was the one thing she hadn't been certain he knew. Ivo was not present in the square when Arwin had pled with the king in Hod's behalf.

"You said yourself . . . he is addled," she whispered. She could not believe it was true. Hod would have told her. Hod would have said. She would have seen it.

"I did not say it was true. I did not say I believed it." He frowned and clacked his nails together, ten tiny blades engaged in battle.

Desdemona had proclaimed Bayr to be Banruud's only son. But that was not something Ghisla was supposed to know, and it was not something Ivo seemed willing to divulge. She wondered if he and Dagmar had discussed Arwin's ramblings. She thought not. Instead they stewed, interpreting signs and keeping their secrets. She was weary of it all.

"Hod is not a god. He is just a man," she said. "And he is gone."

"And you mourn him."

"I mourn many things."

He glowered at her, but his chin trembled, like he couldn't decide whether to scold her or sympathize with her.

"I will draw a rune to help you forget him."

"No." She shook her head. "I don't want to forget him."

He sighed and threw up his hands.

"I am afraid for him. I have not known how he fares since that day. And he will not understand why I have not called out to him." She turned her hand again so he could see her awful scar.

"It is better this way, Daughter," he warned.

"Better for whom, Master?"

"Better for Saylok!"

"I want only to know that he is well. And then . . . I will do my best to forget him." *For now.* "Can you help me, Highest Keeper?"

He grumbled and sighed again.

"Sit down and close your eyes," he ordered. "And hold out your hands."

She obeyed, sensing he was going to help her.

She heard him rise from his throne, and a moment later felt the wet of his blood against the flesh of her palms. He was drawing runes and he did not want her to see.

"Press the runes to your eyes, Daughter," he instructed. "Then ask the Norns to show you what—or who—you seek. Each rune drawn in blood will only work once—if it works at all. The fates decide."

She hesitated, half-euphoric, half-afraid.

"Do not let them dry, and do not pull away. The moment you do, it is done," Ivo barked.

She raised her palms to her eyes and pressed them against her lids. "Show me Hody," she said.

There was a sense of falling, as though she'd thrown herself from a cliff, but the landing never came. Instead, she became formless, and the sanctum around her was no more. She resisted the urge to withdraw her hands—she still felt them there—to catch herself, just as Ivo had instructed.

His back was bare, and he stood in the water up to his waist, his arms to his sides, palms touching the waves as they rolled past him. She despaired that she could not see his face, only to find herself looking at him from a new direction. His shoulders and chest were muscled and his abdomen notched from top to bottom, but his ribs and collar bones were too pronounced, and he'd let his hair grow. It bristled from his head and jaw like he'd just emerged from months of hibernation. She saw it then, a resemblance to Banruud, and she almost lowered her hands.

He shuddered, his back stiffening like he'd caught a chill. He cocked his chin, the way he did when he was listening, and his pale eyes were striped with shadows like they'd been that night on the hillside.

"Ghisla?"

"I am here," she said, but her voice had not made the journey with her, and the runes were played out. The sanctum settled back around her and the sound of the sea and the scent of the brine was replaced by incense and old men.

The blood on her hands was smeared, and the Highest Keeper stood over her, his hands folded on his scepter.

"He could not hear me."

"No."

"But he looked well," she whispered. She would not cry in front of Master Ivo.

"It is better this way," he said again, almost pleading with her, and she wiped the blood from her hands and face. But it was not better for her.

Later that night, when she was alone and the temple was slumbering, she returned to the sanctum. She had a ceremony of her own to perform and didn't want to do it huddled in the cellar or creeping through filthy tunnels. She had sharpened her small knife so it would not require too much skill or pressure to break the skin. Carefully, her lip tucked beneath her teeth, she drew the rune Master Ivo just taught her—the rune of the blind god—into her left palm. From left to right and top to bottom, one crescent, and then the other, with the arrow piercing them both through. Blood beaded in the wake of her blade, but she was pleased with the result. Neat, exact, and centered, just like Hod himself.

She set down her blade and with a deep breath, she said his name.

She hadn't known what to expect or if she should expect anything at all. But if she had to wear the king's mark on one hand, she would wear Hod's mark on the other.

The world went black—the darkness sudden and absolute—and she gasped, both elated and afraid.

"Hod?" she whispered. The rune was working.

She waited, sightless, resisting the need to catch herself. But she wasn't falling. The smell of incense still warmed the air around her, and the stone bench was firm beneath her thighs. She wasn't falling or flying; she was blind.

She closed her fist around her bleeding left hand and patted the area around her with her right. She was still in the sanctum. She blinked, trying to restore her vision, but the inky darkness was complete. She had given her eyes to the blind god.

"Hody. Hody. Help me," she moaned. But Hod was far away. Her hand was wet with her blood, and she blotted it frantically, trying to wipe away the effects of the rune, but it wasn't just a mark made in blood. It was a mark carved into her skin.

She stood and felt her way forward with searching feet and one hand. At the altar, her knuckles grazed the side of the bowl where the Highest Keeper washed his hands. The bowl rocked and water sloshed, splashing her feet and dousing her hands. She steadied it with her right hand and carefully immersed her left, washing the blood from her shallow cuts, but it wasn't enough.

She stepped back so her movements would not upend the bowl or brush against anything else and awkwardly loosened the sash at her waist. She wrapped the fabric around her hand, making a bandage from the cloth and pulling it tight. She needed the blood to stop.

She waited for an hour, hovering in the sanctum, listening to every groan and creak of the floors, to every whisper of the wind against the colored panes high on the stone walls. If the candles kept vigil beside her, she did not know, though the incense remained.

It was only when her tears came, the darkness and her fear breaking her down, that the idea came too. She unwrapped her hand and held it to her face. The salt of her tears stung her wounded flesh, but she began to sing, holding it there.

> Cry, cry, dear one, cry,
> Let the pain out through your eyes.
> Tears will wash it all away,
> Cry until the bruises fade.

Her tears came harder, and the sting intensified briefly, but then, with her song, the rune began to close and the darkness began to lift.

When she crept into bed just before dawn, her eyesight completely restored and her new rune scabbed over, she vowed to never tempt or test the runes again. The blind god had finally answered her.

18

SPELL SONGS

Arwin did not recover quickly. His ribs were broken and his heart was weak, or mayhaps it was his ribs that were weak and his heart that was broken. But he was not himself. He was shaken, scared, and befuddled.

"We will not give up, Hod. We will not give up," he groaned, and Hod wondered if Ghisla had felt the rage that filled his breast when he'd said the same thing to her.

He nursed Arwin for months, his days and nights running together until he lost all sense of both. Arwin was asleep more than he was awake, and he was so weak and unwell that Hod feared that if he left for any length of time, Arwin would slip into the great unknown.

Ghisla was as silent as she'd been in the early days, and his fear for her well-being and his longing for her voice was almost unbearable. He comforted himself with the strong heartbeat he'd heard on the hill just before he'd found Arwin; whatever the clansmen from Adyar had been referring to, she was in the temple—alive and well—when he carried Arwin down the hill.

He slept little, and when he finally succumbed to exhaustion and slept for hours at a time, he would wake in horror thinking Arwin had cried out or Ghisla had sung, and he'd been too unconscious to hear either of them. He traced the rune on his palm in blood and tried to will her to answer, but there was never any response, no burning on his palm or tingling in his fingers. And there were no songs. It was as if their link had been completely severed.

He grew so desperate to know how she fared that he drew a seeker rune on his palms that sent him hurtling into the darkness. But the seeker rune did not give him eyes, and the things he heard and felt were muted and distorted by distance and dissonance. What sounded like a voice lifted in song could just as easily have been birds cawing in the bell tower.

One night he fell asleep in the chair beside Arwin's bed and woke to his master moaning and tugging on his hand.

"I have failed you, Hod," he whispered, and Hod could hear his tears. He disentangled his fingers and checked his mentor for fever. His head was warm, but not alarmingly so, and Hod pressed a drink to his lips and wiped his mouth. Warm tears dribbled from the corners of Arwin's eyes, and he wiped those too.

"I have failed you, Hod," he said again and reached for Hod's hand. This time Hod let him hold it, sinking back down into the chair beside him. It was clear that Arwin wanted to talk.

"You have not failed me. You have been the only family I have ever had, and you have cared for me all these years."

"They have failed us."

"Who, Master?" But he knew who. When Arwin was lucid, he talked of little else.

"The Keepers of Saylok. The mighty Keepers of Saylok. They have failed us all," Arwin murmured. "They have failed my little boy." He brought Hod's hand to his lips and pressed a kiss to his palm, his tears pooling again. The gesture was something he'd done when Hod was small, a way to reinforce pride in his work. It'd been years since he'd kissed Hod's hand; but these days Arwin was lost in the past far more often than he resided in the present.

But his lips stilled and he pulled his face away, his thumbs smoothing Hod's palm, over and over, like he worried a rabbit's foot or summoned wishes from a rock.

"You have a rune on your palm," he gasped. "It is a soul rune."

Hod sighed. It revealed the fragile state of his own health that he could summon no excuse for his teacher.

"Yes, Master," he said. "I do."

When he tried to withdraw his hand, Arwin clung to it, drawing it back to his face. He pressed his right eye into Hod's rune, the act a similitude of Odin dropping his eye into the well of Mimir in exchange for the wisdom of the runes.

"Take my tears in lieu of my blood, and show me your other half," Arwin beseeched the rune. Hod did not stop him or yank his hand from his trembling grasp. He had begged the rune for the same thing, day after day, in hopes to simply hear a heartbeat or sense Ghisla there on the other side.

"There is nothing there," Arwin said. "I see only frayed tendrils."

"No . . . there is nothing there," Hod answered, and his voice broke.

"It is forbidden. Have I not taught you this? It is forbidden. What if the Highest Keeper had seen this?"

Hod rose and washed his hands. He could smell Arwin's breath on his skin, sickly and sour, and there was nothing more to say.

"She is the king's witch now," Arwin hissed. Hod froze, his hands dripping, his hackles raised.

"Who, Arwin?"

"Ghisla the Songr. The girl who sang to you. She sings to the king now. She has addled his brain. He is mad. We have a mad king and the keepers put him on the throne. They put him on the throne and brought daughters into the temple."

"What do you know of Ghisla, Arwin?" he pressed, trying to keep his tone even. He dried his hands, keeping his back turned to his teacher.

"She is the king's witch now," Arwin repeated. "He has marked her."

"Marked her how?"

"He will make her the new queen. I have seen it."

"You have *seen* it?" It was an old manipulation. Arwin always claimed to have "seen" something when he tired of Hod's questions, and Hod had always resented it. Mayhaps it was because he could see nothing and thus had no use for visions meant to mold belief or obedience.

"How has he marked her?" Hod insisted, refusing to be distracted by Arwin's prophecies.

"She wears his emblem. She is his."

Arwin was trying to wound him; Hod could hear it in the words he chose. Arwin did not lie . . . but he evaded, and his erratic heartbeat exposed him.

"I am going out, Master. I am going to hunt. I won't be far," he said, retrieving his staff.

"I told the king he has a son . . . but he does not care," Arwin shouted. He did not want Hod to leave yet. "He did not believe me. Just like you do not believe me."

"When did you speak to the king?" Hod gasped.

"I spoke to him in the square when he brought the Songr back. I warned him about her. And I told him about you. But he just laughed."

"You warned him about her?" Hod fell back into the bedside chair.

"The king did not believe me. He is mad. She has addled his brain."

"Oh, Arwin," Hod said. "What have you done?"

"He put me in the stocks. No one would listen to me. The Highest Keeper told me to leave. They have let us down. They have let us all down."

~☉~

Months passed.

Five months. Six. Seven. Arwin's condition continued to deteriorate. He orated the eighteen spell songs of Odin one day, reciting them without mistake, only to forget his own name the next. And through it all, Ghisla failed to sing. Hod grew more and more desperate, going so far as to ask his master on a more lucid day to draw the rune of the seeker and tell him what he saw. Arwin did not seem surprised, nor did he argue the wisdom of such a request. He simply sighed and stroked the rope of his beard.

"I cannot . . . remember . . . the rune, my boy," Arwin whispered, regretful and almost sweet.

"I will draw the rune. I need only for you to tell me what you see," Hod reassured him.

"But I have been banned from the mount, and you have been shunned by the Highest Keeper."

"I know, Master. They have shunned us both, and yet . . . I still know the runes."

Arwin cackled, pleased at this truth. "They cannot strike the knowledge from our minds," he crowed, the irony lost on him.

Hod nicked his finger and drew the seeker rune on Arwin's palms, careful to be precise.

"Just . . . hold the runes to your closed eyes."

"Yes. Yes. I remember now."

"Find Ghisla, Arwin."

"You seek the Songr. The little girl washed up on the shore," Arwin said slowly. His voice was low and the sound came from just above his heart, as though he'd tucked his chin to study the runes Hod had drawn.

"Yes, Master. Do you remember her?"

"I shunned her. She begged me to let her stay. But I was afraid. I was afraid she would make you weak."

"Yes," Hod said, trying not to weep.

"We sent her to the temple . . . and now . . . the temple is barred from us."

"They cannot bar your eyes, Master."

"No. They cannot bar my eyes," Arwin sighed, and lifted the runes to his lids. "Show me . . ."

"Ghisla," Hod finished for him, and Arwin repeated the plea.

"Show me Ghisla," he asked.

He stiffened and swayed, and Hod feared he would drop his hands. Then he stilled and his breath whooshed from his lips.

"She is there."

"Where, Master?"

"She is . . . on the temple steps. I can see the castle and the square and the spires . . . The columns are behind her. She sings the song of supplication. All around her are the keepers . . . the keepers and daughters . . . all around."

Hod wished he could hear her, but he did not interrupt, barely breathing as Arwin continued.

"She has . . . grown. She is not a waif anymore . . . but a beautiful woman." He sounded confused. "She was so small . . . bones and blue eyes . . . when I took her to Leok. And now she . . . she is grown."

"Is there a babe in her womb?" He had to ask. He had to know.

"A babe?" Arwin asked, befuddled. "There is no babe! She is but a child."

"No, Master. No . . . she is grown, remember? Tell me what you see, not what you remember."

"She is slim . . . but not tall. I see the swell of breasts . . . but not the swell of a child. Her hair is woven into a golden crown. Her eyes are lifted to the sky. They are blue. So blue. She wears the robe of a keeper. She wears the robe of a keeper!" Arwin's voice became agitated. "All the daughters wear the robes. Yet my Hod has been rejected."

"Arwin," Hod warned, trying to refocus his teacher, but it was too late. Arwin's hands fell from his eyes and flopped onto the bed beside him.

"There are daughters in the temple . . . and none in Saylok. And my Hod has been rejected."

❧

In late spring, on a day which promised more sunshine than rain, Arwin asked, quite lucidly, to visit the grave of Bronwyn of Berne for a while and eat some berries from the bushes nearby. Arwin wearied about halfway, and Hod carried him the final distance, settling him on the big stone where his mother was laid to rest.

"This is where I buried her," Arwin said.

"Yes, I know."

"She was a good mother to you."

"I hardly remember."

"Bronwyn. Bronwyn of Berne. The fates gave her time . . . but not enough."

Hod rose and began collecting berries from the bushes nearby.

"You were so small. And she did not want to leave you."

He'd heard this before, but it meant little to him.

"She called you Baldr."

Hod's hands stilled. He had no faces in his head. But he had voices. *Baldr the Beloved. Baldr the Brave. Baldr the Good. Baldr the Wise. You are all those things.*

He remembered a voice saying those things. Saying that name. Sweet. Patient.

"She called me Baldr," he mused. "I had forgotten. It doesn't seem . . . real. It is more like a story someone once told me."

"The Highest Keeper told her you were not Baldr. You were Hod. So that is what I've called you."

Baldr the Beloved or Hod the Blind. Hod vastly preferred the first and wished the Highest Keeper had left well enough alone.

"One day the Highest Keeper will summon you. He will realize his mistake, and he will summon you," Arwin said, and Hod kept gathering, his hands moving swiftly over the leaves, avoiding the thorns and plucking the berries.

"Hod is the most misunderstood of all the gods," Arwin said.

"Do you speak of me . . . or Odin's son?" he said, because Arwin often spoke as if he *were* the blind god.

"I believe Hod knew what he was doing when he shot Baldr. He was not tricked. One cannot trick a blind god, a god who hears every heartbeat and knows every voice."

Hod was hardly listening. Arwin liked to ramble on. "If he was not tricked, why did he do it?"

"It was his destiny."

"His destiny?"

"Yes. He knew that his brother's death would bring about his own destruction. But he did it anyway. In many ways . . . it was a selfless act."

"A selfless act?" This was new.

"Baldr's death was necessary. It marked a new beginning . . . the death of the gods and the rise of man. The rise of . . . woman."

Hod returned to his teacher's side and put the berries beside him. The sun felt good on his face, and he tipped his chin upward, letting the rays rest on him. Arwin smacked his lips, eating the berries in happy silence.

"You cannot stay here, Hod. When I am gone . . . you must go too. You must save Saylok."

"How will I do that, Master? Where will I go?" Hod asked, humoring his old mentor. It did no good to argue.

"You are Hod. The brother of Baldr. If Saylok is to free itself and rise again, Baldr must die."

"And who is Baldr, Master? How shall I slay him?"

"Do you not know?" Arwin stopped eating.

"You said my mother called *me* Baldr. Must I kill myself?"

Arwin slapped at him and pulled his hair, knowing that his sticky fingers would irritate Hod more than anything else. Hod grimaced and stood, making his way to the place where a small spring trickled between the rocks.

After he'd been sent from the temple, he'd begun to grow his hair. The hair had bothered him until it grew long enough to slick it down.

He kept the sides of his head shaved smooth—he couldn't stand the whisper around his ears or the way it altered sound—but the hair on top remained; if he could not be a keeper, he did not want to look like one.

"You look like a skunk," Arwin had complained, but Hod had just tugged on his teacher's braided beard and patted his bald head, reminding him that he had no room to criticize.

He splashed water over his face, up his arms, and down his tight center braid, removing the residue of the berries and filling up his flask so he could clean Arwin's hands as well.

When he returned to the rock, Arwin had risen and was ready to leave. Hod helped him wash and hoisted him up on his back. It wasn't until they were almost to the cave that Arwin spoke again, his voice sleepy, his beard tickling Hod's cheek.

"Baldr is the Temple Boy, Hod. Bayr. Bayr is Baldr."

Hod had never shared the things Ghisla had told him with Arwin. In the beginning it was because his knowledge would have had to be explained. Now it was simply . . . useless. The temple was closed to him, Ghisla lost to him, and Arwin would not remember tomorrow what Hod said today.

"Bayr is not the son of Odin, Master. He is the son of a lying, murderous king. And I would never harm him."

Arwin grew lax against his back, and Hod doubted he heard.

⟲

He had intended to hunt, but when he settled in a thicket, waiting for the wind to shift so he could approach his prey undetected, he'd fallen asleep. He awoke with a start sometime later, and immediately knew something was amiss. He cast his senses wide, sifting, searching. He'd been so tired and slept so deeply that he had no sense of how much time had passed. Though the wind pressed cold fingers into his sides and pinched at his cheeks, he didn't think night had fallen; the sounds were different in the darkness—the creatures that woke and those that slept were not the same—and the temperature had not yet dropped. The air wasn't balmy, but it wasn't cold.

He couldn't hear Arwin. But that did not alarm him. He was a ways from the cave and the rock walls muffled the sound from inside, especially deeper within.

The crashing of the surf was a sound that became almost invisible after living in the cave all these years. Like the sound of his own breath or his ongoing, never-ending stream of consciousness that never quieted, even when he was asleep.

The waves still broke and billowed over the rocks and sand, but there was another sound . . . like water against a hull. There were boats in the bay. Longships, like those of the Northmen. He listened again and, once satisfied that his immediate surroundings were clear, rose, secured his bow, and made his way out of the thicket and down the mountain path toward the cave.

Every few feet he stopped, listened, and began again.

He could hear the men now, though water, wind, and distance made it impossible to tell how many. More than a dozen—maybe two—and their heartbeats hugged the shore, indicating they'd disembarked. They must have caught a perfect tide, and those were rare. The inlet near the cave was not conducive to visits by travelers. The sea beyond the mouth usually carried vessels east toward Adyar or west to the tip of Leok. The area in between was a churning eddy above a sandbar that made natural access difficult and kept the bay beyond it mostly unexplored. In the time he'd lived in these cliffs, the sea had only washed up a single traveler: Ghisla.

But there were boats and men in the bay now, that much was clear, and Hod would need to investigate.

He hurried into the cavern, dropping his bow and unsheathing his blade without pausing. He carved a rune of cover in the dirt near the entrance and dripped his blood at its center. He did not want a cave full of curious Northmen.

"Arwin?"

Hod could not hear him moving about, but he felt him and knew he was near. He washed quickly, scrubbing his forearms before moving to his neck and his face and running soap and water over the stubble on the sides of his head. He was dirty and his sweat had dried on his skin; he didn't want his smell cloaking his senses when he left again.

"Arwin?"

His only answer was a gurgling breath and an erratic pulse.

He strode toward Arwin's chamber, suddenly alarmed. He'd been distracted by the boats and men, and he'd been gone too long.

Arwin was in his bed, but he did not answer when Hod touched his face.

His heart was beating, but his breath was shallow and his time was short.

Hod shoved his nightshirt aside and drew runes across Arwin's thin chest—one for strength, one for healing, one for his failing heart—and Arwin inhaled, deep and long, and set his hand on Hod's arm.

"This is not an illness you can drive out or a wound you can close, my boy." His words were slurred, but he was coherent.

"I can. And I will."

"You have never been especially obedient," Arwin sighed. "But maybe that is for the best."

"Drink, Master."

Arwin let him lift his head, but the water dribbled from his mouth and soaked the pillows beneath him.

"I am tired, Hod. And your runes will not keep me here long. Sit beside me while I speak."

Hod collapsed into the chair beside Arwin's bed, listening to the old man breathe and gather the last of his strength.

"You must go to him and tell him who you are."

"Who, Master?"

"Banruud."

"Banruud?" Hod gasped.

"I *told* him he was your father . . . but he did not believe me. He knows he is cursed. But you can break the curse. It is your destiny."

"Arwin," he contended. "I am not Banruud's son."

Arwin fell silent, and for a moment, Hod thought he was gone. He took his mentor's hand, not wanting the king's name to be the last words between them.

"You were born before Banruud was king. Before the drought. Before the troubles," Arwin murmured.

"Before Bayr?" Hod pressed, shaking his head in disbelief.

"Before the Temple Boy," Arwin agreed. He jerked as if he were trying to nod, but he was unable to control the motion. "You are his half-brother. And his . . . other half."

Hod scoffed, unable to believe what he was being told.

"With Bayr came the curse," Arwin insisted.

That drew Hod up short.

It was exactly what Ghisla said Dagmar feared.

Bayr's birth marked the beginning of the drought. What if his death marks the end?

"We are brothers," Hod whispered, the truth dawning slowly.

Desdemona had cursed the king. She'd cursed all of Saylok, but she had not known about Hod.

"Yes . . . Hod and Baldr . . . two sides of the same sword."

"Why didn't you tell me?" Hod mourned. He was sick to the soles of his feet.

"I wanted to protect you. Your mother wanted to protect you. She was afraid your father . . . would reject you because of your blindness. And it wasn't . . . time."

"The Highest Keeper rejected me."

"Yes. He rejected both of us. But you don't need the Highest Keeper, Hod. He needs you. The king needs you. All of Saylok needs you. You are the blind god."

∞

The fates were not generous, and they did not honor the runes Hod drew on Arwin's breast. The cave keeper died quietly, a rattle in his chest and a hopeful fluttering in his breath.

Hod could not bury him, not immediately, and he had no time to grieve him. There were strangers on the beach and crawling up the cliffside.

He added blood to his rune and sat near the opening, listening as men moved beyond the walls, hesitating, and then continuing on, searching for something to bring back to their boats, disappointed by the austerity of the cove. They were Northmen, just as he'd suspected, and they talked of gold and gluttony, but they would find none here. They fished from his creek, roamed his hill, and saw his tracks—he heard their discussion—but they did not find the cave, and they did not leave. They spoke of conquest and combat, but beneath their bravado was a weariness that made him suspect they had not been home in a while.

Hod rolled Arwin's body in the blankets from his bed and carried him through the main tunnel and past chambers filled with runes to a deep recess bigger than most tombs where Arwin kept his treasure. A ledge stretched from one side to the other, and Hod laid Arwin's body upon it, covering him with his keeper's robe. Arwin had been proud of his robes, and should anyone find him, they would know what he'd been.

Arwin had spent his life in the cave. Hod did not think he would care that he was buried in it too. Arwin was a cousin of the late king of Adyar—"Of royal heritage all the way back to Saylok himself!"—but he had a pauper's heart. He'd spent his life hoarding treasure, tucking it away deep in the cave; for what, Hod never knew. Hod thought it useless. He could not see it, or eat it, or burn it. It had no warmth and it smelled of time and blood. In that way, treasure wasn't much different from the runes, though in Hod's estimation, the runes were a thousand times more useful.

He sang one of Ghisla's songs, his voice bouncing back at him in gentle mockery, and then he said the Prayer of the Supplicant one last time. Mayhaps it was a prayer for Arwin, mayhaps it was a vow to himself.

No man can follow.
No man can lead.
No man can save me,
No man can free.

For five days, the Northmen camped on the beach, their fires sending smoke billowing up the cliff face, warning him away, urging him to stay hidden. They were big men, the sound of their chests and the tenor of their voices like the drums of war beating up from the sand. But they had no one to fight and nothing to take, not here. The tide that had brought them in was making it hard for them to leave. They'd tried to make it out of the cove only to turn back, the bellies of their boats scraping on the bar that kept the sea at bay.

It was Arwin's treasure, tucked in chambers beneath ancient runes that gave Hod an idea. He spent half a day moving caskets and trunks to the entrance of the cave. He shouldered a chest so rotted, it threatened to burst and rain its contents down his back. But he knew the goblets, chalices, and chains would be of interest to the Northmen. Then he washed and readied himself.

He valued soap more than gold, but he packed some of both. He added two clean tunics, some trousers, and two pairs of wool socks to the pile and wrapped them in Ghisla's robe before tucking them into his sack. He'd been unable to part with it then and found he could not do so now.

He tucked his blade into his belt, sheathed his sword and his staff across his back, and bled into another rune to obscure the entrance, though the protection would fade in time. When he came back—if he came back—the cave would still be here, though its contents may not. Mayhaps the Highest Keeper would send a new cave keeper to tend the runes and live among the rocks. Eventually, he would discover that Arwin was gone and his blind apprentice too.

Hod could not find it within himself to care.

Men powered the runes with their blood and their belief. The runes should not power man, and he would not sit by, waiting for the fates to tell him what to do. Arwin had believed in prophecy, but Hod did not want to be the blind god, brother of Baldr the Beloved. He did not want to be son of the king or a keeper of the cave. And he did not want to harm Bayr.

He had promised Ghisla he would return . . . but he had nothing to give her and nowhere for them to flee. And until he did, he would not come back.

He heard the moment he was spotted and tossed the small chest of treasure he'd brought with him down onto the sand. The casing ruptured and the contents spilled, clinking and clattering at his feet. He unsheathed his staff, not bothering with his sword. If they decided to kill him, he would die. If they decided to poke at him, he would do better with his stick.

"I am Hod. The treasure is yours. And there is more where it came from," he yelled. "You can kill me, but then you won't find it. You also won't get out of this cove. But if you let me come with you, I will help you do both."

PART THREE

PART FIVE

19

Northmen

"I do not like coming to Berne," Alba sighed, peering out the carriage window. "Just once, I would like to go to Dolphys."

Ghisla said nothing. They did not go to Dolphys because Bayr was the clan's chieftain. The king always sent an official emissary to Dolphys instead, and when the chieftains gathered on the mount, Bayr sent his grandfather in his place. Bayr had never returned to Temple Hill, and over the years, Alba had slowly ceased talking about him. Ghisla understood. It hurt too much to forever hope and endlessly wait. Six years had gone by since Ghisla had seen or heard from Hod. Bayr had been gone even longer, and Alba had grown up without him. But every now and again, she revealed her inner longing. She had not forgotten Bayr.

"I have even been to Joran and Ebba. Ebba is overrun by the Hounds, and we still go to Ebba. But not"—Alba sighed—"Dolphys." Alba smoothed her dress nervously. It was something both she and Ghost did, like they smoothed their emotions with their hands. Alba turned from the window and her eyes met Ghisla's. The black of the royal robe she wore would look like a funeral shroud on many, yet somehow Alba's white hair shined a little brighter and her brown eyes glowed a little deeper beside the dark velvet.

"But we are here. And the Bernians await." She settled her crown on her head and grimaced. "And we must smile."

"I never smile. I sneer." Ghisla curled her lip and raised one eyebrow in a disdainful dismissal. "I am the least favorite daughter of the temple . . . and I intend to keep my title."

"You sneer at them, but Juliah carries a sword. She terrifies them. I think she might be the least favorite."

They both laughed, giggling into their hands. The carriage had stopped, and they could hear the preparations being made for them to alight.

"I miss them," Ghisla admitted.

"So do I . . . but at least they did not have to come to Berne. You'll walk beside me, Liis?"

"I will walk behind you as I always do."

"The people will want to see you too," Alba said. "The purple of your robe makes your eyes so vivid, you'll hypnotize them. One look from you and mayhaps the Northmen will leave for good."

Alba was teasing, but her smile slipped. The Northmen were known as Berserkers, and the villages on the northern coasts of Saylok had felt their wrath. Both Lothgar and Aidan had beaten back the raids, but Benjie had used another strategy—appeasement—and Banruud had allowed and even abetted it.

"I fear it will take more than a look from me," Ghisla murmured. "Benjie has allowed the North King to take whatever he wants."

"And yet my father comes to Berne—the king himself—to talk of trade and feast and give the North King even more. One of these days, they won't leave. They'll stay. And they won't remain in Berne."

Ghisla knew Alba was right; the Northmen always left for a time, but they always came back wanting more. Still, the princess's grasp of the situation surprised her. Someone in Adyar had been whispering in her ear. King Banruud did not discuss such things with his daughter or the occupants of the temple. What they knew they learned from scattered conversations and their own observations. The keepers attempted to shield the daughters too, though their efforts had ceased to be effective since the king had started demanding the daughters accompany Alba and appear before the clans.

This time, the king had brought only Alba and Ghisla on the visit, insisting it was because he was only traveling to the clans they represented. They had gone to Leok first, then Adyar, and had expected to return to the mount. Instead they had continued on to Berne. The Bernians would be disappointed that Bashti was not with them, though Ghisla doubted they would see many of the clanspeople. She feared this was not that kind of trip.

Alba clearly feared it as well. "Father has even promised the Northmen land in Berne—land that Bernians own—if they will come with their families and stay. Saylok is dying. We need women and children . . . and I suppose this is a way to accomplish that, but . . . I have yet to see any families from the North. I've seen only warriors."

Beyond the windows a huge crowd had formed, and King Banruud was already moving through the gathering on his horse. Benjie of Berne rode toward him, a parade of red-clad warriors behind him. The Northmen, if they were present, would not be mounted. They came to Berne in boats.

"Master Ivo says it is not the women of Saylok who are the problem. It is the men," Ghisla murmured. To say such a thing in front of the king or the chieftains—in front of any of Saylok's men—would not be wise. "King Banruud and the chieftains keep negotiating with, and raiding, other lands for their women, but that has not lifted the scourge."

The carriage door opened abruptly and a member of the king's guard poked his head through the opening.

He extended a hand to help Alba disembark. She did so, and then the guard turned to Ghisla. Ghisla followed the princess, trying to quell the nervous jangling in her veins. She would be glad when the visit was through.

⤴

Hod heard the beat of her heart before the carriage even came to a stop and almost fell to his knees. He did not stand with the Northmen who had assembled to observe the arrival of the king but hugged the edge of the Bernian part of the crowd, wearing a drab cloak with his head covered and his eyes closed.

Arwin had taught him to close his eyes when he trod among other men. "They will remember your eyes, and you don't want them to remember. You don't want them to notice you at all. That is where true freedom lies. When you're invisible, you come and go as you please."

Arwin had not been right about everything, but he was right about that. Hod was overlooked and ignored in almost every situation, and he played the part of the harmless blind man quite well. It also helped that he wore no ornamentation—no bones or leather or rings in his ears like the other Northmen—and he leaned upon his staff like his back was bent and his body weak. Of course, he wasn't a Northman at all, though he'd won acceptance over the years.

Banners flapped in the wind, the carriage wheels squeaked, and the horses shifted and shimmied, chuffing at their bits, their breath harsh and their big hearts thundering. Hod had expected the arrival of the king—the villagers and the Northmen had talked of nothing else for days—but he had not expected Ghisla.

"Tell me what you see," he begged the old woman beside him. He kept his eyes shuttered so she wouldn't be frightened, but he felt her suspicious gaze and smelled the ale on her breath. He also heard the exact moment she took pity on him. Her tension eased and her attention shifted, and she began to speak.

"Oh, it's grand, it is. Flags of every clan, but the red flag of Berne first. King Banruud is of Berne, he is. He's a big man and fine looking . . . like most of us Bernians. You have a look of a Bernian. Who was your mother?" she asked, getting too close and peering into his face, her nose almost touching his.

"I am a Bernian. Full-blooded. My mother was Bronwyn. She was a harlot, but she has assured me my father was of good Bernian stock."

"Oh. Well then," the woman said, and immediately shifted away, just as he'd intended.

"Tell me more," he pled.

"The king is riding a black horse. No carriage for him. The princess has just disembarked. Oh, she's a beautiful girl. She's grown! A lady now, tall and slim. Her robes are black, but she is dressed in white. Her hair is white too . . . such an odd color. Like silver."

"Moonlight," he offered.

"Yes! Like moonlight," she said, and clucked her tongue in approval.

"Is there . . . another woman?" he asked, striving to keep his voice even. "Perhaps . . . the queen?" He steeled himself.

Arwin had predicted Ghisla would be queen, and she was traveling with the king and the princess. There were no other daughters present. It was a logical conclusion to draw.

"The old queen? Queen Esa? No. No. She does not travel when the king visits the clans."

"No, not the old queen," he said. "Not Esa. Another woman."

"I cannot see . . . Oh, there. She's just stepped out of the carriage. Yes. The king has brought a daughter of the temple."

"Describe her," he insisted, though he needed no confirmation that it was Ghisla. "Please."

"It is Liis of Leok. She does not smile or wave." The woman sniffed. "Cold as ice, she is. I've seen her once before at the Tournament of the King, and she was just the same."

"Cold as ice?" Hod asked. His chest was ice. Ice and fire, and he struggled to keep his tone politely disinterested.

"She's pretty, I suppose. Her eyes are quite blue, but her cheekbones are too sharp and her hair too severe. The daughters all wear their hair in braided crowns, but it does not suit her. She's a little on the small side. Too thin, if you ask me. She wears the purple robe of the keepers and a dress in Leok green. Some say the king favors her. But I don't know why."

"Ghisla," he breathed.

"No, no. Liis. Liis of Leok," the old woman corrected, like he wasn't just blind but deaf too.

"You said the king favors her?"

"Yes. It is said she has a beautiful voice. Mayhaps she will sing . . . and I will form a more favorable opinion."

"But she is not . . . his queen?" he asked.

The old woman cackled. "She mayhaps thinks she is. She acts as though she is our better. But no. She is not the queen. Banruud has not taken another queen. Not since poor Alannah, Odin keep her."

Hod followed Ghisla's movements, tracking her thrumming heart through the press of people on every side. The old woman kept prattling on, describing things he cared nothing about. He wanted only to know about *her*.

He had not allowed himself to nurse hope these last years. He'd done nothing but survive. But now he was here. And *she* was here.

"The daughters have gone into the keep," the old woman announced. "The king and Chief Benjie are approaching the Northmen. The North King is a fearsome man. He blackens his eyes like the keepers and wears bones in his hair and rings in his ears. I hardly dare look at him. Be glad you are spared that, blind man."

Had he not been so distracted he might have smiled.

"Some think there will be an announcement soon. A betrothal. Perhaps that is why Liis of Leok is here. Then mayhaps . . . the Northmen will go," the woman added, wistful.

"Thank you for helping me," he said, bowing slightly. He began moving away. There were plans to be made.

"I've not seen you before in the village," the woman said, moving with him. She wasn't ready to stop talking now that she had someone to listen to her. "Did you come from the inlands?"

"No. I came with the Northmen." He opened his eyes and smiled, showing her his teeth and his empty gaze.

She gasped, and he heard her shuffle back. She would not follow him now.

"Liis of Leok is not cold," he said as he turned away.

The old woman huffed as if to say, "How would you know?"

"And her voice will make you weep."

He found Gudrun, the North King, sprawled on a pile of skins in the company of a handful of his men. They'd taken possession of a chateau overlooking the port of Garbo and the North Sea not far from the chieftain's keep. Benjie had promised the ousted landowner it would be returned to him when the Northmen left. Hod doubted the man would want it. The Northmen were filthy, and they had no regard for the possessions of others. They'd taken it, and it was theirs now.

They'd burned the furniture that got in the way; they required space to sleep and there weren't enough bedchambers for so many. The iron tub off the kitchen had not seen a single use, except for a place to piss when the hour was late and the pisser was lazy. The great hall of the keep reeked of sweat and waste and animal fat, and Hod steeled himself against the barrage on his senses as he stepped inside. The Northmen did not live this way in their own lands; they had wives to scold them there. But none of them seemed to mind the mayhem or the stench, and they stretched themselves in front of the fire, discussing the day's events.

When they were not on the boats, Hod did not sleep among the other men. He'd learned he was safer—and a good deal cleaner—when he pitched his own tent and kept his distance from the others. In the beginning, he'd not had that luxury. The North King had kept him under constant watch, but slowly that had changed. Hod had earned his solitude and the king's trust, and he was mostly left alone. He was greeted when he walked into the room, and Gudrun told him to sit.

"I would rather stand, Sire."

The men laughed. It was an ongoing joke they never tired of. Hod did not sleep among them . . . and he rarely sat. In the beginning, the Northmen had amused themselves by throwing things at him, trying to catch him unaware. He'd sustained more cuts and bruises that way than from all the fists and fights put together. He'd learned it was best not to ever let down his guard. So he didn't sit, and after a particularly brutal barrage, he'd begun to carry a shield strapped to his shoulders. He could ward off a great deal with his staff, but it was nice to have something always at his back.

"I wish to speak with you, King Gudrun. Alone, if I may," he added.

The others grumbled, but the king made a curious noise and rose, leading Hod from the room to the chamber he'd taken for himself. It was not nearly so filthy, and the breeze from the sea wafted through an open window. Hod breathed more freely, but his anxiety did not relent. Circumstances had forced his hand.

Gudrun threw himself into a chair and rested his heavy feet on the desk positioned beside it. It was a lovely piece of work with smoothed edges and an intricately inlaid map of Saylok. Hod had explored each inch with the pads of his fingers when Gudrun demanded a refresher on the clans. He'd wanted to know every chieftain and every keep, every cove and every climb. And he'd wanted to hear all about the temple.

He did not bother to insist Hod have a seat but launched into his own update.

"The King of Saylok has brought women with him. He thinks he will give them to me and I will leave," Gudrun said.

"Yes. I know. The Bernians who were gathered to see the arrival hope there will be a betrothal. They are very proud of their princess and the daughters of the temple."

"Banruud does not realize I do not need—or want—his women. I want his throne. I want Saylok. And I am going to take it."

Hod nodded. None of this was news to him. He knew precisely what Gudrun wanted and exactly why they'd come to Berne. The Northlands had suffered their own plague. They'd lost entire populations. Men, women, children. Villages. The sickness that had taken Ghisla's family had taken many. Fields lay fallow, animals wandered free, and Gudrun had taken to the seas to plunder the riches of other lands to fill his empty coffers. Saylok, with all its troubles and inner tribulation, was prime for the taking. And Gudrun could have it. Hod had convinced himself Saylok might even be better off if it was overrun. But the North King could not have Ghisla.

"I want the woman," Hod said. He could not see Gudrun's face, but Hod could still hear his stunned response.

"What?"

"I want the woman," Hod repeated.

Gudrun barked in disbelief. "*You* want the woman? Which one?"

"The one they call Liis of Leok."

"The small one. The unsmiling one," Gudrun said slowly. "The plain one."

Hod nodded, not bothering to correct the description. Gudrun liked to twist the knife and invoke a reaction. It was the risk Hod took in telling him the truth. Gudrun valued Hod, but he was ruthless too, and he would not hesitate to exploit Hod's desires to achieve his own ends. In fact, Hod was counting on it.

"You have not wanted a woman in the six years I have known you, Hod," Gudrun argued. "I thought you committed to your solitude and your stick. You are hung like a man . . . but you do not act like one."

"I have not wanted a woman . . . because . . . of her."

"Because of *her*?" Gudrun was incredulous. "Liis of Leok?"

"Because of her," Hod said again.

"You know her." It was not a question but a realization.

"Yes." Hod took a deep breath, praying his instincts were right. "And she is not of Leok. She is a Songr."

Gudrun stiffened in surprise. "There are no Songrs left."

"There is at least . . . one."

"How do you know this?"

"Her family died from the plague that swept your land. She was left alive . . . in Tonlis. She had nowhere to go. She boarded a ship, was tossed overboard in a storm, and washed up onto the shore . . . where you found me."

Gudrun's big boots hit the floor, like he'd straightened abruptly. But he said nothing. His heartbeat had quickened, and his gaze was sticky on Hod's face. He was listening.

"My master took her to Leok. And she was taken to the temple . . . for safekeeping. She has been there ever since. She is known for her song. The king . . . values her, and he will not be inclined to let her go. But I want her."

For a moment, Gudrun was quiet, sucking on his teeth the way he was prone to do when considering. "Does this woman, this Songr . . . does she want you?" he asked finally.

"No."

Gudrun laughed at his honesty.

"She wanted me . . . once," Hod said. "But it has been many years. And she has given me no reason to hope."

"You have been of great use to me," Gudrun said. "But mayhaps— if she is a Songr—I will want her for myself."

Hod could hear Gudrun's exaggerated shrug in the repositioning of his body and the shift in the air. He was goading him, and Hod did not rise to the bait. Gudrun needed him, but he liked to remind Hod who was servant and who was king. Hod also knew if the North King heard Ghisla sing, he would most decidedly want her for himself. Hod was staking his claim. His only claim.

"The Songrs belong to the Northlands," Gudrun added.

"That is where I intend to take her. It is where I have always intended to take her. But I did not think I would . . . meet her again . . . here."

"You thought you would have to go to the temple . . . and get her," Gudrun surmised slowly, the truth dawning.

"Yes. And I knew I could not go alone."

Gudrun did not suck his teeth or worry his lips, and Hod suspected from the shape of his inhalations, his jaw was gaping. "How long have you been planning this?" he whispered.

"Since I threw myself—and my treasure—at the feet of nineteen Northmen."

Gudrun gasped and stood. He drew his blade and twirled it over his fingers as he strode from one end of his commandeered headquarters to the other. With no warning, he pivoted and threw it at Hod, grunting with exertion. Hod swung his stick and lunged to the side, knocking the blade from the air. It clattered and spun back toward Gudrun, across the floor. Gudrun bent, picked it up, and sheathed it at his belt. Hod waited, tensed, ready. In six years, he'd evaded death at least once a day.

"I do not like being taken by surprise," Gudrun stressed. It was the only justification Hod would get for the sudden attack.

Hod nodded once, acknowledging his complaint. It would not be the last time Gudrun would fling something sharp or heavy at him.

"I have always believed it was . . . hate . . . that drove you. Now you tell me . . . it is a woman."

"I have no use for Banruud, and I have no use for the keepers. Both have failed Saylok."

"So you will help me overthrow the king—who is your father—and take his lands . . . and you want only the *girl*?" Gudrun scoffed. "Your ambition disappoints me, Hod."

"I am a simple man."

The North King laughed and shook his head, making the bones that ran down his matted braids click and clack. He had allowed Hod to touch them once, even hacking one free so he could "see" it better. Gudrun was *not* a simple man; he could be kind one moment and kill a man in the next, and Hod had not allowed himself to form an attachment or expect one in return. He also had no illusions about the risk he had just taken. He'd told Gudrun about his father, King Banruud, in the early days of his captivity. It had helped Gudrun understand him—and trust him—even though Hod hardly understood himself.

"No. Not simple," Gudrun grunted. "Not at all. You are far too clever, and I do not trust you, Blind Hod. Not completely. But I understand you better now. Tonight . . . we will feast with your father. And we will see what can be done about retrieving the Songr."

20

THORNS

Ghisla and Alba were escorted to a well-appointed chamber on the back corner of Chief Benjie's keep and told to enjoy a brief respite before dinner. Berne rose up from the water's edge in green shelves, and the chieftain's keep occupied the perfect vantage point, with water on one side, meadows edged in forest on the other. The windows of their room were guarded by huge trees, and Ghisla thought if they were so inclined, they could climb from the window and scale them, which oddly comforted her. She liked the idea of an escape route, even if she had nowhere to escape to. The branches were fat and sprawling, perfect for climbing, unlike the prickly pines on Temple Hill.

Water for bathing was brought in by a handful of aging porters, and Ghisla and Alba washed and changed into fresh gowns because they dared not sleep and be caught unprepared when they were summoned. Ghisla unwound, brushed, and rewrapped her hair and then assisted Alba with her tresses.

"I would like nothing better than to crawl into that bed and be done with this evening," Alba said as Ghisla ran a brush down the silvery length. "But I am too hungry to beg off, and Father will insist I make an appearance. Benjie is odious, but I don't mind his wife, Lady

Beatrice, though I would have liked a small repast to tide us over." Ghisla's stomach growled in agreement, and Alba laughed, her eyes meeting Ghisla's in the mirror.

"I do not think they planned on us," Ghisla murmured. "This visit seems to have been hastily arranged on every front. They are scrambling to be ready for a feast and have had no time to think of their individual guests . . . even if that guest is the princess herself."

"It was the arrival of the Northmen that necessitated it. Benjie was caught unawares, as usual. I do not know why Father would have brought us here otherwise."

Alba grew pensive and Ghisla's tension mounted. It was an odd visit indeed.

"You don't think . . . you don't think he will just . . . give me . . . to the North King, do you, Liis?"

Ghisla gasped. "No, Alba. A contract would have to be drawn. Such things take ages and planning. There would be celebrations and signings. You are the princess of Saylok."

"They have been given gold and grain and even land. Yet they keep returning."

"You will not be tossed at the North King's feet like a bag of silver. You are the hope of Saylok."

"I am a pawn," Alba said, her voice flat.

Ghisla's hand stilled in the princess's hair. "It would be far more likely that I would be given away. The king is already speaking of a marriage between Elayne and Aidan of Adyar. He will marry us off first. You are his prize."

Alba shook her head, and her white hair danced around her shoulders. "You are the only one of us he has any use for. I don't know if that makes things better for you . . . or worse."

They waited for three hours to be summoned, and when they finally were, it was Benjie and his lady, Beatrice, who knocked on their door to accompany them to the hall where the feast would take place.

Ghisla hated Chief Benjie even more than she despised Banruud, and she made no effort to hide her feelings. The chieftain was bothered by her disdain; he thought she should grovel for his favor. He took every opportunity to demean and dismiss her, and this night was no different.

"She should not be present," Benjie said, not looking at Ghisla. "The other daughters are not in attendance."

"But I will be in attendance," Alba protested. Lady Beatrice did not dare argue with her husband.

"Yes. Of course. You are the princess," Benjie said. "We have not set a place for her at the king's table. She will stay in her room."

"But . . . ," Alba argued.

"It is just as well. I have no wish to be there," Ghisla said. "The company in Berne has never been to my liking." She curtsied deeply, excusing herself from the princess, and bid them all good night.

Alba cleared her throat to hide her laughter, and Benjie sputtered, but Ghisla turned back toward the chamber, grateful to be excused from any official duty. Benjie thought he'd insulted her, but he had given her what she wished for most: an hour or two of solitude.

"You will make sure there is something sent to my quarters?" Alba insisted to Benjie's wife. "Neither of us have eaten all day."

"Of course, Princess," she soothed, and dispatched a servant to see that it was done. Ghisla shut the door, bolted it, and fell across the huge bed, tugging at the heavy coil of her hair. Her head ached and her neck screamed, and the gold pins that kept her braid in place felt like twenty six-inch thorns. She pulled them free and unraveled her braid, running her fingers through it almost frantically, moaning in pain and relief as her hair tumbled down her back. She brushed the tangles free, her eyes closed, sparing a thought for poor Alba, who would have to endure her braid and her crown for several more hours.

Ten minutes later, a knock sounded—supper—and she rose, grateful for Alba's thoughtfulness. She was famished, and she would have gone to bed hungry if not for her. The servant would have to forgive her streaming hair.

She unbolted the door, eager, but it was not a kitchen boy or a serving wench on the other side.

"You will come to the hall," Banruud said, eyeing her unbound tresses.

"I have been disinvited."

"Benjie forgets himself."

"I do not want to sup with him."

"You will sup with me."

"But I have taken down my hair."

"Good. I prefer it that way."

He held out his arm. There was something there, in the set of his mouth and the hollows of his cheeks, even the way his hairline came to a peak directly above the grooves between his eyes, that reminded her of Hod. It had been obvious to her that the king was Bayr's sire—his size, his movement, his midnight hair were all repeated in Bayr—but Hod was there too, and sometimes she studied the king's face too long, too often, trying to see him. The king had misinterpreted her searching look more than once.

"You will not eat if you do not come to the hall. The North King has requested that you sing."

Ah. So that was it.

She didn't want to sing. She didn't want to sit in the hall amid three dozen warriors who ate like wolves and belched like frogs and skewered anyone who disagreed with them. But she was hungry, and if the king said she would not eat, she would not eat.

She settled her hand on his arm and gritted her teeth.

"You are wise, Daughter."

"And you are gracious, King," she purred.

They were announced at the door: "Liis of Leok and His Majesty, Banruud of Berne, King of Saylok." Those who were sitting rose, and there was a quiet clamor about their combined entrance, but Ghisla did not let her eyes rove the hall. She kept her gaze fixed and her face frozen.

She'd learned that looking at men only encouraged them, and the Bernians were the worst of the lot. Their chieftain had allowed the clan to fall into disarray. Mayhaps it was the way he governed, taxing his people into the ground while placating marauders, but his warriors were more vicious and less disciplined than those of any of the other clans. Aidan of Adyar had complained mightily that the Bernians had begun to steal from and plunder the farms and villages on his border. Bayr had sent emissaries complaining of the same in Dolphys, but Banruud ignored Bayr and attempted to bribe the Chieftain of Adyar. Banruud was no fool, and he'd noticed Aidan's interest in Elayne of Ebba. When they'd left Adyar two days ago, she'd heard Banruud's parting salvo: "It is time for the past to be done away with. The daughters of the temple will be given back to their clans—or to new clans in marriage. They serve no purpose in the temple. We must find you a wife, Aidan."

Banruud escorted her to a seat at the high table next to Alba, who was seated on his left. Benjie and Lady Beatrice sat on his right, and thankfully conversation with that end of the table was impossible.

Ghisla sat with her spine straight but her eyes on her plate, wanting only to eat and be done—hopefully Banruud would not keep her or Alba past a song or two.

"There was a seat for you after all," Alba murmured, barely moving her lips. "And Benjie has angered my father. It's been lovely so far."

It was far from lovely. The conversation was stilted, and every man had his hand on his sword. The Northmen did not seem to trust the king or the Chieftain of Berne, and they wouldn't eat what was put before them. Instead, their king stood and traded his plate with Benjie, letting it clatter on the table, food dripping from every side. His men followed suit, trading their plates with the warriors of Berne and the king's party until they were satisfied with their selections. Ghisla had her plate taken three times before the swapping was complete.

Banruud was not amused, but he tolerated the North King's suspicion, as no one had dared to touch his plate. As a result, he finished before everyone else. Ghisla ate as quickly as she could, knowing at any minute she would be called upon and her opportunity to fill her stomach would come to an end, but the king noticed her hunger and her haste and rose to his feet, ever spiteful, ever small. She put down her knife and fork and gulped from the tepid wine in her cup. She wanted water. Her throat was dry and the room was too warm.

"We will have some entertainment," Banruud said, raising his goblet. "As requested by King Gudrun. This is Liis of Leok, a daughter of the temple. She will sing to you."

Banruud offered her his hand, insisting she rise.

She took it but released it immediately, and the king settled back into his chair. All eyes lifted to her face, including those of the North King, who sat directly across from Banruud at a similarly high table, surrounded by warriors with similarly furrowed brows. King Gudrun wore his eyes rimmed in black like the keepers, but his hair hung in braided coils down his back. The top was gathered into a knot pierced by animal bones to keep it from falling in his eyes. His men wore variations of the same thing. Leather hose and tunics studded with metal, swords strapped across their bodies, and blades bound to their boots with long leather straps.

They were a frightening lot, but not at all unfamiliar. She'd been raised in the Northlands, and men like these had roamed Tonlis and every village that had dotted the landscape. She was not unacquainted with the North King either. His name had visited many a charred memory. Once he had let her live, though he had made no attempt to assist her. She doubted he would remember.

She began with the song of Saylok, as was the tradition. Had the chieftains and warriors of the other clans been the audience, they would have pounded their fists and clasped their braids, but Gudrun yawned when she finished, unimpressed. She felt much the same way about the song and could hardly blame him.

"I fear your woman attempts to sing us to sleep, Banruud," Gudrun said, his mouth twisted in mockery. "And I do not wish to have my throat cut while I slumber."

"Mayhaps the lady knows a song of the North?" someone suggested from the table behind King Gudrun. The voice was low, a quiet suggestion for his sire, but Ghisla's heart stuttered in recognition. She craned her neck, breaking her own rule, and then caught herself. She was being foolish. She had stopped hearing Hod long ago.

"What song would you like to hear, King Gudrun?" she asked, her eyes trained on his brow so she wouldn't have to look in his eyes.

"Sing the begetting song," a Northman belched off to the left, and the men around him laughed.

"Yes. Let us hear that song," the North King said, nodding. "I've been assured you know many of the Songr songs."

"It is hardly appropriate for the occasion," she demurred. *Who had assured him of such a thing?*

King Banruud waved his hand, dismissing her reservations. "Give the king what he wants, Daughter."

She raised her chin and lifted her eyes to the back wall. The head of a giant, black bear was mounted on a column, his teeth bared, his snout wrinkled, performing even in death. They had a great deal in common, she and that bear. She took a deep breath and sang the old song, divorcing herself from the memory of the last time she'd sung it, holding Hod's hand on the hillside, letting him see her people dance in his thoughts.

Men who need kisses
Make babes who need kisses.
Babes who grow up
Become men who need kisses.

Men who need kisses
Chase women for kisses.

"And . . . begetting begins again," she sang, folding her hands primly in front of her.

She sang it again, faster, as it was designed to be sung, and the Northmen all joined in on the last line. "And . . . begetting begins again."

"Again!" the North King brayed.

She sang it once more, her tongue skipping over the words so quickly she had no space to breathe, and the whole room clapped and joined in on the ending, cheering the effort.

She inclined her head in a little bow and took a cleansing breath, waiting for his next request.

The demands came, one after the other, all songs of the Northlands, and she sang them, as she'd been instructed.

After a dozen numbers, the North King clapped loudly and banged his cup on the table, and his men followed suit.

"You must sing us another before the night is over, Liis of Leok," Gudrun insisted. "But we must entertain you now."

Ghisla sank gratefully into her chair.

"We do not have a woman with beautiful, golden hair to sing to you," Gudrun said. "But perhaps we can amuse you some . . . other way."

King Banruud nodded, magnanimous, indicating Gudrun should proceed.

"Where is Blind Hod?" Gudrun said, and his warriors shouted, stomping their feet and banging their goblets in anticipation.

If Ghisla had not been seated, she would have fallen.

"Stand up, Hod. You must let our new friends see you." There was a shoving and a shuffle, and a gray-robed man rose reluctantly from the table behind the North King. He was thin and grim, though his furrowed forearms bespoke strength and his shoulders were wide beneath the cowl of his robe. He shoved it back, revealing a tight, black braid that ran down the center of his skull. The sides of his head were shaved smooth above well-shaped ears and a lean, squared-off jaw.

When he lifted his eyes, they were an empty green.

Alba gasped and Banruud leaned forward in interest, but Ghisla could not feel her fingertips or the tip of her nose, and the room had started to darken around the edges. She swayed, knocking into Alba, and reached for the princess to steady herself.

"Liis?" Alba asked. "Liis, are you all right? You are so pale."

But she could not speak. She could only tremble and stare as the Northman made his way around the tables, clearing his way with his staff, until he stood in the middle of the floor, between the two opposing sides.

"Father, Liis is not well," Alba murmured. "May we be excused?"

Banruud ignored the question, or mayhaps he didn't hear. He too was entranced.

"Hod is blind. Do you see his eyes?" Gudrun asked, warming to his game. He had rapt attention on every side, and the Northmen were beaming with anticipation.

"When we first met young Hod on the shores of Saylok, we thought he was a phantom come to kill us. Instead, we tried to kill him, and discovered the lad was quite handy with a stick. He still got beat within an inch of his life, but he gave as good as he got—maybe better—for he lived and one of my men died."

"Two, my king. He killed two," someone said.

"You found him on the shores of Saylok?" Benjie interrupted, like Hod was a box of treasure or an exotic crustacean.

"Indeed we did. He is one of you . . . though now . . . he is one of us."

The Northmen guffawed and banged their fists at Gudrun's flare for drama.

Amy Harmon

"We tried to kill him every day for about a month. Threw him off the boat, told him to swim after us, and left him behind. But he caught up to us hours later when we hit the doldrums. He could hear us—imagine that—for miles."

"And if you hadn't hit the doldrums?" Alba spoke up, her voice ringing with curiosity. "What would . . . Hod . . . have done then?"

"He would have died or learned to swim faster," the North King leered. The men around him laughed again.

"I saw him once . . . years ago. In a contest on the mount. He is an archer. But he cheats," Benjie insisted. The Northmen grumbled and guffawed.

"He cheats?" the North King repeated, and he laughed loudly. "How does a blind man cheat, Hod?"

"Well, I do hear far better than most," Hod answered, and the sound of his voice crashed over her, tossing her about like a boat on the sea. She was going to be sick, but Hod continued, seemingly unbothered by her presence.

"Tell us what you hear," Gudrun insisted, enjoying himself immensely.

"Three Bernian warriors stand near the doors," he said. "They do not trust me. I can hear it in their heartbeats and the way they have shifted their weight to the balls of their feet. They are ready to rush me if need be. The man behind the king has drawn his sword."

"You can hear a man's thoughts?" Benjie sneered.

"No. I can hear his intention. His indrawn breath, his dry mouth, his disbelieving huff. His pounding heart and his grinding teeth. Sometimes, I can hear the blink of an eye. I can hear the whisper of an arrow in flight and the snick of a blade. I can smell the wine on the breath of your cook. I hope he is your cook. Otherwise, you have a stranger preparing your food."

The Northmen laughed.

"Where is my cook?" Benjie looked around the room. "I don't see him."

"He is in the kitchen," Hod answered. He cocked his head. "But he is heading here now. His belch is wafting behind him."

Alba laughed, just a tinkling of sound that was hardly more than a sigh, but Hod turned his head toward her, acknowledging her appreciation. An instant later he was spinning away, his staff circling his head, and several blades clattered to the stone floor, swatted from the air with Hod's stick.

Three of Gudrun's men had thrown their knives, each from a different direction, and they all stomped their approval.

"You see?" Gudrun said, turning his palm. "He is quite difficult to surprise."

"Do you know how to kill a man . . . or only to evade killing?" King Banruud asked.

"I did not think you would appreciate such a demonstration," Hod said evenly.

Gudrun roared with laughter. "Would you like him to kill one of your men, Banruud? Perhaps one of yours, Chieftain?"

Hod removed the bow across his back and sheathed his staff in its place. He withdrew an arrow from his quiver, and the room stilled. Every man was armed, but no one trusted the other, and a nocked arrow was an imminent threat.

"There is a mounted bear on the far wall. I killed him with a single shot through his bawling mouth to the back of his throat," Benjie boasted. "Let me see you put an arrow near his head."

"I can't," Hod answered.

"It is a mere fifty feet," Benjie mocked. "Surely you can hit such a target."

"I have never met a dead bear who wants to kill me," Hod said. "I cannot hear what doesn't have a heartbeat."

The Northmen laughed uproariously.

"I do better with living targets. But there is an owl perched above you. He has a fine set of feathers." With a steady swing, Hod brought his bow up and released an arrow toward the rafters. A rush of feathers and a flapping of wings was evidence of how close he came.

"You missed," King Banruud mocked.

"I didn't. I simply had no desire to kill him, though he left something behind."

A feather drifted lazily above Hod's head, and he plucked it from the air.

Alba clapped, delighted, but before the others could join in, Hod lifted his bow again and shot another arrow into the network of beams above them. A rat the size of a man's foot fell with a clatter and a thud onto Lady Beatrice's plate, completely skewered by the arrow.

Her shriek and Benjie's howl were confirmation of his success.

He sheathed his bow and retrieved his staff, and when Benjie flung the dead rat at him, he neatly sidestepped the gory projectile and bowed to the king, indicating his demonstration finished.

Banruud clapped, appreciative.

"Impressive, very impressive," Banruud said. But Gudrun was not finished. He projected his voice above the praise for Hod and raised his arms to gather all eyes once more.

"Hod has been my valued servant for many years. But I will lend his services to you, King Banruud. I will return him to Saylok. In exchange for the Songr." The North King pointed at Ghisla.

The room was silent for a single, indrawn breath. A stunned second passed before Banruud exhaled on a disbelieving laugh. "The singer?" he asked. "You wish to trade me a blind man for a daughter of the temple?"

Ghisla had already been rendered senseless by Hod's presence, and the North King's words fell around her, meaningless and surreal.

Hod was also unmoved. His chest didn't rise and fall like he was winded from his efforts or from distress. He simply stood, perfectly still, listening without expression, but Ghisla could not drag her eyes from his face.

"What use have I for a blind archer?" Banruud persisted. "You offend me with this suggestion."

"A king and country can never have too many loyal sons," Gudrun said. "Especially ones so skilled in staying alive."

"I cannot trade a daughter of the temple. She belongs to her clan first."

"She belonged to the Northlands first. You should return her to us."

"She is of Leok," the king spat out.

"No. She is a Songr. Of Tonlis. I spared her life myself. Many years ago." Gudrun's voice was perfectly mild and without accusation. He looked at Ghisla. "Do you remember Tonlis, Songr? Do you remember your king?"

Ghisla's throat had closed and her memory wailed. *Do you remember Tonlis?* She remembered Tonlis. She remembered the soldiers and the smoke and the stench. She remembered it all, though she had tried for a decade to forget it. Alba reached for her hand beneath the table.

"I am her king! She belongs to me," Banruud said. His voice was hard and his words dripped with displeasure.

"And your daughter? Does she belong to you?"

Alba flinched, and Ghost's face filled Ghisla's thoughts. It was as if the North King knew all and was quietly enflaming Banruud, ember by burning ember.

"Princess Alba is the hope of Saylok. The pride of our people. But as her father . . . it is my duty to make a match that will aid the country and my daughter. I have great hope for a union between the Northlands and Saylok. One that will benefit both lands."

"And she is very beautiful," Gudrun said. "It would not be a hardship to bed her."

Even Gudrun's men were stunned into silence at their leader's provocative disrespect. The North King waited for Banruud to respond, a slight smile around his lips, but his eyes were sharp and his hand was on his sword.

But it was Alba who rose slowly, her shoulders back, her hand still in Ghisla's. Ghisla rose beside her immediately, and the clatter of steel and the scrape of chairs created a sudden maelstrom in the hall as the men around them also stood.

"I will bid you all good night," Alba said evenly. "It has been a trying day, and we will be leaving on the morrow."

The North King stood as well, inclining his head. His men rumbled to their feet around him.

"Of course, Princess. Let us save this talk until we are alone."

It was another blow, another volley oozing with inuendo, but it was not answered by the king, the chieftain, or their men.

On wooden legs, Ghisla followed Alba from the room, several members of the king's guard falling in around them, and the earth-shattering summit came to a close.

21

STRIDES

"I have never heard such a song," Alba said. "The one about begetting." They lay side by side in the large bed, the chieftain's keep creaking around them, the wind nudging the trees, and the leaves hissing back. Neither of them had been able to talk about the events that had transpired. They'd readied themselves for bed with nary a word, but the shock had worn off with their silence.

"It is a song for weddings," Ghisla answered. "For marriage."

"I've never been to a wedding," Alba mused, wistful, and Ghisla was startled into silence once more. Such a commonplace thing in any culture had become so rare that a sixteen-year-old princess had never witnessed it.

"I did not know you weren't from Leok," Alba whispered. "Do the others know?"

"Master Ivo does. I'm sure it has been discussed among the keepers. I once was afraid I would be sent away if anyone found out. But it hardly seems important now."

"Is it as King Gudrun said?"

"Before I came to the mount—when I was a girl—I lived in a place called Tonlis. In the Northlands. But that was long ago, and I am not a Northlander anymore. King Gudrun has no claim to me."

"And Father will never give you away."

The knowledge was not a comfort to her, though she knew Alba sought to reassure her even as she feared it would be her own fate.

"It is not the king or the Northlands or even leaving Saylok that frightens me," Alba whispered.

"No?"

"No. I am afraid I will never see Bayr again," Alba confessed. "I do not speak of him because it hurts too much. But that is what I fear most."

Ghisla reached out and took Alba's hand. She did not tell her all would be well. She couldn't. Not when she was convinced all would not be well.

"Will you sing to me, Liis?" Tears leaked from the corners of her eyes.

"Of course. And tomorrow we will go home," Ghisla murmured. "You have nothing to fear." *Yet.*

"Sing the one about the little bat," Alba begged, sounding like the child she'd been.

"Oh, Alba. Not that one," Ghisla moaned. She couldn't sing that one. Not tonight. Not while she clutched Alba's hand.

"He cannot see, but he's not scared, he swoops and glides up in the air. His joy is full, his wings are strong. He dances to a distant song," Alba sang. "I always thought it such a lovely little song. To be free and surrounded by those who love us most. What more could a living creature want?"

"What indeed?" Ghisla murmured.

"Please, Liis. Please sing it. It comforts me," Alba pled, and Ghisla relented as she always did, but Alba was not consoled. Her misery echoed in her memories, and Ghisla, with their hands clasped and the song reverberating between her and the princess, could not escape them.

Six-year-old Alba sat atop Bayr's shoulders. Her arms were spread and her hair streamed out behind her. He was running, making her fly, and her remembrance was painted in joy.

"Bayr promised me he would come back," Alba cried as the song ended. "He promised."

"Someone I loved once promised me the same thing," Ghisla said.

"What happened?" Alba almost sounded afraid to ask, as if she knew.

"He never did." Until now. But *had* he come back?

"Why?" Alba asked, mournful.

"I don't know. Some promises . . . are impossible to keep."

"I fear that's true," Alba murmured. "But . . . you're not angry?"

"Sometimes I am angry," Ghisla admitted. Sometimes she was so angry she lay facedown and sang her anger into the earth until the grass turned brown and the ground around her cracked with her furious song. "But most of the time, I simply miss him."

Oh, how she had missed him.

He had lived among the Northmen, that much was evident. But why? And why was he here? How would she see him? How would she tell him she had given up long ago?

"I miss Bayr every day. There is a hole in my heart," Alba said. "And I fear it will always be there."

"You were very close," Ghisla said, her voice strangled.

"And now . . . we are nothing," Alba said dully.

For a time, they lay together in the dark, their hands clasped, and when Alba finally found relief in sleep, Ghisla allowed herself to grieve.

Hod did not leave the chieftain's keep with the Northmen but doubled back on his own. In the darkness, everyone was a threat, and he did not want to be seen lurking in the shadows. He found the room where Ghisla and the princess were quartered and climbed a tree where he could eavesdrop without being observed.

The North King had created a spectacle in the hall. He'd dangled Hod like a carrot with his ridiculous talk of a trade, insulted the princess, and tossed Ghisla's history onto the pyre all to provoke the king. She'd had no warning of his presence, and Hod had heard her distress, her racing heart and her constricted breath, and he'd put up a wall against her, unable to concentrate on his audience—and the things they hurled at him—and still listen to her. But he was listening to her now.

The two women were comforting each other, their voices bleak and their conversation quiet. Alba begged for the song about the bat, and Hod was catapulted back to the temple mount, standing in the shadow of the temple listening to little Alba plead for the same song.

"Bayr promised me he would come back," Alba mourned.

Bayr had never returned to the mount?

"Someone I loved once promised me the same thing," Ghisla murmured.

Someone she loved once. Did she love him still?

"What happened?" Alba asked, almost fearful.

"He never did."

Hod's heart cracked and bled, knowing Ghisla spoke of him. No, he never had . . . and she'd given him no reason to believe she would welcome him.

"You're not angry?" Alba asked.

"Sometimes I am angry. But most of the time, I simply miss him," Ghisla answered.

He was angry too. The anger had become a constant companion. But he had missed her more than he hated her. He had loved her more than he hated her. And right now, he could not hate her at all.

Eventually, Alba fell asleep, the cadence of her breathing and the tempo of her heart signaling she'd succumbed to slumber. But Ghisla did not sleep. She cried. Her weeping was not a moan or a wail. It was a catch in her chest and an ongoing, valiant attempt to breathe quietly so Alba would not hear her distress.

A soft knock on her chamber door came after she'd just begun to drift off, her tears finally abating, her weariness deep. She woke immediately, her pulse quickening.

"The king is asking for you, Liis of Leok," the guard murmured.

Her heart raced, but she rose and, after a moment of shuffling, followed the guard down the corridor to the king's chambers.

Hod's anger rose again, so palpable it flooded his mouth. He should have left then and saved himself the agony of their interaction. But he couldn't pull himself away. He couldn't bear not to hear her, even if it meant burning himself alive while he listened.

Their voices were obscured by walls and the patter of rain that had just begun to fall, making his perch in the tree even more precarious, but he did not leave.

"Lie beside me," the king demanded.

She did not protest and her heartbeat did not alter; the king's request was not out of the ordinary. The taste in Hod's mouth became metallic, like he'd licked his blade and cut his tongue. Mayhaps he had. It felt forked behind his teeth.

"What will happen on the morrow?" Ghisla asked the king.

"It does not concern you."

"The North King thinks it does."

"Shall I give you to him?" Banruud hissed. His heartbeat echoed oddly, like it ricocheted in his head, and his breaths were harsh with pain.

"If you wish." Her words were devoid of emotion.

"He would not make you his queen; he seeks only to goad me."

"I do not wish to be his queen. I do not wish to be your queen."

He grunted, like he was all too aware of her wishes, and she didn't press him further. She began to sing, no words, just music, her voice a harp to the anguished, and the bitterness in Hod's mouth became longing in his veins.

She carried on for half an hour before the king slept, the odd echo in his head fading with her song. She eased herself off the bed, moving slowly, painfully, and walked back down the corridors, twenty-one tired strides to her chamber door. The creak of the handle told him she'd entered, but she didn't cross the floor and crawl into her bed. She drank two glasses of water, her throat working; she'd cried and sung herself into a great thirst. Then she washed her face, cleaned her teeth, and dressed, shrugging off one gown for another and pulling on her shoes.

Her movements were almost as intoxicating to him as her voice. To hear her swish about, to breathe, to simply *be*, when she'd lived only in his memory for so long was irresistible.

She stopped in front of her window and unlatched the shutters, and he froze, realizing he'd been careless. He'd lost himself in listening, and though he'd climbed high enough in the tree to escape detection from the ground, he was directly across from her window. She would see him, resting in the tree like the bat in her song.

She opened the shutters inch by inch, as if guarding against the screech of hinges, and he swung down, dropping from the lowest limb an instant before she leaned out into the dark coolness and inhaled deeply. He hugged the wall of the keep directly below her, listening, always listening.

She was climbing out. A tiny huff of exertion, a rustling of leaves, and a murmur in the tree signaled that she had cleared the ledge and settled herself on the branch nearest the window. She breathed for a moment, plotting her course, and he inched back, sliding along the wall until he turned the corner.

Where was she going? The woods were full of Northmen and Bernians, neither of which would hesitate to harm—or kidnap—her. It was not safe in the trees. It was not safe anywhere.

Then she said his name.

She could not see him; he was almost certain of it. He would have heard the moment of sight and the change in her breath. He would have felt her eyes.

"Hod?" she said again, but the word was a moan. "Where have you been?"

His answer hovered on his lips. He would reveal himself. Right now. He would tell her everything and plead for her to come with him. He would take her to Gudrun and insist that he give them safe passage to the Northlands. His hopes soared . . . and immediately sank.

Gudrun would not help him.

When he discovered her gone, Banruud would most likely declare war, which the Northmen were not yet prepared for. They'd brought a small contingent for this meeting with King Banruud and the Chieftain of Berne. They had a plan, and Ghisla was not part of it. Gudrun would probably kill him, and Ghisla would be at the mercy of yet another king.

Hod clenched his teeth and made fists of his hands, denying himself. Denying her. He dared not even speak. Alba slept mere feet away, and the king's men patrolled nearby, bristling at every sound. Nothing would be accomplished in the chieftain's keep, not tonight, and mayhaps not for some time to come.

She sat in the tree until just before dawn, as if she waited for him, but he did not show himself. Instead he stayed, crouched beside the wall, holding his vigil until she slid back along the heavy branch and returned to her chamber, barring the window behind her.

⁓

"Have I made you angry, my blind warrior? Are you sulking because I have attempted to trade you for the Songr?" Gudrun became affectionate and magnanimous when he thought he had won. He was eating like he'd just been through battle, slurping up the grease on a platter of lamb with great hunks of bread, one of which he tossed to Hod. He'd insisted Hod join him for breakfast, but Hod didn't eat with Gudrun for the same reason he didn't sit among his men. He needed his hands free and his senses sharp. He would break his fast when Gudrun left the table.

He doubted the North King had slept. The sun had not yet begun to warm the air, and the mist from the water sat thick on the ground, muting the early morning chatter of the birds and the movement of Gudrun's men in and out of the chateau and back and forth to the docks. They were preparing to sail. A settlement had been reached.

"I am not angry. I simply do not understand your strategy, Sire," Hod responded, voice even.

"I met with King Banruud last night. After the feast. Where were you?" Gudrun's tone changed, suspicion tinging his words. "I sent men to fetch you, but you had disappeared. You could have witnessed the drafting of a momentous agreement."

"I was sitting in a tree, listening to a woman sing."

Gudrun snorted, but the pathetic confession seemed to reassure him. "He will not give me the Songr."

"Imagine my surprise."

"Ahh. You *are* angry." Gudrun tsked as he hacked off a large piece of lamb and fed it to his teeth.

"I don't understand your play," Hod said again.

Gudrun washed his mouthful down with loud gulps of ale and wiped his fingers on his trousers.

"You said he would not want to part with the woman. You were right. I simply wanted to make King Banruud feel as though he'd won and I'd relented. It made negotiations much easier later on. And it provided an opportunity to put your skills on display."

"My skills," Hod said, voice flat.

"I want to make your father love you, don't you see? I am repairing a bond." His tone was mischievous, and Hod heard his grin. When he did not elucidate but began preparing another bite, Hod prodded him, just as Gudrun expected him to.

"He does not know he is my father, Sire, and there is no bond to repair," Hod said.

"He does. I have told him," Gudrun said, swallowing.

"What purpose does that serve?" Hod whispered. He was not surprised. Gudrun used every weapon at his disposal, and Hod had supplied him with it, long ago. It had provided him with a story any man could understand: the blind, bastard son of a king seeks revenge on those who rejected him. It was only a matter of time before Gudrun wielded the information against him.

"It serves my purposes, Hod." Gudrun thumped his chest to emphasize his words. The action made him belch, and he laughed again. He was in fine spirits this morning.

"I have agreed to bed—er, wed—the daughter." Gudrun laughed at his wordplay. "In exchange I have promised to be a very good North King and stay in my own lands. The Northlands will not attack Saylok, and Saylok will not raid the Northlands. It's all very civilized and familial. We will set sail today, and I will return next month to retrieve my bride."

"Retrieve your bride . . . where?"

"I've been invited to Temple Hill." Gudrun spread his arms and sat back in his chair, making the rungs groan against his girth. "To the castle of the King of Saylok. The mighty Banruud wants to show his people that he has tamed the North King and saved the clans from being overrun by Northmen."

"I see."

"You will not be sailing with us, Hod," Gudrun added.

Hod waited, tensed.

"You will go with Banruud to his hill. I have convinced him I must have a man I trust on the mount to prepare for my arrival and to ensure that no treachery is afoot. If he kills you, he can't very well expect me to hold to my end of the bargain."

"You do not intend to hold to it regardless."

"Yes. But he thinks he has the upper hand. He has invited us to the mount during his Tournament of the King. He informs me that the fiercest warriors from every clan will be in attendance. I have told him I worry I will be ambushed." The irony was as thick as the grease on his plate.

"It is a valid concern," Hod murmured.

"The king insists that a wedding at the end of the tournament will be well received by the chieftains. Coronations and celebrations are done during the week, as I understand it."

"This is true."

"I have agreed to his plan with great . . . reluctance."

"Understandably."

"Banruud has asked that you be ready to depart today. I doubt he will welcome you. But you must make yourself useful to him . . . until I arrive."

Hod's fingers flexed around his staff, but he nodded, impassive. "Very well."

Gudrun wanted a reaction, and Hod did not give him one. The king's irritation was evident in his exhale. "You will have until then to make the Songr want you again," he murmured. "You should thank me. Of course, if she is the king's Songr, you may not want her." He sucked at his teeth. "She is rather appealing, Hod. Not plain at all. Long hair like spun gold. Sweet little bottom and enough breasts to fill a man's hands. Her eyes are the bluest I've ever seen—shocking, how blue—and her mouth is a rosebud, soft and pink and plump; it is a shame you cannot look at her."

"I've always seen her well enough."

Gudrun chuffed, and Hod did not know whether the man grinned or glowered. He was silent, studying Hod, and when he leaned toward him, his voice intimate and low, Hod did not shrink.

"Do not fail me, Hod." His greasy breath wafted over Hod's lips. "And do not cross me."

"I have never crossed any man," Hod replied softly. "They have crossed me."

Gudrun chuckled, this time in earnest, and he sat back in his chair, the tension leaving him. "If you do, the little Songr is mine. I may take her yet."

If Banruud and the North King had addressed terms of an accord, they were not announced. Instead, the Northmen prepared to sail, and the king's party prepared to depart from Garbo. The Bernians seemed relieved—overjoyed even—to see both, and they'd gathered on the docks and around the chieftain's keep to point and speculate.

The king's men were in their saddles and the wagons loaded, and the North King and his men, including Hod, were lined up to bid them adieu. The only point of contention seemed to be who would leave first.

Ghisla and Alba had been escorted to the carriage, and they watched from behind the parted drapes they'd drawn over the open windows.

"Do you think they are really leaving?" Alba whispered, flabbergasted.

"Yes. I think they are." And Hod would be leaving with them. She had not slept at all, hoping he would find her. He stood beside the North King, his hand on his staff, a shield, his bow, and a small satchel slung over his shoulders. She wondered suddenly if he was listening.

"Father must have promised them something," Alba said, and her fear was palpable.

Ghisla had lain beside the king in his chamber, but she had not touched him while she sang—she always tried not to—and she had not divined his thoughts. Mayhaps next time, for Alba's sake, for both their sakes, she should.

Banruud reined his horse around and halted in front of the North King, obscuring the view from the carriage, but his words were clear.

"We have saddled a horse for your man, Gudrun. I hope his skills extend to riding."

"I will walk," Hod answered.

"You will not be able to keep up, blind man," Banruud argued.

"I will keep up well enough."

"Hod does not trust the horse between his legs," Gudrun inserted. His men laughed as he intended for them to do.

"Why not?" Banruud asked. "Surely you are not afraid?"

"I can only hear the horse," Hod explained evenly. "Their hearts are like cannons and their instincts interfere with my own. I will be of more use if I walk."

"He'll make it eventually, Highness," Gudrun said, and the Northmen laughed again.

"It is three days' hard travel to reach the hill," Banruud protested.

"Yes. I know. If I fall behind, I will catch up to you by day's end," Hod replied, unbothered.

Banruud was silent for a moment, and his horse shimmied, impatient.

"You will ride on the carriage. There. On the footman's stoop." Banruud pointed toward Ghisla and Alba. "It will not be pleasant for travel, but you will not be left behind, and you can guard the rear."

"Very well," Hod said. And without another word, he approached the carriage and swung up onto the tiny platform. The carriage bounced beneath his weight, and Alba stared at Ghisla, dumbfounded.

"The blind man is coming with us," she whispered.

Ghisla could only nod, her hand pressed over her racing heart. "It seems he is."

࿐

She was intimidated by the knowledge that Hod would hear her every word. The bumps and jostles of the wheels and the thundering clap of horses' hooves would not be enough to shield their conversation from his ears. She sat in agonized silence, unable to believe the turn of events, and unwilling—for a multitude of reasons—to speak of them to her young companion. Alba's mood improved with each mile from Garbo, and she chattered about this and that for the first hour but then curled herself up into an impossible ball and fell asleep, her hands folded beneath her chin and her head against her knees. Ghisla had not slept in ages, and quickly succumbed as well, waking only when they stopped at midday to water the horses and eat a hasty meal. Hod was coated in dust and spent several minutes shaking out his clothes and washing the grit from his skin. The driver goaded him good-naturedly.

"Ye'll be covered again, Northman, within the hour."

Hod nodded, acknowledging the truth of the man's statement, but he washed anyway. Alba worried that he'd had nothing to eat and made sure he was given food from the provisions. She was so thoughtful that Ghisla was shamed, but she had no notion of how to speak to him when there was so much to say. And there were eyes and ears everywhere.

Before resuming their journey, Alba and Ghisla were escorted to the trees to find some seclusion to relieve themselves. It was always a difficulty for the guard when they traveled; they had to keep their distance while maintaining a protective presence. Hod was recruited to the detail, the captain of the king's guard remarking dryly that his blindness made him the perfect escort for such things. The fact that he was Gudrun's man did not seem to bother him overmuch.

It bothered Ghisla, but she did not protest. She and Alba hurried through their privacies and washed with him standing watch. It was also Hod who extended his hand to assist them back into the carriage. He helped Alba first, and when he offered his hand to Ghisla, palm up, the lines of the rune he'd made a decade before were still visible to her eyes. Very softly, she rested her hand on his. His reaction was immediate, a tightening of his lips, a flutter of his lids, and Ghisla's breath caught.

His fingers brushed over the thick, star-shaped scar on her palm, and his brow furrowed. She dared not stand with her hand clutched in his and climbed the steps quickly so she could let go, but his hand tightened around hers.

"What happened to your hand, Ghisla?" he insisted, his voice flat. It was the first time he'd acknowledged her at all, and he'd used her real name, the name only he knew.

"You called her Ghisla. She is Liis," Alba corrected. "Release her please, Northman."

Hod did so immediately, but he didn't move.

"What happened to her hand?" He directed the question at Alba instead. He stood in the doorway of the carriage, his face perfectly void of emotion, but his voice was lethal.

"It was burned," Ghisla said.

"You had best keep your distance, Blind Hod," Alba murmured, urging him to close the carriage door. The guard was mounted and the driver in place.

"When did this happen?" He was addressing Ghisla now, but Alba answered.

"It was many years ago. It does not pain the lady anymore. Now . . . please. Retreat."

The driver called down, impatient. "Are you ready, Northman?"

Hod stepped back and shut the door without another word. They felt him hoist himself onto the footman's stoop, and the driver cracked

his whip. The carriage lurched forward, falling into line with the caval-
cade, armed riders taking up positions on each side.

Alba frowned at Ghisla in confusion.

"How odd . . . and impertinent. He should not have asked something so personal. And what was it he called you? *Ghisla?*"

Ghisla was too shaken to speak. She could still feel Hod's fingertips
against her palm.

Alba tipped her pretty head, studying Ghisla with new eyes.

"Was that your name? Do you know Blind Hod?"

"His name is not Blind Hod," Ghisla said, her voice low. She hated
when people called him that, as if his sightlessness was part of his name.
"He is Hod. And I do not . . . know him." Once she had. Once she'd
known him better than she knew herself.

"But you did," Alba guessed, nodding, warming to her conclusion.
She crowed and clapped, thrilled at the surprising discovery.

"Alba," Ghisla protested softly. "Please. Please. Let us not speak
of this." Hod would be able to hear, but that was not what scared her
most. Any familiarity between them would be noticed and punished.
Alba knew this. It was why she'd immediately warned Hod to not linger.

"He does not act like the other Northmen. He is quiet and . . . very
clean. He reminds me a little of Bayr too. He is humble, though he has
every reason to be proud. He does not boast or brag like most men do."
She paused and then made her pronouncement. "I like him very much."

"You would, Alba. You have a soft spot for the strange." Ghisla
winced at her own words. Hod would think them critical when they
were not. She too had a soft spot for the strange, and Hod's peculiarities
had always been precious to her.

"No." Alba shook her head. "Not for the strange. For the good.
He is good."

He once was. Once, he was very good. But Ghisla didn't know
anymore. They'd been parted too long, and he was too removed. Too
different.

"I thought you seemed nervous around him. That is not like you. You are so self-contained," Alba said, prying, curious.

"I will not speak of this," Ghisla insisted again.

"All right, Liis," Alba sighed. "We will not speak of it. Your secret is safe with me."

Her sisters did not know about her past with Hod. She'd never confessed to having feelings for him, never spoken of him at all. But Ivo knew. Dagmar knew. And if Dagmar knew, Ghost knew.

It would be seen as an omen when they discovered he'd returned to the mount.

She would be warned to stay away from him and watched even more closely than before.

It made her angry. Hod had done nothing but supplicate the keepers for a place among them. He was blind, but he was fully capable and supremely well-trained in the art of the runes as well as for the defense of the temple. He'd been raised up for a purpose, and his purpose had been denied him. He'd been branded a risk, a threat, a portent, and he'd been rejected.

They could not reject him now.

He would not need or seek their acceptance. For whatever incomprehensible reason, he was now a servant of the North King, an emissary between lands, and Master Ivo would have no influence over him whatsoever.

For the first time since she'd seen Hod's face in Chief Benjie's great hall, Ghisla smiled.

22

MILES

Twenty-two miles beyond the border of Berne and a day's travel to the mount, Hod began to shout for the king's company to halt. The rain had drizzled from before sunup, and the dry, late-summer earth drank greedily, gorging itself, but by midafternoon, the road to the mount had turned to mud.

"Halt," he shouted. "King's guard, halt."

"What is it, man?" the driver hollered back. "If I stop, we'll be stuck."

"Pull up," Hod insisted, but the driver and the mounted guard around him paid him no heed.

"There are men concentrated in the trees half a mile ahead," he yelled, but the driver cracked his whip, still spurring the horses forward. "I don't like it."

He'd not traveled from Berne to the temple mount, and the way was unfamiliar, but the distant, clustered heartbeats he could hear—two dozen to the left, another dozen on the right—seemed to float above the ground, indicating bodies in the trees. The men hiding in the trees did not converse, and he couldn't divine their motives, but it was obvious that they were awaiting the caravan.

"What are you shouting about, Northman? We are one hundred strong and we ride under the king's banner. 'Tis naught but a few scared clanless taking shelter beneath the boughs," the guard nearest him grumbled back.

The caravan trundled along, the slog—and the messenger—making them foolish and resistant to his warning.

"Banruud!" he shouted, but the king, near the front of the convoy, did not rein his mount or give any indication he'd heard the warning, and the men around Hod protested his disrespect.

"The king doesn't take orders from a blind Northman," another man reprimanded him.

"Who does he think he is?" This comment came from a guard in front of the carriage. They were hearing him, but they didn't draw up.

"He rides like a lady all day but can't abide the wet," someone else mumbled. They'd laughed at his refusal to use a horse and mocked him when they thought he couldn't hear.

The driver kept on, ignoring his pleas, and the guard on either side demanded that he cease his yammering.

They weren't going to listen or even alert the riders in front of them, and he wasn't going to run alongside them, waving his arms. He'd do more good right where he was.

He could hear the women inside the carriage. They were awake and listening.

"Princess Alba," he directed. "Liis of Leok, get down on the floor and brace yourselves."

Their immediate movement indicated they had not disregarded his instructions, praise Odin. He scrambled up onto the carriage roof, grateful it was sturdy and well constructed, with cleats for an archer to balance between. He shrugged off his bow and centered his shield beneath his quiver.

The driver cursed and swung his whip, thinking Hod had come to take his reins. Hod could only turn his head against the snap, unable to guard against it, balanced as he was.

"Mind the road, man," he ordered, and he nocked an arrow and drew back on his bow. Then he waited for the hiss that confirmed his instincts. He would not be the first to shoot.

"The Northman's taking the carriage," someone yelled, and for a second he feared they would turn their weapons on him.

"Ambush!" someone yelled a moment before his voice caught in a gurgling sigh. His horse shrieked beneath him, and a volley of arrows rained into the king's caravan.

"In the trees!" the captain of the guard boomed. "They're in the trees."

The carriage driver started to pull up, but it was too late for that.

"Go, go, go," Hod roared. "And don't slow."

An arrow nicked his sleeve and he returned fire, his legs screaming as the carriage rocked, and the horses bolted. One, two, three thundering hearts. One . . . two . . . three shots. One, two, three falling bodies.

Banruud was trying to give orders, hollering from the back of his rearing horse. An arrow whistled toward him as another sank into the chest of the man to his left. Hod swiveled and aimed again, releasing three more arrows in quick succession in the direction of the wailing, incoming volleys. The man who'd almost killed the king careened from his perch and another landed in the undergrowth, the crash and snap signaling his fall.

Hod found three more beating hearts and silenced them, one by one, and thought for a moment the skirmish had been quelled; the attackers in the trees were falling or fleeing, but the dead and dying littered the way, and the carriage was not built for the battlefield. Ghisla screamed his name and Alba begged Odin for protection as the front axle snapped and a wheel split in two. The carriage flipped, tossing

Hod and the driver into the air and sending the women inside on a perilous ride.

Hod landed on his back in the mud, his bow still clasped in his hands, but his shield sent him spinning across the mire like a child sledding across the snow and tossed him into a hedge. He lay stunned for five seconds, his breath knocked from his chest, his senses scrambled.

"Hod!" Ghisla screamed his name again, and he rolled, coming to his knees to meet the ongoing threat. Horses reared and men ran, and all was chaos and cacophony around him. He couldn't distinguish foe from friend, not when the men he fought beside were as unfamiliar as those who sought to kill him. The trees had emptied.

Someone ran at him, swinging a blade, and he brought up his bow and released an arrow, point blank, into his assailant's chest. The man fell on top of him, his breath rattling through his lips, as an arrow meant for Hod hissed through the air and buried itself in his back.

"My thanks, kind sir," Hod whispered, patting the dead man's cheek. He heaved him to the side and reached for his staff, but it had come loose in his fall. He gritted his teeth, raised his bow, and held his position as he listened to the mayhem around him, trying to distinguish who needed killing. It was like sifting through sand looking for a seed, and he raged against his limitations.

Banruud had dismounted. His heart pounded, the only recognizable rhythm in the thunderous haze. Hod couldn't hear Ghisla or Alba. His terror ballooned and he bit it back, forcing them from his thoughts. He was no good to them if he was dead.

Someone rushed the king from behind, lungs rasping, heart wailing, and Hod released his arrow, glad to have an obvious target. He listened as it found its mark; the man's heart slowed . . . then dropped . . . and his howl of attack became a whoosh of air that bid goodbye to the ground.

Banruud swore and said Hod's name, acknowledging the rescue. The ruckus swelled to a fever pitch, dancing feet and clashing blades, the movements too intermingled for Hod to enter the fray, and then someone yelled, the sound triumphant, and a chorus of cheers rose in answer.

The battle was won.

Thank Odin.

Hod rose to his feet, unsteady, and went to find Ghisla.

Had Hod not warned them, it would have been much worse. The carriage was broken, the wheels split and the door caved in, but Ghisla and Alba were unharmed. They'd knocked heads as the carriage rolled, and Alba's eyes were already blackening, but they crawled out of the window and climbed down the wreckage when the cry of victory went up.

The driver limped toward them, his whip still clutched in his hand, his left arm tucked against his side, and Ghisla searched the wreckage for Hod, dread and terror warring within her. She'd screamed his name when the carriage rolled, unable to help herself, but she dare not call for him now.

One horse had a broken leg, one a broken neck. Two still stood in their harnesses, waiting to be rescued, and they nibbled at the grass at their feet as if nothing were amiss, but the worst of the battle scene was behind them.

Three dead men were still draped in the trees, arrows protruding from their chests, but most of the slain lay beneath them, piled and pinioned by other dead, including some of the king's guard. She found his staff first. It protruded from the ground like a spear, the sharpened end buried deep, and she ran to it, pulling it free before she saw him, moving toward her from the edge of the wood, covered in mud and navigating the dead with searching steps.

Then she and Alba were spotted and swarmed, the soldiers of the king rushing to inquire after their welfare, and Hod was lost to her view.

"The Northman tried to warn us. But we didn't listen," the driver confessed to the captain of the guard. "I thought he just wanted a break to stretch his legs and take a pisser, and the mud was too deep to slow."

"Were they Northmen?" someone asked, suspicious. "Maybe he was in on it."

"The Northmen sailed from Berne two days ago," Ghisla shot back. "And we left before them. How would they get ahead of us, with no horses, and hide in the trees? I also recall the blind man pleading with you to halt."

The guard had enough conscience to look ashamed, and Ghisla bit down on her cheek so she wouldn't say more. The king was pushing through his men, giving orders and demanding answers, and the speculation began.

"They're clanless," someone else suggested. "They wore no colors."

"They're Bernians," Hod said, working his way through the gathering crowd. The king turned and his men shuffled, parting for him. Ghisla stepped into the space they made, using the staff she held to clear the way. When she reached him, she took his hand and placed it on the stick.

He grimaced slightly, almost like her touch pained him, and she immediately stepped away, afraid she would bring him unwelcome attention with her care. His face was battered and one of his empty eyes was swollen shut, but he did not move like he was greatly injured, and the blood he wore did not appear to be his own.

"How do you know they were Bernians?" the captain challenged.

Hod pointed his staff toward a captured, wounded man propped against a tree. He was gray and grim, and he wouldn't live long. "He told me they were Bernian."

"And you believed him?" the captain retorted.

"He sounds Bernian, smells Bernian, and I'm guessing he looks Bernian too," Hod responded, his voice dry. "There are a few of the clanless mixed in, I'd suppose, but the Bernians knew we would be coming this way and thought they could kill a few soldiers, take the wagons, and ransom or sell two valuable women."

"Aidan of Adyar said Bernians have been attacking settlements on his border," Alba interjected. "He claimed they've been doing the same in Dolphys too. They won't fight the Northmen but are all too happy to harass their neighboring clans." The men around her shifted in discomfort, but ceased their arguing.

"String them all up," Banruud said. "Wounded and dead."

There was nowhere to go, nowhere to hide from the macabre display, and she and Alba made their way among the wounded of the guard, trying to avert their eyes from one horror as they tended to another. As instructed, the king's men dragged the Bernians, both dead and alive, to the trees they'd hidden in and strung them up, one by one, a lesson to the next band of rovers and raiders who might seek to do the same.

Two wounded Bernians, seeing their unavoidable fate, jumped up and rushed the king, who stood with his back to the gruesome work of his men, Hod at his side.

Ghisla wasn't sure if it was instinct or duty, but Hod swung his stick at their feet, taking the first man's legs out from under him. The second man was wilier, and he dodged Hod's staff as he lunged for the king. Hod pivoted and brought the stick down hard across the man's shoulders and the backs of his arms. His head bounced off the ground, and he wasn't conscious when his clansman rose up again and launched his blade at Banruud. Hod paddled the knife from the air and, with both hands, skewered the man through the back with the sharpened tip of his staff, ending the scuffle.

Hod pulled his staff free with a grimace, and the king's guard cried out, staggered by the exhibition . . . and then they clapped.

Alba shielded her eyes and Ghisla turned away, sickened by the unending death, but she heard the king commend Hod, wonder and wariness underlining his praise.

"That is three times today, blind man, that you have saved my life. It seems the North King has done me a great service. I would not have believed it had I not seen it with my own eyes."

"Indeed, Majesty. Indeed," the captain of the guard cried, his own amazement evident.

But Hod said nothing at all.

With the carriage destroyed and some of the horses scattered or deceased, the wounded rode and Hod and many others walked, including Ghisla and the princess, who shunned the suggestion that they ride with the king or one of his men. They'd seen too much killing and staunched too much blood, and they walked huddled together, averse to everyone else. Hod had felt Ghisla's revulsion and her surprise when he killed the two Bernians. He was aggrieved by it . . . and unsettled.

Shock was settling in for everyone, and they didn't get far before the king called a halt and they set up camp, circling the few wagons and erecting tents in a clearing near a creek. Hod was sent to guard the women as they washed, his blindness a convenience for the other men.

He would wash later, when the camp was sleeping, but he longed to be clean now. The driver's whip had left a long slice from his right ear to his nose, and the brambles of the hedge had marked his brow. His left eye was swollen shut, not that he needed it. He vaguely remembered his staff connecting with his cheekbone as he was tossed from the carriage roof. He was fortunate he hadn't impaled himself.

He listened to the women and the trees around them, standing watch in the only way he could, logging the creatures and sorting the sounds. Fires had been started, the scent of smoke and stew wafting up into the air. Both warmth and food would do the women good. They had submerged themselves completely, dresses and all, scrubbing at the bloodstains on their skirts and sleeves before soaping everything else.

They said very little as they washed, their splashing, their chattering teeth, and the squelch of their clothes their only communication.

They emerged from the river, the water sluicing from their limbs, and wrung out their skirts before wrapping themselves in blankets and trudging back to the tents. He followed them silently, a shadow with a staff, and when they ducked into the enclosure prepared for them, he made a shelter for himself, grateful for the provisions he'd been allotted. He'd retrieved his possessions from the carriage, and the women's trunks had been transferred into a wagon. They had dry clothes, and furs to sleep on.

But Hod didn't rest. He washed and ate and crawled into his tent. His face throbbed and his muscles ached, and he could hear Ghisla's troubled heart as she drifted off and woke again, restlessly dreaming, hardly sleeping. When she said his name, knowing full well he would hear, he rose and went to her.

The sentry outside their tent had fallen asleep an hour after he arrived, and Hod shook him awake. It would be hours before the next watch came.

"I'm awake. I'll take this shift," he reassured the man, who stumbled off toward his tent, mumbling a grateful good night.

When he entered her tent, Ghisla was awake, and when he crouched down beside her, she sat up, silently greeting him. Her heart quickened, but it did not race, and her scent prickled his skin. She was warm and close, and he felt her eyes on his face.

"Alba sleeps deeply," she murmured, "but you must listen and leave if she begins to stir."

He nodded, his throat aching, his hands on his thighs. This was not what he wanted, this hushed conversation after all these years, but he would take it.

"You are hurt," she whispered.

"I am fine."

She raised her hands slowly, communicating her intentions, but when she rested her palms against his cheeks, he had to grit his teeth. It was not pain that made him harsh when she touched him. It was impatience. He had wanted to be near her for so long that he didn't trust himself to be still. To be sane. To maintain the separation.

"Do not pull away. Please. I can help you." She misinterpreted his discomfort.

"I will not pull away," he ground out. It was the last thing he wanted to do.

She began to sing, the words so soft she barely said them, and his eyes began to stream.

Cry, cry, dear one, cry,
Let the pain out through your eyes.
Tears will wash it all away,
Cry until the bruises fade.

He groaned in relief, embarrassed by his tears, but she continued, her hands cool, her song tender, and he thought she might be crying too. He raised his hands and found her face, mirroring her position.

She *was* crying too, but she kept singing, softly coaxing his pain away.

Her face was small between his palms, the line of her jaw, the point of her chin, the tips of her brows, the lobes of her ears, all within his grasp. His thumbs rested at the corners of her mouth, feeling her words until her song ended. She did not move her hands. He did not move his.

"My rune is gone, Hod," she whispered.

He nodded, a sob in his throat.

"Banruud burned his amulet into my hand."

He nodded again.

"I tried to re-create the rune, but I could not. I sang and I sang . . . but you weren't there."

May the gods smite him now. He could not bear it.

"You thought I didn't want you," she moaned, and he knew she'd plucked the thoughts from his head as she'd leached the pain from his face.

He pulled away from her and dropped his hands, forcing her to drop hers.

He felt too much. *He felt too much.*

He couldn't hear. He couldn't smell. He couldn't sense anything but her.

He rose and staggered from her tent, pulling air into his lungs and order to his thoughts as he walked deeper into the trees until he found a little clearing. For several long minutes he stood with his back to a big oak until his senses returned.

The camp was quiet, the night peaceful, the creatures stirring. He sensed no danger, no listening ears, no lurking strangers, but Ghisla had followed him.

"Hody," Ghisla mourned, so softly. So sweetly. "Please don't leave."

He moved back toward her, wanting his staff, needing his shield, and knowing neither would help him now. He stopped several feet away, close enough to speak softly, far enough to not lose his mind.

"I thought you had . . . given up hope. That you had . . . given up . . . on me," he whispered, trying not to scald her with the truth. "Arwin told me you would be queen of Saylok. He said you wore the king's mark. Now I know what he meant. But I spent the last six years believing you were Banruud's queen."

"They call me Banruud's harlot. His guards. They know I sing . . . but they are convinced, after all these years, that I do more."

He did not want to hear it. It turned his belly into a gaping wound, and his rage into a mindless swarm. He could not afford to be senseless. He wanted to back away from her again, not in repudiation, but in self-preservation. He stepped forward instead, knowing that if he distanced himself now, she would think she'd repulsed him.

"I do not do more. I sing. I try not to be alone with him or to get too close to him. But there are times when I am . . . and . . . I do. I have navigated both as best I can."

He dare not touch her, not in comfort or in support. He didn't know if she would welcome it. She was rigid in front of him, her voice low, her breaths shallow. He let her speak, let her tell him what she wanted to say, and he kept his hands to his sides.

"The first time he kissed me, I told Master Ivo that it happened, and I swore I would never go near him again. Ivo agreed, but a week later, the king had a terrible headache and he kept sending for me. I held out strong until I found out he was giving ten lashes to every sentry who came back without me. Master Ivo scolded and stomped his feet, but the next week it became twenty lashes, then thirty, and one guard, not much more than a boy, died.

"I stopped threatening to quit singing and told him that if he forced himself on me, I would kill myself. You cannot coerce the dead. He must have believed me, for he has spared me that. But he is also afraid."

"Afraid of what?" Hod asked, his voice barely above a whisper. He was trying to simply listen, to not react, to not lose his mind. Banruud would die. If it was the last thing he did, Banruud would die.

"He is afraid of lying with me and making me with child," Ghisla said, so tremulously her words didn't leave her lips. "Queen Alannah had one dead son after another until it killed her. If Banruud takes another queen and the same thing happens again . . ."

"It begins to look as though *he* is the problem," Hod finished for her.

"Yes. And calls into question Alba's parentage. He fears, more than anything else, losing the power her birth gave him. He took her from Ghost. I've seen it time and time again in his thoughts. He stole a daughter and rejected a son. Two sons, though he didn't know about you . . . No one knew about you."

He wasn't sure how or how long *she'd* known . . . but Ghisla knew most things. She carried Saylok's secrets on her small shoulders.

"Did you know, Hod?" she asked softly.

"It is what my mother told Arwin. It is what Arwin told me the day he died."

She swallowed her sympathy. He heard it in her throat and in the tightness of her jaw, but she forged ahead, setting Arwin aside.

"And you feel nothing for him?" Ghisla asked.

"For my father?"

He heard her curt nod.

"I feel curiosity. And I feel disgust. For him . . . and for myself. I do not like the similarities between us. I do not like that we both love the same woman."

He heard Ghisla's heart leap and wondered if it was horror or hope . . . or both.

"He does not love me," she said.

"I think he does. In his way."

"And *you* do not love me." She sounded so sure, so adamant, and he wondered how she could know so much and not know that.

"You are the only thing on this earth that I love."

Her hands fluttered to her lips and then slid to her throat. But she did not profess her love in return.

"I don't know where your allegiance lies," she said, and the words were a quiet sob that she tried desperately to suppress.

"I have none. I have no allegiance to Saylok. I have no allegiance to Banruud, or the temple, or a clan."

"You could have let Banruud die today," she whispered. "Why didn't you?"

"I don't know," he confessed. "It was instinct more than . . . anything. And his death . . . today . . . was not part of the plan."

"What plan? Do you have any allegiance to the North King?" she cried.

"No. I care naught for the North King or his ambitions. I care only that it all . . . ends."

"Then why? Why have you done this?"

"Done what, Ghisla?" He had not done any of the things he had dreamed of, and suddenly his weariness was so deep he could barely stand. An angry horde of screeching giants could descend upon the clearing and he wouldn't hear them coming.

"You have aligned yourself with him. Gudrun is not a good man. Banruud is . . . not a good man." It was too tepid a criticism, but Hod agreed.

"No. They are not good men."

"Are you still a good man, Hod?" she whispered, almost begging him to reassure her. But he couldn't.

"I have tried to be, but I don't always know what is right. Sometimes . . . there is only survival."

"And there is truth. The truth is right. The truth is good. That is what Master Ivo told me once, and that is what you must give me now."

"The only truth I know is you, Ghisla. I have spent these last years trying to get back to you."

She wanted to believe him. He could hear it in her sob and smell it on her skin. But she was afraid too. She was afraid of him. She was afraid for the future. And she was afraid that, in the end, there was nothing anyone could do to save them.

"Rest now, Ghisla of Tonlis," he said. "Go back to your tent. There is nothing that must be decided tonight. And I can't think when you are near."

"I blind you," she said sadly, the echoes of Arwin and a long-ago clearing all around them.

"Yes. And yet . . . you are the only one who makes me see."

She turned away then, but she paused after a few steps.

"You will not leave?" she asked.

"I will not leave. I've come too far to turn back now."

23

Rooms

They broke camp at daybreak, uneasy by their diminished numbers and obvious vulnerability to attack. The king kept Hod at the front of the caravan, insisting he ride in the wagon of provisions and listen for threats. Ghisla and Alba shared the saddle on a huge, battle-tested charger who'd lost his rider in the skirmish the day before, but more than their mode of transport had changed; they were guarded on all sides by men who now viewed Hod with wide eyes and spoke of him with hushed praise.

He did not get closer to the women than his assigned duties required and maintained a careful posture of cold reserve when he guarded their privacies. He did not speak to Ghisla or even incline his head in her direction throughout the arduous day of travel, and she resolved to do the same, if only to protect him. But his words of the night before ricocheted continually in her head, and tenderness and terror warred in her chest.

By the time the bugles sounded from the walls and the final ascent to the mount began, she was weak with strain and trembling with fatigue, and Alba was drooping in her arms. The caravan rumbled into the cobbled courtyard, the king's guard shouting for porters and grooms, and she and Alba were assisted from the saddle, their legs buckling and their backs bent. She saw Hod then, near the castle steps, but he followed at the king's heels, already consigned to duty.

She did not see him for several days, and she did not dare inquire after him, but word of the attack on the road from Berne had begun to spread among the king's men and the residents of Temple Hill, and Hod's notoriety seemed to grow with each retelling. He was the new Temple Boy, his feats rivaling those in the old stories of Bayr, who was still a legend on the mount. The only difference was one of note: King Banruud had hated Bayr, and he seemed quite attached to Hod.

Ghisla was summoned to the king's chamber to ease his aching head three days after their return from Berne and was made to endure an hour in his arms with Hod standing watch outside his door. Banruud's thoughts were tangled, and he buried his face in her neck like he was drowning, but from the flickering impressions she saw as she sang, he was reassured by Hod's presence. He felt . . . safe.

She did not.

She was unmoored. She was back in the North Sea, bobbing between two lives, begging for heaven, and knowing there was none.

When she left Banruud's chamber, Hod stood in the shadows a mere ten feet from the door, but she called for the sentry at the top of the stairs and turned away like she didn't see him there. Banruud's sticky breath clung to her throat, and she didn't want Hod to smell him on her skin.

The following morning, Master Ivo requested her presence in the sanctum.

"The Blind Hod has returned," he said without preamble, his hands wrapped around the arms of his chair. His papery skin and black eyes absorbed the shadows that the flickering candles did little to alleviate. She had oft wondered how he could endure the gloom and had come to realize he welcomed it. The darkness hid his uncertainties.

"Yes. He has. He is in the employ of the king." Her voice was steady. She'd prepared herself for this interrogation.

"And how did that come to be?" Ivo pressed.

"You ask me, Master?" she responded, dumbfounded. "I am not privy to the inner workings of the castle or the king."

"You did not expect him?"

"I did not expect him."

He pondered this for a moment, seeming to forget she was even present. The skies rumbled, and rain began to spatter against the temple walls. The smell of wet stones and dry earth seeped into the space, and the gloom around them intensified.

"There is a storm coming," he remarked.

"The storm is here," she answered. It was not meant to be provocative, but he peered at her, stooped and suspicious, and the truth of her statement resonated in her chest. The storm had arrived, and she almost . . . welcomed it.

"I do not know what to make of it," he confessed, and for the first time in her recollection, he seemed scared and unsure.

"The storm, Master?"

"The blind man," he snapped.

"Mayhaps . . . there is nothing to make of it. Mayhaps it has nothing to do with you, or the gods, or the runes, or the king." She spoke evenly, doing her best to remain circumspect.

"Do you know why Loki chose the blind god to do his bidding?" Master Ivo asked, scowling at her.

She waited, knowing he would remind her. Resentment bubbled in her chest. Hod was not the blind god. He was a man. And Master Ivo could be a fool.

"Loki realized that the fates could not see him," Ivo muttered. "And what they could not see . . . they would not prevent."

She remembered the story as Hod had told it so many years ago. He'd been frying fish, preparing dinner, sharing the simple tale of the blind god for whom he had been named. *We can only see what can be seen.*

"I cannot see him either," Master Ivo confessed. The revelation startled her.

"You cannot see . . . Hod?"

"The runes reveal many things, but not all. Not nearly all." He spread his hands, and uncurled his talon-like fingers, signaling he knew nothing. "He is a mystery to me. An unknown quantity. And I did not anticipate his return."

"What will you do?" Ghisla asked. She pictured him summoning Hod, demanding that he leave the mount, and her anger bubbled again. The intrigue had gone on too long, and nothing—nothing—had changed.

The Highest Keeper raised his eyes to hers. "The question is . . . what will *you* do, Daughter?"

"There is naught I can do," she cried. "I have been on this mount for more than a decade, waiting for salvation. Day after day, night after night, singing my songs, sleeping beside my sisters, and sitting with a tortured king. Tell me, Highest Keeper, what should I do?"

He nodded. "I fear there is naught any of us . . . can do."

⁃᪥⁃

The king gave Hod a small room on an upper floor in the castle equally distanced between his own chambers and the servants' quarters. He was not an honored guest—that wing of the castle was empty—nor an acknowledged member of the family; the Queen's Tower where Alba and the old queen slept was up a winding set of stairs off the main entrance. Still, a room of his own in the castle was far better than Hod had expected, and it was far better than sleeping in the barracks with the king's guard. A narrow bed and an iron tub were all he needed, and the room was more than sufficient, but he was required to work for his prime lodgings.

The king seemed eager—anxious even—to have him near. He stood sentry while Banruud ate and hovered in the hall while Ghisla sang. He guarded the king when he spoke with his advisors and trailed him when he walked the grounds. He was even asked to rove the corridors and walk along the temple wall to listen for approaching threats before he retired at night.

It was odd how so many feared him . . . and how Banruud feared him not at all. King Banruud did not think him a threat; Hod suspected he did not think him a man. It was as if he considered Hod a trained raptor, skilled and useful but without emotion or humanity. As if, having no eyes, he had no soul.

He was good at being useful and invisible at the same time. It was how he'd survived in Gudrun's realm all those years. The temple mount was not the Northlands; it was simultaneously more civilized and more remote, more open and more oppressed. He did not dodge blades and evade blows at every turn, but the quiet desperation on the hill was much harder for him to endure. Mayhaps it was simply his proximity to Ghisla.

The temple itself teemed with worried hearts. He could hear Ghost and Dagmar and Master Ivo. He could hear the keepers and the daughters, and he could hear Ghisla. Even when he lay down to sleep in his strange bed in his strange new room he could hear her, and her nearness filled him with both elation and grief.

She had no freedom. He knew she could not seek him out. But twice she'd seen him in the corridor outside Banruud's chamber, and twice she'd run from him. She was upset by his presence. He could hear it in her heartbeat and in her shallow breaths. But she had avoided him long enough.

When Banruud summoned her again, he was waiting when she exited the king's rooms. The halls were quiet, the sentry sleeping, and Hod stood directly across from the door so she would not flee.

"I must go," she whispered.

He shook his head. "Not yet."

"Banruud will hear."

"He will not. But let us walk." He held out his hand, inviting her to come with him, and she moaned, the sound barely audible, as if she stood on a precipice from which she desperately wanted to jump.

She did not take his proffered hand but turned and walked deeper into the corridor, away from the stairs and the heat of the sconces. She sought the shadows, and he followed her. When she stopped, he stopped too, keeping a safe distance between them. He did not want to push her. He just wanted to be near her.

"What do you want, Hod?" she asked quietly. The words wounded him, but he did not flinch.

"I have missed you," he confessed. "I don't want to miss you anymore."

Again the faint moan.

"And why . . . are you here?"

"You know why I'm here, Ghisla."

"You cannot call me that out loud. I am Liis of Leok."

"We are alone. And you are Ghisla to me."

"Why are you here?" she insisted again. He knew she didn't mean the corridor or even the castle. She wanted to know his intentions.

"I knew no other way to be near you. Arwin is dead. Saylok is dying. I cannot be a keeper. I have no clan. I have no family. I have only you. You are the only thing that matters to me. So I am here."

"It has been years," she said, her words a hushed wail.

"I am here," he said again.

"You are the North King's man."

"No. I am Hod. The same Hod you have known for a decade. The same Hod you once loved."

"You are the king's man!" she said, adamant, but Hod could hear the tears in her throat.

"I am Ghisla's man. I have only ever been yours."

Her heart was pushing, pulsing, pulling at him, and he could smell the want on her skin and feel the weight of her stare. He reached out toward her again, beseeching, but this time he turned his palm up, exposing to her gaze the rune that had connected them for so long. For a moment he thought she would reject him again, that she would flee.

The corridor was quiet. The king was in his chamber, his breaths steady and his sleep deep. Below them, in the kitchen, the hum of voices and the heat of bodies radiated up through the floor. Food was being prepared for people who would sleep for hours yet. But they were alone. Finally. Blessedly. Alone. And he heard the moment she raised her hand, her sleeve whispering against the bodice of her dress, and then her fingertips touched his.

For a heartbeat, he allowed himself to exult, but he could not wait any longer, and he pulled her to him, seeking her mouth, and her heat, and her substance.

But he was not prepared for the reality of Ghisla, her breasts and her belly and her hips pressed against him; the collision rocked him, radiating in his legs and emptying his thoughts, and he groaned her name in wonderous disbelief.

She was no longer in his head and his heart but in his hands. She gripped his face like she too was clinging to a dream, and then his mouth found hers, soft and insistent, and violet rose behind his eyes and surged beneath his tongue.

She dragged her mouth away and moaned his name, "Hody, Hody, Hody," the way she often called him in song, and for a moment, his own face rose in his mind, as if he looked at himself in that moment through her. Harsh angles and empty green eyes, his back bent to hold her, his lips wet with her kisses. Then his face was gone and her lips returned, consuming him.

Salt—were they her tears or his?

He couldn't kiss her fast enough, hold her close enough, or taste her well enough, and impatience guided his hands over her hips and around her waist, up the cage of her ribs and over the swell of her breasts only to retrace the same path, seeing her in the only way he could. She bit at his lips and nipped at his jaw, and her words came back to him from so many years ago.

I want to be inside you. And I want you to be inside me.

She ripped her mouth from his and pushed herself away only to immediately return to his arms and bury her face in his neck, her hands clutching his back, almost clawing.

"I do not know when you lie," she said.

He stiffened.

"You know when I lie, but I don't know when *you* lie," she whispered, keeping her face buried against him.

"I have not lied to you." He had not told her all of the truth, but he had not lied.

"Everyone lies. Do they not? But you have the advantage of hearing what most cannot . . . what *I* cannot."

"The advantage? My lack is what created my advantage . . . so it is hardly an advantage."

"I do not know when you lie," she insisted again.

He eased her back, his hands bracketing her small face. Her jaw was locked and her chin jutted out against his thumbs. He wanted to kiss her again, but there were words in her throat. He could feel them gathering beneath her chin.

"And I cannot read your mind, woman. So you must tell me what you are trying to say." His voice was gentle even if his words were dismissive. She had made her name an issue; she could hardly argue now about him calling her *woman*.

"You say you have love for me."

"No. I said I love you."

She swallowed, her throat moving beneath his hands. "But how do I know if you lie?"

"For what purpose would I lie?"

"Why does anyone lie? Because the truth is too hard."

"You *know* I love you."

"I know nothing."

"Do you love me, Ghisla of Tonlis?"

"No," she snapped, defensive.

"You lie," he shot back.

He grinned, and she . . . laughed, the sound brushing his lips with surprised mirth, and he kissed her again. She met his mouth with all the desperation and wonder he felt, but fear hounded her, and she pulled back almost immediately.

"Someone will hear us," she lamented. "If you are seen with me . . . if you are seen kissing me . . . he will kill you."

She stepped away, and he let her retreat. Not because he feared for himself, but because her distress was palpable. For a moment they simply breathed, bringing their emotions under control.

"I will walk with you," he said. "Back to the temple. I have guarded you before. It will not raise alarm if I do so now."

"All right," she whispered. Disappointment limned her words, but she touched his hand, a glancing caress, and turned toward the stairs. He followed her, staff in hand, still enveloped by the rosy waft of her scent.

The sentry near the stairs didn't even raise his head. The guard at the castle doors had left his post, and the watchman on the wall was not doing his job. His snores would not be audible to anyone else, but to Hod they were as clear as a pig rooting at his feet.

The courtyard was empty, and in the distance between the palace steps and the temple columns, there were no indications that he and

Ghisla were observed with alarm or even interest. The mount was accustomed to her late-night crossings.

He could not feel eyes the way he heard hearts or breath or movement, but he felt safe enough to speak before she reached the temple doors.

"I will wait for you on the hillside. If you cannot come . . . I will wait tomorrow. And the day after that. Until you know whether I lie."

∾

Dred of Dolphys and a handful of sweat-soaked, dust-coated warriors arrived on the mount three weeks after the king's return from Berne. Dred demanded an audience with Banruud, who insisted Hod stand in front of him to deter a sudden attack.

"I do not trust Dred of Dolphys. He's wanted to kill me for years, and he's not afraid to die. He will keep his distance. If he doesn't . . . you will respond accordingly."

Hod did as he was told, positioning himself in front of the dais as Dred was ushered in and made to address the king from more than a hundred paces. Hod heard the moment Dred took note of him and the scoff of derision the old warrior released beneath his breath. Hod remembered Dred of Dolphys from the tournament years before. He'd liked him greatly. He wasn't sure if the old warrior's disdain was for him or for the king—or for both—but it bothered him all the same.

King Banruud listened with feigned boredom and blatant hostility as Dred made his complaint.

"We've had attacks from Berne on our borders, and we've had word that your caravan was attacked as well. Surely you know the conditions across the countryside. Yet nothing is done. Benjie sits in his keep and gets fat while his clansmen die . . . or prey on others," Dred stated. "We went to him first. Now we come to you."

"Are you the chieftain, Dred of Dolphys?" King Banruud said, yawning. It was a pretense; Hod could smell his nervous perspiration.

"You know I am not, Banruud."

"Yes. I know you are not. Yet you come to me as if you are."

Dred ground his teeth but simply waited for Banruud to continue.

"I have not seen the Temple Boy in all these years. Mayhaps he sits in his keep and gets fat as well?"

"What will be done, Banruud? I come to you in deference to your throne. I do not want war among the clans, but if things persist as they are, we will have no choice but to engage with Berne."

"Is that a threat, Dred of Dolphys?"

"Yes, Majesty. It is. A threat and a warning. You have been a chieftain. Your father was a chieftain. I did not like him—we were fierce rivals—but I respected him, and he was a good chief. Benjie has not been a good chieftain. And now we all suffer."

The men behind Dred shifted and rumbled in agreement, and the king's guards at the doors seemed to acknowledge his words as well, many of them having been on the road from Berne when the caravan was attacked. But Banruud sighed heavily, as if Dred overreacted and asked too much.

"I will go to Berne again—before the tournament—and I will see to the matter myself," the king grumbled. He was stalling. He would go to Berne to meet the North King and bring him back to the mount. The only consequences for the Chieftain of Berne would be administered by the disintegrating conditions in his clan . . . and the Northmen who would overrun him. Hod considered it another reason to let events unfold.

When the king dismissed Dred and the handful of warriors, Hod was instructed to follow them out.

"Make sure they leave the mount," Banruud insisted. "I also want to know who Dred confers with and what is said. You can hear him?"

"I can hear him," Hod confirmed.

"Good. Then see to it."

He did so, not appreciating his new role as Banruud's pup . . . though he supposed that's exactly what he was. He had no intention of stirring up trouble or informing on Dred or his men, but he was curious about their sudden arrival and about Bayr, who had kept his distance all these years. In the end, that distance would serve him well, and it comforted Hod greatly, knowing what was to come. When Banruud fell, Hod did not want Bayr to be anywhere near him.

They saw him coming and rose in distrust. They'd pitched a tent in the meadow where the clans converged during tournament, clearly having expected the king's reception. They would not be sleeping in the castle, though there were twenty-three empty rooms. Their horses grazed nearby—they were hobbled by the sound of it—and someone had built a fire.

"Banruud has sent his blind henchman to dispatch us," a warrior crowed, and Hod recognized his voice. He was a loudmouth, a pup that had nipped at Dred's feet, and time had seemingly not changed him. The others—there were four in all—said nothing, but their hands were on their swords as he approached.

"You are Dred of Dolphys. We met years ago," Hod greeted, amiable.

"I remember," Dred answered, cautious. "Your skill was impressive then. I suspect it is more impressive now. I did not expect to see you here."

Hod extended his hand toward the man, and Dred took it. It was like clutching the branch of a tree—rough and ridged and unforgiving.

"Dystel," Hod said, greeting the man to Dred's left. He'd been at Dred's side through the competition. He was a good archer and had been among the final contestants.

"Archer," Dystel grunted. "How did you know it was I? I've not said a word."

"I never forget a heart."

The youngest man scoffed, and Hod turned his face toward him.

"You didn't like me then either . . . Daniel, was it?" Hod said. "And you weren't much of a shot. You got out in the first round."

Daniel gasped, affronted, but the other men laughed.

"I remember now that I liked you, blind archer," Dred said, a smile in his voice.

"We have not met, Dakin," Hod said, addressing the silent man at the edge of the group. "But you were there too. You have a heart like a gong."

"That is uncanny," Dred marveled.

"It is theater," Daniel grumbled.

"Your stomach is growling, young Daniel," Hod said. "Perhaps some supper would make you less hostile?" The men laughed again, as he'd intended, but it didn't make his assertion any less true. They were all hungry, and he was delaying their dinner.

"Please . . . eat with us. We have enough," Dred invited.

"I cannot stay. But please . . . eat. I wished only to greet you."

"And make sure we leave?" Dred added. He was not a fool.

"Aye," Hod said.

Dred exhaled, as if relieved by Hod's honesty. Most men were.

"You look like a keeper. Except, mayhaps, for your braid," Dystel remarked. "I thought years ago that is what you were."

"I was raised by a keeper. A cave keeper in Leok. I thought one day I would go to the temple and become a supplicant." Hod shrugged. "But that was not to be."

"The Dolphys was raised by a keeper too," Dred said. "By a whole temple."

"They called him the Temple Boy, archer. Surely you've heard the stories," Dakin said.

"Yes. I've heard the stories," Hod answered. And he had loved the stories.

"You wanted to be a keeper . . . but now you work for the king," Dred said. "I find that surprising." His voice was neutral, but he did not like Banruud. Understandable, considering their history. His daughter, Desdemona, had been rejected by the king. Her death was on Banruud's hands. The death of Saylok was on his hands.

"There aren't many options for a blind henchman," Hod replied. The men laughed again.

"No," Dred answered. "Though I daresay . . . there aren't many options for any of us. A warrior or a keeper, a farmer or a fisherman. It is a hard life, whether a man is born blind or with a stuttering tongue. We all have our battles."

"Yes. We do." Hod hesitated, wanting to warn them, and not certain how to do so. "The mount is not a safe place, Dred of Dolphys."

The men stiffened.

"Saylok is not a safe place," Dred shot back.

"No. It isn't. Not for a warrior or a keeper, a farmer or a fisherman. Not for a blind man or a man with a stuttering tongue," he repeated, using Dred's own words. He lifted his face to the breeze, listening. It was time to go. Dagmar was coming, and Hod had no wish to be in his presence or draw attention to himself.

"Your son approaches, Dred of Dolphys. Eat. Rest. But when you are done . . . it would be best to gather your tent and leave the mount. Sleep in the Temple Wood, if you must. But don't return. Not even for the tournament."

"Do you threaten us, archer?" Dystel asked, baffled.

"No." Hod shook his head. He had to tread carefully, to ward off but not warn. To pressure but not pique. "I seek only to impart the king's warning. I seek only to . . . protect you."

The men were hushed as he departed, and he felt their wary eyes as he picked his way across the meadow in the opposite direction from whence he'd come. When Dagmar reached them, he was well out of sight.

24

Moons

Ghisla was able to creep away to the hillside three times in the following weeks, and each time, Hod heard her waiting and arrived shortly after. Her fear was a constant flogging, her hope a stinging salve, but she could not stay away from him.

He tasted the same, and his very existence filled her mouth, swelled in her chest, and burned in her veins. When he was beside her, that moment was the only thing that mattered, and they volleyed between frantic kisses and desperate words, trying to catch up on all their years apart.

He told her of his adventures in the Northlands, the journey that got him there, and the luck that brought him back.

"I will never be a sailor; I'm useless on the open sea. I have not learned to hear my way across it. I cannot see the sky, the stars do not speak or breathe or live, and beneath them I am truly blind."

"You can't sense them."

"No. I can feel the sun on my face, and when it is bright, I can plot its course across the sky. But when the clouds are thick, and the sun is hidden, time is harder for me to gauge. The tools of a sailor are lost on me."

"Can you feel the moon?" she asked.

"If I am very still—I can feel its pull."

"It is full tonight. Fat and slow, and so bright it hurts my eyes to gaze on it too long." She sang about what she saw, the size, shape, and glow of the orb that rolled across the heavens, a sated circle in a sky of lesser beings . . . until the sun rose and shooed him away.

> I am the moon and the moon is me.
> I am young and I am old.
> I am weak and I am bold.
> I am distant. I am cold.
> I am the moon and the moon is me.

"I have not heard that one before," Hod said. "But you are not the moon."

She laughed, but the sound contained no mirth. "I am just like the moon. Young and old. Weak and bold. Distant and cold. I am a constant contradiction, even to myself."

"Mayhaps. But you are not distant or cold."

"I am. It is how I've survived. Just like the moon. The less I feel, the easier it is to go on. I have been this way for so long . . . I hardly remember if I was ever someway else."

"You are not cold, Ghisla. Not to me. You are color. You are sound. You are the song on the wind and the hope in my heart."

"Oh, Hody," she whispered, moved. "How can you still hope? Life has given us no reason for such belief."

"How can you not?" he said. "When we are together . . . how can you not?"

She clasped his hand and pressed it to her lips, moved by his sweetness and reminded of the boy who'd pled with her to never give up. He had changed, her Hod, but in so many ways, he was exactly the same.

"When Odin gave his eye to the well in exchange for the meaning of the runes, he took a chunk of the twenty-fourth moon to make himself another," Hod murmured. His eyes too could have been carved from the orb. They reflected the white light and gleamed at her softly.

"What have you received in exchange for your eyes?" she asked. "What has the well shown you?"

He grew silent, as if the conversation had turned to ground he didn't want to tread. They had not talked about Gudrun or the Northmen while on the hillside. They'd avoided Banruud altogether. They'd inhabited a world of lovers, of kisses and caresses and careless whispering, like time would wait until they'd caught up.

"In one week, King Banruud will go back to Berne. I will be going with him," Hod said.

Ghisla brought their clasped hands to her chest, and he soothed her quickening heart with the back of his hand.

"I will return with him . . . and with Gudrun. And when I do . . . you must be ready to flee, Ghisla. Gudrun plans to overthrow the king and take the hill. I will not stop him. In fact, I will help him. And when Banruud has fallen, I will kill Gudrun myself."

"But Banruud will not be the only one to fall."

"No. Men will die. Chieftains who have done nothing but suck the teat of Saylok will fight beside the king. Their warriors, the king's guard, the clanless . . . some of them will die too."

"What of the temple? What of the daughters? There are more women in the temple now than just my sisters. It is a sanctuary. What will the Northmen do to them, Hod?"

"You will go. All of you. Alba, Ghost, the women, and the keepers. You will go to Bayr in Dolphys. And when the battle is done . . . those who wish will return. And you and I will be free. Mayhaps Saylok will finally be free."

"You think Banruud's death will break the curse?"

"Arwin says the scourge began with Bayr, and it will end with him. He even believed . . . that I would be the one to take his life. Like Hod, the blind god."

"Hod . . . no. Oh no." It was what Master Ivo feared. What Dagmar feared. What she had come to fear as well.

"Shh, my love. Listen to me," he urged, and she did her best to control her terrible dread.

"I have puzzled over Desdemona and her runes all these long years. I have thought of my own mother. Of her sacrifices for me. A mother does not curse her son. She seeks only to bless him." He was quiet, pondering. "I do not think the scourge will end with Bayr's death, Ghisla, but with his ascendance to the throne."

Her breath caught, and her eyes clung to Hod's face. He touched her cheek, ever so softly, as if needing to reassure himself she was there.

"It is the story of Baldr and Hod, two brothers, two gods. One who ushered in the end, and one who rose again. It is the tale that has followed me all my life. I cannot escape it."

"And . . . which one . . . are you?" she asked.

"I am the one who ushers in the end," he said gently.

"I am afraid," she moaned.

"As am I. It is not my destiny to kill Bayr . . . but to help him rise again."

"If we are going to be apart, you must make a new rune on my hand," Ghisla pled with Hod the next time they met.

"I fear it will only bring you trouble, my love." He'd thought about the matter a great deal.

No matter what happened—if Banruud fell or Banruud prevailed—it would not end well for Hod. His allegiance would be questioned, and rightfully so. His only loyalty was to Ghisla and to the brother that didn't know he existed, and he would be hard pressed to defend himself among any of the opposing factions. The best outcome would be for Banruud and Gudrun to both fall in battle, but Hod would be branded a traitor on either side.

He did not want Ghisla branded with him. It was bad enough that she had the rune of the blind god, however faint, scarred into the lines of her left palm.

"You already wear the mark of Hod," he whispered.

"I wear the king's mark." She traced the star of Saylok in her palm. "I wanted to wear yours."

"It is a rune, that star. And it does not belong to Banruud. It belongs to Saylok," he said, pulling her right hand into his lap.

"A rune?"

"Yes . . . A seeker rune."

"A seeker rune?" she gasped. "I have had a seeker rune on my hand all this time?"

"Start at the tip of Adyar, North, the top of the star, and move around it, from east to west, tracing the lines, until you rejoin the tip of Adyar." He traced the grooves as he spoke, showing her.

"And what of these lines?" she asked, using his finger to trace spokes that ran from the tip of each leg and met in the middle.

"Those connect the star to the center."

"To the temple?"

"Yes." The idea pained him. "After you have traced the star, start again at the tip of Adyar, where you began, and draw the line to the center. Then go to Berne and do the same. Then Dolphys, Ebba, Joran, and Leok, until every line has been traced.

"When you have traced the star with your blood, just like I've shown you, press the rune to your brow, where the star is drawn at coronations or at a child's birth, and ask the Star of Saylok to show you one of her children or a place within her shores."

"I could have seen you . . . all this time?" she gasped.

"Mayhaps . . . but I was not in Saylok, love. The star only works in Saylok. Every rune has its limits, and the fates decide whether to answer the summons."

She shook her head in disbelief, and he wrapped her hand in his, covering the scar burned there. He hated it as much as she; he felt scalded each time his fingers brushed it.

"You know the runes. Did you ever try to see me?" she asked quietly.

"Seeker runes do not give a man eyes. I have been taught to make and unlock the runes, but knowledge is not always enough. I did try to see you. I even begged Arwin to reassure me."

"And did he?"

"Somewhat. His mind was going, and he was sick. He was never the same after Master Ivo turned me away. He lost his faith."

"Master Ivo taught me the rune of the blind god. Left to right, top to bottom. I carved it in my hand, hoping I could summon you."

"It is not that kind of rune."

"No." She shook her head. "I pressed it to my eyes . . . the way I'd done with the seeker runes, and I said your name. It did not give me sight. It took my sight. I was blind until the bleeding stopped."

"When was this?" he gasped.

"Months after you left, after the tournament. Master Ivo showed me how the runes of Hod and Baldr were the same."

"He sought to make you understand why . . . I am the enemy."

She exhaled heavily, but she did not argue.

"You lost your sight," he breathed, realization dawning.

"I was terrified. I bound my hand and sat in the sanctum for hours, scared the king would send for me, terrified that my sisters—or Ivo—would find me, and afraid I'd lost my eyes in my foolishness."

"But your sight came back."

"Yes. I sang the song, and as the rune healed, my sight returned. Had I not sung the song . . . it might have taken days instead of hours. Had I done it sooner, I would have saved myself a great deal of fear."

"That was the day I saw," he said, understanding washing over him, an answer to a mystery that had baffled him for years.

"You saw?"

"For two hours, around that same time frame that you've just described, I could see."

"I gave you my eyes?" she said, flabbergasted.

He could not stop the bubble of incredulous laughter that escaped his throat.

"The rune of the blind god does not seek sight or take sight. It gives sight to the blind," he explained, awestruck. "It is not a seeker rune . . . it is a sacrificial rune. You carved it into your hand and then . . . said my name?"

"Yes. And I was immediately blind."

"You gave me sight that day, Ghisla. For two blessed hours, I saw the sky and the hillside. I saw Arwin and the runes. I saw my reflection in the glass. My hands and skin. My . . . life. And I didn't know why. It was a gift amid a very bleak time. I was . . . devastated by your absence. And then, out of nowhere, the blind god gave me a respite from the darkness. You gave me a respite. I did not let myself mourn when it was gone, though I hoped it would return someday. You gave me a thousand pictures that day, Ghisla, and I didn't even know it was you."

Banruud was irritable, demanding comfort from her presence as well as her voice, while he stewed over whether he could bring her with him to Berne. He abandoned the idea only after Hod quietly reminded him that it would not be safe for "the Songr."

"If you value Liis of Leok, Majesty, it would not be wise to put her anywhere near the North King. He will not hesitate to take what he believes is his."

The king dismissed Hod with a surly "Get out," but he did not persist with his plans. She would stay on the mount. When Liis left the king's chamber near midnight, she was worn from evading his hands and his mouth and weary from trying to sing him to sleep. He was a child throwing tantrums, and when he finally succumbed, she washed herself in the basin in his chamber, though she feared he might wake and she would have to do it all again.

Hod waited for her in the hallway, his face pensive, his jaw tight, his staff in his hands, and his shield on his back.

"There must be somewhere we can go," she whispered. "Surely . . . there is some place where we can lie behind a locked door. Where we don't have to run. Or fear. Or speak in whispers. Where you don't have to carry your shield and staff. Just for a while."

She didn't want to run to the hillside or hide in the Temple Wood. To be gone too long would result in chaos, and to go too far was too great a risk. And they had so little time; Hod would leave in the morning.

He turned, listening to the sentry who nodded off in the alcove, and then took her hand and pulled her down the corridor and up a flight of stairs. He stopped beside a small room at the end of a hushed hallway.

"There is no one on this floor but me, and those stairs lead all the way down to the yard at the rear of the castle."

He ushered her inside, barred the door, and set down his staff and his shield as she surveyed the simple space.

A surge of tenderness welled in her chest. He always asked for so little, and he'd been given even less. A bed with a worn blanket was neatly made. A tub filled the corner, and a set of three drawers stood against the back wall. A basin sat atop the drawers; a bar of soap and a neatly folded towel were placed beside it. Everything was ordered and nothing was extra, except for the long, oval looking glass that hung on the wall adjacent to the door. She turned toward it, and he moved behind her, resting his cheek in the crown of her hair. It was odd to look at them together this way, framed in glass, as though they were a painting, permanent and fixed.

"There is a looking glass on your wall," she said.

"I thought it might be," he murmured. "It's broken, though. When I look in it, I can't see anything."

He began to take down her hair, and she watched him, her blood warming beneath her skin. When he ran his fingers through the tresses, spreading them over her shoulders, she loosened the ties between her breasts.

There was no question, or even caution, no hesitation between them at all. He did not ask, and she did not instruct. He was suddenly impatient to touch her skin, and she didn't shimmy or shy away or giggle at his urgency when he drew her skirts up in his hands and pulled her dress over her head. She helped him, tugging at her stays and loosening the sash at her waist.

Her underthings intrigued him, but only for as long as it took to remove them, and then she stood naked in the looking glass, shivering with anticipation, the cool night air whispering through the shutters that kept the wind from watching them.

"I want to see you," he said.

She brought his palm to her heart and stroked the back of his hand.

"I have no songs that describe my flesh," she said, "or capture the look of my face. But if you look into the glass while I sing, maybe you'll see us the way you saw my sky."

"Violet," he breathed, remembering.

"Yes."

He lifted his face and waited, hopeful.

"I am Ghisla . . . I am . . . small," she sang, feeling her way into a song. "I am . . . summer . . . more than fall."

He smiled. His grim face and empty eyes were transformed by the flashing of his teeth and the parting of his lips.

"There you are," he cried. "There . . . we are?"

She nodded, humming softly.

"My eyes are blue, just like the sky. My hair is gold . . . don't . . . ask me why." She wrinkled her brow, trying to write lyrics even as her breath caught and his hands began to rove.

"Your waist is small, your hips are round," he murmured, helping her. She repeated his line with a bit of melody and a smile.

"Your beauty doesn't make a sound," he added.

"Very good," she said, and sang it back to him.

"Your breasts are full enough to hold," he composed, and she moaned the words as he tested their weight.

"And these?" he asked, stroking the peaks of her breasts with the tips of his fingers. "Tell me about these."

"Pink berries . . . on a . . . bed of . . . snow," she sang, her face flushing.

The song was silly and she felt like a fool, but watching Hod's face in the looking glass as his hands moved down her body—not just touching her, but seeing her, seeing them, their bodies together—made the song feel almost sacred, like the keeper's praises at the end of the day.

"You are looking at me . . . and I am looking at you," he marveled.

She nodded, overcome, and they began again, her song and her eyes, his hands and his touch. She followed his movement, letting him match sight with sound, resisting the urge to direct his hands.

"I hear your blood coursing and your heart galloping, but I see the flush of your skin and the heaviness of your lids. And I see myself, loving you," he rasped.

She continued on as long as she could, letting him see what he did to her, what she did to him, but when he found the place where her pleasure was centered, she couldn't sing anymore, and she closed her eyes against the onslaught of sensation.

"Your eyes are my eyes," he implored. "Don't close them. Let me see you."

She opened them again, searching his face in the mirror, and he waited for the image to return, his arms wrapped around her, his lips to her hair.

"Don't look away."

She didn't. Not again. Not when her limbs quaked and her belly trembled. Not when he had to help her stand. She watched him touch her, unblinking, murmuring the song of supplication all the while.

Then he lifted her in his arms and laid her across the bed, needing her mouth more than he needed her eyes, and they forgot about the mirror and the magic of their connection and simply made love, Ghisla and Hod, in the quiet of his humble room.

He covered her with warmth and kisses until she wept his name, and he saw her pleasure and his own in the purring length of her sighs. In the woods she saw stars; in the castle bed, she saw only him, his mouth and his sharp edges, the brow that was lowered in concentration, trying not to take his pleasure too fast when the journey was so sweet. But she wanted to watch the moment he came undone, and she hummed louder and clutched his hips to push him over the edge. He kissed her, mouth open, tongue seeking, and she answered, anxious and eager, before pushing him away again so she wouldn't miss it.

"Ghisla, I'm waiting for you," he begged. She laughed and writhed against him, trying to oust his restraint only to lose her grip on her own. She clutched his face in her hands and saw the shudder that rippled past his eyes and down the harsh lines of his face before she captured his mouth and let the tide take them both.

They slept briefly, wrapped around each other in sated exhaustion, only to wake each other again with lovemaking, unwilling to waste their time in sleep, but when Hod stiffened and cocked his head, listening to the castle halls, she held her breath and he rolled away from her to clear his senses. After a moment, his shoulders relaxed and he turned back toward her, but she saw the ending in his grim expression.

"The cock has crowed. The mount is stirring."

She sighed but rose and began to dress, and Hod did the same. She braided her hair with flying fingers and wrapped it around her head, tight and neat; if she was seen, she wanted to look like she'd risen early instead of not sleeping at all. She washed her teeth and splashed her face before pushing her feet into her shoes. Hod stood by the door, his head bowed, and she thought he was waiting for the path to clear. She slipped her hand into his, signaling her readiness without speaking. His fingers tightened around hers, and he brought them to his cheek.

"I love you, Ghisla," he said. They'd whispered the words over and over again through the night, but his tone was different now, and she tensed, expectant, as he continued. "I have thought many times that the gods had forsaken me . . . or never cared to begin with. But I cannot think thus when I am with you."

"You are my only joy," she whispered, and pressed her mouth to his, needing for him to believe it. For a moment they were lost again, kissing as if time had stopped beyond the door.

Then he lay his forehead against hers, as though drawing the strength he could not muster.

"When I go, use the star if you must. But only if you must. It is easy to lose oneself to the runes, to stare into them all day, and forget the world around us. And sometimes what we see does not free us . . . but destroys us."

She thought of the keepers, moldering away in their temple.

"Arwin said you blinded me . . . and it is true to a point. When I am with you, you consume me, my senses, and my attention. But I think it is better to be blinded by love than by the runes. I fear many of the keepers—Master Ivo too—have been blinded by them; they believe every answer is in a rune, and they don't see what is right in front of them. They have lost all perspective. But the answers . . . are not in the runes."

"Where are they, Hod? Where are they, my love?" she lamented. She had given up on clear answers.

He brought her hand to his chest, to the heart that pounded steadily beneath his skin, and pressed his other hand against her breast.

"They are almost always right here," he whispered.

Then he opened the door and drew her out into the corridor, down the rear stairs, and out into the cool predawn, bidding her goodbye before he slipped away.

25

KINGS

Ghisla stood at the window in her room that overlooked the north gate and watched Hod leave. The hazy greens and blues of a distant Adyar were no more than a wistful suggestion, and she watched until the convoy disappeared into the dust. She resisted the urge to prick her finger and trace the star so she could follow his every step. If she gave in to the impulse, she would never be able to stop. Hod was right; she would drive herself mad.

She sang a simple prayer, beseeching the blind god to guard his namesake, and then she turned away.

It was in the same spot, standing at the window a week later, the amber light of the fall afternoon making the world soft, when another rider, this one alone, emerged from the dust and began his climb to the mount.

As she watched, drawn to the ever-nearing approach, the bells began to sound, clanging merrily, joyously, and as the rider drew near on a horse as black as his braid, she recognized him. He had aged and grown—he was a muscled bear of a man—but the Temple Boy was still there in the set of his eyes, the width of his smile, and the peak of his brow.

"I am Bayr, Chieftain of Dolphys, here to see King Banruud," he boomed to the gate watchman, and though he paused every third or fourth word, he did not stumble.

"Open the bloody gate!" Dagmar bellowed to the winchmen who lifted the grates, and she knew he'd been the one ringing the bells.

"The king is not here, Chieftain," the gate watchman replied good-naturedly. "But Keeper Dagmar has vouched for you and has bid me open the gate." With a holler slightly more subdued than Dagmar's had been, he granted Bayr entry.

Then Bayr was coming through the gate, his eyes trained on Dagmar, who had placed himself directly in his path. He slid off his horse and ran, sweeping his uncle up in his arms, laughing and saying his name.

"I see Dolphys in you—the clan is in your blood—but you are still Bayr, though you are more boar than cub," Dagmar choked, laughing through his tears. He kissed his nephew's cheeks as though he were still a child and not a great, hulking man, and Bayr embraced him in return.

"I am no bear. I am a wolf, Uncle. Though I do run a bit b-bigger than most of them." Bayr's grin was blinding, and his stutter was much improved.

"Bayr has returned," Ghisla whispered, flabbergasted. Overjoyed. Horrified.

"Bayr has returned!" Juliah cried.

Ghisla's sisters ran from the room, and she ran to catch up with them as they clattered down the stone steps to the wide entry below. They were not the only ones who had heard the bells and witnessed Dagmar's joyous shouting. From the west staircase, a stream of keepers began to pour, voices raised in welcome, hands clasped in excitement at Bayr's return.

Master Ivo was waiting in the foyer, watching the reunion through the wide doors. Bayr strode forward and enveloped the Highest Keeper in an embrace that should have reduced him to dust, but Ivo curled his winged arms around the big chieftain and uttered not even a peep of protest.

"We've been waiting, Bayr of Saylok," he murmured as Bayr released him and turned to greet the others hurrying toward him. Ghost reached him first and held out a hand in greeting, her smile as careful and quiet as it had always been. Bayr bowed above it, kissing her pale white knuckles. Her joy was as clear as her gossamer skin.

"You are s-still beautiful, Ghost," Bayr said softly. "Thank you for l-looking after him." He cast a brief glance at Dagmar so there would be no question to whom he referred.

"Your uncle looks after all of us," she replied, and pink suffused her pale cheeks.

"You are all . . . w-women," Bayr stammered, raising his eyes from Ghost to Ghisla and the other daughters, who had stopped a few paces behind her. He gripped his braid as though he greeted the king, his reverence and fealty bringing to mind the day so long ago when they'd been brought to the temple as scared little girls.

"You are all beautiful women, g-grown," he marveled.

In response, Juliah grasped the heavy coil that circled her head.

"Mine is not a warrior's braid, but a warrior's crown," she said, a smirk twisting her soft lips.

"The Warrior Queen?" Bayr asked, and Juliah's smile widened.

"There has been no coronation, but I accept your title," she said, lifting her chin like royalty, but her eyes caught on Alba, who stood framed in the light of the gray afternoon beyond him. The heavy temple doors had been pushed wide upon Bayr's entry and never closed, and no one had even seen her enter in their eagerness to greet their returning friend.

"Bayr?" Alba called.

Bayr froze, as though he knew exactly who spoke. He seemed to brace himself before turning, but the shudder that wracked him was visible to all who observed.

"Alba?"

She was tall for a woman, taller than many of the keepers, and straight and strong in her carriage and character. She wore her hair loose around her shoulders, the pale waves like moonbeams against her deep-blue gown. The light at her back shadowed her features, but her eyes, dark as the soil of Saylok, were fixed on Bayr's face.

A heartbeat later, she was hurtling through the entrance hall, her skirts clutched in her hands to free her flying feet, her hair streaming behind her. Then she was in Bayr's arms, caught up against him, her feet no longer touching the floor, as though she'd leaped past the last few steps.

All was silent around them, as the stunned observers watched a reunion that was as wrenching as it was wonderful. Bayr and Alba did not speak at all, but stood, locked in a desperate embrace, clinging to each other in quiet commiseration. Ghisla could not see Bayr's face, but Alba had begun to weep, her shoulders quaking, her face buried in Bayr's neck. Bayr simply turned, still clutching her to his chest, her feet still dangling, and strode across the wide foyer and into the sanctum. He closed the double doors behind him with a shove of his boot.

They sat in the sanctum all afternoon, their voices and Alba's laughter trickling out and echoing over the stone walls. The keepers moved in hushed happiness, keeping their ears attuned to the glad sound, and the Highest Keeper instructed those on kitchen duty to prepare a feast for the return of the favorite son.

No one seemed to know what to do—decorum dictated that a man and woman not be alone together behind a closed door, yet no one wanted to deny or diminish the joyous reunion, and so Master Ivo left it ajar. Ghost hovered near the sanctum door, shamelessly eavesdropping, and Dagmar kept finding reasons to join her, though the front entrance hall contained nothing but stone, space, and staircases.

At sundown, Ghisla joined the daughters and the keepers in songs of worship and took Ghost's hand as they sang the final praise.

Ghost's thoughts spun in dizzy wonder, sugared and pink, her joy for her daughter the constant in her unfiltered musings.

Mother of the earth be mine, father of the skies, divine.
All that was and all that is, all I am and all I wish.

Ghost wished for one thing above all others: Alba's happiness. Ghisla suspected it was the mantle of motherhood, to gladly sacrifice for the sake of your child.

Or mayhaps it was just the mark of true love; Ghisla would endure the rack to save Hod from it. He would do the same for her, and the simultaneous terror and joy of having and holding such devotion was more than she could comprehend most days.

But yes, she would endure the rack for Hod. It couldn't be worse than the torture she felt now.

Bayr had returned. Of all the times to finally come home. And she could not warn him. Not yet. Not at all? How would Bayr handle such a warning? She suspected he would handle it the way he'd handled every duty placed on his shoulders throughout his life. He would battle the Northmen, defend the mount, and protect his king. He might die doing it, but that would not be his concern. It would be Hod's concern. Saylok's concern. To warn him would be to seal his fate and destroy all chance of a peaceful revolution—if there was such a thing. So somehow, Hod had to get him off the mount.

Ghisla succumbed to her worry and went to the rune. She pricked her finger, traced the star, and said Hod's name, grimacing in anticipation. One didn't always know what waited on the other side of an unlocked rune.

She was suddenly doused—rather unpleasantly—in the sights and smells of unwashed men, seawater, and dark shores. A group of Northmen were gathered around a huge fire, drinking and belching and speaking of people and things she cared nothing about. Hod stood on the edge of the circle, his hands on his staff, his shield on his back, and his feet planted in the sand like he expected a bottle to be thrown at his head at any moment.

They were in Berne, and he was whole. She wiped the blood from her scar and severed her sight. It did her no good to look on him if she could not warn him or even talk to him. She vowed not to look again.

The gathering bell was rung for supper, and she joined the others in the dining hall, taking her usual place at her regular table and, like everyone else, spent the meal watching Bayr, who sat at the head. He was completely at home among the shiny pates and narrow shoulders, and the keepers peppered him all through the meal, making him answer question after question, though Bayr struggled through each one.

"Brothers. I am w-well. Dolphys is well. I want to hear from all of you. P-please don't torture me thus."

"But . . . why now, Bayr? Why have you come now?" the Highest Keeper asked softly, saving his question for last. The room fell silent as if each man and woman had wondered the same thing.

"We cannot continue as w-we have done. Saylok is . . ." He seemed to be searching for the right word, and he held up his big palms in frustration.

"Collapsing," Ghisla blurted out. Heads swiveled toward her in surprise, and Bayr raised his eyes to hers across the long table. She bowed her head, mortified that she had spoken aloud. She had not meant to. The word had risen to her lips and jumped of its own accord.

Bayr nodded, his mouth pursed in concern. "Yes, Liis of Leok. Saylok . . . is . . . collapsing."

The mood in the room flattened like an underbaked cake.

A frown dripped from the Highest Keeper's face, and his eyes searched Ghisla's before he thumped his scepter on the stones.

"We have survived twenty-five kings. Surely we can survive this one," the Highest Keeper refuted. "Sing for us, Liis of Leok. Tonight is not a time for dour predictions. Let us celebrate."

⁀℥

Hod and King Banruud did not return with the Northmen. Not the next day or the next. The grounds began filling with the tents and wagons of tradesmen preparing to sell their wares at the games, and overnight, the mount was flooded with clans and chaos as the Tournament of the King commenced without the king. The temple opened her doors to travelers making their yearly pilgrimage to worship in her walls, and the keepers heard the complaints and the confessions of the disconsolate.

Three chieftains arrived on the first day of competition—Aidan of Adyar, Lothgar of Leok, and Josef of Joran. Elbor of Ebba arrived at dusk on the second day, and he surrounded himself with soldiers, doing his utmost to avoid the other chieftains. Benjie of Berne was notably absent.

Alba greeted the crowds with upraised arms and a welcoming smile, fulfilling her role as welcoming monarch without a hitch. When she declared the tournament open to "all of Saylok's people, to her clans and her colors," no fear or discomfort tinged her voice, and the people threw flowers at her feet and sang her praises. At the commencement of each contest she wished the entrants "the wisdom of Odin, the strength of Thor, and the favor of Father Saylok," and they battled as though they had all three.

It was not until the fourth day of the tournament and well into the afternoon when a lone horn sounded from the watchtower and a cry went up.

"The king has returned! Ready the mount for His Majesty, King Banruud of Saylok."

From the King's Village to the top of Temple Hill, one trumpeter signaled another, each wailing a note that rose on the end like a question, the sound growing louder and louder as it climbed the long road to the mount. Along the ramparts, another chorus of horns sounded, verifying the message had been received.

The grounds were thick with clansmen and villagers, but every contest was halted as people ran to the gates and spilled down the hill. No clan wanted to be accused of not honoring the return of His Majesty, and the courtyard was flooded with clansmen mere minutes after the horns were sounded. Master Ivo clanged the gathering bell, summoning the keepers to their formation amid the columns; the daughters were required to make their presence felt as well, and Ghisla awaited the king's arrival standing among her silent sisters in a sea of purple on the highest row. It gave them a perfect view of the entire square.

Across the courtyard on the palace steps, Aidan, Lothgar, Josef, Elbor, and Bayr awaited the king as well, their most trusted warriors behind them.

The king's guard began to clear the enormous courtyard between the temple and the palace, forcing the curious and the clustered to move out onto the grass and the grounds to give the king and his retinue wide berth. To return during the tournament created a chaos the king's men clearly weren't accustomed to, and more than one villager was shoved to the ground in an attempt to clear the square. From outside the walls of the mount, a rumble began to swell and spill through the gates, a wave of shock and speculation that tumbled from one mouth to the next.

Ghisla's stomach groaned and her palms dripped. She knew what was coming.

The horns bugled again, indicating the king was nearing the gate, and Alba appeared at the top of the palace steps in full regalia. She had opened the tournament wearing only a long white dress and a simple gold circlet on her brow. King Banruud expected a more formal greeting. Her crown was a smaller replica of her father's, six spires with jewels that matched the colors of the clans embedded at the bases and the tips. Emeralds for Adyar, rubies for Berne, sapphires for Dolphys, orange tourmalines for Ebba, brown topaz for Joran, and golden citrines for Leok.

The chieftains moved to the sides, creating an aisle for Alba to descend between them, but she stopped in their midst, Bayr on her left and Aidan of Adyar on her right. Ghisla's attention was drawn away from the princess when the villagers who had been cleared from the central courtyard began to point toward the entrance, to clutch each other and cower.

"He's brought the Northmen to the temple mount," Juliah hissed, outraged.

"It is King Gudrun," Elayne whispered.

It was indeed, and a contingent of fifty Northmen.

Ghisla resisted the urge to crane her neck—she'd been trained to remain still and draw no attention to the daughters—but her eyes bounced from man to man, looking for Hod. He'd found a perch on a supply wagon; he'd probably ridden in it all the way. His staff was across his knees, his hood pushed back, and when her eyes settled on him, he lifted his chin as though he heard her too.

"My people. My daughter. My chieftains. My keepers," Banruud boomed, his arms raised to call the crowd to attention. "In the spirit of peace and negotiation, I have brought King Gudrun of the Northlands to see our temple and to take part in the tournament. I bid you to welcome him and his people. We are in need of strong alliances. May this be the first of many such visits."

The people murmured nervously. No one jeered, but there was no jubilance in their greeting, no cheers or waving of their colors. Many began shuffling toward the wide gate only to be cowed by the bone-studded, leather-clad Northmen who spilled out onto the drawbridge.

Alba began to descend the final palace steps, her sense of duty demanding she bid the visitors welcome, but Bayr moved forward with her. Aidan must have been of the same mind, for he too remained at her side. Josef and Lothgar trailed them as they walked out into the courtyard to present the princess of Saylok to the king of the Northlands. Elbor, evidently not wanting to be left behind, hurried to join them, though he cowered behind Lothgar.

As Alba neared, King Banruud dismounted and extended his hand toward her.

"Father, I thank Odin for your safe return," Alba said, projecting her voice to the crowd. She stepped away from the chieftains and pressed the back of Banruud's outstretched hand to her forehead in traditional greeting. Turning to the North King she curtsied, low and lovely, and rose up gracefully. "King Gudrun, we welcome you."

There was an appreciative murmur among Gudrun's men, and the North King slid unceremoniously from his horse and grasped Alba's fingers as though to press a kiss on her knuckles. At the last moment, he turned her hand so her palm was facing up. With exaggerated pleasure, he licked upward from the tips of her fingers to the pulse at her wrist, and his men roared in rowdy approval.

Bayr growled, a deep, guttural rumbling that caused Gudrun to raise his eyes and withdraw his tongue.

"Is that not how it's done in Saylok?" the North King asked Bayr, sardonic. "Or is she yours, Chieftain?"

"May I present my daughter, Princess Alba of Saylok," the king interrupted, but his eyes censured Bayr, his expression hard, his mouth tight. "The Temple Boy has fallen back into his old ways. He returns to the mount after a decade and immediately considers himself the princess's protector."

"Temple Boy?" Gudrun repeated, his eyebrows raised in query.

"I am Bayr. Chieftain of Dolphys," Bayr said carefully. Slowly. He did not acknowledge the king but kept his gaze on Gudrun.

"Ah. I have heard of you, Dolphys. You are known for your strength. I should like to test it." Gudrun sucked at his teeth.

"These are my chieftains—Adyar, Joran, Leok, and Ebba. You've met Berne," the king introduced, tossing his hand toward the men who trailed his daughter. Bayr was not the only one who bristled at the introduction. The clan chieftains were subordinate to the king, but the implication that they were "his" did not sit well.

Banruud offered his arm to Alba, who took it without hesitation, though her fingers barely touched his sleeve and her posture did not relent. Banruud nodded toward the keepers standing in silent observance on the temple steps. Ivo had moved out in front of them, a stooped crow bent around his scepter.

"Gudrun, may I present the daughters of the clans," Banruud said, striding toward the robed assembly. Gudrun followed eagerly. Some of the Northmen dismounted, eyes suspicious, hands on their weapons, and trailed after their king.

"I see only old men," Gudrun mocked. The daughters' hair was the only thing that set them apart—Master Ivo had dispensed long ago with any clan-colored distinctions—and they'd raised their hoods to cover their heads.

"We want to see the daughters, Master Ivo," Banruud ordered, coming to a halt before the Highest Keeper.

"They are not yours to command or display, Majesty," Ivo replied, his tone mild, as though he spoke to an insistent child.

Banruud moved so close to Ivo, he appeared to be speaking to a lover, whispering assurances in his ear, but Master Ivo raised his eyes to Gudrun, who stood over the king's shoulder, and spoke to him directly, ignoring King Banruud.

"What is your purpose here, Northman?" the Highest Keeper queried. His tone was so cold the crowd shivered.

"I want to see your temple, priest."

"I am not a priest. I do not save souls or speak for the gods. I am a Keeper of Saylok."

"And what treasures do you keep, old one?" Gudrun grinned, and his men laughed around him.

"Let us see the daughters," Elbor hollered, showing his support for the wishes of the king. "They belong to the people. Not the keepers."

A few clanspeople cried out in agreement. Others protested, frightened by King Banruud's company, unnerved by the Northmen inside the walls of their precious mount.

Benjie, still seated on his horse, among a handful of Gudrun's men and Banruud's guard, raised his voice in agreement.

"You worship the gods, but you obey the king, Highest Keeper," he said.

Lothgar of Leok grunted his agreement and Josef of Joran stepped forward, demanding a viewing as well.

"Daughters of the clans, come forward," Banruud bellowed, his hand on his sword. The keepers shifted, a pathway opening among them, and Ghisla and her sisters, their eyes fixed above Banruud's head, their purple robes hiding them from neck to toe, descended the steps.

The crowd strained to get a better view, and Gudrun smirked as they stopped in a straight line before him, not shrinking but not acknowledging him in any way.

The North King touched the fiery coils of Elayne's hair. Ghisla heard her whimper slightly, but she did not pull away.

"Elayne of Ebba," Banruud said.

"Elayne of Ebba," Gudrun grunted, his eyes shrewd. He moved on.

"Liis of Leok," Banruud announced, almost dismissing her. He seemed eager for Gudrun to move along, but the North King moved his face within an inch of hers, willing her to meet his gaze. He blew a stream of warm air against her lips.

"Hello, Songr," he whispered.

She did not respond or even deign to look at him.

"Such an icy wench," he hissed. He laughed and moved on to Juliah as the king introduced her.

Juliah was not ice, she was fire, and when Gudrun paused in front of her, she glowered at him disdainfully, her top lip lifted in the smallest of sneers.

"Juliah of Joran does not like me," he murmured. "Though I might enjoy changing her mind."

"Dalys of Dolphys," King Banruud intoned.

Dalys had begun to shrink, her slim shoulders bunching around her ears, but Gudrun ran the tip of his finger along the silky underside of her jaw and demanded she lift her face.

When she did, his lips curled.

"Your chieftain is so big." He shot a look toward Bayr. "But you are a runt. I want a woman," he said, dismissing her without another word. The crowd rumbled, and the Highest Keeper gnashed his teeth, but Gudrun wasn't finished. He moved to Bashti, who met his gaze with all the disdain he'd just shown Dalys. She was not a big woman either, but she demanded attention. Gudrun gave it to her.

He pressed his thumb to the swell of her full lips as though he intended to check her teeth. When she snarled and snapped at him, he laughed and lifted his eyes to Banruud, releasing her before he lost a finger.

"You have six clans, Banruud . . . but only five daughters," he mused.

"The princess is of Adyar," Aidan spoke up. "She represents our clan among the daughters of the temple." Aidan had remained by Bayr's side, though his eyes had clung to Elayne throughout the North King's inspection. His voice was controlled, but his hand clung to the hilt of his sword, and Ghisla knew she and Hod were not the only ones who nursed secret affections.

Gudrun turned and considered Alba once more. Like the daughters, she was unflinching beneath his scrutiny. "I think you lie, Chieftain. Who is that?" Gudrun pointed, his eyes sharp. "Do you seek to hide her from me?"

Ghost stood among the keepers, Dagmar beside her, but the hood of her robe had fallen back a few inches, and her thick, white braid was a stark contrast to the vivid hue of her robe.

If Ghisla had not been facing him, she might have missed Banruud's response. He recoiled beside Alba, drawing her back with a vicious jerk, his eyes wide with horror.

"I want to see her, priest," Gudrun insisted, curling his fingers at Ghost, beckoning her forward. Ghost had already ducked her head, shrinking back into her robe, an ivory slice of cheek the only visible part of her face. Dagmar was rigid beside her.

"She is not a daughter of the temple, King Gudrun," Master Ivo replied, but his eyes were glued to Banruud.

"No?" Gudrun sneered. He began mounting the stairs, shoving keepers aside. The crowd cried out, frightened by his aggression. Gudrun stopped in front of Ghost and pulled her hood from the wreath of her silvery-white hair. Her chin snapped up, her eyes gleamed, and Gudrun cursed and stumbled back, almost falling when his foot glanced off a step. The crowd in the courtyard gasped, the collective inhale like a crack of angry thunder.

"She is not a daughter, Majesty," Master Ivo repeated, though it was not clear to which king he referred. "She is a keeper." He paused, his gaze still clinging to King Banruud. "We call her . . . Ghost."

"I want to see the temple," the North King demanded, his voice ringing imperiously, but he had retreated several more steps. Ghost did not recover her hair or drop her gaze, but Dagmar had taken her hand in his, and without a word, the robed keepers moved back around her protectively.

"And you shall see it, King Gudrun," Banruud promised, finding his voice, though it rattled oddly. "It is open to all during the tournament. But we've traveled far, and you are hungry. We will dine first and enjoy the games. The temple can wait."

Banruud turned away, dismissing the Highest Keeper the way he had been dismissed. He gripped Alba's arm and drew Gudrun and his men forward with a wave of his hand. The North King followed reluctantly, turning back more than once to study the temple, her daughters, and her rows of huddled keepers.

26

Soldiers

The ship was sinking, and secrets were oozing through the widening cracks in the bow like terrified rats. Ghisla's own secrets trembled on her lips, but she clenched her teeth and bit them back, willing the rodents to swim.

Ghost had been careless. She should have kept her head down. Instead, she'd stood among the keepers on the temple steps, and the North King had seen her. Banruud had seen her. He'd seen her, and he'd known her. She would not be able to hide from him any longer.

Odin help them all.

Ghisla could feel the listing of the ground beneath her feet, and she clearly was not the only one. Ghost must have fainted or swayed, because Dagmar had swooped her up into his arms and was carrying her into the temple. Ghisla and her sisters hurried after him, and Master Ivo wasn't far behind, his scepter clacking against the stones.

"Are you unwell, Ghost?" Elayne asked, hovering at Dagmar's side. She passed a gentle hand over Ghost's brow. Ghost shook her head in shame.

"I'm a fool, Elayne. I was afraid, and I forgot to draw sufficient breath. I'm fine. See to the others. You were all so brave . . . and I am so proud."

"Go, Elayne," Dagmar urged kindly, laying Ghost on a cool bench in the sanctum. "See to the others. I'll look after Ghost."

Elayne hesitated and looked at her sisters.

"Do not send us away," Juliah said. "Tell us what is happening."

"We deserve to know what is happening," Bashti agreed.

Ghisla already knew what was happening.

She knew, and her heart raged in her chest. She needed to find Hod, but she didn't move. None of them moved.

Dagmar seemed at a loss, and Ghost stared up at him, her terror evident.

"What are we going to do?" Ghost whispered, but Dagmar rose from her side and stepped away, turning as Ivo entered the sanctum, his black robes melding with the shadows that jumped from stone to stone in the flickering light.

Ghisla pulled her sisters back, retreating to the shadows, but they did not leave.

Ivo did not sit upon the dais, and he did not ask Ghisla and her sisters to go. Ghisla wasn't even sure he noticed they were still in the sanctum. Instead he stopped in front of Ghost, his hands wrapped on the ball of his scepter, his chin resting on his hands. Ghost tried to rise, but her strength seemed to fail her.

"Why does Banruud fear you, Ghost?" he whispered.

"He does not fear me," Ghost choked.

But he did. Ghisla knew he did.

"Banruud will give the princess to the North King to stop their advance into Saylok, and young Bayr can do nothing to stop it," Master Ivo said, staring down at Ghost.

"I will go with her," Ghost panted.

Elayne moaned softly and Juliah took a step toward her, but Ghisla laid a hand on her shoulder, restraining her, afraid they would be asked to go. Dagmar, Ivo, and Ghost were oblivious to them.

"You are a keeper—you will not," Dagmar shot back, incredulous. "You've been entrusted with the knowledge of the runes. And that knowledge stays here, in the temple."

"I gave my word to the princess," she ground out, her jaw locked.

"You gave your word to me," Ivo hissed. "To Dagmar. To Saylok."

"I care nothing for Saylok," she cried. "I care nothing for the bloody runes. What good are the runes if they can't protect us? If they cannot right these wrongs?"

Ivo swayed as though he too had lost the strength to stand, and he turned away from her and walked up the long aisle to the dais, his head bowed, his shoulders stooped, and Ghost rose and followed him, Dagmar beside her, as if unable to resist the pull of his displeasure.

"Bayr is going to Alba," Ivo said, sinking down into his chair. "Even now. And you say nothing." Ivo raised his black gaze to Dagmar. "Have you not seen the way they look at each other?"

Dagmar flinched as though he'd been struck, and Ghost moaned.

"These secrets have been kept too long, and this one will destroy them, Dagmar. And still . . . you . . . say . . . nothing," Ivo marveled.

Ghisla's guilt sprouted like green vines, winding their way up her throat. She too had said nothing. They had all said nothing for far too long.

Tears had begun to course down Ghost's cheeks.

"Bayr and Alba do not understand that the connection they feel is a connection of the blood, of the heart, but it can never be a connection of the body," Master Ivo admonished.

"It is . . . not . . . a connection of the blood," Ghost wept, the words so faint Ghisla wasn't sure she'd even said them.

But she had. She'd finally said the words aloud. Dagmar turned shattered eyes to her, and Ivo beckoned her forward, curling his fingers toward his palm.

"Tell me!" Master Ivo bellowed.

"Alba is not Banruud's daughter," Ghost shouted back. "She was not Alannah's daughter. She is not a daughter of Saylok at all. She is the daughter of a slave."

"What are you saying?" Ivo whispered.

"Banruud took her from her mother only days after she was born," Ghost panted, as if the words were a torrent she could no longer contain. "And you made him king," she mourned. "You made him king. You made her a princess. And I could not take that away from her."

"But . . . in my vision . . . I saw . . . her mother's . . . joy," Ivo stammered. "Alannah gave birth to a child. I saw it."

"And I saw . . . her mother's pain," Dagmar whispered, as though he finally understood. "You are the slave girl, Ghost. *You* are Alba's mother."

"Odin help us," Elayne whispered, the words so faint only Ghisla and her sisters could hear. Ghisla feared Odin had abandoned Saylok long ago.

"Yes. I am Alba's mother," Ghost breathed. "I am Alba's mother." She told the truth like it was precious, too sacred for sound, and when she said the words again—"I am Alba's mother"—they were hardly more than a whisper.

"Tell me everything," Master Ivo demanded, harsh, exacting, and Ghost submitted, spilling the story with the relief of the long damned.

"My masters . . . a farmer and his wife . . . brought the babe to the Chieftain of Berne. They told me it was custom—law—and that they would return with the child and a piece of gold. I waited for hours. I worried. I needed to feed her. I went to the chieftain's keep and watched them come out. They didn't have my daughter. They said . . . they said the chieftain wanted to bring her to the Keepers of Saylok to determine whether she was a changeling . . . a monster . . . or a blessing."

Dagmar cursed, but Ghost continued.

"I watched her—I am called Ghost for my skin and my hair. But I have become one. I have learned how to blend in, to disappear, to be invisible. I waited and I watched. I planned. And then one day, I got my opportunity. But I couldn't do it. As much as I hated the king for what he'd done, what he'd taken from me. I could not hate the queen, a woman who so obviously loved and cared for my daughter. She held her so gently. She was so patient . . . and kind. And she was able to give her a life . . . that I could never give her."

Ghost raised her eyes to Dagmar and then to the Highest Keeper, pleading for them to understand. She didn't look toward Ghisla and her sisters. They did not exist. In that moment, it was only Ghost and her confession, and the daughters witnessed it in silence.

"My daughter was a princess. And I was a ghost. I could not take her from the people who loved her so perfectly. There would have been nowhere I could go, no place to take her where I wouldn't have been hunted down. In this world, in this temple . . . she had a protector."

"Bayr," Dagmar supplied.

"Yes. And all of you."

"That is why you are here. That is why Banruud dreamed of pale wraiths who came to take his child. Today the king . . . has seen his ghost," Master Ivo said, sinking back into his chair, his staff clattering to the floor.

"He thought I was dead. He sent men to kill me then. He will send them to kill me again."

"What have you done?" Ivo moaned.

"I have watched my daughter grow," Ghost shot back, defensive. "I have seen her raised as a princess of Saylok. She is loved. She is protected. She is safe." The final words rang false, and Ghost closed her eyes as if to hide her doubt.

"She isn't safe, Ghost. You aren't safe! Banruud saw you, and Alba is about to become queen of the Northlands," Dagmar lamented.

"Better queen of the Northlands than the daughter of a ghost," she retorted, wounded, and Dagmar touched her hand as though he'd forgotten all of them observed. But the Highest Keeper was already speaking, his voice a weary wail.

"We made Banruud king. We made him king. And the curse upon the clans continues. We have failed the people. Bayr was our salvation. And I knew it. I did not listen to the gods. Now it is too late."

"You m-made Banruud king," Ghost stammered. "You gave him his power. Can you not . . . take it away?"

"How?" Master Ivo asked, raising his clawed hands to the heavens. "We are a temple of aging keepers and hunted women. We have no power to remove Banruud. Should we seek to remove him by the sword? We have lost the faith of the people and the support of the chieftains. You heard the crowd today. The keepers have failed them. The Northmen are at our door, the king conspires to sell our daughters, and the temple—even Saylok—hangs in the balance."

"Surely . . . surely the runes . . . ," Ghost stammered.

"The runes are only as powerful—and as righteous—as the blood of the men and women who wield them. And we have tried every rune, beseeched every god, and bled into the soil of every clan," Master Ivo said. "The keepers have failed. I have failed. And Saylok will fall."

The mount was crowded and Hod's senses reeled. He was no good in a crush—not to himself or anyone else. One heartbeat reverberated into another, and he climbed from the wagon of provisions and, using his staff and his general ability to repulse, moved among the masses.

He tracked the dulcet tones of Ghisla's heart and the butterfly wings of her indrawn breath. She was still among the keepers; they'd withdrawn from the steps after Gudrun's inspection, and twenty-six soldiers now guarded the temple doors. The North King's arrival had struck terror into every breast: the chieftains, the princess, the keepers, the citizenry. And Bayr. Bayr was not supposed to be on the mount.

He left the courtyard and drew a pail of water from the well and took the stairs to his room, addressing the servants who bustled in and out of the yard with a terse "good day." The king's return had sent them all into a frenzy. He washed the dust from the journey off his skin and patted himself dry. Ghisla's scent still lingered on his bed and in the towel beside the basin. He tracked her heart again, unable to help himself.

"Hody, Hody, Hody." She was singing his name. It wafted in on the breeze, and as he listened, she grew closer.

She was trying to find him. Or mayhaps . . . she already knew where he was.

He heard her climb the steps, her treads soft but hurried, like she dashed to avoid detection.

He turned and strode to his door, pulling it open as she reached the corridor. She tumbled into his arms a moment later.

"I knew you would hear me, and I prayed you would be here," she cried.

"You could have been seen," he chided, shoving the door closed behind her, but he was too glad to see her, too eager to greet her, and he kissed her, allowing himself a brief respite from his crippling concern.

She smelled of rosewater and incense, of panic and tears, and he lapped at the salt of her mouth and shuddered beneath the clutch of her hands. Her breasts were pebbled against his chest, and her limbs were trembling with need. It was not anticipation or desire, though he felt that too.

She was afraid.

"Ghisla," he soothed, stroking her silken cheek as he softened his kiss, but she shook her head, resisting his comfort and seeking her own. Her hands dug into his hips, urging him to her. And he understood. He gathered her skirts in his hands and found the slick heat of her body beneath them. She shuddered against his mouth, and he urged her onto his bed, freed himself from his breeches, and sank inside her without another word.

She quaked against him, her mouth on his mouth, her chest to his chest, her legs cradling his hips, and for a brief, mindless moment, unparalleled pleasure drenched a month of unbearable strain.

Then the present returned, the tower bells tolled, and their pleasure fled in the face of their fear.

Hod smoothed Ghisla's skirts and gathered her into his arms. Her heartbeat made love to his, though their time together was gone.

"You must go, my love," he urged.

"I know."

"You must gather the daughters and the keepers, bar the temple doors, and leave through the tunnels. You must get off the mount tonight."

"What of Alba?"

"Ghost must decide if she wants to keep her secret or save her daughter."

"She told Master Ivo. She told Dagmar. Just now, in the sanctum. Her secret is out. Banruud saw her. She has haunted him all these years. I think he convinced himself she wasn't . . . real."

Hod had heard the exchange on the temple steps. He'd heard Banruud's gasp and smelled the terror that rose on his skin, but he had not known how to interpret it. "He's shaken. But it will only harden his resolve. He will announce the betrothal tonight, and there will be a wedding in the morning. He thinks the Northmen will leave and his troubles will be averted."

Ghisla groaned with such pain that he tightened his arms, as if he could protect her from it all. He couldn't.

"Alba and Bayr . . . He is in love with her. She's in love with him. They've tried to keep it hidden, but . . . I know it's true."

"Oh no," Hod rasped. "This cannot be."

"The betrothal will destroy them both. She cannot marry the North King."

"We will get her off the mount. She must go with the daughters," Hod said, scrambling to process the unraveling of his plans.

"But Hod, what of Bayr? If the Northmen attack, he will fight! He will fight for the mount. He is a chieftain of Saylok. He will fight."

"I will take care of Bayr," he vowed, though he didn't know how. Bayr should be in Dolphys. In ten years he had not come to the mount! "I will protect Bayr. I will guard him with my life."

"And who will guard you?" Ghisla wailed, her hands clutching her face. For a moment he gave her his mouth, pressing his entreaties into her lips and her skin.

"You must not give up," he whispered, and her tears began to fall. "Shh. Ghisla. You promised you would not give up on me."

She groaned again, her teeth grinding, her fists clenched against his chest.

"I will do . . . whatever . . . you say," she bit out, "but you promise *me* that I will not have to live without you again."

He wrapped his hands around hers and drew them to his lips, trying to control the quaking in his chest.

"If you fall . . . I will follow. Do you understand me?" she cried, fierce even as her tears fell unchecked.

"I understand you," he whispered.

He rose and pulled her from his bed, kissing her mouth and her eyes and wiping her tears. She pushed him away like she could not bear the agony of parting one more time, and when the coast was clear, she fled his room as quickly as she'd come.

"Do not fall, Hod," she whispered as she ran. "Do not fall."

He did not fear a fall. He could endure that. He could endure the end. But he could not fail.

27

ATTACKS

The feast was raucous and rowdy, the North King taunting the chieftains and refilling his goblet with abandon. Banruud made no effort to subdue him, though he dismissed Alba before the first course was finished. Hod listened to her go, his stomach in greasy coils. He was not alone in his tension, for when the meal was done and Gudrun stretched out, snoring by the fire like the castle was already his, Lothgar of Leok and the Chieftain of Adyar pushed their chairs back from the table and demanded an audience with the king. When Bayr added his voice to Aidan and Lothgar's and Chief Josef concurred, the king sighed and rose.

"So be it."

"Benjie and Elbor should be p-present as well," Bayr demanded.

"By all means," Banruud mocked. "It will be your first council, Temple Boy. We welcome you."

Banruud snapped his fingers, instructing Hod and half his guard to accompany him. He bade the other half remain behind with the sleeping North King and his unruly cadre.

The chieftains, rattled by the king's sentry, signaled for their own men to follow, and every man eyed the others with open distrust, clan colors and weapons on full display. Aidan pounced as soon as the council chamber doors were closed and the chieftains were seated.

"You bring the Northmen to the mount, you parade the daughters of the temple in front of their bloody king, and you have not consulted about it with any of us."

Banruud was slow to answer the Chieftain of Adyar.

"I am the king. I do not take instruction from Adyar, or Leok, or Dolphys, or Joran. I will hear your complaints. But I will do as I wish, just as other kings have done before me. Just as other kings will do when I am gone."

"Do you take instruction from Berne?" Bayr interjected.

Benjie scoffed, but the other chieftains were silent, waiting for Bayr to continue.

"Between Ebba and Berne, we have s-suffered twenty-seven attacks over these last few years. Benjie d-denies it, Elbor throws up his hands. But our villages have been attacked. Our farms. Our fishermen. We repel attacks on our shores only to be attacked on our f-flanks by these clans." Bayr had to pause several times and speak more slowly than the king had patience for, and Hod found himself gritting his teeth, willing the room to hold, to listen, to respect the stuttering chieftain.

"Benjie cannot be blamed for rogue bands of marauders," Banruud said, disdain dripping from the words.

"He can," Bayr argued.

The king snapped his teeth at the chieftain's insolence, but Bayr continued, undeterred.

"Benjie encourages it. He is . . . em-emboldened . . . by his . . . relationship to you, S-sire, and has no r-respect for other c-clans or other chieftains."

"Do you stutter because you are frightened, Temple Boy?" Banruud mocked.

Dakin and Dred grunted at the insult to their chieftain, and the king's guard drew their swords, a rippling of steel that stiffened Hod's back.

"He is the Dolphys. Not the Temple Boy, Banruud," Dred growled.

"And I am the king, Dred. And you will address me as such, or you will lose your tongue."

"I care n-not what you call me, Majesty. But you will not be k-king of Saylok if the c-clans destroy each other."

"You threaten me?" Banruud growled.

"If the clans fall, the k-kingdom falls."

"And who will be king when I am not, hmm? You? The next king will be from Dolphys, and you believe the keepers will choose you. Is that why you've finally taken your place at the council table, Temple Boy? You wish to kill me and let the keepers make you king?"

The room became tomb-like with the accusation, and Bayr did not seek to break the silence. Hod thought that wise; to protest was to give credence to the king's claim.

"You are naught but a hulking ox, Bayr of Dolphys. An ox has great strength, but we do not make an ox our king," Benjie mocked.

Again, Bayr did not react, but Hod could hear Dred's outrage. It rumbled deep in his throat like a hungry wolf.

"I have no w-wish to be king," Bayr stated firmly.

"A king must command his people, and you can barely speak. The tribes of our enemies would breach the temple mount before you could call out the order for attack," Elbor snickered.

"Better a hulking ox than a blathering idiot," Josef of Joran murmured.

"Better a good man than a glib man," Aidan of Adyar purred.

"Better a tangled tongue than a forked one," Dred growled.

Hod knew every man in the room had his hand on his sword, and for a moment no one breathed, as though wondering who would be the first to lunge. The king's chair scraped against the floor; the vibration skittered up Hod's legs. He rose, for his voice came from several feet higher than moments before.

"What do you want me to do?" Banruud asked. "I am a king, not a keeper. I am but a man. I am not a master of runes. We support the temple on the mount, the people worship the keepers, and yet they cannot answer our prayers. My daughter is the last girl child to be born to a son of Saylok. In twenty-four years, she is the only one." Banruud paused, letting the reminder sink in around him. It was almost as if he believed his own lie.

"Yet you come to *me* as though I can heal *your* seed," Banruud continued. "Why do you not ask the keepers what they have done to end the scourge? Do they not guard the holy runes? Do they not commune with the fates? Do they not have Odin's ear?"

Banruud waited again, fervor ringing in his voice, and when no one disagreed with him, he continued.

"Five daughters have grown to womanhood in the temple walls, yet they have not been returned to you, to their clans. Their wombs are empty. What hope have they given you, Chieftains of Saylok? What hope have they given your people? Our sons turn on each other. And you come to *me* with your hands extended, asking *me* to cure this ill. Why do you not ask the keepers?"

The men behind Elbor all began to grunt in raucous agreement, the sound like a herd of starving pigs.

The chuff and growl of the warriors of Berne, the Clan of the Bear, became a competing swell, and Hod resisted the urge to cover his ears. Lothgar of Leok threw back his head and roared just to compete, the sound reverberating like the lion he claimed to descend from.

"There . . . is . . . no . . . order," Bayr said, each word succinct, and the cacophony ceased.

"It is not the keepers who rape and pillage. It is not the keepers who send their warriors to plunder the lands of their neighbors," Dred added, his fury billowing over his grandson's head.

"We take what we must to survive," Benjie barked.

"You are lazy, Benjie. Your land is overrun with young men who follow your lead. Our women are few, but it is not the women who plow the fields or trap or fish or fight the Northmen. It has never been the women. So what is your excuse?" Dred argued.

"You are not a chieftain, Dred of Dolphys!" Benjie yelled, and the scraping of chairs and the rattling of swords indicated a battle of some sort had ensued.

Bayr bellowed, and from the sound of it, Benjie had made the mistake of lunging for Dred of Dolphys and had been tossed head over tail and landed with a crash behind Lothgar of Leok. His blade rattled across the floor and thudded against Hod's foot. Hod kicked it back toward him as gasps of shock rippled from the table to the warriors who lined the walls. Hod wasn't certain if it was awe at Bayr's feat or fear at what it would incite.

Lothgar roared again, but this time in laughter. "I didn't know bears could fly, Benjie."

From Benjie's silence, Hod could only ascertain that he was not conscious or he too had been stunned by his newly discovered ability.

"Help the man off the floor," Lothgar instructed his men.

"The chieftain from Dolphys is not wrong," Aidan contended as Lothgar's merriment subsided. "We too have been beset by raiders from Berne. The fish have not stopped filling our nets. There is bounty in the land, and our men continue to be fierce in battle. But there are too many of them without families or female companionship. And some grow aimless . . . and vicious."

Josef of Joran, a man who was more farmer than warrior, raised his own weary complaints to the king. "We are under constant threat from Ebba. Some of the Ebbans who seek refuge have nothing but the clothes on their backs, but they are willing to work and we welcome them. Others who come want only to take what does not belong to them. We have had to put warriors on the border, and now all who seek entry are turned away. We simply cannot absorb all of Ebba. Elbor sends his poor to me, and he sits like a pig on the spit, an apple in his fat snout."

"We have been suffering attacks from the Hinterlands for more than a decade," Elbor shot back.

"As have we," Josef replied wearily. "It has always been thus among the clans on the southwestern shores. We battle the Hinterlands, Dolphys battles the Eastlanders, Berne and Adyar battle the Northmen, Leok battles the storms. But we have never come against each other, clan on clan."

"You t-tax your people into the ground, Elbor, while you do l-little to protect them," Bayr leveled.

"I collect coin for the keepers. And what do they do for us?" Elbor shouted, echoing the accusations of the king.

It was a lie. The keepers lived on very little, herding their own sheep, milking their own goats, and tending their own gardens. Whatever coin came from the clans by way of the king was a pittance. Alms were collected during the tournament, and every farthing went to the preservation of the temple itself. There were no wealthy keepers.

"You collect coin for yourself and for the king. As do we all," Bayr replied. "The k-king requires far more than the keepers."

"Careful, Temple Boy," the king whispered, the words slithering from his mouth.

"This is all true," Lothgar interrupted, oblivious to the tension that coiled around him. "Yet . . . I have wondered why the keepers can do nothing to end the scourge among our women."

"As have I," Josef admitted.

"Aye," Elbor agreed, eager to turn the subject away from his own failures.

"Something must be done," Benjie agreed, and his acquiescence had the king sitting back in his chair as though he pondered the question. The chair squeaked with the motion.

"And something has been done," the king said. "I have reached an agreement with the North King. The princess will be a queen."

Hod held his breath, sick for his brother.

"She will leave with King Gudrun for the Northlands in two days. In return, the North King has agreed to pull his warriors from Berne. An announcement will be made after the melee tomorrow. Your precious daughters of the temple will be left to age beside your useless keepers," the king mocked.

Silence wrapped the room in guilty relief, and the chieftains began to murmur like it was the only feasible course of action. Benjie stood from the table as though it were settled, and Elbor lumbered to his feet as well, clearly eager to escape further condemnation.

"She should not be sold," Bayr said, stating the words precisely, breathing between each one, speaking slowly even though Hod could hear how his heart raced.

"She is not being sold. She is going to be a queen, and she will help her country in the process," Benjie argued.

"She should be queen of Saylok. She is the only one . . . of her kind," Bayr insisted.

Banruud laughed, sitting back in his chair; it squealed against his weight.

"And how . . . exactly . . . would she be queen of Saylok?" Banruud sneered. "Did you think . . . *you* . . . might have her? Did you suppose *you* could marry the princess . . . and when I die . . . *you* and she could reign in my stead?" Banruud's voice was hushed with mock surprise, and Elbor grunted.

"That will never be, Temple Boy. Alba's destiny does not include you," Banruud said, his tone flat.

Bayr was silent. Hod knew he had never wanted to reign. But it was evident that he *did* want Alba.

"You are a bloody cur, Banruud," Aidan of Adyar growled. He stood abruptly, his chair scraping the stone, an echo of his disgust. He left the council table without another word, striding for the doors with his men trailing after him. Lothgar was slower to leave, but he did not argue the king's decision or seek to offer an alternative solution. He followed Aidan from the room.

"We're done here," Banruud said, dismissing those who still lingered. Bayr did not leave the table. His heart was a counterrhythm to the king's, and Hod listened to them both as the room emptied around them and the two men sat, alone but for Hod and a handful of the king's guard, who hovered near the doors, and Dred and Dakin, who remained in silent support of their chieftain.

"Don't do this . . . to Alba. To Saylok. The people . . . look . . . to her. She is their . . . only hope," Bayr pled, his voice low. His heart brayed in his chest.

"It is done," Banruud said, enunciating each word with a thump of his fist upon the long table. "Leave me."

"P-p-please," Bayr stuttered, unable to keep the desperation from the word, and in his desperation, he was not a chieftain but an abused child.

"P-p-please," Banruud mimicked, exaggerating the sounds so he spat with every syllable. "You dare question me? You love my daughter, and you think I don't know? She is your sister, you fool. You cannot wed your sister."

Bayr grunted as though he'd been lanced.

The king laughed and threw his feet up on the table, feigning indifference.

"Surely you knew. Surely your beloved Uncle Dagmar told you who you are? I thought you slow but not entirely ignorant."

Bayr stood in horrified disbelief.

"You are my son, Bayr. You are Alba's brother." Banruud said the words like they were of no consequence at all.

Heaviness spread through Hod, numbing his lips and his neck, his shoulders and his chest, hollowing out his veins and hardening his blood. He would kill Banruud himself. He would kill him, and he would free the mount from his tyranny. He would free his brother from his lies.

"I am n-not," Bayr denied, aghast.

"Oh, but you are. You are of the Clan of the Bear. Named for me, your father. Desdemona was a passionate wench . . . and so dramatic. Even in death, I'm sure."

Dred howled in fury, and Dakin grunted in protest, wrapping his arms around the incensed warrior to save him from taking vengeance upon the man who could have him put to death. The king's guard leaped forward, protecting the king and dragging Dakin and a thrashing Dred from the chamber. Hod listened, bereft, wanting to gnash his teeth and bellow the injustice alongside them.

"You will leave the mount, Temple Boy," Banruud ordered. "And take the old man. If you want to live—if you want him to live—you won't return."

Hod could not feel his legs. He could not feel his hands or his heartbeat. He felt nothing at all. No sensation. No sadness. No breath. No being.

He could hear the king's guard circling around Bayr, their swords drawn, but no one dared to engage him. They'd all heard the tales. They'd all seen proof of his power. Yet he stood, hardly breathing, like he'd been carved from stone.

Then someone gasped and something fell, and Bayr turned and strode from the room, his heartbeat fading as his distance from Hod grew.

"He cut off his braid," someone whispered, and Hod hung his head in shame.

For a moment, the king sat in silence, his breathing harsh, his heart oddly echoing that of the man who'd just exited the room, severing all ties.

"Balfor, make sure my daughter is in her chambers for the rest of the night. Put a guard at her door," Banruud ordered.

"Yes, Majesty."

"The rest of you . . . leave me."

Hod moved to go with the others, but Banruud called him back.

"Hod," Banruud said. Hod tensed and turned, but the king did not continue until they were the only two left in the room.

"Follow him."

"Who, Sire?"

"The Temple Boy."

Hod waited, knowing there was more.

"Follow him. Make sure he leaves the mount. And when he does . . . end him."

"Yes, Sire."

"And Hod?"

"Sire?"

"It would be better if he were not found."

&

When the warriors of Dolphys came to the temple not long after sundown in search of their chieftain, Ghisla's alarm continued to build. Dagmar had slipped away to pray, but everyone else was present to hear the warriors relay their account of the king's council.

"He knows, Master Ivo," Dred of Dolphys confessed. "I should have told him long ago. But Bayr knows the truth now, and I fear it has broken him." Dred's face was streaked with worry and wear, and the warriors around him shifted in distress. Their faces held traces of their own shock and disbelief, as if they too had been seared by the mistreatment of their chieftain. The Highest Keeper did not have to ask of what truth Dred spoke.

"The king has banished him," Dakin said, grim. "But he is the Dolphys, and our allegiance is to him first. We will not let this stand."

"What should we do, Highest Keeper?" Dred asked.

"Wait for him near the Temple Wood," Ivo answered. "He will not go far. His heart is here. His . . . fate . . . is here too."

391

When the men from Dolphys left the sanctum, Ghisla followed them. It was a testament to their dazed devastation that they didn't notice her hovering behind them until they neared the east gate. Those who saw her would simply assume the men were acting as guards, if they took notice of her at all. No one milled around; the east wall overlooked the winding climb above the Temple Wood, darkness had fallen, and the festivities were elsewhere.

"Dred of Dolphys, I would have a word, please," she said, touching his sleeve.

The men turned as one, startled, and the youngest one stepped on the back of the red-headed warrior's shoe, causing them both to stumble and the elder one to curse.

They all clutched their braids in confused respect.

"Liis of Leok," Dred said, bowing.

"Please, I know you are worried about Bayr. But I must know . . . in the council . . . with the king . . . was the blind man there?" she implored.

Dred frowned and cocked his head. His face had aged in the last hour. In the torchlight his hair was that of a silver wolf, but his form was as muscled and hard as a warrior half his age. He was a man who'd spent his life wielding a sword and had never had a woman to make sure he fed more than his hunger for battle.

It was the redheaded warrior who processed her question first. "Aye. He was there. He stood back from it all, behind Banruud's chair."

"He is the king's man," the warrior they called Dystel added softly.

She dared not dispute that and simply thanked them, turning away. The liquid feeling in her legs became acid in her stomach.

Hod knew what had transpired. He would be aware that Bayr had left the mount.

"Why do you ask, daughter of Leok?" Dred pressed, detaining her with a hand on her arm.

"She is the king's harlot," the youngest one blurted. "I've heard the tales about her."

Dred swung on the warrior, knocking him back. "Ye'll not be speaking that way to a daughter of Saylok, Daniel. The king has abused and abandoned many. I've a mind to cut out your tongue."

Daniel was immediately repentant. "Forgive me, Dred. Forgive me, Daughter."

She nodded once, caring little for his opinion of her, one way or the other.

"Things are not what they seem," she whispered. "Bayr is . . . not the only son of Banruud."

It was the only thing she could think to say to convey the complicated nature of Hod's involvement. His relation to Banruud would not condemn him with these men. Not when their beloved chieftain had just found himself in the same position.

"What do you mean?" Dred rasped.

"Exactly what I say. The king has abused and abandoned many," she repeated, raising her eyes to his.

The guard on the east gate peered over at them, curious.

"Do not judge too hastily," she said. "I beseech you." She didn't dare warn them away from the hill. It would only make them want to remain. They needed to do as Master Ivo—and the king—had demanded. They needed to leave the mount, and she would not delay them further.

"Find Bayr . . . and go. There is nothing to be gained by warring with this king. Eventually, he will reap what he has sowed."

"He warned us as well, Daughter. Mayhaps now . . . I understand," Dred murmured. He was reeling, and there was no time.

"Go. Please," she urged. Her sisters would notice her gone, and already two sentries approached. It was not every day that she made two successful escapes.

Dred grabbed his braid, a signal of his respect, and the other men did the same.

Then they left through the east gate, their swords swinging and their strides long.

28

DAUGHTERS

Bayr was moving quickly, almost running. He'd hurtled through the east gate and bounded down the mountainside like a sheepdog, and Hod, for all his skill and ability, was a man of distinct limitations. He could go great distances . . . but he could not go quickly. Within minutes, Bayr was out of range, and Hod could not hear him anymore.

At the bottom of the hill, Hod stopped and listened, trying to find his brother in the miasma of life that was the wood.

He could not hear him.

But his scent lingered, the smell of incense and cedar, as if the trees in Dolphys and the temple sanctum had converged in him. Both scents bled from his skin with his despair. It created a tang not so different from that of a wounded animal careening through the brush.

Hod entered the wood and picked his way along, reassuring himself that Bayr would stop, and when he did, Hod would find him. It might take all night, but he would find him. And when he did, he would tell him everything.

It was a comfort to know he'd left the hill. Hod could only pray Ghisla and the keepers would soon do the same.

Princess Alba was missing.

No one was allowed in the temple, and no one was allowed out.

Minutes after Ghisla had returned, the king had ordered the doors barred.

King Banruud now paced from room to room, checking the progress of his men, demanding they look again when their efforts yielded nothing. When they came up empty handed after an hour, he returned to the sanctum, his men trailing behind him, their tension echoing his.

"Where is she, Ivo?" Banruud clipped, towering over the weary Highest Keeper.

Master Ivo stared at the king balefully. "Where is who, Majesty?"

"My daughter," Banruud ground out.

"But Majesty . . . you have no daughter," Ivo murmured. "Only a son. And he has been sent away."

Banruud's countenance darkened, and his gaze swung to the women gathered at the rear of the room. Over the last years, the temple had become a sanctuary for an assortment of females who had nowhere else to go. Twenty-eight had been added to their numbers.

The king walked toward them, pushing them apart as though Alba hid among them. He then searched the keepers the same way. Ghisla and her sisters were next. Banruud glowered at her last and sniffed the air around her like he could smell Hod on her skin.

Mayhaps he could.

His eyes narrowed and his nostrils flared, but he turned away, and walked back toward the keepers.

"Remove your robes," the king ordered. The keepers gaped and shrank from him. "All of you, remove your robes," he insisted again, yanking their hoods from their heads, their gleaming pates vulnerable in the orange glow of the guards' torches.

Banruud wanted to intimidate them, to demoralize them, and he was succeeding.

Ghisla watched the old men obey—everyone but the Highest Keeper. They opened their robes without argument and dropped them on the sanctum floor. They all stood in their simple white sheaths; Dagmar was not among them. Nor was Ghost. Ghisla took heart that they were gone. She had little doubt the king was searching for Ghost too, and she would be struck down if he found her.

"Separate the keepers!" the king instructed his men, and they immediately began spreading the disrobed keepers from one end of the sanctum to the other. Then he demanded the same to be done with the women.

As Banruud searched, his anger grew, and he turned back to the Highest Keeper once more, his boots echoing across the stone floor like a spike being nailed home.

"Where is she?" Banruud snapped, his face pressed up to Ivo's, spittle flying in the Highest Keeper's face.

"Who, King Banruud? Who is it you seek?" Ivo asked, his voice barely audible and perfectly mild.

"The white woman. The wraith. Where is she?" Banruud hissed.

"Ah. The white woman. You have sought her for some time. Mayhaps she has taken your daughter. Or . . . mayhaps . . . you . . . have taken . . . hers."

Banruud's nostrils flared and something flickered in his eyes, and Ghisla moaned. The Highest Keeper had confirmed the one thing the king feared most. Ivo knew what the king had done, and that could not stand.

The king's hand shot out, plunging and retreating, and Ivo stilled even as Ghisla's scream rent the air. The king stepped back and watched Ivo crumple, folding into himself without so much as a grunt.

"We're done here," the king called to his guard. "Keep men at the doors. No one goes in or out until the princess is found."

The rattle of stone against stone indicated a reentry from the tunnels, and Keeper Amos, the senior-most member of all the keepers, rose from the throng surrounding Master Ivo's body and walked toward the dais. Ghisla noticed numbly that his feet were coated in Ivo's blood.

When Dagmar and Ghost stepped out of the opening and into the sanctum, they were met with a room crowded with kneeling keepers and quiet condemnation.

"The king has killed the Highest Keeper. His men stand at every door," Keeper Amos cried, his voice ringing with accusation.

Dagmar and Ghost stared back, brows furrowed in disbelief, unable to make sense of the sight before them and process the keeper's unfathomable claim.

"Master Ivo is dead," Juliah said, rising. Her face was grim, but her voice was strong. In the orange glow of the flickering light, she was far fiercer than any keeper in the room. Ghisla rose beside her.

Ghost cried out and ran toward the circle of mourners, stepping over and between them until she halted, her hands clutching her robes, her eyes on the ground. Dagmar followed more slowly.

Master Ivo's black robes were soaked in blood, making them shine in the candlelight. In death he was not powerful; he was not the Highest Keeper. He was an old man, an abandoned shell, his skin spotted with age, his features flaccid, the black stain from his lips smeared across his papery cheeks.

Dagmar crouched beside him and lifted him from the floor as if he were no more substantial than a child, and every bit as dear. Then he carried him to the altar. Ghisla, Ghost, the daughters, and the keepers followed in an impromptu processional.

Ghost rushed to help straighten his limbs and smooth his robes as Dagmar laid him down and presented him to the gods. His sleeve caught on Dagmar's front clasp, and Ivo's thin white forearm was revealed.

"There are runes on his arm," Ghost gasped, pushing back the voluminous folds. "He has carved them here, above his wrist."

Ghisla gaped at the bloody whorls and lines.

"I don't know these runes," Ghost murmured.

Ghisla knew them. One was the soul rune, used to connect one spirit to another. It was the same rune Hod had carved into her hand. Ivo had been reaching out to someone in the final minutes of his life. The other rune—man, woman, and child separated by a serpent—was Desdemona's. She'd seen it too, in Dagmar's thoughts, a lifetime ago.

"Someone tell me what happened here," Dagmar demanded, and his voice shook. Amos, always the most outspoken among the keepers, proceeded to describe the events that had unfolded.

By the time Amos had finished his account, Dagmar had sunk to Ivo's chair on the dais and the daughters and the keepers had gathered around him, as stricken and lost as he. But Ghost remained beside the altar, her white head bowed, holding Ivo's gnarled hand. The hem of her purple robe was black with Ivo's blood; a long crimson streak stretched from the altar where she now stood to the rear of the sanctum where he'd lain, marking her path.

"Who will come to our aid?" Dalys asked, her voice small.

"We must save ourselves," Ghisla implored.

"But . . . even Bayr has forsaken us," Keeper Bjorn complained, and Ghost raised her head, her eyes meeting Dagmar's across the altar.

"The gods have forsaken us," Amos intoned. "We have failed to lift the scourge."

"The king must die," Juliah growled.

"We must get a message to the chieftains. We must tell the people what he has done," Elayne pressed.

"None of them will care," Keeper Dieter argued.

"Aidan of Adyar will care," Elayne shot back. "Lothgar and Josef will care."

"No one will stand against Banruud," Ghisla said. The time had come. She could wait no longer. "There are Northmen on our mount. The clans are afraid, and the king has offered a solution."

"What solution is that?" Dagmar asked, harsh.

"He has announced the marriage of Princess Alba to the North King. Gudrun has promised to leave the mount and to withdraw from Berne," Amos supplied, a hint of admiration tingeing his words. "It is really the only solution."

"Why would the North King agree to such a thing?" Dagmar hissed.

The keepers gaped, not understanding, and Amos was the first to recover. "The princess is beautiful. She is a great prize, a valuable treasure. She is the hope of Saylok," he stammered, outraged.

"The hope of Saylok," Dagmar repeated softly. "And what assurances does the king have that Gudrun will leave?" Dagmar asked.

The keepers had no answer, and their aging faces grew grim. Ghost turned from the altar, her gaze clinging to Dagmar's.

"He wants the temple," Juliah muttered.

"And the mount," Bashti added.

"He wants Saylok," Ghisla said. "He won't leave."

"And if no one will stop Banruud . . . who will stop Gudrun?" Dalys asked, and her cry echoed in Ghisla's chest.

"We will stop him," Dagmar whispered, but there was no victory in his voice. He bowed his head and closed his eyes. "Master Ivo has already begun."

"We have to leave the mount," Ghisla insisted. "All of us. If Gudrun will not leave, there will be a battle. The keepers cannot stand against the Northmen. We can't hide in the temple any longer. We have to go."

Her sisters stared at her, stunned. It was so rare that she voiced her opinions or took the lead.

"Where will we go?" Dalys whispered.

"We must go to Dolphys . . . with Bayr." With Bayr and Hod. *Oh, gods.* She prayed Bayr would keep on going, and Hod would follow.

But they could not leave without Alba, and Alba was missing.

Dagmar solved that problem the same way Master Ivo had to find Bayr—with a seeker rune—and he raised weary, blood-streaked eyes to Ghost mere seconds later.

"She was waiting on the hillside . . . probably for Bayr, but he was not with her. She is coming back now."

"I will go to her. I will tell her what has happened. And we will go. We will all go," Ghost said.

But when Ghost came back an hour later, her face streaked with tears and her white hair escaping her braided crown, she shook her head.

"She will not leave."

"She has to!" Ghisla shot back.

"She won't," Ghost whispered. "She is convinced if she leaves, war will follow, and she will not bring death to Dolphys. She is the princess, and a princess has a duty to her people."

"She is right," Dagmar whispered. "Banruud will not let her go. He will declare war on Dolphys, the clans will take sides, and Saylok will . . . collapse."

He looked at Ghisla, using her word from the night they'd celebrated Bayr's return.

Ghisla's legs could no longer hold her. It was all spiraling out of control. If Alba would not leave, Ghost would not leave. If Ghost would not leave, Dagmar would not leave. The keepers were already murmuring among themselves that their duty was to the temple.

"We do not know that the North King will break his word," Keeper Amos argued, hopeful. "Mayhaps he will marry the princess as the king has announced, and he will take his filthy soldiers and leave."

"Mayhaps we are anticipating an attack that will never come," another keeper protested.

Ghisla did not know the plan or the precise way events would unfold. She doubted even Hod knew the specifics. Mayhaps the attack would come after the nuptials, and mayhaps it would happen during. Images of the Northmen wreaking havoc in the temple, striking down keepers and congregants swelled in her thoughts. Whenever it happened, she had no doubt an attack would come.

"He does not have enough men to take the mount. There are three hundred clan warriors on the hill right now, not counting the king's forces and the clanspeople. It makes no sense to attack this way," Dagmar agreed.

"He has seen inside the walls now. He knows the position of the king's men. He knows the strength of his forces and the numbers in the clans," Ghost murmured.

"Mayhaps . . . he is simply gathering information for a . . . future . . . attack?" Amos sounded so wistful at the thought of pending—and not immediate—doom.

"We need to go," Ghisla urged. "All of us. Together. Now!"

"I'm not leaving," Juliah argued. "If there is to be a battle, I want to fight."

"You will be hewn down or worse!" Ghisla cried. "I will drag you from this hill if I have to, but we are leaving."

"No. We will stay in the temple," Keeper Amos said, assuming the mantle of leader. "We are as safe here as anywhere."

"We have never been safe here!" Ghisla shouted, desperate. *Why would they not listen?*

The others stared at her as if she'd sprouted wings and a forked tongue. She closed her eyes and prayed for deliverance. Mayhaps her tongue *was* forked. She was complicit, and her guilt was almost as great as her fear.

"The women must go," Dagmar agreed. "Gather whatever you can easily carry."

"The king will notice immediately if Liis is gone," Elayne said quietly. "If there is a wedding . . . we . . . all . . . must be in attendance."

Ghisla hung her head in defeat.

"Very well." Dagmar nodded. "Go and prepare. Rest if you can. As soon as the ceremony ends and the temple empties, you will go through the tunnels and into the wood. If the North King leaves . . . you can return. If he does not, you will keep walking until you reach Dolphys."

⌒⥀

When Hod heard Bayr again, he'd stopped moving altogether. The hour was late, and the forest was both sleeping and waking. Hod had followed the stream which would keep widening and strengthening until it reached the river Mogda in Dolphys and, beyond that, the East Sea that lay between Saylok and Eastlandia.

Bayr's breaths were slow, like he'd stopped to rest and fallen into exhausted slumber. From the position of his heartbeat and the angle of his breath, he'd fallen asleep propped against a tree.

Hod did not want to approach; it would startle him. Hod was many things, but he was not especially stealthy when he navigated unfamiliar surroundings.

His own weariness burned in his back and dulled his senses. He could not remember the last time he'd slept. It was only yesterday he'd climbed aboard the provisions wagon and rolled the final miles to the mount, surrounded by Northmen and two repugnant kings that thought they each held the better hand. They'd circled each other warily for the better part of two weeks, each of them pulling Hod aside to divulge the other's secrets. Gudrun had threatened and Banruud had implied, and Hod had kept his mouth closed.

Hod needed rest and food, even if it was just an hour, propped against a tree like Bayr. He found a thicket not far from the water and crawled behind it. In minutes he was asleep, dozing in the embrace of his shield and his bow.

When he surfaced again, he did not move or stretch but found his brother's heart.

It had quickened and Bayr breathed through his nose, as though he tried to hide his presence.

The woods were crawling with drumming human hearts.

A thick wall of them moved toward the mount. Big men, from the echoes in their chests. They did not speak, but they rustled and rattled distinctly as they walked. Bones. Leather. Blades. They were Northmen. Gudrun had brought an army after all.

Hod didn't move, not even when one man stopped and urinated into the bush he was stretched out behind. The foul stream kicked up the dirt and shook the brambles; a few drops pinged against his shield. He prayed the man would not investigate the inconsistent sound. He didn't. He shook himself and proceeded on.

When Bayr began to follow them, staying a safe distance back, Hod picked up his staff and trailed after them as well.

$\sim$

The Northmen stopped before they reached the forest's edge, and they waited as morning grew into day. For what they waited, Hod didn't know. A signal? A sign? They created a sort of sound barrier between Hod and the mount.

He could hear Bayr, hovering at the rear of the small army. Within the group were recognizable rhythms—he knew some of the Northmen—but his range was interrupted by the sheer number of them.

There were Bernians among the Northmen too. It seemed some of Benjie's men had seen the shift in the winds and thrown in with the conquerors. They'd been the ones to guide them in.

Mayhaps Benjie knew. Mayhaps he didn't. It mattered little now. It was yet one more example of how fragmented the clans had become.

Hod put his palms to his ears for a moment, trying to focus his senses. He breathed in and out, his back to a tree, his feet planted. Then he focused, narrowing in on the hearts he needed to hear.

There was Bayr. *Boom, boom, boom, boom.*

He let his awareness rise over the drone of the Northmen.

Ghisla . . . Where was Ghisla? He suspended his breath.

Ah. The sound was faint, like tinkling glass in a storm, but he found her.

She was still in the temple.

He wanted to shout in fear and frustration. Instead he breathed, in and out, in and out, and found her sisters and Ghost. Alba too. They all remained on the mount.

Mayhaps it was better, he realized suddenly. Had they entered the Temple Wood, they would have come face-to-face with the Northmen.

Panic bubbled but he bit down on it and beat it back.

He had to get around them. He had to get back onto the mount. He was useless this way. He couldn't stop an army, and he couldn't guard his brother if Bayr ran headlong into the battle.

And that was exactly what Bayr would do.

Hod scanned the mount with his ears, trying to feel his way into a strategy. It was an anthill, crawling with clansmen and chaotic sound.

He had to warn them.

That realization brought a wash of helplessness more debilitating than all his years in the dark. He didn't know what to do.

The bells began to clang and horns sang from the ramparts. The Northmen in front of him began to shift, moving north toward the village at the entrance to the mount, hugging the tree line all the way. They didn't hurry, but they were clearly moving into position, and Bayr trailed behind them.

Suddenly, from just above the base of the hill, he detected a familiar cadence, and then another, and another, and another. He listened, and hope sparked in his chest. Dred, Dakin, Dystel, and the insufferable Daniel hunkered—the smell of a small campfire tickled Hod's nose—on a shelf about fifty feet from the bottom of the east slope. He'd missed them behind the wall of Northmen.

He began to pick his way toward them. He couldn't run; he would fall flat on his face. They would see him coming, and they would think the king had sent him. Again. But there was no help for that.

He heard the moment they saw him, and he felt their eyes throughout the rest of his climb. They did not cry out or warn him off as he approached, but they shuffled and stood, wary, withdrawing their swords with a whispering snick.

"There are Northmen in the woods," Hod said as he neared. There was no time for greetings or reassurances.

Dystel swore.

"I have followed Bayr all night and kept watch all day," Hod continued. "He has seen them. He knows. And he's circled around to the entrance to the mount. I cannot protect him, and I cannot protect you."

"Son of Frigg," Dystel swore again.

"There are Bernians with them. They led the Northmen in. I don't know who to trust, and I don't know what to do," Hod confessed. He was not interested in excuses.

"You knew," Dred said. His voice was not an accusation but a grim statement.

"I have known this was coming, and I did not seek to prevent it. I wanted only for Banruud to be overthrown."

"Bloody hell," Dakin said, but his voice trembled with excitement, not fear.

"You plot against the king?" Dystel gasped, but Dred followed his question up with another.

405

"And who will take Banruud's place if he falls, Hod? The North King?" Dred asked, quiet.

"My hope was that Gudrun and Banruud would destroy each other," Hod answered.

"And who will sit on the throne?" Dred pressed. "You?"

"No. I am a blind man. Not a king. But I see some things clearly. Bayr must sit on the throne."

"Bloody hell," Dakin said again, and he was practically vibrating with anticipation.

"Praise Odin," Dred growled. "Long live the Dolphys, future king of Saylok. Now tell us where to go, blind man."

No matter what, they had to protect Bayr. And if Hod was going to save anyone, he had to get on the wall. With his bow, he could thin the numbers of the Northmen as they climbed.

"I am going up on the wall where I can be of use," Hod explained. "I need you to protect your chieftain. Bayr cannot fall."

29

Deep

He heard the moment Ghisla reached the wood. At least thirty women—hearts thrumming—were with her. A wash of relief followed by a rush of anger flooded him. No keepers walked among them. Even now, they huddled in the temple, clustered in the sanctum, but Master Ivo was not among them. Hod searched for his signature sound, for the hitch and hollow drumming of his ancient heart, but it was not there.

No one had questioned Hod when he returned to the mount. The bridge had been lowered for much of the tournament. It was lowered now. The portcullis was at half-staff, and he easily rolled beneath it. Someone greeted him—a young sentry who sometimes stood at the temple door—and Hod waved him over.

"Where are the archers who should be on the wall?" he asked.

"I don't know, sir. I'm stationed at the gate today. But half the hill is sozzled. The melee was a bit of a bust, and weddings aren't as entertaining as wine."

He'd insisted that the sentry—Edward from Ebba—send archers to the wall immediately.

"As many as you can find. On the king's orders."

"Y-y-yessir," Edward stammered. "I'll do my best. Elijah is here. He's my brother. He won the archery contest. He wants to meet you. I'll get him!"

"Have him bring his bow," Hod grunted.

Hod climbed the stairs to the top of the ramparts and found a spot where he could hear the traffic from the entrance road and the goings-on in the courtyard equally well.

There was no panic on the temple grounds. No urgency at all. The mood was celebratory but with a sleepy edge, like the clanspeople were ready to be done with it all. Then the temple doors opened, and Northmen and warriors streamed out.

The bells began their clangor again.

Alba was escorted into the courtyard, Gudrun beside her. She cried out in distress as he lifted her into the saddle with a careless toss. Her horse whinnied in sympathy, and she patted and shushed him almost hypnotically.

She was in shock. Why had she not left the mount with the other women?

"It will be better this way," she whispered, almost as if she answered him. She was praying. "Freya watch over the daughters," she murmured. "And keep Bayr far from this hill."

Gudrun was nervous. His pulse whined with adrenaline, and he kept sucking at his teeth. His behavior alone made the hair stand up on Hod's neck.

As the North King and his men mounted their horses, Banruud and his men exited the temple and climbed the palace steps to oversee the departure. The grating sound of the swinging doors followed on their heels, and the clap of bars being lowered behind the entrance to the temple made Hod shudder. Ghisla had warned the keepers. They'd simply chosen not to go, but they were barring the door.

An old woman was crying, moaning like she was at a wake instead of a wedding.

"I do not want to go," she wailed. "I've not left the mount in fifteen winters. I shan't leave it now."

Someone shushed her, impatient. "I've not left the mount in thirty, and you don't see me crying." This boast became a blubbering wail.

They were most likely servants, chosen to accompany the princess; they weren't happy about it.

Lothgar of Leok, Aidan of Adyar, and some of their men mounted their horses as well. Apparently the chieftains of the northern clans were riding with the princess as far as the fork. Benjie of Berne was already in the saddle.

He was not nervous. He was drunk. Fumes billowed up around him. He was not the only one. Many of the clanspeople had not stopped drinking since the feast the day before. Few had abandoned their libations since the melee, and the merriment would continue until the people collapsed in drunken piles. It was always thus when the tournament ended.

Hod gripped his bow, shifting behind the ramparts. He was still the only archer on the wall. Odin's eyes. *What a disaster.*

The portcullis was raised all the way—the winch squealed and the horses chuffed and danced in anticipation—and the Northmen began to descend the mount.

They were . . . leaving.

༄

When Ghost walked out of the tunnel, squinting against the late-afternoon light, Ghisla and her sisters were waiting for her. But when she stepped forward and clutched their hands, Ghisla knew what she was going to say.

"I'm not going with you," Ghost said.

Bashti cried out and Juliah gaped, but Ghisla nodded slowly, and Elayne took Ghost's hand as if she too had expected as much.

"But . . . you cannot stay here," Dalys cried. "You are in more danger than all of us."

"No. I can't stay here," Ghost agreed.

"You are going with Alba," Elayne murmured, and Ghost nodded again.

"She is my daughter, and she is alone," Ghost said, looking at each woman in turn.

"I want to fight," Juliah insisted suddenly, her impatience billowing around her. "I am staying here."

"No, Juliah. You are not," Ghost shot back. "You will fight for them!" She pointed at the women waiting on the hillside. "You will fight for each other." Ghost pointed at the trees. "Now go."

Ghisla bit back tears as the others broke down around her.

"Don't cry," Ghost begged, her voice shaking. "Please. We must all be strong. If the gods will it, we will see each other again."

She embraced them fiercely, kissing their cheeks and professing her love before she hastened them toward the Temple Wood, willing them to hurry. Then she set off, cutting across the hillside toward the northern entrance to the mount, the drab brown of her old shepherd's cloak covering her hair and shielding her face.

Ghisla sang softly, willing the fates to spare her and all the others, and followed her sisters toward the Temple Wood.

༄

Aidan rode on Alba's right, Lothgar on her left, and Benjie led the way, belching and swaying as though he were already half-asleep. King Gudrun rode at the front, a group of his warriors leading the way, another bringing up the rear.

"Halt!" Aidan of Adyar bellowed suddenly, his voice ringing with tension, but the party continued down the road without him, and a Northman grunted and urged him along. The trumpeters ceased their heraldry, their duties done, and the horses quickened their pace, the downhill pull urging them forward. A handful of clanspeople spilled out the gates behind them, and the portcullis stayed open for the ebb and flow.

They were halfway down the temple mount when Hod heard it. *Whoosh. Whoosh. Whoosh.*

Fire.

Fires were being set. Bodies swarmed from the mouth of the village, rushing up the road toward the North King's entourage as though they fled the fire behind them.

"Those aren't villagers," Aidan shouted.

"Close the gates," Hod screamed.

"Close the gates!" Lothgar repeated.

But the Northmen were already falling upon the confused clansmen.

Hod began to shoot, letting arrows fly into the climbing horde, doing his best to ignore the clash and the shrieks and the stench. The smell of blood threatened to overwhelm everything else.

Then Bayr was among the throng, his heart thundering, and Hod knew he battled though Hod could not see him fight.

Alba screamed, Bayr roared, and Gudrun laughed.

Hod released one shrieking dart after another, picking off the men around Bayr as best he could before the heartbeats combined to one pulsating swell. It was like a line of drummers, one thumping out the tempo that all the others marched to, and he pulled back, thwarted.

Suddenly there was an archer by his side, and Hod pled for direction.

"I'm no good in a fight like this. I can't determine which heartbeat to aim at," he shouted.

Then Bayr was running through the gates, his grunts echoing the slice of his sword.

"There you are," Hod breathed, relief straightening his aim.

"Is the Dolphys surrounded?" he yelled at the archer beside him.

"Aye. He's twenty-nine deep, at least," the archer said.

And Hod could hear them, the *rat-at-tat* of their hearts striking against the anvil that was Bayr. One by one, Hod started picking them off, hearing the moment each fell and a new one took his place.

"The Northmen are breaking down the temple doors! Do you hear that?" the archer yelled.

Hod nodded with a quick jerk of his head.

"There's not one of ours near him."

But Gudrun was among them; Hod knew his heart well.

"Make it rain, blind man. Make it rain!" the archer beside him bellowed.

He let another stream of arrows fly, but Gudrun was inside, the door giving way beneath his axe.

The archer who'd been beside him was racing down the rampart, and Hod turned back to Bayr but didn't dare shoot.

"I need your eyes, archer," he bellowed, but the man was gone.

In the cacophony of swords and shrieks, he could not determine the warriors from the Northmen, friend from foe. The stench of blood overwhelmed his senses, and he roared in impotence at his own weakness.

"I need your eyes."

The trumpets wailed, the sound sitting on the breeze, and the women quickened their pace. Minutes later, another sound rose in the wind, a sound Ghisla could not immediately identify. It was a collective bellow bristling with shrieks and cries, like the sound of gulls caught in a gale or a frenzied crowd at a tournament. She couldn't see the front of the mount or the northernmost edge of the village, but the sound curled the hair on her nape and curdled the contents of her stomach.

She stopped to listen, eyes turned up to the temple walls, but nothing looked amiss. The sound swelled, and she knew what it was. The attack had begun.

The women began to run, but Ghisla fell to her knees and pulled out her blade.

"Liis," Dalys shrieked. "Get up."

But she couldn't. She had to know. She pricked her finger and traced the star on her hand just the way Hod taught her.

"What are you doing?" Elayne moaned.

She held the rune to her brow and whispered her imperative.

"Show me Hod."

The square swam in blood. Everywhere blood and bodies—horses and men. A severed head, an arm clutching a sword, and then feet, legs, running, lunging. Sound ricocheted between her ears.

She saw a hand fitting an arrow against a bowstring, and knew it was his, even beneath the blood and dust that coated his skin. It was like she sat beside him, surveying the courtyard below. He was on the wall. She watched the arrow fly, and Hod grunted as it found its mark. He was keeping the Northmen off Bayr, who was bathed in blood and gore. Only the blue of his eyes and his size separated him from the men around him. His braid was gone and his hair, no longer weighted and bound, flew around him, as red and matted as his skin.

Hod nocked another arrow and it pierced the back of the man in Bayr's path. Bayr raised his eyes to the wall, acknowledging the help, even as he spun with both hands on the hilt of his sword and cut a Northlander—his bone-studded braids rattling with his death throes—in two. The torso flew as the legs collapsed.

"I need your eyes, archer," Hod shouted, though she couldn't see to whom he spoke. "I need your eyes," he begged.

She drew her palm from her brow, and her vision cleared with a dizzying snap.

"He needs my eyes. I have to give him my eyes," she babbled, trying to make her sisters understand. She traced the rune of the blind god and said Hod's name.

Her eyes went dark.

Elayne was shouting at her, and Bashti tried to wipe the blood from her palm.

Ghisla kicked out with her legs, the way Bayr had taught them to do so long ago. Willing them to understand, she began to sing:

> Take my eyes and give me wisdom.
> Take my heart and give him strength.
> I will fight beside my brothers.
> I will battle with my men.

"Go! I will stay with her," she heard Juliah shout. "She is singing for them. Let her sing."

∽

He had eyes. Suddenly he had eyes.

Ghisla.

He raised his bow, exulting, and realized he might have eyes but he was out of arrows.

He crawled, moving along the wall. He could see his hands, and it made him dizzy. He could not make his mind accept the new source of information. He pulled an arrow from the breast of the watchman; the poor sod held a horn in his hand. He found two more and let them fly, the hiss and the pull matching his exhalations.

Hod bellowed, and his eyes—Ghisla's eyes—followed his flight as he threw himself from the wall into a sea of swords and writhing flesh. He tripped and cursed and rose again, feeling like a man just learning to walk instead of a man trying to see. He wiped his hand across his face.

A man ran toward him, sword upraised, and Hod closed Ghisla's eyes. He was better without them once he knew where to shoot. The man collapsed with a sliding thud, and Hod narrowly missed being hewn in half by the force of his momentum. He opened his eyes again and chose his next battle before it chose him.

A smattering of clansmen fought nearby, their braids swinging, their shields bearing the mark of the wolf. All were sorely outnumbered. Aidan of Adyar fought with the same madness that seemed to beset them all, back to back with a son of Lothgar, hacking and skewering, trying to withstand the assault of too many Northmen. Clusters of clansmen dotted the grounds, treading on their own dead as they struggled to beat back the enemy.

The wide entrance was littered with bodies. Benjie of Berne, recognizable to Hod only because his cloak was made from the fur of a bear, was missing the top half of his head. An old woman lay staring at the indifferent sky, her eyes fixed and her chest gaping.

She had not left the mount after all.

Someone had attempted to lower the portcullis, but there were bodies in the way, and it rested on the backs of two temple guards who'd been hewn down, one on top of the other. From all sides, screams and cries for mercy were interspersed with the clashing of shields and the grunts of men.

A man stood alone and was entirely encircled, though he seemed to be holding his own against the warriors surrounding him. He was awash in blood and gore and armed with an axe in each hand. His hair was short and unadorned—no braids or bones—and for a moment, Hod gaped, dizzied once more. It was Bayr. Of course it was Bayr. He bellowed, bringing his axes together and felling three Northmen simultaneously.

More kept coming.

Hod pulled a quiver of arrows from a crumpled sentry and began to shoot, peeling the Northmen from around his brother. He used his new eyes to pick his target and immediately shut them before he let go. He sensed the motion a hair too late and was missed by the blade of an axe but battered by a Northman's shield.

"You didn't hear me coming, Blind Hod?" the man yelled, spittle flying, a moment before Hod ran him through with a fallen clansmen's sword. He shoved the man off, his hand slick with blood, his head spinning. He dropped the sword, picked up his bow, and sent a dozen more men to their deaths.

When the cobbles buckled beneath his feet, he thought it just another dizzy spell.

Then his eyes—her eyes—caught and held on the temple.

A keeper stood with his hands braced on the pillars of the temple. The image began to shake, bouncing and blurring. Dust billowed and the screaming changed. Hod closed his eyes, listening to the keeper's heart. He didn't know faces.

"Dagmar!" he heard someone scream.

It was Dagmar. Of course. The man propped between the pillars was Dagmar, and he was about to bring down the temple.

"Run!" Dagmar roared. "Go!"

The sound was that of a mighty storm, like thunder and lightning, like Thor himself was taking his hammer to the temple walls. Hod stumbled back, the quaking beneath his feet worse than the tossing of the North King's ship upon an angry sea. The fighting in the courtyard had ceased, the warriors around him more frightened of the quaking mount than the swords of their enemies.

He thought he heard Gudrun yell, cursing the gods, his voice echoing out through the entrance door, and Hod saw Alba and Ghost run, keeping each other upright as the temple continued to buck and break. Northmen began fleeing the mount, racing for the gates as the cobbles beneath them writhed, tossing the dead into the air and the living to their knees.

A groaning arose, inhuman and earsplitting, and the roof of the temple crashed down, abandoning the walls that had once supported it, a cloud of dust and debris mushrooming into the sky and coating the mount in white powder.

And then the world went still.

⁓

Hod could not hear the living, if any living remained, and the dead did not have heartbeats. He couldn't hear, and he couldn't smell.

The world was white instead of black, shallow instead of deep. Nothing existed but wintery silence.

The silence was almost worse than the screams.

"Bayr?" he whispered, but he could not feel his lips or hear the word when he released it.

"Ghisla?" he tried again.

She would not forgive him. He had fallen after all.

30

PACES

Ghisla curled herself around her palm, guarding her sacrifice as she crooned her song.

Her sisters sat with her, frightened but not willing to leave, confused but not willing to flee. When the forest began to quake beneath her, sending waves of fury up her legs, some of the women began to scream. But she did not. Her eyes were still sightless, the rune of the blind god still wet on her palm. She dared not stop feeding it. Hod needed her eyes.

The trees shuddered and the leaves shook, and the relentless black abated with a jolt. But the trembling continued, and the gods roared. She blinked, horrified, and tried again, tracing the shape of the rune with her bleeding finger and saying Hod's name.

"Hody, Hody, Hody."

But her eyes remained her own.

She traced the scar of the amulet on her right hand, shaking so hard she had to wipe away the blood and try again. But instead of dark she saw light. Instead of black she saw unrelenting white.

"I cannot see the mount," she mourned, raising her gaze to her terrified sisters. She could not see the mount, and she could not see Hod.

Hod awoke in stages. His left foot screamed, and his right ear burned. Then his legs were being stung by a thousand bees, and his stomach repeatedly fell over a cliff. Someone beat against his back with a rod, and Ghisla's eyes were gone. His own were flaming shards in his skull.

His throat tickled next, and he hummed, trying to clear it. Dust billowed from his lips and he began to choke.

"I dare not move him," someone said.

He listened for their heartbeats and heard only his death rattle instead. He bucked and arched, desperate for breath, and his body responded with a lurch and a lungful of air.

"We thought you a dead man," the stranger said.

"What's wrong with his eyes?" another worried.

"There's naught wrong with his eyes that wasn't wrong before. He's Blind Hod."

"What happened?" Hod rasped.

"The temple . . . is no more."

Then he remembered Dagmar, standing between the writhing pillars.

"Oh no."

"Aye."

"Where is Bayr of Dolphys?" he said, trying not to weep.

"He is here."

"And the princess?"

"She lives too, blind man."

"What of . . . the keepers?"

"They're all gone," the man sighed. "Buried with the Northmen."

"Buried with their runes," another man mourned, and Hod closed his burning lids and slid back into the inky abyss.

They slept in the clearing where Desdemona died, huddled together like rabbits in a warren. But Ghisla did not sleep. She never slept; she sang instead, one lullaby after another, and pled with Odin to spare his sons.

The daughters dared not return to the hill, and they could not head for Dolphys. Bayr was on the mount, and if he lived there would be a new king. If he died . . . Saylok was finished. Hiding in Dolphys would not save them.

She tried to give Hod her eyes again, tracing the rune of the blind god throughout the night, but her sight remained and darkness began to fill her chest.

Promise me you will not give up.

I will not give up today.

She persisted, and just before dawn she fed the star on her palm, pressing it to her brow in one last attempt at hope, and she found him.

Alive.

~

When he woke again, warmth brushed his cheeks and tickled his nose. He was back in the clearing near his mother's grave, Arwin at his side.

"Baldr's death was necessary. It marked a new beginning . . . the death of the gods and the rise of man. The rise of . . . woman."

The sun felt good on his face, and he tipped his chin upward, letting the rays rest on him. Arwin smacked his lips, eating his berries in happy silence.

"You cannot stay here, Hod. When I am gone . . . you must go too. You must save Saylok."

Hod listened, coming awake to the reality that was the temple mount.

Arwin was dead.

The keepers were dead.

But Banruud was not.

He could hear his heart, pulsing inside the castle walls.

People moved around Hod, and a robe had been shoved beneath his head. He patted the ground for his staff and realized it was still sheathed on his back.

He rolled to his side, thrilled when his limbs obeyed him, *groaning* when his limbs obeyed him.

The warmth had intensified, and he lifted his face to it, gauging the hour. Morning had broken. He lifted his hand to his brow and located the source of his most pressing pain. His braid was still intact, but his brain was now a throbbing, rotting corpse. The reek of death was all around him, and he welcomed the return of his senses even as he retched.

He scanned the hearts that pulsed and pummeled his head. He'd been left for dead or deemed a lost cause . . . or mayhaps there were simply not enough hands to help all that had fallen. He found his brother, and his chest swelled in grateful adulation.

Bayr lived. He moved. And his loyal band of warriors walked with him.

Hod found Alba, Ghost, and the archer from the wall. Aidan of Adyar moved amid the rubble as well. There were others, and he was thankful.

He turned his attention to the king.

Banruud huddled in the cellars beneath the castle floor. From the galloping chorus that seeped out through the walls, down the steps, and over the bodies that now lined the courtyard, a dozen men were with him.

Hod pushed himself up with his staff.

No one halted his progress or delayed his climb. No one called his name. He took tortured steps to the castle doors, wobbling and weak. But his resolve grew as he went.

The men in the cellar heard him coming and scrambled for swords and shields. He did not descend. Stone steps led down into the dank underground, and he opened the door above them and called down to the king.

"Gudrun is dead, Sire. The Northmen are gone."

Elbor cried out in sodden relief. Even from Hod's position at the top of the stairs, he smelled of piss and spirits, but he began to climb the cellar steps as if he'd been pardoned. Hod moved aside to let him pass, but he hovered nearby, waiting for the others.

"And the Temple Boy?" Banruud asked, still uncertain.

"The Temple Boy is no more," Hod said, unflinching. The Temple Boy *was* no more. He'd long ago become a man. A chieftain. And soon he would be a king.

"You must come out now, Majesty," he demanded, using the same quiet, emotionless voice Banruud seemed to expect from him.

He would make Banruud stand in front of his people, those that were left. He would force him to face the chieftains and the warriors who remained. And then he would end him, the way Banruud had insisted Hod end Bayr. If Hod was condemned to die with him, then so be it, but Banruud would die.

The king began to climb the steps.

"You will find Liis of Leok, and you will bring her to me in my chambers," he insisted.

"The temple is gone, Majesty. And all the keepers with it. Did you not hear it fall?" he murmured.

"But the daughters?" Banruud gasped.

"I know not," Hod whispered, and he spoke the truth. He knew not. "You must come and see for yourself. The people need to see their king."

Banruud stank of long hours of sweat and tortured sleep, but he brushed off his tunic and straightened his robes before he left the palace. His cowardly cadre followed.

Hod trailed thirty paces behind, not able—or desirous—to walk among them.

When Ghisla and the other women emerged from the Temple Wood, Alba and Ghost were on the eastern slope. They began to run, the daughters up and the princess down, laughing and crying at the welcome sight of each other.

Ghost was slow to follow, but no less exuberant.

"We couldn't do it," Juliah said. "We couldn't leave. We watched from the wood, and we heard the screams."

"We felt the earth quake and saw the dome of the temple fall," Bashti added, her face grim.

"We waited all night. We didn't know what to do," Elayne said. "And then we saw you on the hillside and knew it was safe."

"Is it . . . safe?" Dalys asked, hesitant.

Ghost began to weep, and Alba clutched the girls to her. For a moment, neither of them spoke.

"What has happened?" Ghisla whispered. "Please . . . tell us what has happened."

"Dagmar is gone. The keepers too," Ghost choked out.

Gone? Odin, no.

"And Bayr?" Juliah asked softly, fearfully. "What of Bayr?"

"He is here," Alba said, and her obvious relief rippled among the women. "He is here. And we are . . . safe. As safe as we can possibly be."

"What of the Northmen?" Juliah asked.

"Vanquished," Alba said with a pallid smile. "Come," she gestured. She turned back toward the east gate and began to climb. They all followed, their steps slow and heavy, their thoughts unbearably loud.

"Where will we live?" a child asked from amid the tired group, voicing the fears of many. "The temple is gone."

"You will stay in the palace," Alba said, her shoulders set, eyes steady. "There is room enough for all of you. And we will take each day as it comes."

The destruction within the walls had them clinging to one another again and weeping in disbelief, but as they walked into the courtyard, the clanspeople gaped, and the warriors clutched their braids.

Aidan of Adyar rushed forward, oblivious to everyone but Elayne, and pulled her into his arms, his composure destroyed.

"I thought you were gone," Aidan rasped. "I thought you were in the temple."

Ghisla searched the faces, pausing in the place where she'd seen Hod. He'd been sitting up. Talking. Whole. But he didn't sit by the wall any longer. He was not in the courtyard at all.

Bayr greeted the daughters one by one, clasping their hands and expressing his thanks. His gaze settled on Alba, and devastation rippled over his face before he bit it back.

He still didn't know.

He turned away, as if the sight of her was too much to bear, and then he froze, his broad back obscuring Ghisla's view. Dred cursed beside him, his voice trembling with loathing, and the men around him shared his sentiments. Ghisla shifted, stepping around the men to see what had so upset them, and her stomach plummeted.

King Banruud descended the palace steps, his clothes slightly rumpled but his shoulders back. He still wore his cloak and his crown, and he clutched the hilt of his unsheathed sword. A handful of his men, all able bodied and weapon wielding, made a sloppy perimeter around him, their eyes skittering to the unclaimed dead and the ruin of the temple. The Chieftain of Ebba followed a few steps back, weaving as he went. He looked as though he'd barricaded himself in the cellar with a cask of the royal wine. Limping behind them, a short ways off, was Hod, leaning heavily on his staff.

Ghisla jerked and stumbled toward him, but he stiffened as if he heard her heart and raised a hand, palm up, bidding her stay.

No one spoke as the king approached, but every chieftain turned to face him, their tattered clansmen—most still wearing the gore and grime of battle—falling in behind them. Alba moved to Bayr's side, signaling her allegiance, and Ghisla watched as Ghost drew a dagger from the bodice of her gown as if preparing for battle.

"We've defeated the Northmen. Praise Odin. Praise Thor. Praise Father Saylok," the king boomed, nodding at the chieftains as though he'd fought beside them. Banruud's retinue shook their swords at the indifferent sky, shouting in celebration.

"Praise the Dolphys. Praise the keepers. Praise the clans," Dred shot back, his voice raised above the king's guard. Then he spat at Banruud's boots and wiped his chin.

"You were told to leave, Dred of Dolphys, under threat of death, as was your chieftain," Banruud said. His tone was mild, as though Dred caused him no real concern, but his eyes were on Bayr. He leveled his blade, but Bayr did not flinch before his sword.

"You severed your braid, Temple Boy. You're a traitor to your king, and yet you stand on my mount, eyeing my daughter and my crown," Banruud ground out.

"She is not your daughter," Ghost said, drawing the king's gaze. "And that is no longer your crown," she added.

Banruud's face paled. His eyes skittered from Ghost to Ghisla, as if she might rescue him with her song.

He looked away again when he found no softness in her gaze.

"The keepers made me king," Banruud bellowed, his hand tightening on his sword. Ghisla thought for a moment he would try to strike Ghost down. Ghost lifted her chin, as if willing him to do it.

"You lied to the keepers. You lied to the clans. You lied to your son, and you lied to my daughter. We will take your crown, and we will choose a new king," Ghost spat.

"The keepers are gone," he sneered back. "And you are a slave."

"The keepers are not gone," Juliah called out, moving behind Ghost. Elayne, Bashti, and Dalys were right behind her, their purple robes attesting to Juliah's claim. "Master Ivo made us keepers. And as keepers, we declare that you are no longer king of Saylok."

Banruud's eyes jumped to the chieftains, as if gauging their support. Aidan of Adyar gripped his braid and sawed his knife across it, and he tossed the thick blond plait at Banruud's feet. Logan of Leok and Josef of Joran did the same, their mouths twisted in disdain. One by one, every warrior cut his braid, throwing them down and severing their allegiance to the king. Elbor began to stumble back, and Banruud's men dropped their swords in surrender, unwilling to stand against the clans.

Banruud had no one. He had nothing, and the thing he had feared most had come to pass. Bayr would take his crown, and the wraith that had haunted him was no longer lurking in his tortured conscience but standing in front of him, fearless and unopposed. With a desperate roar he lunged at her, seeking to use her as a shield as he thrust his sword at Bayr's chest.

But Banruud had failed to notice the dagger in Ghost's hand. His actions had trapped her hand between them and drawn her knife into his belly.

Ghisla heard the wet clasp and suck of the blade being turned.

The clatter of his sword on the cobbles was accompanied by his dumbfounded groan. He should have pled for forgiveness, but he only wanted answers.

"Who . . . are . . . you?" he gurgled, the words soaked in blood.

"I am the daughters of the clans, and the keepers of the temple. I am Alba's mother, and Dagmar's friend." Ghost's voice broke on Dagmar's name, but she pressed on. "I am everyone you have wronged. And I am Ghost, the new Highest Keeper."

The king brayed, the sound terrible in its dread and dismay, the bawl of a downed bear, and he fell to his knees, swaying and searching the faces of his condemners.

"Hod?" he moaned. "Where are you?"

"I am here," Hod said softly from the edge of the circle. He made no move to approach his father, and he did not weep, but his face was lined with compassion.

"Liis . . . Liis of Leok," Banruud groaned. "You must sing to me. You must sing to me. I am dying."

He reached a hand toward her, beseeching, but the effort made him topple onto his side. She clutched her hands to her chest, unwilling to touch him and unable to comfort him.

There was no time for a song.

Banruud groaned again, a deep, pained rattle, attempting to ward off what was to come, and then his eyes closed and his body softened, sighing against the stones.

For several long seconds, no one moved or breathed or spoke.

"The king is dead," Hod said. "His . . . heart . . . beats . . . no more."

The eyes of every man, woman, and warrior turned to look at him, and Ghisla moved toward him, desperate to guard him from their wary gazes. But Hod did not shrink or slink away. He used his staff to pick his way to the body of the king, and when he reached her side, Ghisla stood over him, guarding his back as he crouched beside Banruud.

Ghost had begun to weep. Alba too. Bleak, stunned faces, blood-streaked and coated in ashy grime, surrounded them. No one rejoiced at the king's death, and no one argued its justice.

"Who are you?" Bayr asked. "You fought beside us . . . but I do not know you." His words were slow, careful, the way they'd always been, but he did not stumble over a single word.

"He is the confidant of Gudrun and henchman of the king." It was the captain of the king's guard who accused Hod; he feared his fate would be the same as Banruud's.

A rumble of agreement swelled among some of the sentries and clansmen.

"He sailed with Gudrun and guarded the king," a warrior of Berne protested.

"But he fought with us," Dred said.

"I was with him on the wall," another man vouched. He was the archer Ghisla had seen with the rune.

"But who *are* you?" Bayr repeated softly, still gazing at Hod, and Hod answered without argument or defense.

"I am called Blind Hod. I was an apprentice to Arwin, the cave keeper of Leok. And I am the devoted servant of Ghisla of Tonlis, Liis of Leok."

Ghisla's sisters gasped, and Ghisla held her breath, but Bayr simply waited for him to continue.

"I am also the son of Bronwyn of Berne . . . and the late Banruud."

A hiss snapped and sizzled among the small crowd, but Dred of Dolphys raised his sword to the sky, as if signaling his support.

"And I am elder brother of Bayr of Dolphys, the rightful king," Hod finished.

"Bayr of Dolphys, the rightful king," Dred boomed, and the men of Dolphys raised their swords beside him.

From Banruud's lolling head Hod slipped the amulet of the king, the one he'd used to burn Ghisla's hand, the one that had been passed down through all the rulers of Saylok. Hod rose, swaying but solemn, and drew it over Bayr's matted, blood-soaked hair.

"You have always been the rightful king, brother. The Highest Keeper knew it when you were brought to him the day of your birth. And our father knew it too. It destroyed him, but it did not destroy you."

"Long live the Temple Boy," Alba said, tears streaming down her dusty cheeks.

"Long live the Dolphys," Dakin cried.

"Long live King Bayr," Ghost choked, her bloody blade raised in agreement.

"Long live Baldr and Hod," Ghisla whispered.

And Hod stepped back and reached for her hand.

EPILOGUE

He had not grown accustomed to happiness; mayhaps he never would. He and Ghisla had said their vows at the altar uncovered from the rubble of the temple, and King Bayr had pronounced them man and wife, though he'd stumbled over Ghisla's name. She would always be Liis of Leok to Bayr and her sisters, and she answered to both. She did not want to return to Tonlis, though he'd offered to take her. He was confident he could make his way across the sea now, especially with her eyes to guide him.

"This is my home. You are my home," she said without hesitation, and he had vowed to make it a good one.

They'd been given a room in the palace—a room for honored guests—though he would have been happy in the little chamber by the stairs. Ghisla had never had a room of her own or even a space of her own, and she had easily adjusted to the order he required.

"I find it amazing that you can hear when I am hungry but you trip over my shoes," she teased him.

The palace was teeming, but they had a corner to themselves. A happy, glorious corner. It was all he'd ever wanted.

He'd been welcomed by all and shunned by none, though Ghost had reservations. She was mourning. She had made herself Highest Keeper, and she worked tirelessly day after day, but her heart was broken. She did not trust Hod—his strangeness was too much like her own—and Master Ivo's suspicions, and probably Dagmar's too, had colored her view of him.

He'd been raised up to be a keeper, and he offered to assist in preserving and cataloging the rubble of the temple. He knew the names of the runes and how to draw and unlock them, but Ghost was not ready for his companionship or his counsel, and Hod kept his distance. He was not even certain he cared whether the runes were preserved.

It was a conundrum; to rebuild without understanding the past—both the triumphs and failures—was to start over instead of moving ahead. Saylok could learn from the runes, but they would be better served not to worship them. Saylok needed keepers to hold a king's power in check, but mayhaps they should be keepers of faith and justice instead of keepers of runes.

Princess Alba—Queen Alba—had embraced him with open arms. She asked him almost daily to put his hands upon her belly and listen to the child within her.

"Can you tell today if it's a daughter?" she would ask.

"I have no experience with such things, Majesty," he always said. "But the heart is strong and steady . . . and if I had to bet upon it, I would say it is a girl child. A daughter's heart is . . . different."

A heartbeat thrummed in Ghisla's womb as well. Two of them. And if he had to guess again, he would wager they were boys. Brothers.

"We will call them Baldr and Hod," Ghisla proclaimed, and he could not sway her against it.

He had not grown accustomed to such happiness. Mayhaps he never would.

He was getting to know his brother. Bayr had no artifice and very little ego. He was fierce in his duty, fierce in his love, and mild in his manner. Sometimes Hod would hear his mighty heart and think of Banruud—the sound was the same, like the sea in a storm, the wind moaning through the cave where he'd been raised. Their voices were the same too—the gravel tones and the rumble from their chests. Ghisla said Hod sounded the same, though he couldn't hear it.

"You share the same voice, all of you. It is one of the things that convinced me, all those years ago, that Arwin spoke the truth."

Bayr was bothered by his paternity. "He was not a good man, our father," he said to Hod not long after his coronation, as he studied his kingdom. He liked to climb up on the wall and survey the lands around him. Hod simply liked to be at his side.

"No. He was not. He caused great grief. Great suffering," Hod answered.

"Does it bother you . . . that we . . . are his?"

"It did. Once. But then I thought of you."

"Of me?" Bayr asked, surprised.

"Yes. I knew long ago you were Banruud's. And I knew all the stories of the Temple Boy. So strong. And good. To belong to Banruud meant I also belonged to you. It made me happy. I was honored."

Bayr did not speak, but he wrapped his hand around the back of Hod's neck, clasping him like the bear from which he'd descended.

"You could have come to me, Hod. You did not have to sail to the Northlands," Bayr said, his tone gentle.

"Arwin was always adamant about my training. I have now served three kings," Hod replied. Then he smiled. "Two of them are dead, though . . . so I don't know if that is much of a recommendation."

Bayr laughed, but he grew tender again almost immediately.

"You do not have to serve me, brother," he murmured.

"But I will. I will guard your heart—and your back—all the days of my life," Hod promised.

"You sound like Dagmar." Emotion limned Bayr's voice. "But surely you want more than to serve yet another king."

"I have everything I have ever wanted," Hod professed. "A home on the mount. A woman I have loved from the moment I met her. And hope in Saylok."

"Ah, brother, we are exactly the same," Bayr said, setting his hand upon Hod's shoulder. They stood together thus, listening to Ghisla usher in the dusk with keeper song.

All that was and all that is, all I am and all I wish.
Open my eyes to see, make me at one with thee,
Gods of my father and god of my soul.
Give me a home in hope, give me a place to go,
Give me a faith that will never grow cold.

AUTHOR'S NOTE

As with *The First Girl Child*, the book that introduced readers to the land of Saylok, *The Second Blind Son* centers on Norse mythology—Odin, Loki, Thor and all the rest—while veering off into a fantastical world of its own. But when I stumbled upon Hod, the blind god, and Baldr the Beloved in my research, I was stunned! I had already named and plotted *The Second Blind Son* without even knowing about the mythical Hod or his relationship with Baldr. The story of Hod and Baldr isn't deeply fleshed out in Norse lore—at least not in any sources I could find—but the bones of the myth fit so perfectly into my own tale that I jumped on the chance to use it as a foundation and build upon it. I hope you love *my* Hod as much as I do.

ACKNOWLEDGMENTS

I wrote this book in the first six months of a global pandemic, and it informed the way the story unfolded. I keenly felt the desperation and hopelessness of being trapped in a world and circumstances I had no control over. When Hod pleads with Ghisla over and over to not give up, I was really talking to myself. Writing books and meeting deadlines always feels like climbing Everest to me. I love it, I'm challenged by it, but it's hard. It's *so hard* every single time. But oddly, this time around, in the midst of so much uncertainty, it became less so. Maybe it was because I put the "hard" in its proper perspective. The truth is, I'm ridiculously blessed to be able to write stories for a living, and each time I sit down at the computer to write, I am reminded of just how lucky I am. My gratitude for that truth is what I most want to express.

Of course I also want to thank my agent, Jane Dystel, and my beta reader/editor Karey White, as well as my 47 North and Amazon Publishing team—Adrienne Procaccini and Jenna Free most of all. I've worked with Jenna on the developmental edit for six books now, and she always makes my stories better without dispiriting me in the process. A real talent, that. My continual thanks to Tamara Debbaut Bianco, my assistant, who is faithful and steady and doesn't seem to mind my tendency to shut out the world for long intervals. She is simply there when I need her, and I am grateful.

And for you, dear reader, I am also grateful. Thank you.

ABOUT THE AUTHOR

Amy Harmon is the *New York Times*, *Wall Street Journal*, *USA Today*, and Amazon Charts bestselling author of seventeen novels, including *Where the Lost Wander*, *What the Wind Knows*, *From Sand and Ash*, and *The First Girl Child* in The Chronicles of Saylok. Amy is also the recipient of four Whitney Awards and several Goodreads Best Book nominations, among many other honors in multiple genres. Her books have been published in two dozen languages—truly a dream come true for a little country girl from Utah. For more information, visit Amy at www.authoramyharmon.com.